What a Chr...

Tall, Dark

Rich

Three fabulous novels
from international bestselling author

CAROLE MORTIMER

CAROLE MORTIMER'S
TALL, DARK & HANDSOME COLLECTION

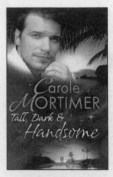

August 2013

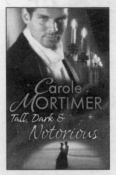

September 2013

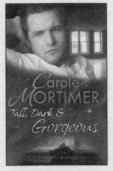

October 2013

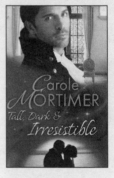

November 2013

December 2013

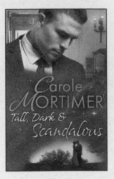

January 2014

A beautiful collection of favourite Carole Mortimer novels.
Six seductive volumes containing sixteen fabulous
Modern™ and Historical bestsellers.

Carole MORTIMER
Tall, Dark & Rich

MILLS & BOON

Published in Great Britain 2013
by Mills & Boon, an imprint of Harlequin (UK) Limited, Eton House,
18-24 Paradise Road, Richmond, Surrey TW9 1SR

TALL, DARK & RICH © Harlequin Enterprises II B.V./S.à.r.l. 2013

His Christmas Virgin © Carole Mortimer 2010
Married by Christmas © Carole Mortimer 1998
A Yuletide Seduction © Carole Mortimer 1999

ISBN: 978 0 263 91026 1

024-1213

Harlequin (UK) policy is to use papers that are natural, renewable and recyclable products and made from wood grown in sustainable forests. The logging and manufacturing processes conform to the legal environmental regulations of the country of origin.

Printed and bound by
CPI Group (UK) Ltd, Croydon, CR0 4YY

Carole Mortimer was born in England, the youngest of three children. She began writing in 1978 and has now written over one hundred and eighty books for Mills & Boon. Carole has six sons, Matthew, Joshua, Timothy, Michael, David and Peter. She says, 'I'm happily married to Peter senior; we're best friends as well as lovers, which is probably the best recipe for a successful relationship. We live in a lovely part of England.'

His Christmas Virgin

CAROLE MORTIMER

CHAPTER ONE

MAC came to an abrupt and wary halt halfway down the metal steps leading from the second floor of her warehouse-conversion home. She'd suddenly become aware of a large figure standing in the dark and shadowed alleyway beneath her.

A very large figure indeed, she noted with a frown as a man stepped out from those shadows to stand in the soft glow of light given out by the lamp shining behind her at the top of the staircase.

The man looked enormous from where Mac stood, his wide shoulders beneath the dark woollen overcoat that reached almost to his ankles adding to that impression. He had overlong dark hair brushed back from a hard and powerful face that at any other time Mac would have ached to put on canvas, light and piercing eyes— were they grey or blue?—and high cheekbones beside a long slash of a nose. He also possessed a perfectly sculptured mouth, the fuller bottom lip hinting at a depth of sensuality, and a firm and determined chin.

None of which was of the least importance—except maybe to the police, Mac wryly acknowledged to herself, if the man's reasons for being here turned out to be less than honest!

She repressed a shiver as the chill of the cold wind

of an early December evening began to seep into her
bones. 'Can I help you?' she prompted sharply as she
finished pulling on her cardigan, using both her hands
to free the long length of her midnight-black hair from
the collar. All the time wondering if she was going to
have to use the ju-jitsu skills she had learnt during her
years at university!

The man shrugged broad shoulders. 'Perhaps. If
you can tell me whether or not Mary McGuire is at
home?'

He knew her name!

Not that any of her friends ever called her Mary. But
then, as Mac had never set eyes on this man before, he
was hardly a friend, was he?

She glanced at the brightly lit studio behind and
above her before turning to eye the man again guardedly. 'Who wants to know?'

'Look, I understand your wariness—'

'Do you?' she challenged.

'Of course,' he confirmed. 'I've obviously startled
you, and I'm sorry for that, but I assure you my reasons
for being here are perfectly legitimate. I simply wish to
speak to Miss McGuire.'

'But does Miss McGuire wish to speak to you?'

The man gave a hard, humourless smile. 'I would
hope so. Look, we could go back and forth like this all
night.'

'I don't think so.' Mac shook her head, deciding that
perhaps she wouldn't need to use those self-defence
lessons on this man, after all. 'The Patels shut up shop
in precisely ten minutes and I intend to be there before
that.'

Dark brows rose over those light-coloured eyes. 'The
Patels?'

Mac elaborated. 'They own the corner shop two streets away.'

'The significance of that being...?'

'I need to get some groceries before they close. That being the case, would you mind stepping aside so that I can get by?' She stepped down two more of the stairs so that they now stood at eye level.

Blue. His eyes were blue. A piercing electric blue.

Mac's breath caught in her throat as she stared into those mesmerising blue eyes, at the same time screamingly aware of the subtle and spicy smell of his aftershave or cologne. Of the leashed power he exuded. Even so, Mac was pretty sure she could take him; it was skill that mattered when it came to ju-jitsu, not size, and she was very skilled indeed.

The man looked at her beneath hooded lids. 'The fact that you're obviously leaving her home would seem to imply that you're a friend of Miss McGuire's.'

'Would it?'

Jonas deeply regretted the impulse of his decision to call and talk to Mary McGuire this evening. It would have been far more suitable, he now realised—and far less disturbing for one of the woman's friends—if he had simply telephoned first and made an appointment that was convenient to both of them. During the daylight hours, and hopefully at a time when one of her arty friends wasn't also visiting!

The fact that the thin little waif standing on the stairs had long, straight black hair that reached almost to her waist, and almond-shaped eyes of smoky-grey in a delicately beautiful face, took nothing away from the fact that she had obviously taken to heart the persona of the 'artist starving in a garret'!

As also evidenced by the overlarge dungarees she

wore over a white T-shirt, both articles of clothing covered by a baggy pink cardigan that looked as if it would wrap about the slenderness of her body twice. Her hands were tiny and thin, the skin almost translucent. The ratty blue canvas trainers on her feet were hardly suitable for the wet and icy early December weather, either.

Jonas had spent the last week in Australia on business. Successfully so, he acknowledged with inner satisfaction. Except he now felt the effects of this cold and damp English December right down to his bones, after the heat in Australia, despite wearing a thick cashmere overcoat over his suit.

This delicate-looking little waif must be even colder with only that thin cardigan as an outer garment. 'I apologise once again if I alarmed you just now.' He grimaced as he moved aside and allowed her to step down onto the pavement beside him.

The top of her head reached just under Jonas's chin as she looked up at him with obvious mockery. 'You didn't,' she came back glibly before wrapping her cardigan more tightly about her and hurrying off into the night.

Jonas was still watching her through narrowed lids as she stopped beneath the lamp at the corner of the street to glance back at him, her face a pale oval, that almost-waist-length hair gleaming briefly blue-black before she turned and disappeared around the corner.

He gave a rueful shake of his head before turning to ascend the metal steps that led up to Mary McGuire's studio; hopefully she wasn't going to be as unhelpful as her waiflike friend. Although he wouldn't count on it!

Mac lingered to chat with the Patels for a few minutes after she had bought her groceries. She liked the young couple who had opened this convenient mini-market two years ago, and Inda was expecting their first baby in a couple of months' time.

Mac's steps slowed as she saw the man who had spoken to her earlier sitting on the bottom step of the metal staircase waiting for her when she returned carrying her bag of groceries, those electric-blue eyes narrowing on her coldly as she walked towards him. 'I take it Miss McGuire wasn't in?' she asked lightly as she stopped in front of him.

It had been fifteen minutes since Jonas had reached the top of the metal staircase to ring the doorbell and receive no response. To knock on the door and get the same result. The blaze of lights in the studio told him that someone had to be home.

Or had very recently been so?

Leaving Jonas to pose the question as to whether or not the young woman in the dungarees and baggy pink cardigan, who had hurried off to the Patels' store to get groceries before they closed, was in fact Mary McGuire, rather than the visiting friend he had assumed her to be.

Something he found almost too incredible to believe!

This young woman looked half starved, and her clothes were more suited to someone living on the streets rather than the successful artist she now was; Mary McGuire had become an artist of some repute the last three years, her paintings becoming extremely valuable as serious collectors and experts alike waxed lyrical about the uniqueness of her style and use of colour.

Her reputation as an artist aside, the woman had also become the proverbial thorn in Jonas's side the last six months.

This woman?

He stood up slowly to look down at her critically as he took an educated guess on that being the case. 'Wouldn't it have just been easier to tell me that *you're* Mary McGuire?'

She gave a dismissive shrug of those thin and narrow shoulders. 'But not half as much fun.'

The hardening of Jonas's mouth revealed that he didn't appreciate being anyone's reason for having 'fun'. 'Now that we've established who you are, perhaps we could go upstairs and have a serious conversation?' he rasped coldly.

Smoky-grey eyes returned his gaze unblinkingly. 'No.'

He raised dark brows. 'What do you mean, *no*?'

'I mean no,' she repeated patiently. 'You may now know who I am but I still have no idea who you are.'

Jonas scowled darkly. 'I'm the man you've been jerking around for the past six months!'

Mac frowned up at him searchingly, only to become more positive than ever that she had never met this man before. At well over six feet tall, with those dark and dangerous good looks, he simply wasn't the sort of man that any woman, of any age, was ever likely to forget.

'Sorry.' She gave a firm shake of her head. 'I have absolutely no idea what you're talking about.'

That sculptured, sensual mouth twisted in derision. 'Does Buchanan Construction ring any bells with you?'

Alarm bells, maybe, Mac conceded as her gaze sharpened warily on the hard and powerful face above hers. A ruthless face, she now recognised warily. 'I take it Mr Buchanan has decided to send in one of his henchmen now that all attempts at polite persuasion have failed?'

Those blue eyes widened incredulously. 'You think I'm some sort of heavy sent to intimidate you?'

'Well, aren't you?' Mac bit out scathingly. 'So far I've had visits from Mr Buchanan's lawyer, his personal assistant, and his builder, so why not one of his henchmen?'

'Possibly because I don't employ any henchmen!' Jonas bit out icily, a nerve pulsing in his tightly clenched jaw as he glared down at her.

He had decided to come here personally this evening in the hope that he would be able to talk some sense into the reputed and respected—and mulishly stubborn— artist Mary McGuire, and instead he found himself being insulted by a five-foot-nothing scrap of a woman who had the dress sense of a bag-lady!

Those deep grey eyes had opened wide. '*You're* Jonas Buchanan?'

At last he had succeeded in shaking that mocking self-confidence a little. 'Surprised?' he taunted softly.

Surprised was definitely understating how Mac felt at that moment; stunned better described it.

She had known of Buchanan Construction— impossible not to, when for years there had been boards up on building sites all over London with that name emblazoned across them—when she was approached by the company's legal representative with an offer to buy her warehouse-conversion home.

Yes, Mac had certainly known the name Jonas Buchanan, and, if she had thought about it at all, she had always assumed that the owner of the worldwide construction company would be a man in his fifties or sixties, who probably enjoyed the occasional cigar with his brandy after no doubt indulging in a seven-course dinner.

The man now claiming to be Jonas Buchanan could only be in his mid-thirties at most, the healthy glow of his tanned face indicating that he didn't smoke even the occasional cigar, and the muscled and hard fitness of his body told her that he didn't indulge in seven-course dinners, either.

Mac looked up at him shrewdly. 'Do you have a driver's licence or something to prove that claim?'

Jonas scowled as his irritation deepened. He had travelled all over the world on business for years now, and never once during that time had anyone ever questioned that he was who he said he was. Until Mary McGuire, that was! 'Will a credit card do?' he snapped as he reached into the breast pocket of his overcoat for his wallet.

'I'm afraid not.'

Jonas's hand stilled. 'Why not?'

She shrugged in that ridiculously baggy pink cardigan. 'I need something with a photograph. Anyone could have a credit card with the name Jonas Buchanan printed on it.'

'You think I forged a credit card with Jonas Buchanan's name on it?' Jonas was incredulous.

'Or stole it.' She nodded. 'I would much rather see a passport or a driver's licence with a photograph on,' she stubbornly stuck to her guns.

Jonas's mouth compressed. 'On the basis, one supposes, that I haven't had either one of those forged in the name of Jonas Buchanan, too?'

She frowned. 'Hmm, I hadn't thought of that...'

No, he definitely shouldn't have given into impulse and come here this evening, Jonas acknowledged with ever-growing frustration as he pulled out the passport that he hadn't yet had the chance to remove from his pocket following his flight back from Sydney yesterday. He had stupidly allowed his success in Australia to convince him, after months of getting nowhere with the woman, that talking personally to Miss McGuire was the right way to handle this delicate situation!

'Here.' He thrust the passport at her.

Mac carefully avoided her fingers coming into contact with his as she took the passport and turned to the laminated photo page. Unlike her own passport photo, where she looked about sixteen and as if she ought to have a prisoner number printed beneath, this man's photograph showed him as exactly the lethally attractive and powerful man that he appeared in the flesh.

She quickly checked the details beside that photograph. Jonas Edward Buchanan. British citizen. His date of birth telling Mac that he had recently turned thirty-five.

She thought quickly as she slowly closed the passport before handing it back to him, knowing she could continue this game, and so annoy the hell out of this man, or… 'What can I do for you, Mr Buchanan?' she asked politely.

'Better,' he rasped impatiently as he stashed the passport back in his breast pocket. 'Obviously you and I need to talk, Miss McGuire—'

'I don't see why.' Mac brushed past him and began to ascend the stairs back up to her home, seeing no reason for her to linger out here in the cold now that she knew—or, at least, assumed—that this man wasn't about to mug her, after all. 'I'll be turning the light out at the top of the stairs in a minute or so; before I do, you might want to get back to the main streets where it's more brightly lit,' she advised without turning as she took the key from the pocket of her dungarees to unlock the door.

Jonas continued to look up at her in seething annoyance for a mere fraction of a second before following her, taking the stairs two at a time until he stood directly behind her. 'You and I need to talk,' he bit out between gritted teeth.

'Write me a letter,' she advised as she unlocked the door before stepping inside and turning to face him, her expression one of open challenge.

Jonas placed his hands on either side of the doorframe. 'I've already written you half a dozen letters. Letters you haven't bothered to reply to.'

She grimaced. 'There's always the possibility that I'll reply to the seventh.'

'I doubt that somehow,' Jonas accepted grimly. 'I don't think so!' He put his booted foot between the door and the frame as she would have closed that door in his face.

She opened it again to glare at him, those smoky grey eyes glittering darkly, bright colour in her normally pale cheeks. 'Remove your foot, Mr Buchanan, or you'll leave me with no choice but to call the police and have you forcibly removed from the premises!'

It was all too easy for Jonas to see that she was more angry than alarmed by his persistence. 'I only want the two of us to sit down and have a sensible conversation—'

'I'm busy.'

'I'm asking for two minutes of your time, damn it!' Jonas exclaimed.

Mac really wasn't being difficult when she said she was busy; she had a major exhibition at a gallery on

Saturday, only two days away, and she had one more painting to finish before then. Besides, no amount of talking to Jonas Buchanan was going to make her change her mind about selling the warehouse she had so lovingly worked on to make into her home.

Her grandfather had left this property to Mac when he died five years ago. It had been one of many warehouses by the river that had fallen into disuse as the trade into the London dock had fallen foul of other, more convenient transportation. Three floors high, it had been the perfect place for Mac to make into her home as well as her working studio. From the outside it still looked like an old warehouse, but inside the ground floor consisted of a garage and utility room, the second floor was her living quarters, and the third floor made a spacious studio.

Unfortunately, the area where the warehouse stood had recently become very attractive to property developers such as Jonas Buchanan, as they bought up the rundown riverside properties to put up blocks of luxurious apartments that had the added allure of a magnificent and uninterrupted view of the river.

It was this man's bad luck that Mac's own warehouse home stood on one of those sites.

She sighed. 'I've already given my answer to your lawyer, your personal assistant, and your builder,' she reminded him pointedly. 'I don't want to sell. Not now. Not in the future. Not ever. Is that clear enough for you?'

Jonas Buchanan's expression was one of pure exasperation as he gave an impatient shake of his head. 'You must realise that the area around you is going to become a noisy building site over the winter months?'

She shrugged. 'You've fenced off this area for that purpose.'

He frowned. 'That isn't going to lessen the noise of lorries arriving with supplies. Workmen constantly hammering and banging as the buildings start to go up, followed by huge cranes being erected on site. Exactly how do you expect to still be able to work with all that going on?'

Mac's eyes narrowed. 'The same way I've continued to work the last few months as you've systematically pulled down all the buildings around this one.'

Jonas's mouth firmed at the implied criticism. 'I offered several times to relocate you—'

'I have no wish to be "relocated", Mr Buchanan,' Mary McGuire growled out between clenched teeth. 'This is my *home*. It will remain my home still, even once you've built and sold your luxurious apartments.'

And, as Jonas was only too aware, be a complete eyesore to the people who lived in those exclusive multimillion-pound apartments! 'In my experience, everyone has a price, Mary—'

'Mac.'

He frowned. 'Sorry?'

'Everyone who actually knows me calls me Mac, not Mary,' she explained. 'And maybe the people you're acquainted with have "a price", Mr Buchanan,' she said scathingly, smoky-grey eyes glittering with contempt. 'I happen to believe that my own family and friends have more integrity than that. As do I!'

Jonas now fully understood the frustration his employees had previously encountered when trying to talk to Mary 'Mac' McGuire; he had never before met a more stubborn, pigheaded and unreasonable individual than this particular woman!

His mouth thinned. 'You know where to reach me when you change your mind.'

'*If* I change my mind,' she corrected firmly. 'Which I won't. Now, if you will excuse me, Mr Buchanan?' She raised ebony brows. 'I really am very busy.'

And Jonas wasn't? With millions of pounds invested in one building project or another all over the world, Jonas's own time was, and always had been, at a premium. He certainly didn't have any more of it to waste tonight on this woman.

He stepped back. 'As I said, you know where to reach me when you've had enough.'

'Goodnight, Mr Buchanan,' she shot back with saccharin—and pointed—sweetness, before quietly closing the door in his face.

Jonas continued to scowl at that closed door for several minutes after she had carried out her threat to turn off the outside light and left him in darkness apart from the lights visible inside the warehouse itself.

He had already invested too much time and money in the building project due to begin on this site in the New Year to allow one stubborn individual to ruin it for him, or Buchanan Construction.

Obviously the money he had so far offered for this property wasn't enough of a reason for Miss McGuire to agree to move. Which meant Jonas was going to have to come up with a more convincing reason for her to want to leave.

CHAPTER TWO

'CHEER up, Mac,' Jeremy Lyndhurst teased as the first of the guests invited to this evening's viewing began to come through the gallery. The fifty-something co-owner of the prestigious Lyndwood Gallery continued, 'A few hours of looking good and being socially polite this evening, and tomorrow you can go back to being reclusive and dressing like a tramp!'

Mac chuckled huskily—as she knew she was meant to—at this reminder of the affront it was to Jeremy's own impeccable dress sense whenever she turned up at his gallery in her paint-smeared working clothes. Which she had done a lot the last few weeks as she came to deliver the individual paintings due to be exhibited at this evening's 'invitation only' showing of her work.

Jeremy's partner—in more ways than one—Magnus Laywood, a tall, blond giant in his forties, was at the door to 'meet and greet' as more of those guests began to arrive; mainly art critics and serious collectors, but also some other individuals who were just seriously rich.

There were twenty of Mac's paintings on show this evening, and all of them expertly displayed by Jeremy and Magnus, on walls of muted cream with their own individual lighting so that they showed to their best advantage.

It was the first individual exhibition of its kind that Mac had ever agreed to do—and now that the evening had finally arrived she was so nervous her knees were knocking together!

'Here, drink this.' Jeremy picked up a glass of champagne from one of the waiters who were starting to circulate amongst the guests in the rapidly filling room, and handed it to her. 'Your face just went green!' he explained with a chuckle.

Mac took a restorative sip of the bubbly alcohol. 'I've never been so nervous in my entire life.'

'Oh, to be twenty-seven again,' Jeremy murmured mournfully.

Mac took another sip of the delicious champagne. 'What if they don't like my work?' she wailed.

'They can't all be idiots, darling,' Jeremy drawled. 'It's going to be a wonderful evening, Mac,' he reassured her seriously as she still looked unconvinced. 'I know how hard this is for you, love, but just try to enjoy it, hmm?'

The problem was that Mac had never been particularly fond of exhibiting her work. Selling it, yes. Showing it to other people, and being 'socially polite' to those people, no. Unfortunately, as Mac was well aware, she couldn't make a living from her paintings if she didn't sell them.

'I'll try— Oh. My. God!' she gasped weakly as she saw, and easily recognised, the man now standing beside the door engaged in conversation with Magnus.

Jonas Buchanan!

He was as tall as Magnus, and dark and dangerous where the other man was blond and amiable, there was no mistaking that overlong dark hair and those hard and chiselled features dominated by piercing blue eyes that now swept coldly over the other guests.

Mac's heart hammered loudly in her chest as she took in the rest of his appearance. Dressed like every other man in the room, in a tailored black evening suit and snowy white shirt with a perfectly arranged black bow-tie at his throat, Jonas nevertheless somehow managed to look so much more compellingly handsome than any other man in the room.

'What is it?' Jeremy followed her line of vision. 'Who is that?' he murmured appreciatively, his longstanding relationship with Magnus not rendering him immune to the attractions of other men.

Mac dragged her gaze away from Jonas to look accusingly at the co-owner of the Lyndwood Gallery. 'You should know—you invited him!'

'I don't think so.' Jeremy's eyes were narrowed as he continued to look across at Jonas. 'Who is he?'

Mac swallowed hard before answering. 'Jonas Buchanan.'

Jeremy looked impressed. '*The* Jonas Buchanan?'

As far as Mac was aware there was only one Jonas Buchanan, yes!

'Ah, I understand now.' Jeremy nodded his satisfaction as a puzzle was obviously solved. 'He's with Amy Walters.'

Mac turned back in time to see Jonas Buchanan placing a proprietary hand beneath the elbow of a tall and beautiful redhead, the two of them talking softly together as they crossed the room to join a group of guests, Jonas easily standing several inches taller than the other men. Mac turned away abruptly.

'Amy's the art critic for *The Individual*,' Jeremy

supplied dryly as he saw the blankness of Mac's expression.

A completely unnecessary explanation as far as Mac was concerned; she knew exactly who Amy Walters was. It was the fact that the other woman had brought Jonas with her this evening, a man Mac was predisposed to dislike, that made things more than a little awkward; Mac was only too aware that she would have to be polite to the beautiful art critic if the two of them were introduced. Something that might be a little difficult for her to do with the arrogantly self-assured Jonas Buchanan standing at Amy's side!

The reason for that current self-assurance was obvious; invitations to this exhibition had been sent out weeks ago to ensure maximum attendance. Meaning that Jonas Buchanan had to have known, when they had met and spoken so briefly together two evenings ago, that he was going to be at her exhibition at the Lyndwood Gallery this evening.

Rat!

If he thought he could intimidate her by practically gatecrashing her exhibition, then he could—

'How nice to see you again so soon, Mac.'

Mac stiffened, her earlier nervousness completely evaporating and being replaced by indignation as she recognised Jonas Buchanan's silkily sarcastic tone as he spoke softly behind her.

Double rat!

Jonas kept his expression deliberately neutral as Mary 'Mac' McGuire slowly turned to face him.

To say that he had been surprised by her appearance this evening would be a complete understatement! In fact, if Amy hadn't teasingly assured him that the delicately lovely woman with her ebony hair secured on top of her head to reveal the slender loveliness of her neck, and wearing a red Chinese-style knee-length silk dress with matching red high-heeled sandals that showed off her shapely legs to perfection, was indeed the artist herself, then Jonas wasn't sure he would have even recognised her!

She looked totally different with her hair up, older, more sophisticated, those mysterious smoky-grey eyes surrounded by long and thick dark lashes, the paleness of her cheeks highlighted with blusher, those full and sensuous lips outlined with a lip gloss the same vibrant red as that figure-hugging red silk gown and three-inch sandals.

In a word, she looked exquisite!

Whoever would have thought it? Jonas mused ruefully. From bag-lady to femme fatale with the donning of a red silk dress.

Although the challenging glitter in those smoky grey eyes as she glared up at him was certainly familiar enough. 'Mr Buchanan,' she greeted dryly. 'Jeremy, this is Jonas Buchanan. Jonas, one of the gallery owners, Jeremy Lyndhurst.'

Mac watched through narrowed lashes as the two men shook hands, finding Jonas's appearance even more disturbing tonight than she had two evenings ago. He was one of the few men she had met who wore the elegance of a black evening suit rather than the clothes wearing him, the power of his personality such that it was definitely the man one noticed rather than the superb tailoring of the clothing he wore.

'Have you managed to lose Miss Walters already?' Mac asked sweetly as she saw that the other woman was talking animatedly to another man across the room.

Those electric-blue eyes darkened with sudden humour. 'Amy pretty much does her own thing,' Jonas Buchanan replied with a singular lack of concern.

'How...understanding, of you,' Mac taunted. Really, she was nervous enough about this evening already, without having to suffer this particular man's presence!

'Not at all,' Jonas drawled with deepening amusement.

'I do hope you will both excuse me...?' Jeremy cut in apologetically. 'Someone has just arrived that I absolutely have to go and talk to.'

'Of course,' Jonas Buchanan accepted smoothly. 'I assure you, I'm only too happy to stay and keep Mac company,' he added as he took a deliberate step closer to her.

A close proximity that Mac instantly took exception to!

One or other of this man's associates had been hounding her for months now in an effort to buy her home—but only so that it could be knocked down to become part of the area of ground landscaped as a garden for the new luxury apartment complex. The fact that Jonas Buchanan himself had now decided to get in on the act did not impress Mac in the slightest.

'You're looking very beautiful this evening—'

'Don't let appearances deceive you, Mr Buchanan,' she interrupted sharply. 'I'll be back to wearing my dungarees tomorrow.' Mac had made the mistake of dating a prestigious and arrogant art critic when she was still at university, and she wasn't about to ever let another man treat her as nothing but a beautiful trophy to exhibit on his arm. 'Exactly what are you doing here, Mr Buchanan?' she asked him directly.

Jonas studied her through narrowed lids. Two evenings ago he had thought this woman looked like a starving waif with absolutely no dress sense, but her exquisite appearance tonight in the red silk dress—which Jonas realised almost every other man in the room was also aware of—indicated to him that she must actually dress in those other baggy and unflattering clothes because she wanted to.

He shrugged. 'Amy asked me to be her escort this evening.'

Those red-glossed lips curled with distaste. 'How flattering to have a woman ask you out.'

Jonas's gaze hardened. 'I'm always happy to spend the evening with my cousin.'

Those smoky-grey eyes widened. 'Amy Walters is your cousin?'

He arched a mocking brow at her obvious incredulity. 'Is that so hard to believe?'

Well, no, of course it wasn't hard to believe, Mac accepted uncomfortably. But it did mean that Jonas wasn't here this evening on a date with another woman, as Mac had assumed that he was...

And why should that matter to her? She had no personal interest in this man. Did she...?

Lord, she hoped not!

The fact that he was one of the most compellingly attractive men Mac had ever met was surely nullified by the fact that he was also the man trying to force her out of her own home, by the sheer act of making it too uncomfortable for her to stay?

She steadily returned Jonas's piercing gaze as she shrugged. 'I don't see any family resemblance.'

He smiled wickedly. 'Maybe that's because Amy is a woman and I'm a man?'

Mac was well aware that Jonas was a man. Much too aware for her own comfort, as it happened. At five feet two inches tall, and weighing only a hundred pounds, in stark contrast to Jonas Buchanan's considerable height and powerful build, she was made totally aware of her own femininity by this man. And, uncomfortably, her vulnerability...

Her mouth firmed. 'I really should go and circulate amongst the other guests,' she told him as she placed her empty champagne glass down on a side table with the intention of leaving.

'Maybe I'll come with you.' Jonas Buchanan reached out to lightly grasp Mac by the elbow as she would have turned away.

His touch instantly sent a quiver of shocking aware-ness along the length of her arm and down into her breasts, causing them to swell inside her bra and the nipples to engorge to a pleasurable ache against the lacy material.

It was a completely unfamiliar—and unwelcome—feeling to Mac. After that one brief disaster of a relation-ship while at university, she had spent the following six years concentrating solely on her painting career, with little or no time to even think about relationships. She wasn't thinking of one now, either. Jonas Buchanan was the last man—positively *the* last man!—that Mac should be feeling physically attracted to.

Her body wasn't listening to her, unfortunately, as the warmth of Jonas's hand on her arm began to infiltrate the rest of her body, culminating uncomfortably at the apex of her thighs as she felt herself moisten there, in such a burst of heat that she gasped softly in awareness of that arousal.

She raised startled eyes to that hard and compellingly handsome face above hers, Jonas standing so close to her now she was able to see the individual pores in his skin. To recognise the lighter blue ring that surrounded the iris of his eyes, which gave them that piercing appearance. To gaze hypnotically at those slightly parted lips as they slowly lowered towards hers—

Mac jerked herself quickly out of his grasp. 'What are you doing?'

Yes, what *was* he doing? Jonas wondered frowningly. For a brief moment he had forgotten that they were surrounded by noisily chatting art critics and collectors. Had felt as if he and the exquisitely beautiful Mac McGuire were the only two people in the room, surrounded only by an expectant awareness and the heady seduction of her perfume.

Damn it, Jonas had been so unaware of those other people in the room that he had been about to kiss her in front of them all!

Her appearance this evening was an illusion, he reminded himself. Tonight she was the artist, deliberately dressed to beguile and seduce art critics and art collectors alike into approving of or buying her paintings. The fact that she had almost succeeded in seducing him into forgetting exactly who and what she was only increased Jonas's feelings of self-disgust.

His mouth thinned as he stepped away to look down at her through hooded lids. 'I really shouldn't keep you from your other guests any longer.'

Mac trembled slightly at the contempt she could hear in Jonas's tone. As she wondered what she had done to incur that contempt; he had been the one about to kiss her and not the other way around!

Her gaze returned to those sensually sculptured lips as she wondered what it would have felt like to have them part and claim her own lips. Jonas's mouth looked hard and uncompromising now, but seconds ago those firm lips had been soft and inviting as they lowered to hers—

Get a grip, Mac, she instructed herself firmly as she straightened decisively. The fact that he looked wonderful in a black evening suit, and was one of the most gorgeous men she had ever set eyes on, did not detract from the fact that he was also the enemy!

She eyed him mockingly. 'I would be polite and say that it's been nice seeing you again, Mr Buchanan, but we both know I would be lying...' She trailed off pointedly.

He gave a humourless smile in recognition of that mockery.

'I doubt very much that you've seen the last of me, Mac.'

She raised dark brows. 'I sincerely hope that you're wrong about that.'

His smile deepened. 'I rarely am when it comes to matters of business.'

'Modest too,' Mac scorned. 'Is there no end to your list of talents?' She snorted delicately. 'If you'll excuse me, Mr Buchanan.' She didn't wait for his reply to her statement but moved to cross the room to where she realised Magnus had discreetly been trying to attract her attention for the past few minutes.

Jonas stood unmoving as he watched her progress slowly across the room, stopping occasionally to greet people she knew. Unlike her behaviour towards him, the smiles Mac bestowed on the other guests were warm and relaxed, the huskiness of her laugh a soft caress to the senses, and revealing small, even white teeth against those full and red-glossed lips.

The tight-fitting silk dress emphasised the rounded curve of her bottom as she moved, and the slit up the side of the gown revealed the shapely length of her thigh. Jonas scowled his disapproval as he saw that most of the men in the room were also watching her, with one persistent man even grasping her wrist and trying to engage her in conversation before she laughingly managed to extricate herself and walked away to join Magnus Laywood.

'So what did you make of our little artist...?'

Jonas turned to look at Amy, compressing his mouth in irritation as he realised he had been so engrossed in watching Mac that he hadn't noticed his cousin's approach. A tall and beautiful redhead, with a temper to match, Jonas's maternal cousin wasn't a woman men usually overlooked!

'What did I think of Mary McGuire?' Jonas played for time as he was still too surprised at his reaction to the artist's change in appearance to be able to formulate a satisfactory answer to Amy's archly voiced question. 'She seems...a little young, to have engendered all this interest,' he drawled with bored lack of interest as he took two glasses of champagne from the tray of a passing waiter and handed one of them to his cousin.

'Young but brilliant,' Amy assured him unreservedly as she sipped the chilled wine.

'High praise indeed,' Jonas mused; his cousin wasn't known for her effusiveness when it came to her job as art critic for *The Individual*.

Amy linked her arm with his encouragingly. 'Come and look at some of her paintings.'

Mac continued to chat lightly with a collector who had expressed a serious interest in buying one of the paintings on display, at the same time completely aware of Jonas Buchanan and his cousin as they moved slowly through the two-roomed gallery to view her work.

It was impossible to tell from Jonas's expression what he thought of her paintings, those blue eyes hooded as he studied each canvas, his mouth unsmiling as he murmured in soft reply to Amy Walters's comments.

He probably hated them, Mac accepted heavily as she politely tried to refer the flirtatious collector to Jeremy for the more serious discussion over price. No doubt Jonas preferred modern art as opposed to her more ethereal style and bright but slightly muted use of colour. No doubt he had only agreed to accompany his cousin this evening in the first place because he had known that by doing so he would undermine Mac's confidence.

He needn't have bothered—Mac already hated all of this! She disliked the artificiality. Found the inane chatter tiresome. And she found herself especially irritated by the opportunistic collector she now realised was unobtrusively trying to place his hand on her bottom…

Mac moved sharply away from him, her eyes snapping with indignation at the uninvited familiarity. 'I'm sure that you'll find Jeremy will be only too happy to help with any further questions you might have.'

The middle-aged man chuckled meaningfully as he moved closer. 'He isn't my type!'

Mac frowned her discomfort, at a complete loss as to how to deal with this situation without causing a scene. Something she knew was out of the question with a dozen or so reporters also present in the room.

In their own individual ways Jeremy and Magnus had worked as hard on producing this exhibition this evening as Mac had. If she were to slap this obnoxious man's face, as she was so tempted to do, then the headlines in some of tomorrow's newspapers would read 'Artist slaps buyer's face!' instead of any praise or constructive criticism on her actual work.

She gave a shake of her head. 'I really don't think—'

'Sorry to have been gone so long, darling,' Jonas Buchanan interrupted smoothly as his arm moved firmly about Mac's waist to pull her securely against his side. He gave the other man a challenging smile, those compelling blue eyes as hard as the sapphires they resembled. 'It's rather crowded in here, isn't it?'

'I—yes.' The older and shorter man looked disconcerted by this unmistakable show of possessiveness. 'I—If you will both excuse me? I'll take your advice, Mac, and go and discuss the details with Jeremy.' He turned to hurriedly disappear into the crowd.

Mac found that she was trembling in reaction—and was totally at a loss to know if it was caused by the unpleasantness of the last minute or so, or because Jonas still held her so firmly against him that she was totally aware of the hard warmth of his powerful body...

Jonas took one look down at Mac's white face before his arm tightened about her waist and he turned her towards the entrance to the gallery. 'Let's get some air,' he suggested as he all but lifted her off the floor to carry her across the room and out of the door into the icy cold night. Something he instantly realised was a mistake as he could see by the street-lamp how Mac had begun to shiver in the thin silk dress. 'Here.' He slipped off his jacket to place it about her shoulders, his thumbs brushing lightly against the warm swell of her breasts as he stood in front of her to pull the lapels together.

Her eyes were huge as she looked up at him. 'Now you're going to be cold.'

She looked like a little girl playing dress-up with the shoulders of Jonas's jacket drooping down at the sides and the bulky garment reaching almost down to her knees. Except there was nothing childlike about the sudden awareness that darkened those smoky-grey eyes, or the temptation of those parted red-glossed lips as she breathed shallowly.

'How old are you really?' Jonas rasped harshly.

She blinked. 'I— What does that have to do with anything?'

He gave an impatient shrug of his shoulders. 'When I met you the other night you looked like someone's little sister. Tonight you look—well, tonight you look more like most men wished their best friend's little sister looked!'

She tilted that long elegant neck as she looked up at him. 'And how is that?' she prompted huskily.

This is a bad idea, Buchanan, Jonas cautioned himself. A very, very bad idea, he warned firmly even as his fascinated gaze remained fixed on those moist and parted lips.

A taste. He just wanted a taste of those sexy red lips—

Hell, no!

He was trying to transact a business deal with this woman, and he made a point of never mixing business with pleasure. And Jonas had no doubts it would have been very pleasurable to touch and taste those full and pouting lips with his own...

His expression was deliberately taunting as he looked down at her. 'In that dress you look like a woman who's ready for hot and wild sex.'

Mac's eyes widened as she gasped at the insult. 'I'll wear what I damn well please!'

That blue gaze moved deliberately down to the split in the side of her dress that revealed the long, bare length of her silky thigh. 'Obviously.'

'You're no better than the idiot whose attentions you

just appeared to save me from,' she accused furiously as she pulled his jacket from about her shoulders and almost threw it back at him before turning on her heel and marching back into the gallery without so much as a second glance.

Rude. Obnoxious. Insulting. Rat!

CHAPTER THREE

'I DON'T give a damn whether Mr Buchanan is busy or not,' an angry voice—that unfortunately Jonas recognised only too well!—snapped in the outer office of his London headquarters at nine-thirty on Monday morning. 'No, I have no intention of making an appointment. I want to talk to him *now*!' The door between the two rooms was flung open as Mac burst into Jonas's office.

Jonas barely had time to register her appearance, in a fitted black jumper and faded hipster blue denims, her hair a silken ebony curtain over her shoulders and down the length of her spine, before she marched over to stand in front of his desk, her cheeks flushed and eyes fever bright as she glared across at him.

She looked like a feral cat—and just as ready to spit and claw!

Jonas tilted his head sideways in order to look over at his secretary as she stood hesitantly in the doorway. 'There's no need to call Security, Mandy,' he drawled. 'I'm sure Miss McGuire won't be staying long...' He looked up enquiringly at Mac as he added that last statement.

Her eyes narrowed menacingly and she seemed to literally breathe fire at him. 'Long enough to tell you exactly what I think of you and your strong-arm tactics, at least!' she snarled.

'Thanks, Mandy,' Jonas dismissed his secretary, waiting until she had quietly left the room before looking back at Mac. 'You appear to be a little...distraught, this morning?'

'Distraught!' she echoed incredulously. 'I'm *furious*!'

Jonas could clearly see that. He just had no idea why that was.

Thankfully Amy had been ready to leave the gallery on Saturday evening when Jonas returned, allowing no opportunity for him and Mac to engage in any more arguments. Or to tempt Jonas into wanting to kiss her...

In the thirty-six hours since Jonas had last seen Mac, he had managed to convince himself that temptation had been an aberration on his part, a purely male reaction to the fact that she had looked as sexy as hell in that red silk dress.

Except that he now found himself facing the same temptation!

Mac wasn't wearing any make-up today, and her hair was windblown, her clothes casual in the extreme—and yet he still found his gaze drawn again and again to the fullness of her tempting lips.

Jonas's fingers tightened about the pen he was holding. 'Perhaps you would care to tell me why you're so furious?' he asked harshly. 'And what it has to do with me,' he added.

'Oh, don't worry, I'm going to tell you exactly why,' Mac promised. 'And you know damn well what it has to do with you!' she said accusingly.

Jonas raised his palms. 'I really am very busy this morning, Mac—'

'Do you have someone else you need to go and intimidate?' she scorned. 'Oh, I forgot—you usually leave that sort of thing to your underlings!' She snorted disgustedly. 'Well, let me assure you that I don't scare that easily—'

'Would you just calm down and tell me what the hell you're talking about?' he cut in coldly, those blue eyes glacial.

Mac was breathing hard, too upset still to heed the warning she could see in that chilling gaze. 'You know *exactly* what I'm talking about—'

'If I did, I would hardly be asking you to explain, now, would I?' Jonas retorted.

Mac's gaze narrowed. 'You knew I wouldn't be at home on Saturday evening because of the exhibition, and you shamelessly took advantage of that fact. You—'

He threw his pen down on the desktop before standing up impatiently. 'Mac, if you don't stop throwing out accusations, and just explain yourself, I'm afraid I'm going to have to ask you to leave.'

The anger Mac was feeling had been brewing, growing, since she'd returned home on Saturday evening. Having no idea where Jonas Buchanan actually lived, she'd had to spend all of Sunday brooding too, with only the promise of being able to visit Jonas at his office first thing on Monday morning to sustain her. Having his secretary try to stonewall her had done nothing to improve Mac's mood.

She drew in a controlling breath. 'My studio was broken into on Saturday evening. But, then, you already knew that, didn't you?' she said pointedly. 'You—'

'Stop right there!' Jonas thundered as he stepped out from behind his desk.

Mac instinctively took a step backwards as he

towered over her, appearing very dark and threatening in a charcoal-grey suit, pale grey shirt and grey silk tie, with that overlong dark hair styled back from the chiselled perfection of his face.

Those sculptured lips firmed to a livid thin line. 'You're telling me that your studio was broken into while you were out at the exhibition on Saturday evening?'

'You know that it was—'

'Mac, if you're going to continue to accuse me like this then I would seriously suggest that you have the evidence to back it up!' he warned harshly. 'Do you have that evidence?' he pressed.

She shook her head. 'The police didn't find anything that would directly implicate you, no,' she admitted grudgingly. 'But then, they wouldn't have done, would they?' she rallied. 'You're much more clever—'

'*Mac!*'

She blinked at the steely coldness Jonas managed to project into just that one word. Shivered slightly at the icy warning she could read in his expression.

But she didn't care how cold and steely Jonas was, the break-in had to have been carried out by someone who worked for him. Who else would have bothered, would have a reason to break into a building that, from the outside, appeared almost derelict?

Jonas was hanging onto his own temper by a thread. Angered as much by the thought of someone having broken into Mac's home at all, as at the accusations she was making about him being responsible for that break-in. She could so easily have been at home on Saturday evening. Could have been seriously hurt if she had disturbed the intruder.

He frowned. 'Did they take anything?'

'Not that I can see, no. But—'

'Let's just stick to the facts, shall we, Mac?' Jonas bit out, a nerve pulsing in his tightly clenched jaw.

She eyed him warily. 'The facts are that I arrived home late on Saturday evening to find my studio completely wrecked. The only consolation—if it can be called that!—is that at least all of my most recent work was at the gallery that evening.'

Jonas nodded. 'So there was no real damage done?'

Mac's eyes widened indignantly. 'My home, my privacy, was invaded!'

And he could understand how upsetting that must have been for her. Must still be. But the facts were that neither Mac nor her property had actually come to any real harm.

He moved to sit on the side of his desk. 'At least you had the sense to call the police.'

'I'm not a complete moron!'

Jonas didn't think that Mac was a moron at all. All evidence was to the contrary. 'I don't recall ever saying otherwise,' he commented dryly.

'You implied it, with your "at least" comment!' She thrust her hands into the hip pockets of her denims, instantly drawing Jonas's attention to the full and mature curve of her breasts beneath the fitted black sweater. Making a complete nonsense of how he had mistaken her for a young girl at their first meeting two days ago.

She was different again today, he realised ruefully. No longer the waif or the femme fatale, but a beautiful and attractive woman in her late twenties. A man could never become bored with Mac McGuire when he would never know on any given day which woman he was going to meet!

He sighed. 'What conclusions did the police come to?'

She shrugged those narrow shoulders. 'They seem to think it was kids having fun.'

Jonas grimaced. 'Maybe they're right—'

'Kids don't just break in, they steal things,' Mac disagreed impatiently. 'I have a forty-two-inch flat-screen television set, a new Blu-ray Disc player, a state-of-the-art music system and dozens of CDs, and none of them were even touched.'

Jonas looked intrigued. 'So it was just your studio that was targeted?'

'*Just* my studio?' she repeated indignantly. 'You just don't understand, do you?' she added as she turned away in disgust.

The problem for Jonas was that he did understand. He understood only too well. Having seen Mac's work for himself on Saturday evening, he knew exactly how important her studio was to her. It was the place where she created beauty deep from within her. Where she poured out her soul onto canvas. To have that vandalised, wrecked, was the equivalent of attacking the inner, deeply emotional Mac.

His mouth firmed. 'But you believe *I'm* responsible for what happened?'

Mac turned to eye him warily as she once again heard that underlying chill in Jonas's tone, the warning against repeating her earlier accusations.

If Jonas wasn't responsible, then who was? Not just who, but why? Nothing of value had been taken. In fact, the living-area part of her home hadn't been touched. Only her studio had been vandalised. Surely whoever had done that would have to know her to realise that the studio was her heart and soul?

Which, as he didn't know her, surely ruled out Jonas Buchanan as being the person responsible for the damage? After all, they had only met twice before this morning, and neither of those occasions had been in the least conducive to them gaining any personal insights about each other. Jonas certainly couldn't know how much Mac's studio meant to her.

She gave a weary shake of her head. 'I don't know what to believe any more...'

'That's something, I suppose,' Jonas commented dryly. 'Why don't we start with the premise that neither I nor anyone I employ had anything to do with the break-in, and go from there?' he suggested. 'Who else could have reason for wanting to cause you this personal distress? Perhaps an artist rival, jealous of your success? Or maybe an ex-lover who didn't go quietly?' he added.

Mac's eyes narrowed. 'Very funny!'

Strangely, Jonas didn't find his last suggestion in the least amusing. Especially when it was accompanied by vivid images of this woman's naked body intimately entwined with another man, that ebony hair falling about the two of them like a silken curtain...

He straightened abruptly and once again moved to sit behind his desk. 'I really am busy this morning, Mac. In fact I have an appointment in a little under five minutes, so why don't we meet up again at lunchtime and discuss this further?'

Mac eyed him suspiciously. 'You're inviting me out to lunch?' she repeated uncertainly, as if she were sure she must have misheard him.

No, Jonas hadn't been inviting her out to lunch. In fact, those earlier imaginings had already warned him that, the less he had to do with the volatile Mac McGuire, the better he would like it!

'On second thoughts it would be far more sensible if you were to talk to my secretary on your way out and make an appointment to come back and see me at a time more convenient for both of us.'

It would be more sensible, Mac agreed, but after arriving back late from the gallery on Saturday evening to find her studio in chaos, and then another hour spent talking to the police, to spend the rest of the weekend alternating between ranting at the mess and crying for the same reason, she wanted to sort this problem out once and for all. Today, if possible.

Her parents, safely ensconced in their retirement bungalow home in Devon, where they also ran a B&B in the summer months, already worried that their move to the south of England had left her living alone in London. They would be horrified to learn that she'd had a break-in at her home.

But was it a good idea for her to have lunch with Jonas Buchanan? Probably not, Mac acknowledged ruefully. Except that he had seemed sincere—no, furious, actually—in his denial that he was in any way responsible for the break-in.

If that were genuinely the case, then she probably owed him an apology, at least, for having come here and made those bitter accusations.

'Lunch sounds a better idea,' Mac contradicted his earlier suggestion. 'In fact, I'll take you out to lunch.'

Jonas raised mocking brows. 'Would that offer be the equivalent of wearing sackcloth and ashes?'

Mac felt the warmth of colour in her cheeks at his pointed suggestion that she should appear penitent for her behaviour. 'It means that for the moment I'm prepared to give you the benefit of the doubt regarding the break-in.'

'For the moment?' Jonas repeated softly, trying not to grit his teeth. 'That's very…good of you.'

'Don't push your luck, Jonas,' she snapped. 'I'm only suggesting this at all because this whole situation seems to be getting out of control.'

Jonas considered her between hooded lids. Mac really had behaved like a little hellion this morning by forcing her way into his office and throwing out her wild accusations. And if Jonas had any sense then he would tell her he would see her in court for even daring to voice those accusations without a shred of evidence to back up her claim. He certainly shouldn't even be thinking of accepting her invitation to have lunch.

Except that he was…

Mac intrigued him. Piqued his interest in a way no woman had done for a very long time. If ever.

All the more reason not to even consider going out to lunch with her then!

She was absolutely nothing like the women Jonas was usually attracted to. Beautiful and sophisticated women who knew exactly what the score was. Who expected nothing from him except the gift of a few expensive baubles during the few weeks or months their relationship lasted; if any of those women had ever harboured the hope of having any more than that from him then they had been sadly disappointed.

Jonas had witnessed and lived through the disintegration of his own parents' marriage. He had been twelve years old when he'd watched them start to rip each other to shreds, both emotionally and verbally, culminating in an even messier divorce when Jonas was fifteen.

He had decided long ago that none of that was for

him. Not the initial euphoria of falling in love. Followed by a few years of questionable happiness. Before the compromises began. The irritation. And then finally the hatred for each other, followed by divorce.

Jonas wanted none of it. Would willingly forgo the supposed 'euphoria' of falling in love if it meant he also avoided experiencing the disintegration of that relationship and the hatred for each other that followed.

Mac McGuire, for all she was an independent and successful artist, gave every appearance of being one of those happily-ever-after women Jonas had so far managed to avoid having any personal involvement with.

'Well?' she prompted irritably at Jonas's lengthy silence.

He should say no. Should tell this woman that he had remembered he already had a luncheon appointment today.

Damn it, it was only lunch, not a declaration of intent!

His mouth thinned. 'I have an hour free between one o'clock and two o'clock today.'

'Wow,' Mac murmured, those smoky-grey eyes now openly laughing at him. 'I should feel honoured that Jonas Buchanan feels he can spare me a whole hour of his time.'

His eyes narrowed to icy slits as he retorted, 'When what I should really do is take your shapely little bottom to court and sue you for slander!'

Mac's eyes widened and hot colour suffused her cheeks at hearing Jonas claim she had a shapely little bottom, making her once again completely aware of his own dark and dangerous attraction...

If anything he seemed even bigger today, his wide shoulders and powerful chest visibly muscled beneath the tailored suit and silk shirt, his face hard and slightly predatory, and dominated by those piercing blue eyes that seemed to see too much.

Did they see just how affected Mac was by his dark good looks, and that air of danger?

Perhaps the two of them lunching together wasn't such a good idea, after all, Mac decided with a frown. She could always claim that she had remembered a prior engagement. That she had to go to the Lyndwood Gallery to check on how the exhibition was going—

'Jonas, I have the letter here from—' The blonde, blue-eyed woman who had entered from the adjoining office, and who Mac instantly recognised as being Jonas's PA, Yvonne Richards—the same woman who had visited Mac a couple of months ago in an effort to persuade her into agreeing to sell her home—came to an abrupt halt in the doorway to Jonas's office as she saw Mac there. 'I'll come back later, shall I?' She totally ignored Mac as she looked at Jonas enquiringly.

'No need, Yvonne; Miss McGuire was just leaving,' Jonas said as he stood up, obviously dismissing Mac.

The fact that was exactly what Mac had been about to do did nothing to nullify the fact that Jonas was trying to get rid of her! Without any firm arrangements having been made for them to meet later today to continue this discussion...

'There's an Italian restaurant two streets over from this one,' she turned to inform him briskly. 'I'll book a table for us there for one o'clock.'

'Perhaps you would prefer me to book the table for the two of you?' the blonde woman offered coolly. 'Mr Buchanan's name is known to the restaurant owner,' she added pointedly as Mac looked at her enquiringly.

Mac gave the other woman a narrowed-eyed glance as

she heard the edge in her tone, recognising that Yvonne Richards, beautiful and in her late twenties, was obviously a typical case of the PA who believed herself in love with her boss. A crush that Mac doubted Jonas Buchanan was even aware of.

Mac gave the other woman a saccharin-sweet smile. 'That won't be necessary, thank you; I know Luciano personally, too.'

'Fine,' Yvonne Richards bit out before turning to her employer. 'I'll come back when you aren't so busy, Jonas.' She turned abruptly on her two-inch heels and went back into the adjoining office, the door closing sharply behind her.

Mac turned back to Jonas. 'I don't think your PA likes me!'

Jonas's mouth compressed briefly. 'She hasn't known you long enough yet to dislike you.' Before Yvonne had interrupted them Jonas had had every intention of refusing Mac's invitation to lunch, and he wasn't at all happy with the fact that, between them, Yvonne and Mac seemed to have arranged for him to have lunch at Luciano's at one o'clock today.

Mac gave an unconcerned grin, two unexpected dimples appearing in her cheeks. 'That usually takes a little longer than five minutes, hmm?'

'Precisely,' he growled.

She raised dark, mocking brows. 'Perhaps she just has a crush on you?'

An irritated scowl darkened Jonas's brow. 'Don't be ridiculous!'

Mac gave an unconcerned shrug. 'She seems—less than happy at the thought of the two of us having lunch together.'

'Will you just go away and leave me in peace, Mac?'

Once again Jonas moved to sit behind his imposing desk in obvious dismissal. 'I'll see you later,' he added pointedly as Mac made no move to respond to his less-than-subtle hint.

'One o'clock at Luciano's,' she came back mockingly before turning and walking over to the door that led out to his secretary's office.

Jonas's scowl deepened as he found he couldn't resist the temptation to look up and watch Mac leave. To be fully aware of his own response, the stirring, hardening, heated pulsing of his thighs, as he watched the provocative sway of those slender hips and pert bottom beneath fitted jeans.

She was an irritation and a nuisance, he told himself firmly. Trouble.

With a very definite capital T!

CHAPTER FOUR

'THIS is nice.'

'Is it?' Jonas asked darkly as they sat at a window table in Luciano's. It was an obvious indication that Mac was indeed known personally to the restaurateur; Jonas had dined here often enough in the past to know that Luciano only ever reserved the window tables for his best and most-liked customers.

Mac was already seated at the table, and had been supplied with some bread sticks to eat while she was waiting, by the time Jonas arrived at the restaurant at ten minutes past one. Not that he had been deliberately late; his twelve-thirty appointment had just run over time.

Everything had seemed to go wrong after she had left his office this morning. His nine-thirty appointment hadn't arrived until almost ten o'clock—which was probably as well when Jonas had spent most of the intervening time trying to dampen down his obvious arousal for Mac McGuire!

He had also found himself closely studying Yvonne throughout the morning as he searched for any signs of that 'crush' Mac had mentioned. Rightly or wrongly, Jonas didn't approve of personal relationships within the workplace—and that included unrequited ones. Which meant, if Mac was right, he would have to start looking for another PA. But if anything Yvonne's demeanour had been slightly frostier than usual, with nothing to suggest she had anything other than a working relationship with him.

Resulting in Jonas feeling annoyed with himself for doubting his own judgement, and even more irritated with Mac for mischievously giving him those doubts in the first place!

Consequently, he was feeling irritable and bad-tempered by the time he sat down at the lunch table opposite his perkily cheerful nemesis. 'Let's just order, shall we?' he grated as he picked up the menu and held it up in front of him as an indication he was not in the mood for conversation.

Mac didn't bother to look at her own menu, already knowing exactly what she was going to order: garlic prawns followed by lasagne. As far as she was concerned, Luciano made the best lasagne in London.

Instead she looked across at Jonas as he gave every indication of concentrating on choosing what he was going to have for lunch.

Every female head in the Italian bistro had turned to look at him when he'd entered a few minutes ago and taken off his long woollen coat to hang it up just inside the door. They had continued to watch him as he made his way over to the window table, several women giving Mac envious glances when he'd pulled out the chair opposite her own and sat down.

Mac had found herself watching him too; Jonas simply was the sort of man that women of all ages took a second, and probably a third, look at. He was so tall for one thing, and the leashed and elegant power of his lean and muscled body in that perfectly tailored charcoal-coloured suit was undeniable.

His irritation told her that he was also not in a good mood. 'We don't have to eat lunch together if you would rather not?' Mac prompted ruefully.

He lowered his menu enough to look across at her with icy blue eyes. 'You would rather I moved to another table? That's going to make conversation very difficult, wouldn't you say?' he taunted.

Mac felt the warmth in her cheeks at his obvious mockery. 'Very funny!'

Jonas placed his closed menu down on the table. 'I want to know more about the break-in to your studio on Saturday night. Such as how whoever it was got inside in the first place?' he asked grimly.

Mac shrugged. 'They broke a small window next to the door and reached inside to open it.'

Jonas noticed that some of the animation had left those smoky-grey eyes, presumably at his reminder of the break-in. 'You don't have an alarm system installed?'

She grimaced. 'I've never thought I needed one.'

'Obviously you were wrong,' Jonas said reprovingly.

'Obviously.' Anger sparkled in those grey eyes now. 'I have to say that I've always found people's smugness after the event to be intensely irritating!' She was still wearing the black fitted sweater and faded denims of earlier, the silky curtain of her hair framing the delicate beauty of her face to fall in an ebony shimmer over her shoulders and down her back.

Jonas relaxed back in his chair to look across at her speculatively. 'Then hopefully I've succeeded in irritating you enough to have a security system installed. Or perhaps I should just arrange to have it done for you?' he mused out loud, knowing it would immediately goad her to respond with the information that he wanted.

'That won't be necessary, thank you; I have a company coming out to install one first thing tomorrow morning,' she came back sharply. 'Along with a glazier to replace the window that was broken.'

His eyes narrowed. 'You haven't had the glass replaced yet?'

'I just said I hadn't,' Mac bit back.

Jonas gave a disgusted sigh. 'You should have got someone out on Sunday to fix it.'

Mac's eyes flashed darkly. 'Don't presume to tell me what I should or shouldn't do!'

'It's a security breach—'

'Oh, give it a rest, Jonas,' she muttered wearily. 'I'm quite capable of organising my own life, thank you.'

'I'm seriously starting to doubt that.'

'Strangely, your opinion is of little relevance to me!' Mac snapped. 'When I suggested we have lunch to talk about this situation I wasn't actually referring to the break-in.'

Jonas managed to dampen down his impatience as he smiled up at Luciano as he appeared beside their table to personally take their order.

'I take it you don't have a date this evening?' He mockingly changed the subject once the restaurateur had taken note of their order and returned to his beloved kitchen a few minutes later.

Mac knew he had to be referring to the fact that there was garlic in both of the foods she had ordered. 'I take it that you do?' she retorted, the Marie Rose prawns and Dover sole he had ordered not having any garlic in at all.

'As it happens, no.' That blue gaze met hers taunt-ingly. 'Are you offering to rectify that omission?'

Mac frowned. 'You can't be serious?'

Was he? Having spent part of the morning in un-comfortable arousal because of this woman, Jonas had once again decided that, the less he had to do with Mac the better it would be for both him and his aching erec-tion! A decision his last remark made a complete non-sense of.

'Obviously not,' he muttered.

Mac looked across at him shrewdly. 'It sounded like you were asking me out on a date.'

Jonas shrugged. 'You're entitled to your opinion, I suppose.'

'You "suppose"?' she taunted.

He scowled darkly. 'Mac, are you deliberately trying to initiate an argument with me?'

'Maybe.'

Jonas narrowed his gaze. 'Why?'

'Why not?' Mac smiled. 'It's certainly livened up the conversation!'

Jonas knew it had done a lot more than that. He was far too physically aware of this woman already; he didn't need to feel any more so. In fact, he was somewhat relieved when the waiter chose that moment to deliver their first course to them.

What the hell had he been doing, all but suggesting that Mac ask him out on a date this evening? Meeting her for lunch was bad enough, without prolonging the time he had to spend in her disturbing company. In future, Jonas decided darkly, he would just stick to taking out his usual beautiful and sophisticated blondes!

'The reviews of your exhibition in Sunday's newspa-pers were good,' he abruptly changed the subject.

She nodded. 'Your cousin was especially kind.'

'Amy is a complete professional; if she says you're good, then you're good,' Jonas said.

'I went to the gallery after seeing you this morning. It seems to be pretty busy,' Mac told him distractedly, still slightly reeling from what she was pretty sure had been an invitation on Jonas's part for them to spend the evening together too. An offer he had obviously instantly regretted making.

Which was just as well considering Mac would have had to refuse the invitation! Going to his office was one thing. Having lunch with Jonas so that they could discuss what was going on with her warehouse was also acceptable. Going out on a proper date with him was something else entirely...

In spite of the fact that Jonas Buchanan was so obviously a devastatingly attractive man, he simply wasn't Mac's type. He was far too arrogant. At least as arrogant, if not more so, as Thomas Connelly, the art critic who had considered her nothing but a trophy to parade on his arm six years ago.

She picked up her fork to deliberately spear one of the succulent prawns swimming in garlic, before raising it to her mouth and popping it between her lips. Only to glance across the table at the exact moment she did so, her cheeks heating with flaming wings of colour as she saw the intensity with which Jonas was watching the movement.

Dark and mesmerising, his eyes had become a deep and cobalt blue. There was a slight flush to his cheeks too, and those sculptured lips were slightly parted.

Mac shifted uncomfortably. 'Would you like to try one?'

That dark gaze lifted up to hers. 'What?'

She swallowed hard, feeling strangely alone with Jonas in this crowded and happily noisy restaurant. 'You seemed to be coveting my garlic prawns, so I was offering to let you try one...'

Damn it, Jonas hadn't been coveting the prawns on Mac's plate—he had been imagining lying back and having those full and red lips placed about a certain part of his anatomy as she pleasured him!

What the hell was the *matter* with him?

In the last fifteen years he had never once mixed business with pleasure. Had always kept the two firmly separate. Since meeting Mac he seemed to have done nothing else but confuse the two, with the result that he was now once again fully aroused beneath the cover of the chequered tablecloth. Hopefully there would be no reason for him to stand up in the next few minutes or his arousal would be well and truly exposed!

'No, thank you,' he refused quickly. 'I would prefer not to smell of garlic during any of my business meetings later this afternoon.'

Mac gave an unconcerned shrug of her shoulders. 'Please yourself.'

'I usually do,' Jonas said dryly.

'Lucky you,' she said.

Jonas considered Mac through narrowed lids. 'Are you saying that you don't?' he taunted. 'I thought all artists preferred to be free spirits? In relationships as well as their art?'

Mac didn't miss the contempt in his tone. Or the underlying implication that, as an artist, she probably slept around.

It would have been amusing if it weren't so obvious that Jonas had once again meant to be insulting!

Oh, Mac had lots of friends, male as well as female,

both from school and university, but that didn't mean she went to bed with any of them. That she had ever been intimately involved with anyone, in fact.

After that fiasco with Thomas, Mac had become completely focused on what she wanted to do with her life. Which was to be successful as an artist in her own right.

From the time she was twelve years old, and her art teacher had allowed her to paint with oils on canvas for the first time, Mac had known exactly what she wanted, and that was to become a successful artist first, with marriage and children second. She had become slightly sidetracked from that ambition during that brief relationship with Thomas, but if anything the realisation of his arrogance and condescension had only increased that ambition.

'If you'll excuse me, I need to go to the ladies' room.' She placed her napkin on the table before pushing back her chair and standing up.

Jonas raised dark brows. 'Was it something I said?'

Mac frowned down at him. 'That necessitates my needing to go to the ladies' room?' she drawled derisively. 'Hardly!'

Nevertheless, Jonas was left sitting alone at the table feeling less than happy, both with himself, and with his earlier biting comment. He knew very little about her personal life—the fact that he had an erection every time he was in her company really didn't count! He certainly didn't know her well enough to have deliberately cast aspersions upon the way she might choose to live her private life.

He forced himself to continue eating his own food as he waited for Mac to return.

And waited.

And waited.

After over ten minutes had passed since she'd left the table, Jonas came to the uncomfortable conclusion that she might have walked out on both him and the restaurant!

Deservedly so?

Maybe. But that didn't make the experience—the first time that a woman had ever walked out on Jonas, for any reason—any more palatable than the prawns he had just forced himself to finish eating.

He stood up abruptly to place his own napkin on the tabletop and make his way across the restaurant to the door through to the washrooms, determined to see exactly how Mac had made her escape. Only to come to a halt in the doorway and feeling completely wrong-footed as he came face to face with Mac, who was standing in the corridor in laughing conversation with one of the waitresses.

She looked at him curiously. 'Is there a problem, Jonas?'

His eyes narrowed. 'Your food is getting cold.'

'Oh, dear.' The waitress gave an apologetic smile. 'I'll talk to you later, Mac,' she said, before hurrying off in the direction of the kitchen.

Leaving Mac alone in the hallway with an obviously seriously displeased Jonas.

Well, that was just too bad!

Jonas had been deliberately insulting before she left the table, and when she'd bumped into Carla as she was leaving the ladies' room Mac had felt no hesitation in stopping to chat; Jonas Buchanan could just sit alone at the table for a few more minutes and stew as far as she was concerned.

She raised dark brows as he stepped further into the

otherwise deserted hallway and quietly closed the door behind him, enclosing the two of them in a strangely tense and otherwise deserted silence. Mac shifted uncomfortably as Jonas walked stealthily down that hallway towards her. 'I thought you said my food was getting cold?' she prompted, suddenly nervous.

'It's already cold, so a few more minutes isn't going to make any difference,' he dismissed softly.

Mac moistened dry lips as Jonas kept walking until he came to a halt standing only inches away from her. Very tall and large, his close proximity totally unnerving. 'Why do we need to be a few more minutes?' She glanced up at him uncertainly.

Jonas was enjoying turning the tables and seeing Mac's obvious discomfort—God knew she had already made his own life uncomfortable enough for one day! Since the moment he first met her, in fact. He had no doubt that leaving him sitting alone at a table in the middle of a crowded restaurant had been deliberate on her part.

A public restaurant wasn't the ideal place for what he now had in mind, either, but to hell with that—Jonas had realised in the last few seconds that he didn't just need to kiss Mac, it had become as necessary to him as breathing.

'Guess,' he murmured throatily as he stepped even closer to her.

Her eyes widened in alarm as she took several steps back until she found herself against the wall. 'Garlic breath, remember,' she reminded him hastily.

He gave an unconcerned shrug. 'That will just make you taste even better.'

'This is so not a good idea, Jonas,' she warned him desperately.

Jonas was all out of good ideas. At this precise moment he intended—needed—to go with a bad one.

His gaze held Mac's as he reached up to cup his hand against the silky smooth curve of her cheek and ran the soft pad of his thumb over her slightly parted lips, the warmth of her breath a caress against his own highly sensitised skin. An arousing caress that made his stomach muscles clench and his thighs harden.

He drew in a sharp breath as he stepped closer still and Mac instinctively lifted her hands to rest them defensively against the hardness of his chest, the warmth of those hands burning through the silk material of Jonas's shirt as he deliberately rested his body against hers.

Mac suddenly found herself trapped between the cold wall and the heat of Jonas's body, her hands crushed against his muscled chest as he slowly lowered his head with the obvious intention of kissing her.

She knew she should protest. That she should at least try to ward off this rapidly increasing intimacy.

And yet she didn't. Couldn't.

Instead her lips parted in readiness for that kiss, her breath arrested in her throat at the first heated touch of Jonas's lips against hers.

Oh, Lord…

Mac had never known anything like the sensual pleasure of having Jonas's mouth moving against hers, exploring, sipping, tasting, teeth gently biting before that kiss deepened hungrily, his body hard and insistent against hers as her hands moved up his shoulders and her fingers became entangled in the dark thickness of his hair as she pulled him even closer. Jonas pushed her against the wall and lowered his body until his arousal pressed into Mac, making her respond with an aching hotness that pooled between her thighs in a rush of moist and fiery heat, her breasts swelling, the rosy tips hardening to full sensitivity as they pressed against the lacy material of her bra.

Her fingers tightened in the silky softness of Jonas's hair as that heat grew, their mouths fusing together hungrily, Mac groaning low in her throat as she felt the firm thrust of Jonas's tongue enter her mouth. Hot, slow and deep thrusts matched by the rhythmic movement of his thighs into the juncture of her sensitive thighs.

Mac groaned again in pleasure as that hardness pressed against the swollen nub nestled there, creating an aching heat deep inside her before it spread to every part of her body, arousing her to an almost painful degree.

God, she wanted this man with a ferocity of need she had never imagined, never dreamt was possible. Here. Now. She wanted to strip off their clothes and have Jonas take her up against the wall, her legs wrapped about his waist as he thrust deep inside her to ease that burning ache.

As if aware of at least some of her need, Jonas moved his hand to curve about her left breast, the soft pad of his thumb unerringly finding the swollen tip and sweeping across it.

Mac whimpered as the pleasure of that caress coursed down to her thighs, and she wished Jonas could touch her there, too—

'Well, *really*!' a shocked female voiced gasped. 'This *is* a public restaurant, you know,' the woman added disgustedly as she walked past them to the washrooms. 'Why don't the two of you just get a room somewhere?' The door to the ladies room closed behind her with a disapproving snap.

Mac had wrenched away from Jonas the moment

she'd realised they were no longer alone in the hallway, burying the heat of her face against his chest now to hide her embarrassment at being caught in such a compromising position.

In a public restaurant, for goodness' sake!

With Jonas Buchanan, of all people.

What could she have been thinking?

She hadn't been thinking at all, that was the problem. She had been feeling. Experiencing emotions, sensations, she had never known before.

If that woman hadn't interrupted them then Mac might just have gone through with that urge she'd had to start ripping Jonas's clothes from his body before begging him to ease the burning ache between her thighs!

Oh, God.

CHAPTER FIVE

'SO, WHAT do you think?' Jonas asked as he stepped back from Mac.

'What do I think about what?' She blinked up at him as she straightened away from the wall to push the tangle of her hair back from her face; her eyes fever bright, her cheeks flushed, and those sensuously enticing lips slightly swollen from the fierce hunger of their kisses.

A hunger that had made Jonas forget, not only who they were, but *where* they were. All that had mattered to him at that moment was tasting Mac, devouring those tempting red lips, pressing the heat of his body against hers, her fingers becoming entangled in his hair as she responded to his desire.

Jonas knew he hadn't been this physically aroused, so totally lost to reason, since he was an inexperienced teenager. And he didn't like the sensation of being out of control. He didn't like it at all.

His mouth twisted. 'The two of us getting a hotel room for the afternoon.'

Mac's eyes widened. 'Certainly not!' she exclaimed indignantly.

'Why not?' he taunted.

'Why not?' Mac repeated as she glared up at him. 'I have no idea what sort of women you usually associate with, Jonas, but I can assure you that I do not go to hotel rooms with men for the afternoon!'

'I wasn't suggesting you went with men plural, Mac, just me,' he drawled.

'I said *no!*' She was breathing heavily in her agitation, the fullness of her breasts rapidly rising and falling.

Something that Jonas was all too well aware of as he looked down at her and his still heavily roused manhood pulsed achingly in response. 'You want me, I want you, so why the hell not?' he rasped.

He would have felt happier about this situation if Mac had just said yes to the two of them going to a hotel for the afternoon. That way he would have found her less of an enigma than he did now. Less intriguing than he did now.

Because Mac had definitely returned his passion. Yet it was a passion she made it clear she had no intention of doing anything about, probably not now nor in the future. He already knew his own afternoon was going to be as uncomfortable as his morning had been, but how did Mac intend dealing with her own unsatisfied arousal?

'Unless you're trying to tell me you don't want me?' he murmured.

Mac wasn't sure which of her emotions was the strongest—the urge she had to slap Jonas's arrogant face or the one she had to just sit down and cry at her own stupidity.

Because he was right, damn him. She did want him. She had never physically wanted a man more, in fact, her whole body one burning ache of need. Something Mac knew was going to bother her long after he had gone back to his office to attend his afternoon meetings.

But she definitely wanted to slap him too. For bringing

that physical awareness down to a purely basic level by suggesting they get a hotel room for the afternoon and satisfy those longings.

She really wasn't that sort of woman. She had never done anything so impulsively reckless as kissing a man so heatedly on the premises of a restaurant before, let alone gone to a hotel room with him, and she had no intention of doing the latter now with Jonas, either. Much as she might secretly ache to do so. It sounded wild. Liberating. Dangerously exciting…

She deliberately fell back on anger as the solution to her predicament. 'Whether I want you or not, an afternoon in a hotel bedroom with a man I barely know—and who I really don't want to know any better—is really not my thing,' she told him scornfully. 'If you're feeling frustrated, Jonas, then I'm sure there are any number of women you could call who would be only too happy to spend the afternoon satisfying you!'

Jonas's eyes narrowed to icy slits. 'I've never been that desperate for sex, Mac.'

Including sex with her, she knew he was implying. Which was no doubt true. Jonas was young, handsome and rich enough to attract any woman he decided he wanted. He certainly didn't need to trouble himself over one stubborn artist, who obviously irritated him as much as she aroused him.

And Mac had aroused him. She'd felt the hard evidence of that arousal pressed against her own thighs as Jonas kissed her.

Her mouth firmed. 'I suggest we just forget about lunch,' she said abruptly. 'I'm really not hungry any more, and I doubt you are either—'

'Not for food, anyway,' Jonas muttered.

'I—' Mac broke off suddenly as the woman who

had interrupted them earlier now came back out of the ladies' room, her gaze averted as she passed them and returned to the dining room of the restaurant. Mac's embarrassment returned with a vengeance. 'Don't worry, I'll explain to Luciano that you had an appointment you had to go to rather than intending any slight to the preparation of his food.'

'I moved my afternoon around. My next appointment isn't for another hour,' Jonas told her.

Her eyes widened. 'You want us to go back to the table and finish eating lunch together?'

After what just happened between us? Jonas inwardly finished Mac's question. And the answer to that was no, of course he didn't want them to return to the table and carry on eating lunch together as if nothing had happened. But neither did he appreciate Mac dismissing him as if the last few minutes had never happened at all.

His mouth thinned. 'Obviously not,' he bit out tersely. 'I'll settle the bill and explain to Luciano that *you* had a previous appointment.'

Mac frowned. 'I asked you out to lunch—'

'I'm paying the bill, Mac,' Jonas repeated firmly.

Mac continued to look up at him frowningly for several long seconds before giving an impatient shrug. 'Fine. Whatever.' Her tone implied she just wanted to get out of here. Away from him. Now.

A need she followed through on as she turned swiftly on her heel and marched down the hallway back into the restaurant, the door swinging closed behind her.

Jonas remained where he was for several more minutes after Mac had gone, eyes narrowed and his expression grim as he recognised that she was no longer just a problem on a business level, but had also become one on a personal level, too.

Perhaps one that would only be resolved once they had been to bed together...

Mac was barefooted and belatedly eating a piece of toast for her lunch when she went to answer the knock on her door later that afternoon, a brief glance through the spy-hole in the door showing her that she didn't know the grey-haired man standing at the top of the metal staircase dressed like a workman in blue overalls and a thick checked shirt. 'Yes?' she prompted politely after opening the door.

'Afternoon, love,' the middle-aged man returned with a smile. 'Bob Jenkins. I've come to replace ya window.'

Mac's brows rose. 'That's great!'

He was already inspecting the broken window next to the door. 'Had a break-in, did ya?' He gave a shake of his head. 'Too much of it about nowadays. No respect, that's the problem. Not for people or their property.'

'No.' Mac grimaced as she recalled the mess that had been left in her studio.

'It will only take a few minutes to fix.' Bob Jenkins gave her another encouraging smile. 'I'll just go and get my things from the van.'

Mac had made him a mug of tea by the time he came back up the stairs with his tools and a pane of glass that appeared to be the exact size of the one that had been broken. 'How did you know which size glass to bring?'

The glazier took a sip of tea and put the mug down before he began working on the window frame. 'The boss is pretty good at judging things like this,' he explained.

Mac sipped her own tea as she watched him work.

'Was that the man I spoke to on the telephone this morning?'

'Don't know about that, love.' Bob Jenkins looked up to give her a grin. 'He just told me to get over here toot sweet and replace the window.'

Mac had no idea why, but she had a sudden uneasy feeling about 'the boss'. Maybe because she didn't recall telling the man at the glazier company she had called this morning what size window had been broken. Or expected anyone to arrive from that company until tomorrow...

She eyed Bob warily. 'Exactly who is the boss?'

He raised grizzled grey brows. 'Mr Buchanan, of course.'

Exactly what Mac had suspected—dreaded—hearing!

After their strained parting earlier Mac hadn't expected to see or hear from Jonas ever again. Although technically, she wasn't seeing or hearing from him now, either; he had just arrogantly sent one of his workmen over to fix her broken window.

Why?

Was Jonas treating her like the 'fragile little woman' who needed the help of the 'big, strong man'?

Or was Jonas replacing the window because he knew that he—or someone who worked for him—was responsible for it being broken in the first place?

'Of course,' Mac answered the workman distractedly. 'If you'll excuse me, Bob?'

'No problem,' he assured her brightly.

Mac was so annoyed at Jonas's high-handedness that she didn't quite know what to do with all the anger bubbling inside her. What did he think he was doing, interfering in this way, when she had already told him that she had arranged for a glazier to come out tomorrow?

An arrangement he had instantly expressed his disapproval of. Enough to have arranged for one of his own workmen to come out and replace the window immediately, apparently! Were Jonas's actions prompted by a guilty conscience? Or by something else? Although quite what that something else could be Mac had no idea. It was enough, surely, that Jonas was sticking his arrogant nose into her business?

Too right it was!

'What can I do for you this time, Mac?' Jonas took his briefcase out of the car before locking it and turning to face her wearily across the private and brightly lid underground car park beneath his apartment building.

He had been vaguely aware, as he drove home at the end of what had been a damned awful day, of the black motorbike following in the traffic behind him. He simply hadn't realised that Mac was the driver of that motorbike until she followed him down into the car park, stopped the vehicle behind his car and removed the black crash helmet to shake the long length of her ebony-dark hair loose about her shoulders. The black biking leathers she was wearing fitted her as snugly as a glove, and clearly outlined the fullness of her breasts and her slender waist and hips. Jonas couldn't help thinking of how they were no doubt moulded to her perfectly shaped bottom, too!

But there was no way that Jonas could mistake the obviously hostile demeanour on her face for anything other than what it was as she climbed off the motorbike; her eyes were sparkling with challenge, the fullness of her lips compressed and unsmiling.

Jonas's afternoon had been just as uncomfortable as he had thought it might be. So much so that he hadn't been able to give his usual concentration to his business meetings.

What was it about this woman in particular that so disturbed him? Mac was beautiful, yes, but in a wild and Bohemian sort of way that had never appealed to him before. There was absolutely nothing about her that usually attracted him to a woman. She was short and dark-haired, boyishly slender apart from the fullness of her breasts, and not in the least sophisticated; she even rode a motorbike, for heaven's sake!

Jonas wasn't particularly into motorbikes, but even he recognised the machine as being a Harley, the chassis a shiny black, its silver chrome gleaming brightly. For what had to be the dozenth time, Jonas told himself that Mac McGuire was most definitely not his type.

So why the hell couldn't he stop thinking about her?

His eyes narrowed. 'Don't you think—whatever your reason for being here—that following me home is taking things to an extreme?'

Her mouth tightened further at the criticism. 'Maybe.'

He raised mocking brows. 'Only maybe?'

'Yes,' she admitted grudgingly.

He eyed her coldly. 'And so you're here because…?'

She glared at him. 'You sent a glazier to repair my window.'

'Yes.'

Her eyes widened. 'You aren't even going to attempt to deny it?'

Jonas grimaced. 'Presumably Bob told you I had sent him?'

'Yes.'

'Then what would be the point of my trying to deny it?' he reasoned impatiently.

Mac was feeling a little foolish now that she was actually face to face with Jonas. Anger had been her primary emotion, as she waited the twenty minutes or so it had taken Bob Jenkins to replace the window, before donning her leathers and getting her motorcycle out of the garage and riding it over to Jonas's office. Just in time to see Jonas driving out of the office underground car park in his dark green sports car.

Frustrated anger had made her decide to follow him home; having ridden back into the city for the sole purpose of speaking to him, Mac had had no intention of just turning round and going home without doing exactly that.

At least, she had hoped Jonas was driving home; it would be a little embarrassing for Mac to have followed him to a date with another woman!

The prestigious apartment building above this underground car park—so unlike her own rambling warehouse-conversion home—definitely looked like the sort of place Jonas would choose to live.

She stubbornly stood her ground. 'I told you I had a glazier coming out tomorrow.'

Jonas nodded tersely. 'And I seem to recall telling you that wasn't good enough.'

Her eyes widened. 'So you just arranged for one of your own workmen to come over this afternoon instead? Without even giving me the courtesy of telling me about it?'

Jonas could see that Mac was clearly running out of

steam, her accusing tone certainly lacking some of its earlier anger. He regarded her mockingly. 'So it would seem.'

'I—but—you can't just take over my life in this way, Jonas!'

He frowned. 'You see ensuring your safety as an attempt to take over your life?'

'Yes! Well…not exactly,' she allowed impatiently. 'But it was certainly an arrogant thing to do!'

Yes, she was definitely running out of steam… 'But I *am* arrogant, Mac.'

'It's not something you should be in the least proud of!'

He gave her an unapologetic, smile. 'Your objection is duly noted.'

'And dismissed!'

Jonas gave a shrug. 'I presume Bob has now replaced the broken window?'

Mac gave a disgusted snort. 'He wouldn't dare do anything else when "the boss" told him to do so "toot sweet".'

Jonas had to smile at her perfect mimicry of Bob's broad Cockney accent. 'Well, unless you want me to break the window again just so that you can have the satisfaction of having your own glazier fix it tomorrow, I don't really see what you want me to do about it.'

Those smoky-grey eyes narrowed. 'You think you're so clever, don't you?'

Jonas straightened. 'No, Mac, I think what I did was the most sensible course of action in the circumstances,' he stated calmly. 'If you disagree with that, then that's obviously your prerogative.'

'I disagree with the way you went about it, not

with the fact that you did it,' she continued in obvious frustration.

He gave a cool nod. 'Again, your objection is duly noted.'

'Right. Okay.' Mac didn't quite know what to do or say now that she'd voiced her protest over the replacement of her broken window.

She should have just telephoned Jonas and told him what she thought of him rather than coming back into town to speak to him personally. She certainly shouldn't—as he had already pointed out so mockingly—have followed him home!

The wisest thing to do now would be to get back on her motorbike and drive back home. Unwisely, Mac knew she wasn't yet ready to do that...

Just looking at Jonas, his dark hair once again ruffled by the breeze outside, the hard arrogance of his face clearly visible in the brightly lit car park, was enough to make her knees go weak. To remind her of the way he had kissed and touched her earlier today. To make her long for him to kiss and touch her in that way again.

To make her question whether that wasn't the very reason she had come here in the first place...

Jonas had been watching the different emotions flickering across Mac's expressive face. First the fading of her anger, which was replaced by confusion and uncertainty. And now he could see those emotions replaced by an unmistakable hunger in those smoky-grey eyes as she looked at him so intently...

A hunger he fully reciprocated. 'I intend to have several glasses of wine as soon as I get up to my apartment—would you care to join me?' he offered huskily.

She visibly swallowed. 'That's probably not a good idea.'

Again, here and now, Jonas was more than willing to go with a bad idea. His body physically ached from the hours he had already spent aroused by this woman today; the thought of an evening and night suffering the same discomfort did not appeal to him in the slightest. Besides, he really did want to see her perfect little bottom in those skin-tight leathers! 'Half a glass of wine isn't going to do you any harm, Mac.'

'Isn't it?'

Maybe it was, Jonas acknowledged with dark humour. If he had anything to do or say about it. 'Scared, Mac?' he taunted.

Her cheeks became flushed. 'Now you're deliberately challenging me into agreeing to go up to your apartment with you!'

He gave her an amused smile. 'Is it working?'

Mac knew that her temptation to go up to Jonas's apartment with him had very little to do with annoyance. Just talking with him like this made her nerve endings tingle, the low timbre of his voice sending little quivers of awareness up her nape and down the length of her spine, the fine hairs on her arms standing to attention, and her skin feeling as if it were covered in goose-bumps. She also felt uncomfortably hot, a heat she knew had nothing to do with the leathers she was wearing to keep out the early evening chill, and everything to do with being so physically aware of Jonas.

All of which told Mac she would be a fool to go anywhere she would be completely alone—and vulnerable to her own churning emotions—with Jonas.

Except she ached to be alone with him.

She nodded abruptly. 'I— Fine. Will it be safe to leave my helmet down here with my bike?'

'I'm sure your bike and helmet will be perfectly safe left down here,' Jonas assured her.

The implication being that it was Mac's own safety, once she was alone with him in his apartment, that she ought to be worried about.

CHAPTER SIX

MAC turned to look at Jonas as he fell into step slightly behind her as she crossed the car park to the lift that would take them up to his apartment. Only to quickly turn away again, her cheeks flaring with heated colour, as she saw the way he was unashamedly watching the gentle swaying of her hips and bottom as she walked.

He eyed her unapologetically as he stood beside her to punch in the security code that opened the lift doors and allowed the two of them to step inside. 'You shouldn't wear tight leathers if you don't want men to look at you!' He pressed the penthouse button.

Mac looked up at him reprovingly as the lift began to ascend. 'I wear them for extra safety if I should come off the bike, not for men to look at. And you know how hot *you* are on safety,' she prodded.

'Hot would seem to be the appropriate word,' Jonas teased.

Mac's cheeks felt more heated than ever at the knowledge that Jonas thought she looked hot in her biking gear. 'Perhaps we should just change the subject.'

'Perhaps we should.' He nodded, blue eyes openly laughing at her.

Mac turned away to stare fixedly at the grey metal doors until they opened onto the penthouse floor. The lights came on automatically as they stepped straight into what was obviously the sitting-room—or perhaps one of them?—of Jonas's huge apartment.

It had exactly the sort of impersonal ultra-modern décor that Mac had expected, mainly in black and white with chrome, with touches of red to alleviate the austerity. The walls were painted a cool white, with black and chrome furniture, with cushions in several shades of red on the sofa and chairs, and several black and white rugs on the highly polished black-wood floor.

Mac hated it on sight!

'Very nice,' she murmured unenthusiastically.

Jonas had seen the wince on Mac's face before she donned the mask of social politeness. 'I allowed an interior designer free rein with the décor in here when I moved in six months ago,' he admitted ruefully. 'Awful, isn't it?' He grimaced as he strode further into the room.

Mac followed slowly. 'If you don't like it, why haven't you changed it?'

He shrugged. 'I couldn't see the point when I shall be moving out again soon.'

'Oh?' She turned to look at him. 'Is that why you haven't bothered to put up any Christmas decorations, either?'

Jonas never bothered to put up Christmas decorations. What was the point? Only he lived here, with the occasional visitor, so why bother with a lot of tacky decorations that only gathered dust, before they had to be taken down again? For Jonas, Christmas was, and always had been, just a time to be suffered through, while everyone else seemed to overeat and indulge in needless sentimentality. In fact, Jonas usually made a point of disappearing to the warmth of a Caribbean island for the whole of the holidays, and, although he hadn't made any plans to do so yet, he doubted that this year would be any different from previous ones.

'No,' Jonas said shortly. Mac really did look good in those figure-hugging leathers, he acknowledged privately as once again he felt what was fast becoming a familiar hardening of his thighs. 'Come through to the kitchen and I'll open a bottle of wine,' he invited briskly before leading the way through to the adjoining room.

He had designed the kitchen himself, the cathedral-style ceiling oak-beamed using beams that had originally come from an eighteenth-century cottage, with matching oak kitchen cabinets, all the modern conveniences such as a fridge-freezer and a dishwasher hidden behind those cabinets, with a weathered oak table in the middle of the room surrounded by four chairs, and copper pots hanging conveniently beside the green Aga.

It was a warm and comfortable room as opposed to the coolly impersonal sitting-room. The kitchen was where Jonas felt most at ease, and was where he usually sat and read the newspapers or did paperwork on the evenings he was at home.

Although he wasn't too sure any more about inviting Mac McGuire into his inner sanctum…

'Much better,' she murmured approvingly. 'Did you design this yourself?'

'Yes.'

'I thought so.'

Jonas raised dark brows. 'Why?'

She gave an awkward shrug. 'It's—warmer, than the other room.'

He scowled. 'Warmer?'

'More lived-in,' she amended.

Jonas continued to look at her for several long seconds

before giving an abrupt nod. 'Make yourself comfortable,' he invited and moved to take a bottle of Chablis Premier Cru from the cooler before deftly opening it and pouring some of the delicious fruity wine into two glasses.

Mac still wasn't sure about being in Jonas's apartment at all, let alone making herself comfortable. And from the frown now on Jonas's brow she thought maybe he was regretting having invited her, too.

She sat down gingerly on one of the four chairs placed about the oak table. 'I'll just drink my half a glass of wine and then go.'

Jonas placed the glass on the table in front of her. 'What's your hurry?'

She nervously moistened her lips with the tip of her tongue as he stood far too close to her, only to immediately stop again as she saw the intensity with which Jonas was watching the movement. 'I just think it would be better if I don't overstay my welcome.' Her hand was shaking slightly as she reached out to pick up the glass and take a sip of the cool wine.

Jonas smiled slightly. 'Better for whom?'

She lifted one shoulder delicately. 'Both of us, I would have thought.'

'Maybe we're both thinking too much,' he murmured broodingly. 'Have you eaten dinner yet?'

Mac looked at him sharply. 'Not yet, no.' Surely he wasn't about to repeat his earlier suggestion that the two of them go out to dinner together?

'I only had a few prawns for lunch,' he reminded her ruefully. 'How about you?'

'I had a piece of toast when I got home. But I'm hardly dressed for going out to dinner, Jonas.'

'Who said anything about going out?' He looked at her quizzically.

Mac felt an uncomfortable surge—of what?—in her chest. Trepidation? Fear? Or anticipation? Or could it be a combination of all three of those things? Whichever it was, Mac didn't think she should stay here alone with Jonas in his apartment any longer than she absolutely had to.

'It's very kind of you to offer—'

'How polite you are all of a sudden, Mac,' Jonas cut in. 'If you don't want to have dinner with me then just have the guts to come out and say so, damn it!' His eyes glittered darkly.

She gave a pained frown. 'It isn't a question of not wanting to have dinner with you, Jonas—'

'Then what is it a question of?' he demanded harshly.

Mac swallowed hard. 'I'm not sure I belong here…'

Jonas scowled. 'What the hell does that mean?'

She gave an awkward shrug. 'I— This apartment is way out of my stratosphere. That bottle of wine you just opened probably cost what some people earn in a week.'

'And?'

'I am what I am. How I am. I hate dressing up in fancy clothes and "being seen".' She winced. 'I've already been through one experience where a man thought I would make a nice trophy to show off on his arm at parties—'

'And you think that's what I want, too?' Jonas asked.

Mac looked a little confused. 'I'm not really sure what you want from me.'

'Then that makes two of us,' Jonas told her with a

sigh. 'For some inexplicable reason you have a strange effect on me, Mary "Mac" McGuire.' His gaze held hers as he reached out and took the wine glass from her slightly trembling fingers, placing it on the table beside his own before grasping Mac's arms to pull her slowly to her feet so that she stood only inches away from him.

Jonas looked down at her searchingly, noting the almost feverish glitter in those smoky grey eyes, the flush to her cheeks, and the unevenness of her breathing through slightly parted lips. Parted lips that were begging to be kissed.

His expression was grim as he resisted that dangerous temptation. 'I'm going through to my bedroom now to change out of my suit. If you decide you don't want to stay and help me cook dinner then I suggest you leave before I get back.' He released her abruptly before turning on his heel and going out of the room in the direction of his bedroom further down the hallway.

Mac was still trembling somewhat as she stood alone in the kitchen. She should do as Jonas suggested and leave before he came back. She knew that she should. Yet she didn't want to. What she wanted to do was stay right here and spend the evening cooking dinner with him before they sat down together to eat it in this warm and comfortable kitchen…

Except she knew that Jonas wasn't suggesting they just cook and eat dinner together. Her remaining here would mean she was also agreeable to repeating their earlier shared kisses.

Mac sat down abruptly, totally undecided about what to do. She should go. But she didn't want to. She knew she shouldn't allow that explosive passion with Jonas at the restaurant to happen again. But she wanted to!

She was still sitting there pondering her dilemma

when Jonas came back into the kitchen, her breath catching in her throat as she saw him casually dressed for the first time. The thin black cashmere sweater was moulded to wide shoulders and the flatness of his chest and stomach, jeans that were faded from age and wear rather than designer-styled to be that way sat low down on his hips and emphasised the muscled length of his legs, and his feet were as bare as her own had been earlier when Bob Jenkins had arrived at the warehouse to replace her broken window. They were long and somehow graceful feet, their very bareness seeming to increase the intimacy of the situation.

Jonas looked everything that was tall, dark, and most definitely dangerous!

Mac raised startled eyes. 'I decided to stay long enough to help you cook dinner at least.'

Jonas's enigmatic expression, as he stood in the doorway, gave away none of his thoughts. 'Did you?'

She stood up quickly, already regretting that decision as she felt the rising sexual tension in the room, her pulse actually racing.

Even breathing was becoming difficult. 'Would you like me to help prepare the vegetables or something?' she offered lamely.

Jonas very much doubted that Mac wanted to hear what he would have liked to ask her to do at this particular moment. He had never before even thought about sitting down on one of the kitchen chairs with a woman's naked thighs straddled either side of him as he surged up into the heat of her, but the idea certainly had appeal right now. Making love to Mac anywhere appealed to him right now!

'Or something,' he murmured self-derisively as he made himself walk across to the refrigerator and open the door to look inside at the contents. 'I have the makings of a vegetable and chicken stir-fry if that appeals?' He looked at her enquiringly.

'That sounds fine.'

Jonas was frowning slightly as he straightened. 'Wouldn't you be more comfortable out of those leathers? Unless of course you aren't wearing anything underneath?' he added mockingly. 'In which case, neither of us is going to be comfortable once you've taken them off!'

It was time to put a stop to this right now, Mac decided. They hadn't even got as far as cooking dinner yet and already Jonas was talking about taking her clothes off!

'Of course I'm wearing something underneath,' she said, scowling at Jonas's deliberate teasing, sitting down to remove her boots before unzipping the leathers and taking them off to reveal she was wearing a long-sleeved white t-shirt and snug-fitting jeans above black socks. 'Satisfied?' she challenged as she stood up to lay her leathers over one of the kitchen chairs and place her heavy boots beside it.

'Not hardly,' Jonas murmured.

'Jonas!'

'Mac?' He raised innocent brows.

She drew in a deep, controlling breath. 'Just tell me what vegetables you want me to wash and cut up,' she muttered bad-temperedly.

'Yes, ma'am!' he shot back.

To Mac's surprise they worked quite harmoniously together as they prepared and then cooked the food, sitting down at the table to eat it not half an hour later. 'You said you'll be moving from here soon?' she reminded Jonas curiously as she looked across the table at him.

He nodded as he put his fork down on his plate and drank some of his wine before answering her. 'By this time next year we should be neighbours.'

Mac's eyes widened. 'You're moving into the apartment complex next to me once it's finished being built?'

Jonas didn't think she could have sounded any more horrified if he had said he was actually moving in with her. 'That's the plan, yes,' he confirmed dryly. 'Unless, of course, you decide to sell and move out, after all.'

Her mouth firmed. 'No, I can safely assure you that I have no intention of ever doing that.'

Jonas frowned. 'Why the hell not?'

'It's difficult to explain.'

'Try,' he invited grimly.

Mac frowned. 'The warehouse belonged to my great-grandfather originally, then to my grandfather. Years ago my great-grandfather owned a small fleet of boats, for delivering cargos to other parts of England. Obviously long before we had the huge container trucks that clog up the roads nowadays.' She chewed distractedly on her bottom lip.

Jonas's gaze was riveted on those tiny white teeth nibbling on the fullness of her bottom lip, that ache returning to his thighs as he easily imagined being the one doing the biting...

For the moment Mac seemed unaware of the heated intensity of his gaze. 'I spent a lot of time there with my grandfather when I was a child, and when he died he left it to me,' she finished with a shrug.

Jonas forced himself to drag his gaze from the sensual fullness of her lips. 'So you're saying you want to keep it because it has sentimental value?'

'Something like that, yes.'

'Your grandfather didn't want to leave the property to your parents?'

It really was difficult for Mac to explain the affinity that had existed between her grandfather and herself. How he had understood the love and affection she felt for the rambling warehouse beside the river. How living and working there now made Mac feel that she still had that connection to her grandfather. 'My parents had already moved out of London to live in Devon when my grandfather died, and so didn't want or need it.'

'No siblings for you to share with?'

'No. You?' Mac asked with interest, deciding she had probably talked about herself enough for one evening.

Jonas's mouth thinned. 'I believe my parents considered that one mistake was enough.'

Mac gasped, not quite sure what to say in answer to a statement like that. 'I'm sure they didn't think of you as a mistake—'

'Then you would be wrong, Mac,' he said dryly. 'My parents were both only nineteen when they got married, and then it was only because my mother was expecting me. She would have been better off—we all would have—if she had either got rid of the baby or settled for being a single mother.' He finished drinking the wine in his glass, offering to refill Mac's glass before refilling his own when she shook her head in refusal.

Mac had continued to eat while they talked, but she gave up all pretence of that after Jonas's comment that his mother should have got rid of him rather than marry his father!

Jonas looked bitter. 'I have no doubts that your own childhood was one of love and indulgence with parents and a family who loved you?'

'Yes,' she admitted with slight discomfort.

Jonas gave a hard smile. 'Don't look so apologetic, Mac. It's the way it should be, after all,' he said bleakly. 'Unfortunately, it so often isn't. I believe it took a couple of years for the novelty to wear off and the cracks to start appearing in my own parents' marriage, then ten years or more for them to realise they couldn't stand the sight of each other. Or me,' he added flatly.

Mac gave a pained wince. 'I'm sure you're wrong about that, Jonas.'

'I'm sure your romantic little heart wants me to be wrong about that, Mac,' he corrected.

He meant his mockery of her to wound, and it did, but Mac's 'romantic little heart' also told her that Jonas's taunts hid the pain and disillusionment that had helped to mould him into the hard and resilient man he was today. That had made him into a man who rejected all the softer emotions, such as love, in favour of making a success of his life through his own hard work and sheer determination. That had made him into a man who didn't even bother to put up Christmas decorations in his apartment...

'Your parents are divorced now?' she asked.

'Yes, thank God,' he replied. 'After years of basically ignoring each other, and me, they finally separated when I was thirteen and divorced a couple of years later.'

Mac didn't even like to think of the damage they had done in those thirteen years, not only to each other, but most especially to Jonas, the child caught in the middle of all that hostility.

'Which one did you live with after the separation?'

'Neither of them,' Jonas bit out with satisfaction. 'I had my own grandfather I went to live with. My father's father. Although I doubt Joseph was the warm and fuzzy type your own grandfather sounds,' he added.

Mac doubted it too, if Jonas had actually called his grandfather by his first name, and if the expression on Jonas's face was anything to go by!

Jonas would have found Mac's obvious dismay amusing if it weren't his own childhood they were discussing. Something that was unusual in itself when Jonas usually went out of his way not to talk about himself. But it was better that Mac knew all there was to know about him now. To be made aware that falling in love and getting married wasn't, and never would be, a part of his future. Jonas had seen firsthand the pain and disillusionment that supposed emotion caused, and he wanted no part of it. Not now or ever.

'You said earlier that you didn't belong in these surroundings,' Jonas reminded her. 'Well, neither do I. My parents were poor, and my grandfather Joseph was a rough, tough man who worked on a building site all his life. I've worked hard for what I have, Mac.'

'I didn't mean to imply—'

'Didn't you?' He gave her a grim smile. 'I probably owe part of my success to the fact that my grandfather had no time for slackers,' he continued relentlessly. 'You either worked to pay your way or you got out. I decided to work. My parents had both remarried by the time I was sixteen and disappeared off into the sunset—'

'Jonas!' Mac choked as she sat forward to place her hand over his as it lay curled into a fist on the tabletop.

He pulled his hand away sharply, determined to finish this now that he had started. Mac should know exactly what she was getting into if she decided to become involved with him. Exactly! 'In between working with my grandfather before and after school and cooking for the two of us, I also worked hard to get my A levels. Then I worked my way through university and gained a Masters degree in Mathematics before going into architecture. I worked my ba—' He broke off with an apologetic grimace. 'I worked hard for one of the best architecture companies in London for a couple of years, before I was lucky enough to have a couple of my designs taken up by a man called Joel Baxter. Have you heard of him?'

Mac's eyes were wide. 'The man who makes billions out of computer games and software?'

'That's the one,' Jonas confirmed. 'Strangely, we became friends. He convinced me I should go out on my own, that I needed to take control of the whole construction of the building and not just the design of it, that I would never make money working for someone else. It was a struggle to start with, but I took his advice, and, as they say, the rest is history.' He gave a dismissive shrug.

Yes, it was. Mac was aware of the well-publicised overnight success of Buchanan Construction—which obviously hadn't been any such thing but was simply the result of Jonas's own hard work and determination to succeed.

She moistened dry lips. 'Are you and Joel Baxter still friends?'

Jonas's expression softened slightly. 'Yeah. Joel's one of the good guys.'

Mac brightened slightly. 'And your parents, surely they must be proud of you? Of what you've achieved?'

Jonas's eyes hardened to icy chips. 'I haven't seen either one of them since my father attended my grandfather's funeral when I was nineteen.'

Mac looked at him incredulously. 'That's—that's unbelievable!'

He looked at her coldly. 'Is it?'

'Well. Yes.' She shook her head. 'Look at you now, all that you've achieved, surely—'

'I didn't say that they hadn't wanted to see me again, Mac,' Jonas cut in. 'Once Buchanan Construction became known as a multimillion-pound worldwide enterprise, they both crawled out of the woodwork to claim their only lost son,' he recalled bitterly.

Mac swallowed hard. 'And?'

'And I didn't want anything to do with either of them,' he said emotionlessly.

Mac could understand, after all that had gone before, why Jonas felt the way that he did about seeing his parents again. Understand his feelings on the subject, maybe, but accepting it, when the situation between Jonas and his parents remained unresolved, was something else. Or perhaps he considered that just not seeing or having anything to do with his parents was the solution?

She looked sad. 'They've missed out on so much.'

Jonas lifted an unconcerned shoulder. 'I suppose that depends upon your perspective.'

Mac's perspective was that Jonas's parents had obviously been too young when they married each other and had Jonas, but it in no way excused their behaviour towards him. He had been an innocent child caught up in the battleground that had become their marriage.

Was it any wonder that Jonas was so hard and cynical? That he chose to concentrate all his energies on business relationships rather than personal ones?

'Don't go wasting any of your sympathy on me, Mac,' he grated suddenly as he obviously clearly read the emotions on her face. 'You told me earlier what you didn't want, and the only reason I've told you these about myself is so that you'll know the things *I* don't want.' He paused, his mouth tightening. 'So that you understand there would be no future, no happy ever after, if you chose to have a relationship with me.'

She raised startled eyes to look searchingly across the table at Jonas as he looked back at her so intensely. She saw and recognised the raw purpose in his gaze. The underlying warmth of seduction and sensuality in those hard and unblinking blue eyes.

CHAPTER SEVEN

THE chair scraped noisily on the tiled floor as Mac suddenly stood up. 'I think it's time I was going.'

'Running scared, after all, Mac?' Jonas mocked, watching her through narrowed lids as she turned agitatedly to pick up her leathers.

She dropped the leathers back onto the chair and faced him, her chin raised challengingly. 'I'm not scared, Jonas, I just don't think I can give you what you want.'

'Oh, I think you can give me exactly what I want, Mac.' He stood up slowly to move around the table to where she stood determinedly unmoving as she looked up at him. 'Exactly what I want,' he repeated as he reached out to curve his arms about her waist and pull her firmly up against him so that she could feel the evidence of what it was he wanted from her. All that Jonas wanted from her or any woman.

Mac gasped as she felt the hardness of his arousal pressed revealingly against her. She felt an instant echoing of that arousal in her own body as heat coursed through her breasts to pool hotly between her thighs.

God, she seriously wanted this man! Wanted him so badly that she ached with it. Longed to strip the clothes from both their bodies and have him surge hard and powerfully inside her and make her forget everything else but the desire that had burned so strongly between them ever since they'd met again at her exhibition on Saturday evening.

She gave a desperate shake of her head. 'I don't do casual relationships, Jonas.'

His face remained hard and determined. 'Have you ever tried?'

She swallowed. 'No. But—' Her protest ceased the moment that Jonas's mouth claimed hers in a kiss so raw with hunger that she could only cling to the hard strength of his shoulders as she returned the heated hunger of that kiss.

Jonas felt wrapped in the luscious smell and heat that was Mac, even as his hand moved unerringly to that strip of flesh between her T-shirt and jeans that had been tantalising him all evening. He needed to know if those full breasts were bare beneath that thin cotton top, and the first touch of her creamy flesh against Jonas's fingertips made him groan low in his throat.

Mac was pure heat. Silk and sensuality as his hand moved beneath that T-shirt and up the length of her bare spine. Jonas felt the quivering vibration of her response in the depths of his body as he pressed her closer against him. He deepened the kiss, his arousal surging in response as his tongue moved skilfully across the heat of Mac's lips and then into the hot, moist vortex beneath.

She took him in, deeper, and then deeper still, as her hands moved up Jonas's shoulders to his nape, her fingers becoming entangled in the thickness of his hair as her tongue touched lightly against his, testing, questioning. Jonas instantly retreated, encouraging, enticing, giving another low groan as that hot and moist tongue shyly followed.

He stroked her satiny flesh beneath her T-shirt, closer, ever closer to the firm mounds that he now knew without a doubt were bared to his touch, loving the way Mac arched into him as his hand moved to cup and stroke one of those uptilted breasts, capturing the soft cry that escaped her lips with his mouth as his fingers grazed across the swollen nipple.

Mac had never felt this way before and felt lost to everything but Jonas as he continued to kiss and touch her, mouth devouring hers, sipping, tasting her, with deep and drugging kisses that drove her wild with longing. While his tongue brushed lightly over the sensitivity of her lips and teeth, his hand— Oh, God, what the touch of Jonas's hard and slightly calloused hand against her naked flesh was doing to her...

Her whole body felt hot, sensitised, and she gasped and writhed, the moisture flooding between her thighs as Jonas rolled her nipple between thumb and finger. Gently, and then harder, the almost pleasure-pain like nothing Mac had ever experienced before.

Her neck arched when Jonas dragged his mouth from hers, his breath hot and moist against her skin as he left a trail of kisses across her cheek, the line of her jaw, before moving down her throat to the hollows beneath, tongue dipping, tasting, as he seemed to draw in the drugging scent of her arousal with his every breath.

Mac could only cling to the power of his shoulders as he swept her along in a tidal wave of desire so strong she felt as if Jonas were her only anchor. All that mattered. Her only reality.

Jonas had never wanted a woman as much as he did Mac. Had never hungered like this before. Had never needed to be inside any woman so badly that he literally seemed to blaze with that need, every cell and nerve in his body aching for her, robbing him of his usual self-control as he longed to feel her hands on him.

His mouth moved back to claim hers in a kiss that was almost savage, Mac offering no protest as Jonas grasped the bottom of her T-shirt to tug it upwards, only breaking that kiss long enough to pull the article of clothing over her head and throw it down on the floor.

He could barely breathe, his eyes glittering darkly blue as he looked down at her tiny breasts. Their naked-ness peaked shyly through that long ebony hair. 'My God, you're beautiful,' Jonas groaned before lowering his head to capture one of those rosy red nipples into the heat of his mouth, intending to drink his fill, to wrest every last vestige of pleasure from her hot and delicious body.

Mac gasped at the first touch of Jonas's lips against her breast, her back tensing now as she arched into him, cradling his head to her as he drew her deeper, ever deeper into his mouth, tasting her sweetness, her heat, the heady smell of her arousal driving him mad with need.

He raised his head to look down at the nipple that had swollen in size, gaze intent as he turned the attention of his lips and tongue to her other breast. At the same time he released the fastening on her jeans to slip his hands beneath the material and grasp her hips before sliding further back to cup the perfectly rounded cheeks of her bottom encased in lacy panties.

Jonas looked up at Mac with darkened and hungry eyes. 'Touch me, Mac,' he growled. He deliberately, slowly, flicked his tongue against that hard and delicious nipple, watching her response as the pleasure vibrated, resonated through the whole of her body.

Mac had never felt so sensitised to the touch of

another, so aroused and needy, her body a single burning ache as she moved eagerly to return those caresses, tugging Jonas's jumper up and off his body to reveal the hard and muscled perfection of his chest before she placed her hands flat against it. He stood immobile in front of her, that glittering blue gaze hidden beneath hooded lids, but the husky exclamation of pleasure he gave as Mac touched him for the first time encouraged her, incited her to explore all of that hard, silken flesh.

He felt like steel encased in velvet, the tiny nipples hidden amongst the light covering of chest hair standing to attention as Mac ran her fingers over them delicately. She wondered curiously whether Jonas would feel the same pleasure as she did if she were to kiss him there.

'Oh, yes, Mac!' Jonas moaned at the first flick of her tongue against that tiny enticing pebble, his hand moving to curve about her nape as he threaded his fingers in the dark tangle of her hair and held her against him, encouraging, demanding.

Mac felt empowered, exhilarated with the knowledge that she could give Jonas the same pleasure he gave her, continuing to flick her tongue against him there as her hands roamed restlessly across the broad width of his back and down the muscled curve of his spine.

Mac's mouth moved down his chest as her fingers moved lightly along the length of the erection pressing against his jeans, able to feel the heat of him through the material as he grew even harder as she touched him.

Jonas stood unmoving beneath the onslaught of those caresses, barely breathing, body tense, hands clenched into fists at his sides as he fought grimly to maintain control as Mac's lips and hands drove him almost wild with need. Knowing he was losing the battle as that image he'd had earlier, of him sitting on a chair with

Mac's naked thighs wrapped about him, caused his thighs to throb and surge in painful need, his jeans too uncomfortable, too tight to contain him any longer.

'We need to be somewhere more comfortable,' he growled before he bent down and swung Mac up into his arms. He moved out of the warm kitchen, down the hallway to his bedroom, kicking the door closed behind them. He walked over to the bed and placed Mac on top of the downy duvet before turning to switch on the soft glow of the bedside light.

He stood looking down at her for several seconds, eyes dark as he looked at that cascade of straight ebony-black hair spread across his pillows, her eyes bright, cheeks flushed, lips slightly swollen from the hunger of their kisses, and then down to the swell of those perfect breasts.

Jonas drew in a harsh breath as he gazed at those orbs with their rosy-hued nipples jutting out firmly, and then down over the curving indentation of her narrow waist, a tantalising glimpse of her lacy panties visible beneath her unzipped jeans.

He sat on the side of the bed, his gaze briefly holding hers before lowering as he slowly tugged those jeans down to fully reveal those white panties with the soft curls dark behind the lace, and the long length of her legs.

Mac was barely breathing as she looked up into the dark intensity of Jonas's face as his gaze slowly, hungrily, devoured every inch of her, from her head down to her toes.

His face was flushed as that glittering blue gaze returned to meet hers. 'I'm think I'm going to have to make love to you until you beg for me to stop,' he muttered gruffly.

Mac longed for that, ached for it, but at the same time she trembled at the depth of the desire she could feel flowing between them. 'I hope you aren't going to be disappointed,' she whispered.

Those blue eyes narrowed. 'Why should I be disappointed?'

Mac shook her head. 'I'm not experienced, and—I—I don't have any protection,' she warned, not wanting to break the spell of the moment, but only too aware now of the reason Jonas's parents had married each other. Of how much he would despise any woman stupid enough to make the same mistake with him.

'You aren't on the pill?' Jonas slid open the drawer in the bedside cabinet and took out a small foil packet.

Her cheeks were flushed. 'I— No, there's never been any need.'

Jonas looked at her suspiciously as an incredulous thought suddenly occurred to him. 'You can't possibly still be a virgin?'

'Why can't I? Jonas…?' Mac frowned her uncertainty as he stood up abruptly.

Jonas stared down at her disbelievingly—accusingly— for several long seconds, before turning away to run an agitated hand through the thickness of his hair. A virgin! Jonas couldn't believe it; Mac McGuire, a beautiful woman in her late twenties, who looked and dressed like a Bohemian, was a virgin!

He turned back. 'And exactly when were you going to tell me that interesting little piece of information?' he bit out angrily. 'Or were you just going to let me find out for myself once it was too late for me to do anything about it?'

Mac gave a dazed shake of her head. 'I don't understand,' she whispered.

Jonas glared at her. 'Virgin or not, you can't be that naïve!'

Mac was too stunned by the sudden tension between them to know what to think. 'I don't believe I'm naïve at all,' she said slowly as she sat up, her hair falling forwards to cover the nakedness of her breasts. 'I thought you realised after I told you about my one youthful disaster of a relationship—Jonas, what difference does it make whether or not I've had other lovers?'

'All the difference in the world to me,' Jonas assured her harshly.

Mac gave a pained frown as she wrapped her arms defensively about the bareness of her knees. 'But *why* does it?'

'Because I have no intention of being any woman's first lover, that's why.' His jaw was tightly clenched.

'All women have a first time with someone—'

'Yours isn't going to be with me,' he reiterated.

'Most men would be only too pleased to be a woman's first lover!' Tears of humiliation glittered in her eyes as she glared back at him and she resolutely blinked them away. She refused to cry in front of him!

'Not this man,' he said fervently.

Mac couldn't believe they were having this conversation. Couldn't believe that Jonas was refusing to make love to her just because she was a virgin!

'Why is that, Jonas?' she challenged. 'Do you think that I'm making such a grand gesture because I already imagine myself in love with you? Or do you think I'm trying to trap you in some way?' Her eyes widened as she saw from the cold stiffening of Jonas's expression, the icy glitter of his eyes, that was *exactly* what he thought—and so obviously feared. 'You arrogant louse!' she scorned furiously.

'No doubt,' he acknowledged. 'But I'm sure you'll agree that it's better if this stops now?'

'Oh, don't worry, Jonas, it's stopped,' she said scathingly as she moved to sit on the side of the bed, grabbed up her jeans from the carpeted floor and started pulling them back on.

'I'm going back to the kitchen; I suggest you join me there once you've finished dressing. You might need this.' He took a black T-shirt out of the tall chest of drawers and threw it on the bed beside her before turning on his heel and leaving the bedroom, almost slamming the door behind him.

Mac stilled, unsure as to whether the tears now finally falling hotly and unchecked down her cheeks were of anger or humiliation, too confused still at the way their heated lovemaking had turned into an exchange of insults.

Did Jonas really imagine Mac was somehow trying to trap him into a relationship with her by giving him her virginity? Into making him feel responsible for her because he'd become her first lover?

If that was what he thought, what he was desperately trying to avoid, then Jonas didn't deserve her tears. He didn't deserve anything but her pity.

Unless you're in love with him, after all? a little voice deep within her wanted to know.

No. She was most definitely not. Mac had felt closer to Jonas this evening. Felt she understood him and his motivations better after hearing about his parents' marriage and his own childhood. And she had physically wanted him. That was undeniable. But none of those things added up to her being in love with him.

Not even a little bit? the same annoying voice persisted.

No, not even a little bit! she answered it firmly.

Jonas was arrogant. Cold. And his behaviour just now proved that he was also completely undeserving of her emotions or her body.

Jonas had pulled his jumper back on and was sitting at the oak kitchen table drinking some of the wine when Mac came back into the room, his gaze narrowing as he took in her appearance in his T-shirt. It was far too big for her, so long it reached almost down to her knees, the shoulder seams hanging halfway down her arms—and yet, somehow, she still managed to look sexy as hell.

Nothing at all like the virgin she was.

Jonas couldn't have known about her inexperience. He would never have guessed it from how she'd responded to him so passionately, so eagerly...

He scowled across at her broodingly. 'Having dinner together was obviously no more successful than our attempt at having lunch.' The food remained half eaten and cold on the plates.

Mac strode across the room to grab her own T-shirt from the back of the chair where Jonas had draped it. 'At least I know who to see now if I ever want to lose weight,' she retorted.

Jonas's jaw tightened. 'You're too thin already.'

Her eyes flashed a deep, smoky grey. 'I didn't hear you complaining a few minutes ago!'

He raised dark brows, his smile sardonic. 'I wasn't stating a preference now either, only fact.'

Mac wanted to slap that mocking smile off his face. No—she wanted to pummel his chest with her fists until she actually hurt him. As he had hurt her when he'd turned away from her so coldly.

She held her T-shirt protectively in front of her.

'Is there a bathroom I can use to change back into my own top?'

He kept one mocking brow raised. 'Isn't it a little late for modesty when I've already seen you naked?'

Her cheeks warmed hotly. 'Not completely!'

Jonas gave a shrug. 'The part you're going to expose, I have.'

Mac's mouth set determinedly. 'Would you just tell me where the bathroom is?'

'The nearest one is down the hallway, first door on the right,' he told her before turning away.

It was a cold and uninterested dismissal, Mac realised with a frown as she turned and walked out of the kitchen. Anyone would think that being a virgin at her age was akin to having the plague! Maybe in his eyes it was...

She wasted no time in admiring the luxurious bathroom as she quickly pulled off Jonas's overlarge T-shirt and replaced it with her own white one, a glance in the mirror over the double sink showing her that her hair was in too much of a mess for her to do any more than plait it loosely in an effort to smooth it into some sort of order.

Her face was very pale, her eyes huge and slightly red from the tears she had shed earlier, her lips full and swollen from the intensity of the kisses she had shared with Jonas.

Most of all she looked...sad.

Which wouldn't do at all, Mac decided as she set her shoulders determinedly before leaving the bathroom to go back to the kitchen. She was a mature and confident woman—even if, horror or horrors, she was still a virgin!—and she intended to act like one.

Jonas was still sitting at the table surrounded by the

remains of their meal, although the level of wine in his glass had definitely gone down in her absence.

Mac placed his T-shirt on the back of one of the other chairs. 'Thank you,' she said stiltedly, her face averted as she sat down to begin pulling on her leathers.

This, putting her clothes back on in a strained and awkward silence, had to be one of the most embarrassing and humiliating experiences of her entire life. More embarrassing than if she and Jonas had actually made love completely? Probably not, she acknowledged with a self-derisive grimace, as she could only imagine his reaction if he had discovered her virginity when it was too late for him to pull back.

Once again Jonas watched Mac broodingly through narrowed lids, easily able to read the self-disgust in her expression, the underlying hurt. Damn it, he had never meant to hurt her. Hadn't wanted to hurt her. He just knew he had nothing to offer a woman like Mac. Beautiful. Emotional. Virginal...

His relationships were always, *always* based on a mutual attraction and physical need. That desire definitely existed between himself and Mac, but the fact that she was still a virgin, and had been willing to give that virginity to him, had also warned him that if they made love together then she would probably want more from him than that. Much more.

Jonas didn't have any more than that to give. Not to Mac or any other woman. But that wasn't her fault.

'I'm sorry.'

She gave him a sharp glance as she straightened from lacing her boots. 'For what?'

Jonas grimaced. 'For allowing things to go as far between us just now as they did. If I had known—'

'If you had known I was a virgin then you wouldn't

have invited me up to your apartment at all!' she finished knowingly as she stood to zip up her leathers.

Jonas winced at the bitterness he could hear in her tone. 'None of what happened was premeditated on my part—'

'No?' she challenged.

'No, damn it!' A scowl darkened his brow.

Mac shrugged. 'Don't worry about it, Jonas. Not all men are as fickle as you; I'm pretty sure I can find one who's more than willing to become my first lover. Maybe I'll come back once I have, and we can finish what we started?' she taunted.

Jonas pushed his chair back noisily to stand up. 'Don't be so stupid!' he rasped harshly.

Mac's chin tilted with determination as she looked up at him. 'What's stupid about it?'

'You can't just decide to lose your virginity in that cold-blooded way!'

'Why can't I?'

He shook his head. 'Because it's something too precious to just throw away. It's a gift you should give to a man you care about. That you love.'

Mac felt a clenching in her chest as she acknowledged that she *did* care about Jonas. She didn't think she was in love with him yet—it would be madness on her part to fall in love with him!—but she definitely cared about him. About the hurt child he had once been, and the disillusioned man he now was.

She looked him straight in the eye. 'I believe that's for me to decide, Jonas, not you.'

'But—'

'I would like to leave now,' she told him flatly.

Jonas stared down at her in obvious frustration. 'Not

until you promise me that you aren't going to leave here and do something totally reckless.'

'Like taking a lover?'

'Exactly!'

Mac gave him a pitying glance. 'I don't believe that anything I do in future is any of your business.'

His mouth was set grimly, a nerve pulsing in his tightly clenched jaw. 'If you're really that desperate for a lover—'

'Oh, I'm not desperate, Jonas,' she said coolly. 'Just curious,' she added, deliberately baiting him.

Jonas wanted to shake her. Wanted to grasp the tops of Mac's arms and shake her until her teeth rattled. Except that he didn't dare touch her again. Because he knew that if he did, he wouldn't be able to stop...

He sighed heavily. 'I thought you understood after the things I told you about my childhood. Mac, I'm not the man you need, and I never could be.'

She frowned. 'I don't believe I ever asked you to be anything to me,' she pointed out.

'But you would.' That nerve continued to pulse in his jaw. 'Perhaps you would enjoy the novelty of the relationship at first, the sexual excitement, but eventually you would want more than I have to give you.'

'You know what, Jonas,' she said conversationally, 'I think you're taking an awful lot for granted in assuming that I would have wanted to continue a—a sexual relationship with you after tonight. I mean, who's to say I would actually have enjoyed having sex with you? Or is it that you're under the illusion you're such a great lover that no woman could possibly be left feeling disappointed after sharing your bed?'

Jonas felt the twitch of a smile on his lips as Mac deliberately insulted him. 'That would be a little arrogant of me, wouldn't it?'

'More than a little, I would have said,' she shot back. 'So, how do I get out of here?' She moved pointedly across the room to stand beside the doorway out into the hallway.

This evening had been something of another disaster as far as he and Mac were concerned, Jonas acknowledged ruefully as he preceded her out of the kitchen and walked with her to the lift.

She grimaced once she had stepped inside the lift. 'I'm not sure if I said this before, but thank you for sending Bob over this afternoon to fix my window.'

Jonas had totally forgotten that was the original reason she had followed him home! 'But don't do anything like it again?' he guessed dryly.

'No.'

He nodded. 'That's what I thought. I—If I don't see you again before then—Merry Christmas, Mac.'

She eyed him quizzically. 'And I'd already marked you down as the "bah, humbug" type!'

'I am the "bah, humbug" type,' he admitted with a quirk of his mouth.

Mac nodded as the lift doors began to close. 'Merry Christmas, Jonas.'

Jonas continued to stand in the hallway long after she had gone down to the car park and no doubt driven away on that powerful motorbike as if the devil himself were at her heels.

He liked Mac, Jonas realised frowningly. Liked the way she looked. Her spirit. Her independence. Her optimism about life and people in general. Most of all he admired her ability to laugh at herself.

Unfortunately, he also knew that allowing himself

to like Mac McGuire was as dangerous to the solitary
lifestyle he preferred as having a sexual relationship
with her would have been.

CHAPTER EIGHT

It was late in the morning when Mac parked her four-wheel-drive Jeep next to her motorbike in the garage on the ground floor of the warehouse after arriving back from a three-day pre-Christmas visit to her parents' home in Devon.

She had felt the need to get away for a while after the disastrous and humiliating end to the evening spent with Jonas at his apartment. And as the men had duly arrived the following day to install the alarm system to the warehouse, and the exhibition at the gallery was going well—Jeremy had informed Mac when she spoke to him on the telephone that the paintings were all sold, and the public were pouring in to see them before the exhibition came to a close at Christmas—she was free to do what she wanted for the next few days, at least.

Just as she had hoped, the time spent with her parents—the normality of being teased by her father and going Christmas shopping with her mother—had been the perfect way to put things in her own life back into perspective. For her to decide that her behaviour that evening at Jonas's apartment had been an aberration. A madness she didn't intend ever to repeat. In fact, she had come to the conclusion that ever seeing Jonas Buchanan again would be a mistake...

Which was going to be a little hard for her to do when he was the first person she saw as she rounded the corner from the garage!

Mac's hand tightened about the handle of the holdall she had used to pack the necessary clothing needed for her three days away, her gaze fixed on Jonas as she walked slowly towards him. She unconsciously registered how attractive he looked in a brown leather jacket over a tan-coloured sweater and faded jeans...

Any embarrassment she might have felt at seeing him again was forgotten as she realised he was directing the actions of the two other men, workmen from their clothing, who seemed to be in the process of building a metal tower beside the warehouse. 'What on earth are you doing?' Mac demanded.

'Oh, hell!' Jonas muttered as he turned and saw her, his expression becoming grim. 'I'd hoped to have dealt with this before you got back.'

'Hoped to have dealt with *what*? What on earth...?' Mac stared up at the wooden sides of the warehouse. Her eyes were wide with shock as she took in the electric-pink and fluorescent-green paints that had been sprayed haphazardly over the dark wooden cladding.

'It isn't as bad as it looks...'

'Isn't it?' she questioned sharply, the holdall slipping unnoticed from her fingers as she continued to stare numbly up at that mad kaleidoscope of colour.

'Mac—'

'Don't touch me!' She cringed away as Jonas would have reached out and grasped her arm. 'Who—? Why—?' She gave a dazed shake of her head. 'When did this happen?'

'I have no idea,' Jonas rasped. 'Some time yesterday evening, we think—'

'Who is *we*?'

'My foreman from the building site next door,' he elaborated. 'He noticed it this morning, and when he didn't receive any reply to his knock on your door he decided to report it to me.'

Mac swallowed hard, feeling slightly nauseous at the thought of someone deliberately vandalising her property. 'Why would anyone do something like this?'

'I don't know.' Jonas sighed heavily.

'Could it be kids this time?'

'Again, I have no idea. These two men are going to paint over it. They should be finished by this evening.' He grimaced. 'I had hoped to have had it done before you got back—'

'I thought I had made it plain the last time we met that I would rather you didn't go around arranging things for me?' Mac reminded him coldly.

Jonas eyed her with a frown, the pallor of her cheeks very noticeable against the red padded body-warmer she wore over a black sweater and black denims. He didn't like seeing the glitter of tears in those smoky-grey eyes, either. But he liked the cold, flat tone of her voice when she spoke to him even less. 'Would you rather I had just left it for you to find when you got home?'

'I have found it when I got home!' Her voice rose slightly, almost shrilly.

Jonas shook his head. 'I wasn't expecting you to be back just yet; I had hoped it would be later today, or even better, tomorrow morning.'

Those huge grey eyes settled on him suspiciously. 'How did you even know I had gone away?'

Jonas knew he could have lied, prevaricated even, but the suspicion he could read in Mac's expression warned him not to do either of those things. 'The Patels,' he revealed unapologetically. 'Once I had seen the mess, and you obviously weren't at home, I went to their convenience store and asked if they had any idea where you were.'

Those misty grey eyes widened. 'And they just told you I had gone away for a few days?'

He gave a rueful nod. 'Once I'd explained about the vandalism, yes.'

'Tarun always puts a daily newspaper by for me,' Mac muttered absently. 'I cancelled it while I was away.'

Jonas smiled. 'So he told me.'

She sighed and ran a hand through her hair. 'Nothing like this ever happened before I met you—'

'Don't say something you'll only have to apologise for later,' Jonas warned through suddenly gritted teeth.

'Even before,' Mac continued as if he hadn't spoken, 'when your assorted employees came here to try and persuade me into selling the warehouse, nothing like this happened. It's only since actually meeting *you*—'

'I said stop, Mac!' A nerve pulsed in his tightly clenched cheek.

Her gaze narrowed as she focused on him. 'Since meeting you, I've had my window broken and my home vandalised,' she said accusingly. 'And now some helpful soul has decided to redecorate the outside of the warehouse for me. Bit too much of a coincidence, don't you think, Jonas?' Her eyes glittered with anger now rather than tears.

Jonas had known exactly where Mac was going with this conversation, and had tried to stop her from actually voicing those accusations.

Damn it, he had considered himself well rid of her once she'd left his apartment on Monday evening. He'd had no intention of going near her on a personal level ever again if he could avoid it. Unfortunately, he hadn't been able to avoid coming here, at least, once he'd received the telephone call earlier this morning from his foreman.

He certainly wasn't enjoying being the object of Mac's suspicions. 'Only if you choose to look at it that way,' he bit out icily.

She eyed him challengingly. 'Did you report this to the police?'

Jonas narrowed cold blue eyes. 'I have the distinct feeling that I'm going to be damned if I did, and damned if I didn't.'

Mac raised questioning brows. 'How so?'

'If I did report it then I was probably just covering my own back. If I didn't report it, then again, I'm obviously guilty.'

Mac was feeling sick now that the shock was fading and reaction was setting in. She didn't want Jonas to be in any way involved in this second act of vandalism. It was the last thing she wanted! It was only that the coincidence of it all was so undeniable...

She closed her eyes briefly before opening them again. 'Your men seem to have everything well in hand,' she acknowledged ruefully as she glanced up at the two men now scaling the metal tower with the familiarity of monkeys, pots of paint and brushes in their hands. 'Would you like to come upstairs for some coffee?'

Jonas raised surprised brows. 'Are you sure it's wise to invite the enemy into your camp?'

Mac straightened from picking up the holdall she had dropped minutes ago. 'Have you never heard the saying "keep your friends close, but your enemies even closer"?' she teased.

His mouth tightened. 'I'm not your enemy, Mac.'

'I wasn't being serious, Jonas,' she assured him wearily.

'Strange, I didn't find it in the least funny,' he muttered as he began to follow her up the metal staircase.

Those psychedelic swirls of paint were even more noticeable from the top of the staircase, evidence that the perpetrator had probably stood on the top step in order to spray onto the second and third floor of the building. They had certainly made a mess of the stained dark wood.

But why had they?

Was it just an act of vandalism by kids thinking they were being clever? Or was it something else, something more sinister?

Mac gave a disgruntled snort as she unlocked the door and entered the living area of the warehouse, dropping her holdall just inside the door before going over to the kitchen area to prepare the pot of filtered coffee.

She was so lost in thought that she didn't notice for several seconds that Jonas had closed the door behind him and come to a complete halt. She eyed him curiously. 'Is there something wrong?'

Jonas was completely stunned by the inside of Mac's warehouse. He had never seen anything like this before. It was—

'Jonas?'

He blinked before focusing on Mac as she looked across at him in puzzlement. 'I—' He shook his head. 'This is—'

'Weird?' she finished dryly as she stepped out from behind the breakfast bar that partitioned off the kitchen area from the rest of the living space. 'Odd? Peculiar? A nightmare?' she concluded laughingly.

'I was going to say *fantastic*!' Jonas breathed incredulously as he now looked up at the high ceiling painted like a night sky, with the moon and stars shimmering mysteriously in that darkness.

The rest of the living area was open plan, the four walls painted like the seasons; spring was a blaze of yellow flowers against burgeoning green, summer a deeper green and gorgeous range of rainbow colours, autumn covered the spectrum from gold to russet, and winter was a beautiful white landscape.

The furniture was a mixture of all those colours, one chair gold, and another terracotta, the sofa burnt orange, with several white rugs on the highly polished wooden floor, that flat-screen television Mac had once mentioned tucked away in a corner. The bedroom area was slightly raised and reached by three wooden steps, the cover over the bed a patchwork of colours, a spiral staircase in another corner of the room obviously going up to the studio above.

And in place of honour in front of the huge picture window was a real pine Christmas tree that reached from floor to ceiling, and was decorated with so many baubles it was almost impossible to see the lushness of the branches.

Jonas had never seen anything so unusual—or so beautiful—as Mac's warehouse home. Much as Mac herself was unusual and beautiful? he wondered...

He firmly closed off that avenue of thought as he turned to give her a rueful smile. 'No wonder you didn't like the décor in the sitting-room of my apartment.'

Mac brought over two mugs of coffee and put one of them down on the low bamboo tabletop before carrying her own over to sit down on the sofa, her denim-covered legs neatly tucked beneath her. 'Obviously I prefer to go with the rustic look!' she teased, sipping her coffee.

Jonas picked up the second mug and sat down in the terracotta-coloured chair facing her. 'Is the studio upstairs like this, too?'

'I'll show it to you, if you like.'

Jonas eyed Mac curiously as he sensed the reluctance behind her offer. 'You don't usually show people your studio, do you?' he guessed.

She grimaced. 'Not usually, no.'

And yet she was offering to show it to *him*...

Jonas wasn't sure if he felt privileged or alarmed at the concession, but his curiosity was such that he wanted to see the studio anyway. 'Perhaps after we've drunk our coffee,' he suggested lightly.

'Perhaps,' Mac echoed uneasily, not altogether sure what to do with Jonas now that he was here.

She had only invited him in for coffee because their earlier conversation had been deteriorating into accusations on her part and defensive warnings on Jonas's. But now that he was here, in the intimacy of her home, she was once again aware of that rising sexual tension between them that never seemed to be far from the surface whenever the two of them were together.

Jonas looked very fit and masculine in his casual clothes, and that overlong dark hair was once again slightly ruffled by the cold wind blowing outside, his face as hard and sculptured as a statue Mac had once seen depicting the Archangel Gabriel. As for those fathomless blue eyes...

She turned away abruptly. 'You never did tell me whether or not you had informed the police about this second incident of vandalism in just a few days?'

His mouth tightened. 'I did call them, yes. Two of them arrived about an hour ago and looked the place over. If I understood them correctly, they were of the opinion that the demolishing of the other warehouses around this one has left it rather exposed and so a prime target for bored teenagers wanting to cause mischief.'

Mac was pretty sure that he had understood the police correctly. 'And what's *your* opinion, Jonas?'

His eyes narrowed. 'I think it's more—personal, than that.'

She gave a rueful smile. 'We aren't back to that disgruntled ex-lover theory again, are we?' she said dryly.

Hardly, when Jonas now knew only too well that there had never been a lover in Mac's life, ex or otherwise! Not even the man who had wanted her to be a trophy on his arm to show off at parties…

He gave a tight smile. 'I prefer to go with the jealous rival theory.'

'We've only been out together once,' she taunted. 'And that was something of a disaster, if you remember? I doubt that would have made any of your other…*women friends* jealous of me.'

Unfortunately, Jonas remembered every minute he had ever spent in this woman's company. 'Very funny.' He scowled. 'I was actually referring to a professional rival of yours rather than a personal angle involving me.'

'That would make sense seeing as we don't have a *personal* relationship—from any angle,' she said cuttingly.

Jonas deliberately chose not to enter into any sort of argument as to what there was or wasn't between himself and Mac. 'I understand your exhibition has been a tremendous success—'

'Understand from whom?' Mac pounced on his comment.

'Mac, you were the one who asked for my opinion, so would you now just let me finish giving it instead of jumping down my throat after every sentence?' he snapped his frustration with her interruptions.

'Fine,' she sighed.

'Is there anyone you know, or can think of, who might be—less than happy, shall we say, at the success of your exhibition?'

'No, there isn't,' she answered snippily. Emphatically.

Which brought Jonas back to that frustrated ex-boyfriend again...

He looked at her through narrowed lids. 'Where have you been for the past three days?'

She looked startled. 'Sorry?'

'I asked where you've been for the past three days,' Jonas repeated firmly.

Mac gave an irritated frown. 'I can't see how that's any of your business!'

'It is if it has any bearing on the unwanted graffiti outside,' he reasoned.

'I don't see how it can have.' Mac sat forward and put her empty coffee mug down on the bamboo table. 'If you must know, I went to visit my parents in Devon,' she explained as Jonas continued to look at her questioningly.

'Oh.' He looked frustrated. 'As you said, that's not particularly helpful.'

It also wasn't the answer he had obviously been expecting. 'Where did you think I'd been, Jonas?' Mac asked.

'How the hell should I know?' he retorted tersely.

Was he being defensive? It certainly sounded that way to her. But why did it? Jonas had made it more than clear on Monday evening that he wasn't interested in becoming involved with her—or indeed with any woman who was so physically inexperienced!

Thinking about what had happened between the two of them that evening perhaps wasn't the right thing for her to do when they were sitting here alone in her home. Well…alone apart from the two men she could see outside the window painting the wooden cladding!

She stood up suddenly. 'I don't think we'll achieve anything further by talking about this any more today, Jonas.'

He looked up at her mockingly. 'Is that my cue to politely take my leave?'

Mac felt the warmth of the colour that entered her cheeks. 'Or impolitely, if you would prefer,' she said sweetly.

What Jonas would *prefer* to do was something he dared not allow himself.

The last few minutes spent here with her, in the warmth and beauty that she had made of her home, made him strangely reluctant to leave it. Or her. Just the thought of going back alone to the cold and impersonal sterility of his own apartment was enough to send an icy shiver of revulsion down the length of his spine.

What was it about this woman in particular that made Jonas want to remain in her company? That made him so reluctant to leave the warmth and vitality that was Mary 'Mac' McGuire?

'Have you ever done any interior designing other than your own?' he heard himself asking.

Mac raised an eyebrow. 'Not really. A room here and there for my parents, but otherwise no. Why?'

What the hell was he doing? Jonas wondered, annoyed with himself. The last thing he wanted—the *very* last thing—when he moved into his new apartment next year was a constant reminder of this unusual woman because he was surrounded by *her* choice of décor!

'No reason,' he replied coldly as he stood up decisively. 'I was just making conversation,' he explained. 'You're right, I have to get back to the office.'

Mac stood near the door and watched beneath lowered lashes as Jonas strode over to place his empty coffee mug on the breakfast bar, her gaze hungry as she admired the way his brown leather jacket fitted smoothly over the width of those shoulders and how his legs appeared so long and lean in his snug faded jeans.

She wasn't over him!

Mac had thought—and hoped—that three days in Devon would put this man and that mad desire she had felt for him on Monday evening into perspective. Looking at him now, feeling the wild beat of her pulse and the heated awareness washing over her body, she realised that all she had done was force herself not to think about him. Being with Jonas again, and once more totally aware of that unequivocally passionate response to him, showed her that she hadn't forgotten a thing about him since she'd last seen him.

She moistened dry lips, instantly aware of her mistake as she saw the way Jonas's dark gaze fixated on the movement as he walked slowly towards her. 'I really do need to go out and get some things in for dinner,' she said desperately.

Jonas came to a halt only inches away from her. 'Why don't I take you out to dinner this evening and you can do the food shopping tomorrow?' he prompted huskily.

Mac blinked her uncertainty, part of her wanting to

have dinner with him this evening, another part of her knowing it would be reckless for her to even think of doing so. 'I thought we had already agreed that the two of us seeing each other again socially was not a good idea?'

'It isn't,' Jonas acknowledged wryly.

'Then—'

'I want to have dinner with you, damn it!' he bit out fiercely.

Mac gave a rueful smile. 'And do you usually get what you want, Jonas?'

'Generally? Yes. As far as you're concerned? Rarely,' he said bluntly.

Mac was torn. An evening spent alone, after being with Jonas again, now stretched in front of her like a long dark tunnel. Alternately, spending any part of the evening with him presented a high risk of there being a repeat of Monday evening's disaster...

'No,' she said finally. 'I—no.'

Jonas eyed her speculatively. 'That's a definite no, is it?'

'Yes.'

'Yes, that's a definite no? Or yes, I've changed my mind and would love to have dinner with you this evening, Jonas?' he drawled.

He was teasing her! It was so unexpected from this normally forcefully arrogant man that Mac couldn't stop herself from laughing softly as she gave a slight shake of her head. 'You aren't making this easy for me, are you?'

Jonas had no idea what had possessed him to make the invitation in the first place, let alone try to cajole her into accepting it. Especially when he knew that spending any more time with this woman was the very last thing he should do.

He had been telling himself exactly that for the past three days. To no avail, obviously, when the first time he set eyes on her again he was pressing her to have dinner with him!

Even now Jonas couldn't bring himself to retract the invitation. 'It can't be that difficult, Mac,' he cajoled. 'The answer is either yes or no.'

Mac looked up at Jonas quizzically, wondering why he had invited her out to dinner when he was so obviously as reluctant to spend time alone with her again as she was with him.

Except the two of them were alone right now...

Alone, and with the sexual tension between them rising just as obviously. The very air that surrounded them seemed to crackle with that awareness; she was so aware of it now that her heart raced and her palms felt damp.

She drew in a sharp breath. 'I think that has to be a definite no.'

'"I think" is surely contradictory to "definite"?' Jonas pressed.

Because Mac was having a problem *thinking* at all in Jonas's company!

Because she really wanted to say yes?

Maybe. No, definitely! But the part of her that could still reason logically—a very small part of her, admittedly!—knew it really wasn't a sensible thing for her to spend any more time in his highly disturbing company.

'I don't want to go out to dinner with you, Jonas,' she stated very firmly—at the same time aware of a sinking disappointment in the pit of her stomach. An ache. A hollowness that instantly made her want to retract her refusal. She bit her bottom lip, hard, to stop herself from doing exactly that.

Jonas looked down at Mac through narrowed lids, physically aware of everything about her; the slender and sexy elegance of her body, the long silky length of her ebony hair, the warm grey of her eyes, her tiny up tilted nose, the satiny smoothness of her cheeks, those full and sensuous lips—the bottom one firmly gripped between her tiny white teeth. Could that be in an effort to stop Mac from retracting her own refusal?

Implying she didn't *really* want to say no to his dinner invitation...

Jonas straightened. 'I'm not asking you out so that you can dress up and be a trophy on my arm, Mac,' he assured her gently. 'How about we eat here instead of going out? I'll come back at eight o'clock with a bottle of wine and a takeaway. Would you prefer Chinese or Indian?'

Mac's eyes widened. 'But I just said—'

'That you didn't want to go out to dinner,' he cut in. 'So we'll eat dinner here instead.'

She frowned. 'That wasn't quite what I meant.'

'I know that, Mac.' Jonas smiled.

'Then—'

'Look, we both know that we would actually prefer not to spend any more time together,' Jonas said neutrally. 'The problem with that is I can't seem to stay away from you. How about you?' he asked, eyes suddenly fierce with emotion in his otherwise calm face.

Mac realised from his careful tone and fierce expression that he disliked intensely even having to make that admission. That he was still as disturbed by their physical attraction to each other as she was. A physical attraction that was going precisely nowhere when he distrusted her sexual inexperience and she distrusted her own ability to resist him. To see him any more than was absolutely necessary would be absolute madness.

She drew herself up determinedly. 'I said no, Jonas, and I meant *no*!'

His mouth tightened, jaw clenched. 'Fine,' he said tersely. 'I'll wish you a pleasant evening, then.' He nodded abruptly before crossing to the door, closing it softly behind him as he left.

That hollow feeling deepened in Mac's stomach as she watched him go. She knew absolutely that the last thing she was going to have was a pleasant evening in any shape or form.

CHAPTER NINE

'I HAVE Miss McGuire for you on line one, Mr Buchanan,' Mandy informed Jonas lightly down the telephone line when he responded to her buzz.

'Miss McGuire?' Jonas frowned as he suddenly realised Mandy was referring to Mac; he had ceased thinking of her as 'the irritating Miss McGuire' days ago!

He and Mac had only parted a few hours ago, and not exactly harmoniously, so why was she calling him at his office now? Had something else happened at her home?

Jonas put his hand over the mouthpiece to look across at Yvonne as she sat on the other side of his desk, the two of them having been going through some paperwork. 'Would you come back in fifteen minutes so we can finish up here?'

'Of course, Jonas.' She stood up smoothly. 'Are you having better luck persuading Miss McGuire into selling?' she paused to ask ruefully.

Jonas gave her an irritated look. 'It hasn't come into our conversation for some time,' he answered honestly. Part of him had forgotten why he had ever met Mac in the first place. Part of him wished that he never had.

'Oh.' Yvonne looked surprised. 'I thought that was the whole point of your—acquaintance?'

'Did you?' Jonas returned unhelpfully. Yvonne was a good PA, a damned good one, but even so that didn't give her the right to question any of his actions. 'If you wouldn't mind, this is a private call…?' he prompted pointedly, regretting the embarrassed colour that entered Yvonne's cheeks, but making no attempt at an apology as he waited for her to leave his office before taking Mac's call. 'Yes?' he said tersely, not sure who he was annoyed with, only knowing that he was.

Mac had been aware of each second she'd been kept waiting to be put through to Jonas—perhaps because he was unsure about taking her call?—and she could hear the displeasure in his voice now as she held her mobile to her ear with one hand and poured two mugs of coffee with the other. 'Have I called at a bad time?'

'No.'

Mac begged to differ, considering that long wait, and the impatience she could hear in Jonas's tone. She knew she shouldn't have telephoned him. Had tried to talk herself out of it. Wished now that she had heeded her own advice! 'I realised after you had left earlier that I hadn't… I just called to say thank you,' she said awkwardly. 'For everything you did for me this morning. Calling the police. Arranging to have the graffiti painted over.'

There was a brief silence before Jonas answered, his voice sounding less aggressive. 'Have Ben and Jerry finished the painting now?'

'Ben and Jerry? That's what they're called?'

'Yes,' Jonas answered dryly.

'Really?'

'Yes, really,' Jonas chuckled softly.

Mac felt slightly heartened by that chuckle. 'They've

almost finished, yes. I was just making them both a mug of coffee.'

'That's very…kind of you.'

Mac bristled. 'You sound surprised?'

His sigh was audible. 'Let's try to not have another argument, hmm, Mac.'

'No, of course not.' She grimaced. 'Sorry.'

'Was that the only reason you called?' Jonas asked huskily.

Was it? Mac had convinced herself that it was before she made the call, but now that she had heard his voice again she wasn't so sure.

They had parted with such finality earlier. Leaving no room for manoeuvre. Something that had left Mac with a feeling of uneasy dissatisfaction.

'I think so,' she answered.

'But you're not sure?' he pressed.

'I am sure,' she said firmly. 'I just— Anyway, thank you for your help earlier, Jonas. It is appreciated.'

'You're welcome,' he said warmly. 'Have you had second thoughts about dinner?'

Second and third ones, Mac acknowledged ruefully. But all of them with the same conclusion—that a relationship between herself and Jonas was going nowhere. Except possibly to a broken heart on her part.

She wasn't sure when—or even how—the feelings she had for Jonas had sneaked up on her. She only knew that they had.

Quite what those feelings were, she had so far shied away from analysing; she only knew, after seeing him again this morning, that her three days away had achieved nothing and that she definitely felt something for him.

She felt energised in his company. A tingling awareness. An excited thrumming. Whether or not that was just a sexual excitement, Mac wasn't experienced enough in relationships to know. She only knew that the thought of never seeing him again, speaking to him again, was a painful one.

It made no difference to those feelings whatsoever that she knew there was no future for the two of them. Jonas undisputedly affected her in a way no other man ever had.

'I'll take it from your delay in answering that you have,' he drawled softly.

'I didn't say that—'

'In which case, Indian or Chinese?' he said authoritatively, rolling right over her vacillation, having no intention of letting her wriggle out of the invitation a second time. Or was it a third time? Whatever. For some reason, Mac had called him, once again opening the line of communication between them, and at the same time renewing Jonas's own determination to see her again. 'I'm waiting, Mac,' he added.

Her raggedly indrawn breath was audible. 'Indian. But—'

'No buts,' Jonas cut in forcefully. 'I'll be there about eight o'clock, okay?'

'I—Yes. Okay.'

Jonas only realised he had been tensed for another refusal as he felt his shoulders relax. 'We're only going to eat dinner together, Mac,' he mocked gruffly—not sure whether he was offering her that reassurance or himself!

Himself, probably, he accepted derisively. Mac had got under his skin in a way he wasn't comfortable with. So much so that he knew he shouldn't see her again. So much so that he knew he *had* to see her again.

She was a magnet he was inexorably drawn to. And resistance on Jonas's part was proving as futile as preventing the proverbial moth from being drawn to a flame...

'Very festive,' Jonas told Mac dryly later that evening once she had opened the door to his knock and he had stepped into the living area of the warehouse, the main lights switched off to allow for the full effect of the brightly lit Christmas tree. The smell of pine was thick in the air, and the branches were heavily adorned with decorations and glittering shiny baubles that reflected those coloured lights.

The dining table in the corner of the huge open-plan area was already set for two, with several candles placed in its centre waiting to be lit, and a bottle of red wine waiting to be opened.

Jonas turned away from the intimacy of that setting to look at Mac instead. Her hair was loose again this evening, and she had changed out of the black jumper, jeans and red body-warmer, into an overlarge thigh-length long-sleeved red shirt over black leggings, with calf-high black boots.

Jonas had spent the remainder of the afternoon telling himself what a bad idea it was for him to come here again this evening. One look at Mac and he didn't give a damn how bad an idea it was, he was just enjoying being in her company again.

'Here.' He handed her the bag of Indian food before thrusting his hands into his jeans pockets in an effort not to reach out, as he so wanted to do, and pull her close to him. Jonas knew that once he had done that he wouldn't want to let her go again. That he would forget everything else but having her in his arms...

Mac turned away from the stark intensity of Jonas's gaze to carry the bag of food over to the breakfast bar and take out the hot cartons before removing the lids with determined concentration, feeling strangely shy in his company now that she was aware of—if choosing not to look too closely at—the feelings she had for him.

'Ben and Jerry did a good job painting over the graffiti,' she told him conversationally as she carried the warmed plates and cartons of food over to the table on a tray.

Jonas shrugged. 'It's too dark for me to tell.'

Mac nodded. 'They were very efficient.' Her gaze didn't quite meet his as she straightened and turned, at the same time completely aware of how vibrantly attractive he looked in a blue cashmere sweater, the same colour as his eyes, and faded jeans of a lighter blue.

'Mac...?'

She raised her eyes to look at him before as quickly looking away again as she felt that familiar thrill of awareness down the length of her spine. 'We should sit down and eat before the food gets cold.'

Jonas frowned at the awkwardness he could feel growing between them. 'Mac, are you even going to look at me?'

She leant back against the table as she turned and raised startled lids, her eyes huge grey orbs in the paleness of her face, her expression pained. 'What are we doing, Jonas?' she groaned huskily.

He gave a rueful shrug. 'Eating dinner together, I thought.'

She shook her head. 'After agreeing only this afternoon that it was a *bad* idea!'

'No, *you* said it was a bad idea. I don't think you asked for my opinion,' Jonas recalled dryly. Although, if asked at the time, he would have said it was a bad idea, too! 'As you said, the food is getting cold, so I suggest that for now we just sit down and eat and think about this again later?' He moved to pointedly pull back one of the chairs for her to sit down.

Mac regarded him quizzically as she sat. 'You really do like having your own way, don't you?'

'Almost as much as you enjoy doing the exact opposite of what you know I want,' Jonas acknowledged with a quick smile as he sat down opposite her before picking up the bottle of wine and deftly opening it.

Mac chuckled softly. 'Interesting.'

'Irritating for the main part, actually,' Jonas admitted as he poured the wine into their glasses. He raised his own glass and made a toast. 'To—hopefully—our first indigestion-free meal together!'

Mac raised her glass and touched it gently against the side of Jonas's. 'To an indigestion-free meal!' she echoed huskily, not too sure about the 'first' part of the toast. It implied there might be other meals to come, and, as Mac knew only too well, she and Jonas always ended up arguing if they spent any length of time together.

Well…almost always. The times when they didn't argue were even more disturbing…

'You really do like Christmas, don't you?'

Mac looked up from helping herself to some of the food in the cartons to see Jonas was looking at her brightly decked Christmas tree. 'I would have said, doesn't everyone?' she replied. 'But I already know that you don't.'

'I wouldn't go that far,' Jonas said.

'No?' Mac eyed him interestedly.

He shrugged. 'I don't dislike Christmas, Mac, it's just a time I remember when my parents were forced to spend a couple of days in each other's company, with the result they usually ended up having one almighty slanging match before the holiday was over. As my grandmother died on Christmas Eve, Joseph wasn't particularly into celebrating it, either.'

'What about your cousin Amy and her family?'

'Amy always goes away with her partner for Christmas, and I'm not close to my uncle and aunt. What can I say?' he drawled at Mac's dismayed expression. 'We're a dysfunctional family.'

It sounded awful to Mac when she thought of her own happy childhood, and the wonderful memories she had of family Christmases, both in the distant past and more recently. 'Why did you call your grandfather Joseph?'

Jonas gave a humourless smile. 'Calling out "Granddad" on a building site didn't go down too well with him, so it became a habit to call him by his first name.'

Looking at Jonas now, so suave, so obviously wealthy from the car he drove and the penthouse apartment he lived in, it was difficult to envision him as a rough and tough teenager working on a building site.

Yet there were those calluses Mac had noticed on his palms three days ago. And there was a ripcord strength about Jonas that didn't look as if it came solely from working out in a gym. Wealthy or not, underneath all that suave sophistication, she realised he was still capable of being every bit as rough and tough as he had been as a teenager.

'What?' Jonas paused in eating his food to look across at her questioningly.

Mac shrugged. 'I was just thinking that maybe you should think about starting your own Christmas traditions.'

From the way Mac had been looking at him so search-ingly Jonas was pretty sure that hadn't been what she had been thinking at all. Although quite what she had been thinking, he had no idea.

She was still something of an enigma to him, he recognised ruefully. There was no sophisticated game-playing with Mac. No artifice. As she had so emphati-cally told him, what you saw was what you got. And what Jonas saw he wanted very badly indeed...

He sighed. 'It's never seemed worth the bother when I only have myself to think about.'

Mac looked at him assessingly. 'I'm taking a bet that you usually go away for Christmas. Somewhere hot,' she qualified. 'Golden sandy beaches where you can sunbathe, and there are waiters to bring you tall drinks with exotic fruit and umbrellas in them. Somewhere you can forget it even is Christmas,' she teased.

'You would win your bet,' Jonas acknowledged with a smile.

She shook her head. 'I can't imagine ever going away for Christmas.'

Neither could Jonas when he could clearly see the distaste on Mac's face. 'What do you and your family do over Christmas?' he asked.

Those beautiful smoky grey eyes glowed. 'Nowadays we all converge on my parents' house in a little village called Tulnerton in Devon. My mother's parents, sev-eral aged aunts. All the presents are placed under the tree, and Christmas Eve we all have a family meal and then attend Midnight Mass at the local church together. When we get back Mum and I usually put the turkey in the oven so that it cooks slowly overnight and the house is full of the smells of it cooking in the morning when we sit down to open our presents. When I was younger, that sometimes happened as early as five o'clock in the morning,' she recalled wistfully. 'Nowadays it's usually about nine o'clock, after we've checked on the turkey and everyone has a cup of tea.'

Jonas's mouth twisted. 'The perfect Christmas indeed.'

Mac eyed him ruefully. 'To me it is, yes.'

Jonas reached out and placed his hand over hers as it rested on the tabletop. 'I wasn't mocking you, Mac,' he said gruffly.

'No?'

Strangely enough, no… It was all too easy for Jonas to envisage the Christmas Mac described so warmly. The sort of Christmas that many families strived for and never actually experienced. The sort of Christmas Jonas had never had. And never would have.

'There are no arguments?' he prompted.

Her eyes glowed with laughter. 'Usually only over who's going to pull the wishbone after we've eaten our Christmas lunch!'

His fingers curled about hers. 'It sounds wonderful.'

Mac was very aware of the air of intimacy that now surrounded the two of them. But it was a different type of intimacy from a physical one. This intimacy was warm and enveloping. Dangerous…

She removed her hand purposefully from beneath Jonas's to pick up her fork. 'I'm sure there must have been arguments; you can't put eight or ten disparate people in a house together for four or five days without there being the odd disagreement. I've obviously just chosen to forget them.' She grimaced.

Jonas looked across at her with enigmatic blue eyes.

'You don't have to make excuses for your own happy childhood, Mac.'

'I wasn't—'

'Weren't you?' he rasped.

Yes, she supposed she had been. Because Jonas's childhood had borne absolutely no resemblance to her own. Because, although he wouldn't thank her for it in the slightest, her heart ached for him. 'If you haven't made other plans yet, perhaps you would like to—' Mac broke off abruptly, her cheeks warming as she realised how utterly ridiculous she was being.

Jonas eyed her warily. 'Please tell me you weren't about to invite me to spend Christmas with you and your family in Devon.'

That was exactly what Mac had been about to do! Impulsively. Stupidly! Of course Jonas didn't want to spend Christmas with her, let alone the rest of her family; with half a dozen strangers there, as well as Mac herself, he would necessarily have to be polite to everyone for the duration of his stay.

Her cheeks were now positively burning with embarrassment. 'I think I feel that indigestion coming on!'

Jonas studied Mac through narrowed lids, knowing by her evasiveness that she *had* been about to invite him to spend Christmas with her and her family. Why? Because she actually wanted to spend Christmas with him? Or because she felt sorry for him and just couldn't bear the thought of anyone—even him—spending Christmas alone?

His mouth thinned. 'I don't recall ever saying that I'm *alone* when I spend my Christmases sunbathing on those golden sandy beaches.'

'No, you didn't, did you?' The colour had left Mac's cheeks as quickly as it had warmed them, her eyes a huge and haunted grey as she gave a moue of self-disgust. 'How naïve of me.'

Jonas knew that he had deliberately hit out at her because pity was the last thing he wanted from her. From anyone. Damn it, he was successful and rich and could afford to do anything he wanted to do. He had never met refusal from any woman he'd shown an interest in taking to his bed. All the things he had decided he wanted out of life years ago when he left university so determined to succeed he had achieved.

Then why did just being with Mac like this, talking with her, make him just as aware of all the things he *didn't* have in his life?

Things like having someone to come home to every night. The same someone. To share things with. To laugh with. To make love with.

'Don't knock it until you've tried it,' Jonas drawled. 'In fact, why don't you consider giving the traditional family Christmas a miss this year and come away with me instead?' he asked as he looked at her over the top of his wine glass before lifting it and taking a deep swallow of the ruby-red liquid.

Mac stared at Jonas, absolutely incredulous that he appeared to be asking her to go away with him for Christmas.

CHAPTER TEN

WAS Jonas serious about his invitation? Or was he just playing with her, already knowing from her earlier remarks exactly what her answer would be?

One look at the unmistakable mockery on his ruggedly handsome face and Mac knew that was exactly what he was doing.

She stood up. 'It would serve you right if I said yes!' she snapped as she picked up her glass of wine and moved across the room to stand beside the Christmas tree.

'Try me,' Jonas invited as he relaxed back in his chair to look across at her thoughtfully. 'I assure you, if you said yes then I would book two first-class seats on a flight that would allow us to arrive in Barbados on Christmas Eve,' he promised huskily.

Mac looked at him scornfully. 'That's so easy to say when you knew before you even asked that I would refuse.'

'Did I?' He stood up to slowly cross the room, his piercing blue gaze easily holding hers captive as he came to a halt only inches away from her.

Mac stared up at him, her breathing somehow feeling constricted. She moistened her lips with the tip of her tongue. 'I had already told you that I couldn't imagine spending Christmas anywhere but at home with my parents.'

Jonas's dark gaze was fixed on those moist and slightly parted lips. 'I'm curious to know what your answer would have been if that family Christmas was taken out of the equation?'

Mac gave a firm shake of her head. 'I hate even the idea of spending Christmas on a beach.'

Jonas had no idea why he was even pursuing this conversation. Except perhaps that he wanted to know if Mac's invitation for him to spend Christmas with her family had been out of the pity he suspected it was, or something else... 'What if I were to suggest we went to a ski resort instead of a beach?'

She smiled slightly. 'I can't ski.'

'I don't recall saying anything about the two of us actually going skiing. I seriously doubt I would have any desire to leave our bedroom once we got there,' Jonas admitted wickedly.

Once again her cheeks coloured with that becoming blush. 'Wouldn't that rather defeat the object?'

He gave a shrug. 'Surely that would depend on what the objective was?'

Mac looked up at him and frowned. 'I believe we had this conversation three days ago, Jonas. At which time, I believe you made it *more* than clear that you're not at all interested in becoming my first lover.'

He hadn't been. He still wasn't. Except he had realised these last three days that he didn't like the thought of some other man being Mac's first lover either! 'Maybe I've changed my mind,' he replied guardedly.

'And maybe you just enjoying playing games with me,' Mac said knowingly.

'Mac, I haven't even begun to play games with you

yet!' he teased. Although whether that teasing was directed at her or himself, Jonas wasn't sure…

He wanted to make love with this woman. He actually wanted it so badly he could taste it. Taste *her*.

Dear God, there were so many ways he could make love to this woman without actually taking her virginity. So many ways he could give her incredible pleasure. And she could give him that same pleasure in return.

But would it be enough to sate the ever-rising hunger inside him? Would touching Mac, caressing her, making love to her but never actually taking her, being inside her, ever be enough for him? Did he really have that much self-control?

Where she was concerned? Somehow Jonas doubted it! The only reason they hadn't already become lovers when she had been at his apartment was because of the realisation of the seemingly insurmountable barrier of her virginity.

Jonas moved away abruptly. 'You're right, this conversation is pointless. Christmas is still two weeks away—'

'And we may not even be talking to each other again by then!' Mac put in with black humour.

'Probably not,' he admitted. 'But even if we are, we still both know that you will be spending Christmas in Devon with your family and I will be sitting on a beach somewhere improving my tan.'

Mac didn't think that Jonas's tan needed improving; his skin was already a deep gold. And from the calluses on his hands and those defined muscles in his shoulders and chest, she didn't think that tan had been acquired sitting on a beach anywhere!

In fact, if she had arrived home a little later than she had this morning, then she was pretty sure that she would have found Jonas up that metal tower outside her home beside Ben and Jerry as he helped to paint over the graffiti. Jonas might now be rich and powerful, the owner of his own company for some years rather than an employee, but his rugged appearance and weather-hewn features were testament to the fact that he still enjoyed getting his hands dirty occasionally.

'I was totally sincere in my invitation for you to spend Christmas with my family, Jonas,' she said huskily.

His eyes were a hard and mocking blue. 'And what do you think your family would have made of you bringing a man home for the holidays?'

Mac's cheeks warmed as she easily imagined her father's teasing, and the whispered speculation of her aged aunts, if Jonas had accepted her invitation and accompanied her to Devon. 'Oh.' She grimaced. 'I hadn't really thought of that.'

'Exactly,' Jonas said, drinking the last of his wine before placing the empty glass on the table. 'It's probably time I was going.'

Mac blinked. 'It's still early.'

As far as Jonas was concerned, it was seriously bordering on being too late!

She looked so damned beautiful, so desirable with the coloured lights on the tree reflected in the glossy curtain of her long black hair, her eyes a deep and misty grey, her skin like a warm peach, and her lips—dear heaven, those full and pouting lips!

Jonas wanted to take those lips with his own, devour them, to kiss her and explore the hot temptation of her mouth until she felt the same need he did. If he didn't leave here soon, in the next few minutes, he wasn't going to be able to withstand that temptation at all.

'You didn't get to see my studio earlier; would you like to see it now?'

Jonas was jolted out of that rising fiery haze of desire to focus on Mac. 'Sorry...?'

She shrugged narrow shoulders. 'Obviously the studio is pretty empty at the moment with most of my recent work being at the exhibition, but you're welcome to take a look. If you would like to,' she added almost shyly.

Did he want to do that? He had evaded taking up the invitation earlier because he didn't want to find himself being drawn into Mac's world any more than he already was. To see where she had created the amazing paintings like the ones he had seen at the Lyndwood Gallery the previous week, and to feel himself being pulled even deeper into the intimacy of Mac's life.

He still wanted to avoid doing that, didn't he?

'I would like to,' Jonas instead heard himself accept gruffly.

Mac smiled. 'It's just up the spiral staircase.' She placed her glass down next to Jonas's on the table before turning to lead the way.

Jonas reached out and grasped her arm to look down searchingly into her face, sure by the way she avoided meeting his gaze, that she was already regretting having made the invitation. 'Don't take me up there if you would rather not, Mac...'

'I—no, it's fine,' she reassured him, not really sure that it *was* fine, but unwilling for Jonas to leave just yet.

Because she could sense the air of finality about him now and she had the feeling that once he left this time he would ensure that it really was the last time she saw him.

Yet wasn't that what she wanted? Didn't she want

Jonas out of her life? To never have to see and deal with this disturbing man ever again?

'It will only take a few minutes,' she told him briskly as she pulled out of his grasp and walked over and switched on the light overhead. She'd rather take him up the spiral staircase to her studio than answer any of her own soul-searching questions.

But she was completely aware of Jonas, every step of the way, as he followed behind her up that metal staircase...

Whatever he had been expecting Mac's studio to look like, after the warmth and colour of the living area below, it certainly wasn't the starkness of the pale cream colour-wash on the three bare brick walls. Or the fourth wall that faced towards the river completely glass, the ceiling also made up of glass panels, and revealing the clear star-lit sky overhead. The only furniture in the room was an old and faded chaise against one wall and a daybed beside another.

Mac's easel was set up near the huge glass window, and she strolled across the room to lightly lay a cover over the painting she was currently working on. 'I never allow people to see my work before it's completed,' she explained ruefully at Jonas's questioning look.

The surroundings weren't quite 'starving in a garret', but the studio was much more basic than Jonas had been expecting after the vividness of colours on the floor below. 'You prefer not to have any outside distractions when you're working,' he realised softly.

Mac turned to him with wide eyes. 'No...'

She hadn't expected him to have that insight, Jonas realised, wondering if anyone else had ever really understood how and why she worked in the surroundings she did. Surroundings that were unique in the way Mac had converted this warehouse to her own individual needs.

Another reason she refused to sell the warehouse to Buchanan Construction. The main reason probably; most of Mac's emotional links to her grandfather would be inside her rather than consisting of bricks and mortar.

This last realisation put Jonas in an untenable position.

Had she done that deliberately?

His mouth thinned as he turned to look at Mac. 'You brought me up here for a purpose.'

Mac briefly thought of denying it, and then thought better of it as she recognised the steely glitter in Jonas's eyes. 'I'm not sure I could work anywhere else,' she answered truthfully.

'Have you ever tried?' he gritted.

'No. But—' She moved her shoulders in an uncomfortable shrug. 'I just thought it might help if you understood I'm not just being bloody-minded by refusing to sell my home and my studio to you.'

'You thought by showing me this that I would back off,' Jonas guessed. 'I don't enjoy being manipulated, Mac,' he said coolly.

She frowned. 'I wasn't—'

'Yes, you were, damn you!' he burst out, suddenly explosive in his anger, taking the two long strides that brought him to within touching distance of her. 'This is just an artist's studio, Mac. It could be replicated just about anywhere.'

She shook her head. 'You're wrong. I've lived and worked here for the past five years—'

'And once this place has been knocked down you'll live and work somewhere else for a lot longer than that!' he said grimly.

'I told you, that isn't going to happen——' Her protest was cut short as Jonas reached out to pull her into his arms before lowering his head and grinding his mouth fiercely down onto hers.

It was a kiss of punishment rather than gentleness, anger rather than passion, Jonas's arms like steel bands about her waist as he held her tightly against him, pressing her to his muscled body, making Mac completely aware of the pulsing hardness of his thighs.

She stood on tiptoe as her hands moved up his chest to his shoulders, and then into the dark thickness of the hair at his nape, her mouth slanting, lips parting beneath his as she returned the heat of that kiss.

Jonas was aware of his shift in mood as the angry need to punish her faded and passion and desire took over, groaning low in his throat as he began to sip and taste the softness of Mac's lips, his tongue stroking those lips as he tested their sweetness before moving deeper into the hot and welcoming warmth of Mac's mouth.

He could feel her delicacy beneath the restless caress of his hands down the length of her spine before he cupped her bottom to pull her up and into him, the soft and welcoming well between her thighs both an agony and an ecstasy as his arousal fitted perfectly against her.

He dragged his mouth from hers to breathe deeply against her creamy cheek. 'Wrap your legs around me,' he encouraged fiercely.

'I don't——'

'I promise I'll lift and support you, Mac,' he looked up to encourage hotly. 'I just need you to wrap your legs around me,' he exhorted her gruffly before burying his lips against the side of her neck.

Jonas's tongue was a fiery torment against Mac's

skin, a rasping, arousing torment that made her feel weak and wanting even as she did as he asked. As promised, Jonas's hands beneath her bottom easily lifted and supported her as she raised up to curve her legs about him and instantly felt the press of his arousal against the centre of her parted thighs.

Her thin leggings and brief panties were no barrier to that firm and pulsating flesh as it pressed against her. Mac felt herself swell there, becoming damp, wet, so hot and aching as Jonas's mouth claimed hers once again.

She was barely aware of him carrying her across the room to press her against the wall, Mac only realising he had done so as the coldness of the brick against her back became a sharp counterpoint to the heated arousal of her breasts and thighs.

His arousal was more penetrating now, pressing into that welcoming well as Jonas moved against her rhythmically, each thrust of his body matched by the penetration of his tongue into the heated inferno of her mouth, so that Mac felt him everywhere.

Jonas wrenched his mouth from hers, breathing hard as he looked down at her with fiercely dark eyes. 'I'm going to pleasure you, Mac,' he promised gruffly as he carried her over to lay her down on the chaise. 'I'm going to make love to you until you beg me to stop,' he vowed as he knelt on the floor beside the chaise.

He pushed her shirt out of the way and took off her boots, then peeled away her leggings and panties before moving up to kneel between her parted thighs. 'You're so beautiful here, Mac,' he murmured throatily as he looked down at her hungrily. He reached out to touch her naked thighs, fingers gentle as he parted her ebony curls.

Mac moaned as she felt Jonas's fingers move against

her in a light caress, heat coursing through her body as that pressure increased, that moan turning to a breathless keening as she felt a burning, aching pressure building inside her, demanding, wanting, needing—

'Jonas!' she cried out at the first intimate touch of his mouth against her, the moistness of his tongue a soft caress against her tender and aching skin.

Her hands moved restlessly, fingers threading into Jonas's hair with the intention of stopping that unbearable torment, but instead finding her fingers tightening her hold as she pressed him closer still, arching into him as she felt the probe of his fingers against her entrance, so close, so very close, and yet circling just out of reach.

'Yes, Jonas!' Mac groaned her torment as she pressed urgently against those tormenting fingers. 'Please…!'

God, how Jonas needed this, wanted this; the taste of Mac in his mouth and the feel of how hot and ready she was beneath his caressing hands.

He entered her slowly as he continued to use his tongue to flicker against her. His fingers began to thrust, slowly, gently to the rhythm of Mac's low encouraging groans as she moved urgently until her muscles tightened and she climaxed in long and beautiful spasms that caused her to cry out in mindless pleasure.

Mac had never felt anything like this in her life before, the pleasure so incredible it bordered on pain. Wave after wave of heat coursing, singing through her body as Jonas continued the relentless pressure of his lips and tongue until he had extracted every last vestige of her climax.

It seemed minutes, hours later, that Mac finally collapsed weakly back onto the chaise, her breath a choking sob, her body so alive to his every touch, so tinglingly aware, that she almost couldn't bear it.

Almost...

Jonas began to kiss his way up the flatness of her belly, unbuttoning her shirt to expose her naked breasts to the ministrations of the heat of his mouth, first one breast and then the other, the rasp of his jeans against her inner thighs as he lay half across her an added torment to her roused and sensitive body.

His hair looked so dark against the whiteness of her skin as Mac looked down at him, his lips fastened about one nipple as his fingers caressed its twin.

Incredibly Mac felt her pleasure rising again. More intense this time, deeper. Every touch, every caress causing her body to quiver in awareness. 'I want to touch you, too, Jonas.' She moved until she was sitting up slightly. 'I need to touch you,' she added achingly as he looked up at her, his eyes dark and heavy with arousal.

Jonas studied her searchingly; her eyes were fever bright, her cheeks flushed, her lips... He had never seen anything as sensual as Mac's pouting, full lips, could feel himself hardening to steel as he easily imagined those lips about him and her hair falling silkily across his hips and thighs as she pleasured him.

The image was so clear, so urgent, that Jonas offered no resistance as she sat up fully to push him down onto the chaise beneath her before unbuttoning and unzipping his jeans to slide them and his boxers far enough down his thighs to fully expose his hard and jutting erection. He groaned low in his throat as he saw the way Mac looked at him so hungrily before she reached out tentatively and wrapped her fingers about him.

She loved caressing him and learning what gave

Jonas the most pleasure as her hand began to move up and down.

Jonas's hands clenched at his sides as that pleasure held him as tightly in its grip as Mac did. His focus became fixed on the expression on her face as she continued to touch him. The fascination. The pleasure. Then the eroticism of seeing the moist tip of her tongue moving over her lips before she slowly lowered her head towards him, before she finally took him into her mouth.

Jonas's back arched as he thrust up into that heat, the past week or so of wanting this woman, making love to her so far but never taking her, making it impossible for him to temper his own response. That response spiralled out of control as she took him deeper into her mouth before slowly drawing back. Then repeating it all over again. Setting a rhythm, a tormenting, heated rhythm that Jonas had no will or desire to resist.

Jonas became lost in that bombardment of sensations, breathing hard, and then not breathing at all when he felt his exquisite release in mindless, beautiful pleasure.

CHAPTER ELEVEN

MAC could feel and hear Jonas breathing raggedly beside her as her head lay against his chest. Jonas's arms were wrapped tightly about her as the two of them lay side by side on the chaise. Her thoughts were racing as she wondered what happened now. Now that Jonas knew her—and her body—more intimately than anyone else ever had. Now that she knew Jonas's body more intimately than she had any other man's...

That she had been able to give him the same pleasure he had given her filled her with an immense feeling of satisfaction. But it was a satisfaction tempered by uncertainty. By the knowledge that her emotions, while she didn't want to look at them too deeply here and now, were most definitely involved. And she had no idea whether or not she would ever see Jonas again after tonight...

Neither of them had spoken as they'd adjusted their clothing into some semblance of order before they lay down together on the chaise. Mac knew her own silence was because she felt a somewhat gauche awkwardness following the intensity of their lovemaking. But she had absolutely no idea what Jonas was thinking or feeling as he lay so silently beside her.

'This is usually the awkward part.' Jonas's chest rumbled beneath Mac's ear as he finally spoke.

Mac could feel the rapid beat of her own heart. The plummeting beat of her heart. Surely this could only be awkward if Jonas didn't intend seeing her again?

'Extracting oneself without embarrassment, you mean?' she guessed huskily.

'Something like that.'

He hadn't intended things to go as far between them as they had. He had wanted to make love to Mac, to give her pleasure. But he hadn't expected to receive that same pleasure back, or for that pleasure to be given so completely. So beautifully. So erotically he had been unable to stop himself from climaxing.

There had been many women in Jonas's life the last fifteen years. Or, rather, in his bed; he didn't allow any woman to actually be a part of his life.

In the past those relationships had always been based on Jonas's need for physical release, and the woman's need for a bed partner who was wealthy enough to treat them out of bed in the way they enjoyed, to be wined and dined and bought the odd piece of expensive jewellery. As far as Jonas was concerned, it had been a fair exchange of needs. Almost as cut and dried as a business proposition, in fact. Something he could definitely relate to.

He didn't understand this relationship with Mac at all...

In fact, Jonas shied away from even calling it that.

That they had met at all had been purely accidental, a business necessity. Their meetings since had, for the main part, been just as incidental. Oh, Jonas had known it was her exhibition he was attending, and after their unsatisfactory conversation a few days earlier he had enjoyed seeing her discomfort when he'd arrived at the gallery with Amy.

But the number of times the two of them had met since weren't so easily explained away.

His desire to see her again after tonight was even less so...

It would be insanity on his part to ask to see her again. A complication he didn't need in his life; Mac was nothing at all like any of the women he had known in the past. Jonas doubted he would be able to extricate himself from a relationship with her as easily as he had with those other women.

No, he couldn't see Mac McGuire again.

Not couldn't, *wouldn't*!

He had told Mac more about himself in the time he had known her than he had ever confided in anyone. Even Joel Baxter, who had become a good friend the past twelve years. He had allowed Mac to get below his defences, Jonas realised. To reach him, know him, better than anyone else ever had.

Sex was one thing, but it was definitely time to sever the unwitting friendship that had been developing between them.

Mac looked up just in time to see the grimness of his expression. And to guess the reason for it. Well, she might have been stupid enough to lose her heart to Jonas Buchanan, but that didn't mean she had lost her pride too!

'You needn't look so worried, Jonas,' she assured him dryly as she pulled out of his arms to stand up. Luckily her shirt was thigh length, long enough to hide her nakedness beneath. 'This evening was—different. But I'm in no hurry to repeat the experience.'

Jonas scowled darkly as he sat up and smoothed the

untidy thickness of his hair back from his face. Hair that had felt silky and soft beneath Mac's fingers only minutes ago!

'Are you trying to tell me you didn't *enjoy* it?' he growled incredulously.

Mac raised a cool eyebrow. 'That would be rather silly of me, wouldn't it? No, Jonas,' she added firmly, chin raised. 'I'm not saying that at all. Only that while this evening was—pleasant, sexual gratification is no reason for the two of us to see each other again after tonight.'

It was exactly the same conclusion that Jonas had come to only minutes ago, but hearing her echo that conclusion so emotionlessly irritated the hell out of him. Mac thought the evening had been *pleasant*! Damn it, he had never, ever lost it in the way he had with her tonight. Had never allowed himself to lose control in the way he had earlier when Mac took him into her mouth.

Jonas could still feel that pleasure. The most gut-wrenching, soul-deep pleasure that he had ever known. He knew the memory of it was going to haunt his days and fill his nights for longer than he cared to think about.

He stood up, eyes glittering angrily. 'In other words, you've had your fun, and thanks for the experience?'

She eyed him mildly. 'You seem angry, Jonas. Isn't this what you wanted?'

Yes, damn it, of course it was what he wanted!

Jonas had wanted to be able to extricate himself from this situation with as little unpleasantness between them as possible. Except he had discovered it was something else entirely for Mac to want to do the same thing!

'Whatever,' he snapped coldly. 'I suggest—what the

hell was that?' He scowled darkly as he heard a loud crashing noise coming from outside.

Mac looked totally bewildered. 'I have no idea...'

Jonas strode quickly over to the window that faced over the river, looking out into the darkness. He couldn't actually see anything, or anyone, and his car was still parked in the street below, but he was pretty sure that crashing noise had been the sound of glass breaking.

He turned quickly, his expression grim as he hurried over to the spiral staircase. 'I think your intruder is back!'

Mac had been rooted to the spot, shocked into immobility by the loud sound. But she moved now, hurrying over to stand at the top of the staircase and look down at Jonas as he reached the bottom step. 'You can't go out there alone, Jonas—'

He paused to look up at her. 'Of course I'm going out there,' he said.

'You can't.' Mac shook her head worriedly. 'What if they have a knife? Or—or a gun—'

'You've been watching too much television, Mac,' he said gently.

'There was a stabbing in this area only a couple of weeks ago,' she protested.

'Reportedly rival gangs sorting out the pecking order,' he reassured her.

'Yes, but—'

'Just put some clothes on and call the police, and then wait inside until I come back and give the all-clear,' Jonas told her grimly.

'But—'

'You are *not* to come outside, Mac,' he instructed firmly. 'Do you understand?'

Mac felt her cheeks warm with displeasure, both with

Jonas's high-handed attitude and the reminder that she still didn't have all her clothes on. 'I'm not stupid, Jonas. Neither do I intend just cowering in here while you go outside and face goodness knows what!'

'You'll do as you're damn well told if you don't want me to come back and deal with you once I've dealt with what's going on outside!' he growled.

'You could try,' she seethed.

Jonas's mouth tightened as there was another sound of glass breaking. 'I really don't have time for this right now, Mac. Just do as I ask and don't complicate the situation by forcing me to worry about your safety when I should be concentrating on putting an end to this!' He didn't stay to argue with her any further before disappearing from the bottom of the stairs.

Mac heard the outside door closing seconds later, her heart pounding erratically as she quickly grabbed up her leggings and panties before hurrying down the metal staircase to use her mobile and call the police, her hand shaking so badly she could barely press the right three buttons.

She had to calm down. Had to at least try to be coherent when she gave the necessary information to the police.

Despite those inner warnings Mac knew she sounded slightly hysterical as she talked to the dispatcher who answered.

She hadn't just sounded hysterical, Mac acknowledged after she had ended the call and hurried over to the picture window to look outside. She had sounded frantic.

Because she didn't care who was outside, or what damage they had done to her home this time. All she cared about was Jonas. That he should come back safely.

Mac might have been uncertain about her feelings for Jonas until tonight, but she had absolutely no doubts now that she had fallen totally in love with him...

Jonas knew he was white-faced by the time he wearily accompanied Mac back up the stairs and into the living area of her home almost an hour later.

Who would have guessed it?

Who could have known?

He gave a heavy sigh. 'I told the police I would join them down at the station as soon as possible.' He picked up his jacket and slipped it on, all without looking at Mac.

He couldn't look at her. Couldn't bear to see the accusation that was sure to be in her face.

It had all been his fault, he realised numbly. The initial break-in. The graffiti. The windows broken this evening on Mac's Jeep parked downstairs in the garage. All of it was Jonas's fault.

He hadn't known. Hadn't realised. Despite Mac's teasing remark earlier in the week, he had still never guessed that Yvonne had feelings for him; the sort of feelings that had prompted his PA into trying to scare Mac into selling the warehouse to Jonas.

'Drink some of this first.'

Jonas looked up to see that Mac had refilled his wine glass and now held it out to him. As if wine were going to erase the horror of finding Yvonne downstairs systematically breaking the windows on Mac's car. Or numb his disbelief at the conversation that had followed. The hysterical conviction Yvonne had that she was helping him. That she loved him. Was sure the two of them were meant to be together.

All of it made worse by the fact that Mac had disobeyed his instruction by then and come downstairs to join him, hearing every word Yvonne said. Along with the police who had arrived only minutes earlier.

Nothing could ever erase the horror of any of that from Jonas's mind!

He grimaced. 'I don't think it's a good idea for me to arrive at a police station smelling of alcohol.'

Probably not, Mac acknowledged as she put the wine glass down on the table.

What an evening! She and Jonas had made love. Mac had realised—and still shied away from looking at it too deeply—that she was in love with Jonas. And now this.

By the time she had dressed and hurried downstairs to the garage, Yvonne Richards had been in full spate, professing her love for Jonas, explaining that she had only terrorised Mac because she wanted to help him. That she had only done those things in an effort to convince Mac into selling the warehouse to Buchanan Construction.

This whole evening had been surreal from start to finish. And it wasn't over yet!

'Would it help if I told the police I have no intention of pressing charges?' Mac asked softly; Yvonne Richards seemed more in need of psychiatric help than prosecution!

Jonas's expression was bleak. 'I have no idea.' He gave a slightly dazed shake of his head as he sat down suddenly. 'I— Do you think Yvonne has done anything like this before? Tried to "help me" like this before?' He frowned darkly as the possibility occurred to him.

Mac shrugged. 'Let's not even go there, Jonas. It's the here and now that we have to deal with,' she added cajolingly. 'Perhaps I should come to the police station with you—'

'No!' Jonas refused harshly as he stood up. He felt humiliated enough for one evening, without Mac having to hear—yet again—how Yvonne had only done the things she had because she was in love with him.

How or why that had happened, Jonas had no idea. Yvonne had worked for him as his PA for almost two years now. She had proved to be particularly good at her job, and as far as Jonas was concerned the two of them had an excellent working relationship. Obviously there had been business trips they had taken together, as well as long hours spent alone together, but Jonas was sure there had never been the slightest suggestion on his part that the two of them had any sort of personal relationship.

He looked across at Mac. 'I've never given Yvonne the slightest encouragement to feel the way she says she feels about me.' He rubbed the back of his neck. 'To my knowledge I've never so much as touched her or spoken to her in a way that could possibly be misconstrued as sexual interest.'

Mac knew that her gaze didn't quite meet his. 'I'm sure you haven't—'

'Don't patronise me, Mac,' Jonas rasped harshly, eyes narrowing to steely slits. 'I do *not* have relationships with the people who work for or with me. Besides complicating things unnecessarily, it's bad business practice.'

'And why bother when there are so many other women willing to give you what you want?' she came back tartly.

'Was that comment really necessary?' Jonas
snarled.

Was it? Probably not. But Mac was feeling less than
composed herself after their lovemaking earlier this
evening.

She and Jonas had made beautiful and erotic love
to each other. At least…it was love on Mac's side. She
doubted Jonas's feelings went any further than lust.

It just seemed too much to now learn that she had
been terrorised this past week by another woman suffering from that same unrequited love for him!

Mac accepted that it wasn't his fault. Jonas had made
it clear from the beginning that he didn't even believe in
love, let alone a committed relationship, and so it wasn't
his fault if the women he met were stupid enough to fall
in love with him.

But that didn't mean Mac couldn't feel a little angry
and resentful about it! 'You had better go,' she said
distantly.

Jonas knew he had to go. That he should drive to the
police station where they had taken Yvonne and try to
make some sort of sense out of this ludicrous situation.
He would just prefer not to leave things so strained between himself and Mac.

'I'll come back later—'

'I would prefer it if you didn't,' Mac cut in firmly.
'We have nothing else to say to each other, Jonas,' she
reasoned as a scowl creased his brow.

'Don't you even want to know what's going to happen
to Yvonne?' he asked tonelessly.

She shrugged. 'I'm sure the police will inform me if
I need to be involved any further.'

In other words, Jonas realised darkly, Mac considered
her 'involvement' with him to be at an end.

Like hell it was!

He reached out and gripped the tops of her arms. 'I'm coming back later, Mac,' he insisted determinedly. 'If nothing else, you and I need to talk about this evening—'

'There's nothing else to say.' Mac wrenched out of his grasp, her cheeks fiery red. Whether in temper or embarrassment, Jonas wasn't sure. 'I'm grateful for the experience, of course, but I certainly don't want to have a post-mortem about it!'

Temper, Jonas acknowledged. Maybe tinged with a little embarrassment...

He should just cut his losses. Take the opportunity Mac was giving him to extricate himself from this situation with a little grace allowed to remain on both sides.

Yet looking at her he couldn't help but remember how he had kissed her. Touched her. Pleasured her. Just as she had kissed and touched and pleasured him.

'I'm coming back later,' he repeated firmly.

'I'm going to bed as soon as I've locked up behind you and cleared away,' she argued just as stubbornly.

Jonas's mouth twisted. 'Then you'll just have to get out of bed and unlock the door and let me in again, won't you?'

Her mouth compressed. 'Don't you understand that I don't want you here, Jonas?'

'I would have to be pretty stupid not to realise that when you've said it three times in as many minutes,' he commented.

Mac had never felt so—so frustrated, so irritated with anyone in her life before. 'Isn't finding out one woman is in love with you enough for one evening?' she shot back.

'Low blow, Mac,' Jonas muttered between clenched teeth, his face paling one more.

It was a low blow. Not only that, it was spiteful when Jonas's shock earlier at learning of his PA's feelings for him had been self-evident. 'Sorry,' she murmured uncomfortably. 'I'm just not sure you should come back here later.'

'Why not?'

Mac moved away restlessly. 'Frankly, I find this whole situation embarrassing,' she admitted. 'I— We— Earlier—' She shook her head. 'Maybe you're used to these situations, Jonas, but I'm not.' And she never would be. Not if the cringing awkwardness she now felt with Jonas was any indication of how traumatic it was to be in the company of a man you had been intimate with. A man you were in love with but who didn't, and never would, love you back...

It was no good telling herself how stupid it was to have allowed her emotions to become involved with a man like Jonas. No good at all when she knew herself to be deeply, irrevocably, in love with him. In the circumstances, her only option had to be never to see him again!

'I really can't take any more tonight, Jonas,' she told him with quiet conviction. 'I just want to go to bed, fall asleep, and hope that when I wake up in the morning I'll find that this whole evening has been just a nightmare.'

Jonas had never heard any woman describe making love with him as a nightmare before, but there had been so many firsts for him with Mac already, why not add that one to the list?

His mouth firmed. 'I'm not quite sure what you're referring to by "these situations",' he said. 'However,

I do accept—for now—that you feel you want some time alone.' He ran a hand impatiently through the dark thickness of his hair. 'If it's any consolation, this evening didn't turn out the way I expected it to, either.'

Mac gave a humourless smile. 'Nothing ever seems to turn out as "expected" between the two of us.' The fact that she had met the owner of Buchanan Construction at all, let alone made love with him, certainly shouldn't have happened.

'No,' Jonas acknowledged heavily as he studied her for several long minutes before turning sharply and walking over to the door. 'I'll ring you tomorrow.'

Jonas could ring all he wanted; Mac had already decided she wasn't going to be here.

No doubt her parents were going to think it a little odd when she turned up in Devon again so soon after her last visit, but what choice did she have? She couldn't stay in London after tonight. Well…she could. If she wanted to have another embarrassing conversation with Jonas like this last one!

'Fine.'

Jonas's eyes narrowed suspiciously on her suddenly expressionless face. 'What aren't you telling me, Mac?'

She gave a brittle laugh. 'Nothing you want to hear, I assure you!'

Jonas continued to look across at her in utter frustration. Would he still be leaving like this if they hadn't heard the sound of glass breaking downstairs, if he hadn't discovered that it was one of his own employees causing the damage to Mac's property, scaring the hell out of her in the process, and if he didn't now have to go to the local police station and sort the mess out? If none of that had happened, would he now be joining Mac in her bed, or would he have left anyway?

It had certainly been his intention to leave before any of those things happened. For him to get as far away from her disturbing presence as possible. Now the only thing he wanted to do was crawl into bed with her and make love to her all over again. Which, in itself, was reason enough for him to get the hell out of here!

'Make sure you bolt and lock the door behind me,' he advised gruffly.

Mac waited only long enough for Jonas to close the door behind him before quickly crossing the room and doing exactly that, to then turn and lean weakly back against it as her legs threatened to buckle beneath her.

She *had* fallen in love with Jonas Buchanan.

A man who would never love her because he had no time for the emotion.

What was she going to do?

CHAPTER TWELVE

As IT turned out, MAC wasn't able to leave London the following morning as planned, after all.

The telephone rang for the first time just after eight o'clock. Fearing, as promised, that it might be Jonas, Mac reluctantly answered the call, immensely relieved when it turned out to be the police asking if she would come down to the police station this morning so that they might talk to her.

Mac was only too happy to agree—the thought of not being at the warehouse to take Jonas's call, or at home if he actually came to the warehouse in person, was definitely an appealing one.

When she received a second telephone call a few minutes later, from Jeremy this time, asking her if she could call round to the gallery in the afternoon and meet a gallery owner from America who was interested in showing some of her work over there, she was only too happy to have an excuse not to be at the warehouse in the afternoon too.

Besides, the request from the police was one that Mac couldn't avoid or simply ignore, and the one from Jeremy was one she didn't want to avoid or ignore. The possibility of taking her work to America, too, would be a dream come true for her.

Consequently, Mac was forced to remain in London even though it was the last place she wanted to be. Forced to remain, perhaps, but at the same time given two legitimate reasons to avoid speaking to or seeing Jonas while she was here.

At least, until she returned to the warehouse at six o'clock that evening and once again found him sitting waiting for her at the bottom of the metal staircase leading up to her home!

Jonas stood up slowly as Mac came to a brief halt before she resumed walking cautiously towards him, her crash helmet tucked under her arm and her hair shaken loose about her leather-clad shoulders. 'You're a difficult woman to track down,' he commented ruefully.

She shrugged those narrow shoulders as she came to a halt in front of him. 'Is this something important, Jonas, or can it wait until another time? I'm rather busy this evening.'

Jonas's mouth thinned at her dismissive tone. He had spent hours at the police station the previous night, talking, explaining, in the hope of avoiding having the situation go any further than it already had. But it had taken until lunchtime today for the police to telephone and inform him they were prepared not to proceed any further with the case as long as Yvonne sought professional help for her behaviour. At the same time making it clear to him that Mac's refusal to press charges concerning the damage to her property had helped them to make that decision.

Trying to speak to Mac and thank her for her intervention had proved more difficult. She hadn't answered any of Jonas's telephone calls. She hadn't been at home when he'd called round earlier this afternoon. When he'd called at the warehouse a second time about an hour ago, and found she still wasn't at home, Jonas had just decided to sit and wait for her.

'Busy doing what?' he grated harshly.

Her eyes narrowed. 'I don't believe that is any of your business, do you?'

The fact that Mac now made no effort to walk up the steps and go into the warehouse indicated she had no intention of inviting him inside. 'It's too cold to stand out here talking.' The cold vapour on his breath gave truth to that statement.

Her chin rose stubbornly. 'I didn't invite you here, Jonas.'

He reached out and took a light hold of her arm. 'Perhaps not, but now that I *am* here you could be polite and invite me inside.'

Mac eyed him impatiently. 'Why change things now?'

Jonas gave her a humourless smile. 'Meaning we've never particularly bothered being polite to each other before?'

'Exactly!' she said. 'I really do need to shower and change, Jonas.'

'You're going out this evening?'

'Not that it's any of your business, but yes, I'm going out,' she snapped.

Jonas felt his hands clench in the pockets of his long woollen overcoat. 'With whom?'

'That's none of your business, either!' Grey eyes glittered with temper.

His jaw tightened warningly. 'I believe what we did last night made it my business.'

Mac tensed indignantly. 'Like hell it did!' She glared up at Jonas, so angry she could have hit him. 'Last night was a mistake from start to finish. The finish obviously being the revelation that it was your own PA who was vandalising my home and property!'

Jonas scowled darkly. 'You're holding *me* responsible for that?'

'Who else?' Mac came back heatedly, knowing she wasn't being completely fair in that accusation, but feeling too unnerved by finding him here waiting for her to even try to rationalise or calm the situation down. 'There's bound to be some sort of reaction when you play games with people's emotions—'

'I've already told you I've never so much as said a word out of place to Yvonne!' A nerve pulsed in his jaw. 'As far as I'm concerned, she has only ever been my PA, never my mistress, and—'

'Jonas, I don't care what your relationship was with Yvonne Richards.' Mac smiled insincerely. 'I'm just relieved to have the whole sorry mess over and done with.'

His nostrils flared. 'You're including our own relationship in that statement?'

'We don't *have* a relationship, Jonas,' she said flatly.

'Last night—'

'We had sex,' Mac finished coolly. 'Interesting experience, but, as I told you at the time, one I'm in no particular hurry to repeat!'

Jonas eyed her frustratedly. He had sought her out today with the sole intention of thanking her for her help in regards to the situation with Yvonne, and then leaving without making any further arrangements to ever see or be with her again. That she was making it more than obvious she was just as anxious to be rid of him definitely rankled.

Which was pretty stupid of him! 'I just wanted to thank you for your help with Yvonne,' he explained.

'You could have done that over the telephone.'

'I wanted to thank you personally.' His eyes glittered. 'Besides, you weren't answering your phone.'

'I've been out all day.'

'Obviously.' Jonas looked at her broodingly as she made no answer, knowing he should leave, and that Mac herself was giving him the perfect opportunity to do exactly that. Except... 'So, are you going out anywhere interesting this evening?' he prompted lightly.

Her eyes narrowed. 'As I believe I've already told you—I'm not answerable to you for any of my actions, Jonas.'

No, and he had never wanted that from any woman, either. Had never asked for exclusivity from any of the women he had dated in the past. But just the thought of Mac going out with another man was enough to cause a red tide of—of what? What emotion was it that was driving him at this moment? Making it necessary for him to know whom she was seeing this evening?

He straightened. 'I'll leave you to get ready for your evening out then,' he bit out, tersely.

Mac's anger and resentment faded as she looked up at Jonas searchingly and acknowledged the finality she could hear in his tone. 'So this is finally goodbye, then?'

His mouth tightened. 'Only if you want it to be.'

Mac's eyes widened. 'If *I* want it to be?'

He shrugged. 'There's no reason why the two of us shouldn't continue to see each other.'

Not for Jonas, perhaps, but for Mac it would be excruciating to see him, be with him as she longed to be, and know that she loved him while all he felt for her was desire. Knowing that once Jonas had completely sated that desire their relationship would come to an end. As all Jonas's other relationships had ended.

No, Mac's pride wouldn't allow her to take the little that he had to give for as long as he chose to give it. Even if her heart squeezed painfully in her chest at the very idea of never seeing or being with him again...

'Until you got tired of me, you mean?' she guessed shrewdly.

He gave her a half-smile. 'Or you tired of me.'

As if that was ever going to happen!

Mac had waited the whole of her twenty-seven years to meet the man she could love. That she *did* love. It was her misfortune that man happened to be Jonas. A man who didn't even believe in love, let alone in a happy-ever-after forever!

'I don't think so, thank you, Jonas,' she refused dryly.

He scowled darkly. 'Why the hell not?'

Mac shook her head. 'What would be the point? You have your life and I have mine, and the two have absolutely nothing in common.'

Jonas's jaw was clenched. 'Except we want each other!'

Mac smiled sadly. 'Wanting something doesn't mean it's good for you.'

His scowl deepened. 'What the hell does that mean?'

She gave a rueful grimace. 'It means that I know how much I enjoy chocolate, while at the same time accepting that eating too much of it wouldn't be good for me.'

'You're comparing a relationship with me to eating chocolate?'

'It was just an example, Jonas,' she said. 'What I'm really saying is that ultimately the two of us wouldn't be good for each other.'

'We *are* good together,' he contradicted, his voice lowering huskily.

'I said we *wouldn't* be good for each other,' Mac reiterated clearly.

Jonas frowned. 'You can't possibly know that.'

Mac gave a humourless smile. 'Inwardly we both know it, Jonas.'

Yes, inwardly he did know it. Just as he knew Mac was everything that he had always avoided in the women he became involved with. Physically inexperienced and vulnerable. Family orientated. Warm. Emotional.

Most of all emotional!

In essence she represented everything that Jonas didn't want in his own life.

Yet at the same time, she was everything he *did* want...

He shifted uncomfortably. 'Admittedly, I can't give you romance and flowers, but—'

'I don't remember ever saying I wanted romance and flowers from you!' she cut in indignantly.

Jonas eyed her intently. 'Then what *do* you want, Mac?' he asked bluntly.

'From you?' she asked shortly. 'Nothing.'

'I doubt you would be this...angry, if it was nothing,' Jonas drawled ruefully.

'I'm not in the least angry, Jonas.' Mac sighed. 'At least, not with you.'

'Then who?'

She shook her head. 'You wouldn't understand.'

'Try me,' he invited huskily.

Mac gave a huff of laughter. 'We simply don't look at things the same way, Jonas.'

'Concerning what exactly?'

She almost smiled at the sudden wariness in his expression.

'Concerning everything that matters,' she elaborated. 'I don't need that romance and flowers that you mentioned but I do want my relationships to matter. *I* want to matter!'

'Didn't our lovemaking last night prove that you matter?' he asked.

Mac gave him a pitying glance. 'Last night proved only that you're physically attracted to me.'

'Don't all relationships start that way?'

'All *your* relationships certainly start *and* end that way! As any relationship with me would too,' she added quietly.

'You can't know that—'

'We both know that, Jonas,' she said wearily.

He couldn't let this go. 'You're making assumptions—'

'I'm being realistic,' Mac corrected firmly. 'I really don't want to have an affair with you, Jonas,' she stated honestly.

His mouth twisted. 'Why don't you just come right out and say that you're holding out for the whole package? Love and romance, followed by marriage?'

Mac felt the warmth in her cheek. 'I'm "holding out", as you put it, for exactly what you said I should hold out for last week—the right man to come along.'

'And obviously that isn't me!'

She swallowed down the sick feeling that had risen in her throat. 'Obviously, that isn't you. Don't you see, Jonas, you've allowed your childhood experiences to colour the rest of your life? To damage you rather than anyone else?'

'Are you a psychiatrist too now?' he sneered.

'No, of course not.' She sighed. 'I just think—you'll never be able to function emotionally until you confront the problem you have with your parents.'

'Forgiveness and all that?' he scorned.

'Yes,' she stated.

Jonas stared down at her for long, timeless seconds before breaking that gaze to glance up at the warehouse. 'Have you given any more thought to selling out to Buchanan Construction?'

Mac was thrown for a minute by the sudden change of subject. But only for a minute. 'None at all,' she said definitely.

'Because it isn't going to happen,' Jonas guessed easily.

Mac's chin rose challengingly. 'No.'

Which left Jonas and Buchanan Construction in something of a dilemma. The same dilemma, in fact, that Jonas had been in when he first met Mac over a week ago...

'That's your final word on that subject, too?'

'Absolutely my final word, yes.' She nodded.

Jonas drew in a harsh breath. 'Fine,' he said.

Mac eyed him uncertainly. 'Does that mean you accept my decision?'

He raised dark brows. 'What other choice do I have?'

None as far as Mac was concerned. 'You seemed so—determined to get me out of here a week ago...'

Jonas's smile was as lacking in humour as her own had been a few minutes ago. 'That was before Yvonne started her sick little game.'

'Oh.'

'And before I knew you...' Jonas added softly.

Before Jonas knew her? Or before he 'knew' her in the physical sense?

Did it really matter which, as long as he accepted that she wasn't going to sell the warehouse?

Mac straightened. 'I really do have to go now, Jonas.'

His expression was remote, those eyes a cold, remorseless blue as he nodded. 'Have a pleasant evening.'

Have a pleasant life, he might as well have said, Mac realised achingly.

Because she knew that after today he wanted no part of her or her life. Just as she knew it wasn't specifically her he wanted no part of; it was simply that the very idea of emotional entanglement with anyone was complete anathema to him.

Mac couldn't even imagine what it must be like to live without love in your life. The love of parents. Of family. Of friends. Of that certain special someone that you loved and who loved you.

Although, after today, Mac was going to have to learn to live without the last one herself...

'You too,' she muttered before turning and hurrying up the staircase, her hand shaking slightly as she unlocked the door before going quickly inside and closing it firmly behind her.

Without hesitation.

Without so much as a single backward glance.

Because she dared not look at him again. Knowing that if she did she wouldn't be able to stop herself from launching herself into his arms and agreeing to continue their relationship—that emotionless relationship that was all Jonas could ever give any woman—to its painful conclusion...

Mac lingered only long enough on this floor to drop her keys and helmet on the breakfast bar before hurrying over to switch on the lights to the floor above and ascending the spiral staircase up to her studio.

The canvas she had been working on the last few days still stood on the easel near the glassed wall, the thin cloth Mac had placed over it when she'd brought Jonas up here yesterday evening still in place. After last night she had stayed well away from her studio today, reluctant to see—to be—where the memories of that lovemaking with Jonas were so strong.

Mac crossed the room slowly now to stare at that blank cloth for several seconds before reaching out and removing it.

The background of the painting was there already in shades of blue, but the focus of the painting was only a pencilled sketch at the moment. Strong, abstract lines that nevertheless caught perfectly the wide brow, intensity of light-coloured eyes, high cheekbones either side of an aristocratic slash of a nose, and the mouth sculptured above that square and determined jaw.

Jonas.

Mac rarely painted portraits, and had no idea why she had felt compelled to do this one of him when those hard and handsome features were already etched deep, and for ever, into her soul. As was the love she felt for him.

Painfully.

Irrevocably.

Tears filled Mac's eyes as she continued to stare at that hard and beautiful face on the canvas.

And she wondered what she was going to do with this portrait of Jonas once it was finished.

CHAPTER THIRTEEN

'COME on, Dad, if you don't hurry we're going to be late,' Mac encouraged her father laughingly as the family gathered in the hallway of her parents' bungalow on Christmas Eve to put on their warm coats and hats and scarves in preparation for going out into the cold and snowy evening. 'And you know how Mum hates to be late—' Mac abruptly broke off her teasing as she opened the front door and saw the person standing outside on the doorstep, one of his gloved hands raised as he prepared to ring the doorbell.

Oh, my God, it was Jonas!

Mac felt the colour drain from her face beneath the red woollen hat she wore. Totally stunned as she stared up searchingly into the grimness of Jonas's face. At the scowl between his brows, the guarded blue of his gaze as it met hers, his mouth and jaw set challengingly.

What on earth was he doing here, of all places?

'Jonas.' Mac's gloved fingers tightened painfully on the door as she moistened dry and slightly numbed lips.

He gave a slight inclination of his head before glancing at the people crowding the hallway behind her. 'I realise you weren't expecting me but—am I in time to join you all at church?' he asked huskily.

'I—yes. Of course,' Mac answered haltingly, her thoughts racing as she tried to make sense of Jonas being here at all.

Apart from the man sent by 'the boss' to collect her Jeep and have the windows repaired almost two weeks ago, Mac hadn't seen or heard from Jonas. Nothing. No telephone calls. No sitting on her metal staircase waiting for her to come home. Just an empty…nothing.

If it hadn't been for the continuous ache in her heart, and the vivid memories she had of their lovemaking, Mac might almost have thought that she had imagined him!

Or perhaps she was just imagining he was here now?

Hallucinating might be a better description!

After all, Jonas was sitting on a beach somewhere on a Caribbean island drinking tall drinks adorned with fruit and pretty coloured-paper umbrellas, possibly with a beautiful blonde at his side. Wasn't he?

'Get a move on, darling, or we're— Oh.' Mac's mother came to an abrupt halt beside her to stare up at Jonas with open curiosity.

Not a hallucination, then, Mac acknowledged with a nervous fluttering in her stomach. Jonas really *was* standing on the doorstep of her parents' bungalow at eleven o'clock at night on Christmas Eve!

The look of total disbelief on Mac's expressive face when she had opened the door and found him standing there might have been amusing if Jonas weren't already feeling so totally wrong-footed himself. If he hadn't already been deeply regretting his decision to come to Devon with the stupid idea of surprising her. But as he was feeling both those things he didn't find that look of embarrassed horror on Mac's face in the least reassuring!

'Mrs McGuire.' He extended his hand politely to the woman who, with her short bob of glossy black hair and smoky-grey eyes, bore such a startling resemblance to Mac that she couldn't possibly be anyone else but her mother. 'Jonas Buchanan,' he explained. 'I hope you don't mind my just turning up like this and joining you all for Midnight Mass? I'm—'

'A friend of mine from London,' Mac put in quickly as she moved to stand at Jonas's side before turning to face her family, linking her arm lightly with his as she did so, and looking very festive in a long white over-coat over a red sweater and black jeans. 'I'm so glad you could make it, after all, Jonas,' she assured huskily. 'Mum, Dad, this is Jonas Buchanan. Jonas, my parents, Melly and Brian.'

To give the two elder McGuires their due, they showed no surprise at finding a complete stranger standing on their doorstep at eleven o'clock at night on Christmas Eve, the tall and still-handsome grey-haired Brian moving forward to shake Jonas's hand warmly. 'The more the merrier,' he assured with genuine hearti-ness. 'I'm afraid we're already late so we'll have to make all the other introductions later,' he added with a rueful smile at the numerous members of Mac's family mill-ing about in the hallway obviously ready to leave for church.

'I can take three other people as well as Mac in my car if that's of any help,' Jonas offered smoothly as Mac's family tumbled outside into the snowy night.

'Perfect,' the beautiful Melly McGuire accepted warmly. 'I won't have to drive the second car now and can have a glass of mulled wine with my mince pie after the service!'

Jonas was preoccupied for the next few minutes helping Mac settle three of her elderly aunts into the back of his car, but conscious all of that time of her puzzled gaze as it rested on him often.

Mac paused out on the icy road. 'Jonas, why aren't you sitting on a beach somewhere on that Caribbean island?' she prompted softly.

Good question.

One that Jonas felt required the two of them being alone when he answered it…

'Never mind,' Mac dismissed as she saw Jonas's hesitation. 'All that matters is you're here.'

He winced slightly. 'Is it?'

'Yes,' Mac answered firmly as she saw that her father had already reversed his car out onto the road and was waiting to leave. 'We had better go,' she said ruefully as she moved to sit in the passenger seat of Jonas's black Mercedes.

Surrounded as they were by so many members of Mac's family, there was absolutely no opportunity for a private conversation between the two of them as they drove the short distance into the village itself, attended the service in the church surrounded by berry-adorned holly and lit by dozens of candles, and then lingered afterwards to chat and enjoy that anticipated mulled wine and those mince pies.

But that didn't mean that Mac wasn't aware of Jonas's presence at her side for that whole time. That she didn't burn with curiosity to know why he was here. And if he intended staying. That her initial uncertainty at seeing him again hadn't begun to turn to hope…

That uncertainty returned with a vengeance once

she and Jonas were finally alone in the sitting-room of her parents' bungalow a little after one o'clock in the morning, the rest of Mac's family having gone to bed. Her mother had already offered the suggestion, 'The small boxroom is empty if Jonas would like to stay for the rest of the Christmas holiday...'

'I did try to warn you,' Mac murmured ruefully as Jonas looked about the sitting-room with its numerous glittering Christmas decorations and enormous and heavily adorned tree with its dozens of presents beneath.

'It's wonderful,' Jonas murmured huskily, his gaze slightly hooded as it came back to rest on Mac as she stood across the room, her hands tightly clasped together in front of her. 'As is your family. I— Mac, I wanted to thank you for my Christmas present,' he said abruptly.

Ah.

Mac smiled a little. 'You didn't have to drive all the way to Devon on Christmas Eve to do that.'

'No.'

Mac shrugged. 'Besides, I had to somehow say thank you for all the help you gave me by having the warehouse painted and the windows on my Jeep fixed. I thought perhaps you might like to hang it in your offices somewhere? In the reception, maybe? A portrait of the head of Buchanan Construction,' she said offhandedly.

'A Mary McGuire portrait of the head of Buchanan Construction,' Jonas corrected softly.

'Well...yes,' she acknowledged awkwardly. 'Just think, if you ever fall on hard times, you'll be able to sell it!' she added jokingly.

Jonas had been surprised when the huge wooden crate was delivered to his office two days ago, stunned when he removed all the packaging and saw the portrait inside. Even so, he hadn't needed to look at the signature in the bottom right hand side of the painting to know it was Mac's work. The style and use of colour were unmistakable.

It was why she had painted it in the first place that Jonas wanted to know...

The last two weeks had been long and...difficult, for Jonas. For numerous reasons. Yvonne Richards. His parents. But most of all, because of Mac.

He hadn't been able to get her out of his mind. Not for a single moment of that time. Her beauty. Her laughter. Her warmth. Her smooth and satiny skin. Her perfume.

This past two weeks Jonas had remembered and re-lived every single moment he had ever spent with her.

As he had always known would happen, memories of Mac had filled his days and haunted his nights!

'I'm not sure I can allow you to give me such a valu-able gift,' he told her gruffly.

Her cheeks flushed. 'I think that's for me to decide, don't you?'

And her temper, Jonas acknowledged ruefully; he hadn't forgotten that fiery temper. How could he, when she had been annoyed or angry with him about one thing or another since the moment they'd first met?

'Yes,' he acknowledged huskily.

Mac's eyes widened. 'Are you actually *agreeing* with me, Jonas?'

He chuckled softly at her obvious incredulity. 'Yes.'

'Well, there's a first!'

Jonas sobered. 'I'm agreeing with you on the un-derstanding that I be allowed to give you something in return.'

Mac eyed him frowningly. Even dressed casually in a dark blue sweater and faded jeans, Jonas was still the most devastatingly handsome man she had ever met. Several other women in the church earlier tonight had obviously thought the same thing as they had eyed him covetously. Admiring glances that Jonas had seemed completely unaware of as he'd stood attentively at Mac's side, his hand resting lightly beneath her elbow.

She shook her head. 'I already told you, the portrait is a thank you for the way you helped me a couple of weeks ago.' It was also a way for Mac to avoid having Jonas's portrait hanging in her studio as a day-to-day reminder of the man she loved but who would never love her in return...

His mouth tightened. 'Help you wouldn't have needed if—'

'We really don't need to talk about that now, Jonas,' Mac rushed in.

'If you wish.' He gave an abrupt inclination of his head.

'I wish,' Mac confirmed firmly. 'What sort of thing are you giving me in return?' she asked warily.

Jonas thrust his hands into his jeans pockets as he shifted uncomfortably. 'I need to explain a few things first.' He frowned. 'I— You told me when we last met that I needed to confront the problem I have with my parents. That the feelings I have for them were—damaging, to me. That—'

'I seem to have made rather a lot of personal remarks that perhaps I shouldn't!' Mac interrupted uncomfortably. 'I was upset when I said those things, Jonas. You really shouldn't take too much notice of me when I'm upset. I inherited my Irish grandfather's sentimental temperament, I'm afraid.'

Jonas gave a twisted smile. 'The truth is the truth, whenever or however it's said.'

'Not if it's in the heat of the moment—'

'But you were right to say those things to me, Mac,' Jonas insisted softly. 'I *have* allowed my parents' disastrous marriage, my unhappy childhood, to affect the man I am now.' He looked her in the eye. 'I've been to see both my parents during the past two weeks—'

'You have?' Mac gasped.

He nodded. 'I've also met my stepfather and stepmother. I still have nothing in common with any of them,' he continued ruefully. 'But I was with them all long enough to know that both second marriages are happy ones. To learn that my parents no longer feel any animosity towards each other.' He sighed. 'I decided that if they can forgive each other for the past then surely I can forgive them too.'

Mac blinked back the tears that threatened to fall. 'I'm so glad, Jonas. For your sake.'

'Yes,' he said. 'Of course, I consider it completely your fault that this reconciliation has now presented me with another set of problems,' he added dryly.

'My fault?' she echoed. 'How?'

'I now have the diplomatic problem of avoiding offending either of my parents. For example, both sets of parents duly invited me to spend Christmas with them,' he drawled ruefully. 'To have accepted one would have insulted the other.'

Mac repressed a smile. 'So as it's my fault you thought you would come here and bother me instead?'

Jonas looked at her consideringly from beneath hooded lids. 'Am I bothering you, Mac?'

Of course having Jonas here was bothering her! Especially as, avoiding offending either of his parents aside, Mac still had no idea why Jonas had chosen to come here tonight of all nights.

Why he had attended church with her family. What he was still doing here...

She moistened her lips nervously. 'You could always have gone to that beach in the Caribbean,' she reminded him huskily.

'No, I couldn't,' he denied quietly.

'No?'

'No.'

'Why not?' Mac breathed softly, the sudden tension between them so palpable she almost felt as if she could reach out and touch it.

'The only reason that matters,' Jonas murmured.

'Which is?'

He drew in a ragged breath, yet his gaze was clear and unwavering as it met hers. 'The only person I want to spend Christmas with has assured me that under no circumstances would she ever spend Christmas sitting on a beach anywhere!'

Mac couldn't breathe as she stared at him incredulously. *'Me?'* she finally managed to squeak.

Jonas gave a genuine smile. 'You.'

Mac stared at him with wide eyes. 'You want to spend Christmas with *me*?'

'And your family. If you'll allow me to,' he added uncertainly. 'Mac.' He crossed the room in two long strides so that he was now standing only inches away from her. 'I know that I'm— Well, I appreciate that my track record for long-term relationships is—'

'Non-existent,' she put in helpfully as a tidal wave of hope began to build inside her.

Jonas's mouth firmed. 'Non-existent,' he acknowledged. 'But that could be a good thing,' he continued encouragingly as he reached out and grasped both Mac's hands tightly in his. 'It means that I don't have any past relationships, any lingering feelings for another woman, to complicate things.'

That tidal wave of hope grew bigger still as Mac easily saw the lingering uncertainty in Jonas's eyes. 'Complicate what things?' she prompted.

'Ah.' He winced. 'Yes. I need my overcoat from the hallway.' Jonas released her hands. 'Your Christmas present is in the pocket—'

'Family rule, no presents to be unwrapped until Christmas morning!' Mac protested before Jonas could leave the sitting-room.

He turned in the doorway. 'It already *is* Christmas morning, Mac,' he pointed out dryly. 'Besides, this present isn't gift-wrapped,' he added confidently.

Mac had no idea what was going on. Just now Jonas had seemed on the point of—well, on the point of something. And now he was totally preoccupied with giving her a Christmas present instead.

When the only Christmas present Mac wanted was Jonas himself!

Jonas returned from the hallway to find Mac still standing where he had left her. His heart pounded loudly in his chest as he walked over to join her, two folded sheets of paper in his hand. 'I'd like your input on this before I submit it for planning approval.' His expression was strained as he handed her the top sheet of paper.

Mac gave him an uncertain glance before she slowly unfolded the sheet of paper, a frown between her eyes as she looked up at him. 'I— It appears to be a building plan of the new apartment complex, one that rather tastefully incorporates my warehouse into the grounds...'

A nerve pulsed in the tenseness of Jonas's jaw. 'It *is*

a building plan of the new apartment complex that—hopefully—tastefully incorporates your warehouse,' he confirmed huskily.

She refolded it carefully. 'And the other one?' She looked at the second sheet of design paper in Jonas's hand.

Jonas's fingers tightened perceptibly. 'These are some alterations to the original plan that don't include your warehouse in the grounds.'

Mac looked at him accusingly as she thrust the original sheet back into his hands. 'And *this* is the present you drove all this way to give me?' she exclaimed. 'You're unbelievable, do you know that, Jonas?' She looked thoroughly disgusted. 'You've come all this way just to have yet another attempt at trying to talk me into selling my home!' She moved away restlessly. 'The answer is no, Jonas. N. O. Is that clear enough for you?' Angry tears glistened in those smoky-grey eyes as she glared at him.

Well that went well, Jonas—*not*! he told himself, wincing. Self-confident to the point of arrogance usually, he had known before he came here tonight that he was somehow going to bungle this. Because it was more important than anything else had ever been in his life before. Because it mattered to him more than anything else ever had in his life before!

'I haven't asked the question yet...' he murmured softly.

'You don't need to,' Mac fired back. 'Just leave, Jonas. Go away and never come back. I never want to see—'

'Mac, will you marry me?'

'—or speak to you *ever*—' Mac abruptly broke off her tirade to stare across at him incredulously. 'What did you just say?'

Jonas swallowed hard. 'I asked if you would do me the honour of marrying me,' he repeated gruffly as he moved hesitantly towards her, the intensity of his gaze searching the paleness of Mac's face as he stood in front of her.

Exactly what she had thought he'd said!

She looked closely at his face, finally seeing the anxiety in those blue eyes, in his tensely clenched jaw and cheeks. 'Why?' she breathed.

Jonas gave a huff of laughter. 'Most women would have said, "No, thank you, Jonas," or, "Oh, Jonas this is so sudden." You, being you, ask me *why!*' He gave a rueful shake of his head.

Mac gave him an irritated glance. 'Well, it *is* rather sudden.'

'Not to me.' Jonas sighed. 'The two weeks since we were last together have been—' He shook his head. 'Hell, is the only fitting description I can think of,' he decided heavily.

'Why?'

'Again with the why!' He briefly raised his gaze to the ceiling. 'Mac, I didn't *want* to fall in love with you. It's the last thing I ever wanted! But you—' He sighed. 'You are the most infuriating, provoking, stubborn, irritating—'

'Do you think we could go back to the "I didn't want to fall in love with you" bit...?' Mac interrupted, her heart beating so loudly, so erratically, she was sure Jonas must be able to hear it too.

'—fascinating, warm, arousing, wonderful woman I have ever met!' Jonas finished. 'How could I not fall in love with you?' He shook his head as he once again reached out to grasp both Mac's hands in his.

Mac felt hot and cold all at the same time. 'You really love me?' she breathed dazedly.

'It's worse than that, I'm afraid,' Jonas muttered. 'Mac, this past two weeks I've come to realise that I want it *all* with you. Love. Marriage. Children. I want to be your last lover as well as your first. I want to wake up and find you beside me for the rest of my life. Most of all I want to be the man you deserve. The man you can love. Will you at least give me the chance to show you that I can be that man?' He looked down at her anxiously.

Jonas loved her! Wanted to marry her! Have children with her!

Mac released one of her hands from his to reach up tentatively and cup one hard and chiselled cheek. 'Are you sure about this, Jonas? Absolutely sure? Love, marriage, children—those things mean for ever to me, you know...'

His fingers tightened painfully about hers. 'I wouldn't settle for anything less!' he assured her fiercely. 'Mac, you totally misunderstood my motives for those two new sets of plans. The first one leaves the warehouse standing, yes, but the second one shows a completely different layout to the penthouse in the apartment complex.'

'Show me,' she encouraged huskily.

Jonas unfolded and smoothed out the second set of plans. 'You see here?' He pointed to the diagram. 'That wall is now completely glass, as is the ceiling in that room. It's a replica of your studio, Mac,' he explained gruffly. 'I went to see my parents because I love you. Because you were right about my needing to confront that situation, to deal with those ghosts from the past, before I could move on with my own life. You are my life, Mac. I'm asking you to give me the chance to show you that, to prove to you how much I love you. To show you how I will always love you, and only you. Exactly as you are,' he added emphatically.

'No dressing up and being a trophy on your arm, then?' she teased a little tearfully.

Jonas really did love her!

'As far as I'm concerned you can live in those damn-awful dungarees and never set foot outside the apartment again as long as I can be there with you. Mac, just give me the chance to show you how much I love you, to persuade you into falling in love with me, and I promise you won't ever have reason to regret it!' he vowed.

'Oh, Jonas,' she groaned.

He gave a pained wince. 'Is that a "no, thank you, Jonas," or a "Let me think about this, Jonas."?'

'It's an "I already love you, Jonas,"' Mac assured him emotionally as she moved into his arms.

'You *love* me?' There was a look of stunned disbelief on his face.

'So much that I really don't care where I live any more, either, as long as it's with you! Jonas, I love you so much that these past two weeks have been hell for me too. I love you, Jonas!' she repeated joyfully.

His arms moved about her like steel bands. 'Enough to marry me?'

'Enough to spend for ever, eternity, with you!' she assured him happily.

Jonas looked down at her searchingly for long, time-less minutes, his eyes blazing with his love for her as he saw that emotion reflected back at him. He buried his face in the perfume of her silky hair as he groaned. 'I can't believe that I let you walk away from me two weeks ago. That I almost lost you!'

'Just kiss me, Jonas,' Mac encouraged breathlessly.

'I intend to kiss you and love you for the rest of our lives,' he promised as his mouth finally claimed hers.

The rest of their lives sounded just perfect to Mac...

Married by Christmas

CAROLE MORTIMER

CHAPTER ONE

'WHO *IS* THAT gorgeous-looking man over there?' Sally gushed eagerly at Lilli's side.

Until that moment, Lilli had been staring sightlessly at a barman across the room as he quickly and efficiently served drinks to the multitude of people attending what had so far been a pretty boring party.

Or maybe it wasn't the party that was boring; maybe it was just Lilli who felt slightly out of sync with the rest of the people here: if the babble of noise was anything to go by they were having such a good time.

She hadn't attended a party like this in such a long while, and so much had happened in the preceding months. Once upon a time, she acknowledged, she would have thought this was a great party too, would have been at the centre of whatever was going on, but tonight—well, tonight she felt like a total outsider, rather as the only sober person in a room full of inebriates must feel. Except she had already consumed several glasses of champagne herself, so that wasn't the reason she felt so out of touch with this crowd with which she had once spent so much time.

As for gorgeous men, the house was full of them—gorgeous and rich. When Geraldine Simms threw a party, this a pre-Christmas one, only the rich and beautiful were invited to attend, in their hundreds. Geraldine's house, in a fashionable part of London, was as huge and prepossessing as its neighbours, and tonight it was bursting at the seams with bejewelled women and handsome men.

Lilli dragged her gaze away from the efficient barman, obviously hired for the evening. It was time she looked away anyway—the man had obviously noticed her attention several minutes ago, and, from the speculative look in his eyes, believed he had made a conquest! He couldn't have been further from the truth; the last thing Lilli was interested in was a fling with any man, let alone someone as transient as a hired barman!

'What gorgeous man?' she asked Sally without interest. Sally was the one who had persuaded her to come in the first place, on the basis that a Geraldine Simms party, an event that only happened twice a year, was a party not to be missed.

'Over by the door— Oh, damn it, he's disappeared again!' Sally frowned her irritation. She was a petite blonde, with a beauty that could stop a man in his tracks, the black dress she almost wore doing little to forestall this.

Lilli had met her several years ago, during the usual round of parties, and, because neither of them had any interest in becoming permanently entangled with any of the handsome men they encountered, they often found themselves spending the evening together laughing at some of the antics of the other women around them as they cast out their nets and secured some unsuspecting man for the evening. Rather a cruel occupation, really, but it had got Lilli and Sally through many a tedious occasion.

'He must be gorgeous if you've taken an interest,' Lilli said dryly, attracting more than her own fair share of admiring glances as she stood tall and slender next to Sally, her hair long and straight to her waist, as black as a raven's wing, eyes cool and green in a gaminely beautiful face, the strapless above-knee-length red dress that she wore clinging to the perfection of her body. Her legs were long and shapely, still tanned from the summer months, the red high-heeled shoes she wore only adding to her height— and to the impression of unobtainable aloofness that she had practised to perfection over the years.

'Oh, he is,' Sally assured her, still searching the crowd for the object of her interest. 'He makes all the other men here look like callow, narcissistic youths. He— Oh, damn,' she swore impatiently. 'Oh, well,' she sighed, turning back to Lilli with a rueful grimace. 'That was fun while it lasted!' She sipped her champagne.

Lilli's eyes widened. 'You've given up already?' She sounded surprised because she was. On the few occasions she had known Sally to take an interest in a man, she hadn't given up until she had got him! And, as far as Lilli was aware, her friend had always succeeded...

'Had to.' Sally grimaced her disappointment, taking another sip of her champagne. 'Unobtainable.'

'You mean he's married,' Lilli said knowingly.

Sally arched her brows. 'I'm sorry to say that hasn't always been a deterrent in the past.' She shook her head. 'No, he belongs to Gerry,' she explained disappointedly. 'As far as I'm aware, no woman has ever taken one of our hostess's men and lived to tell the tale. And I'm too young to die!'

Lilli laughed huskily at her friend's woebegone expression. Sally was exaggerating, of course, although Geraldine's succession of lovers was legendary. In fact, Lilli doubted there were too many men in this room the beautiful Geraldine Simms hadn't been involved with at some time or other during the last few years. But at

least she seemed to stay good friends with them, which
had to say something about the bubbling effervescence
of their hostess!

Sally glanced across the room again. 'But he is *so* gorgeous...' she said longingly.

Lilli gave a shake of her head. 'Okay, I give up; where
is he?' She turned to look for the man who was so attractive that Sally seemed to be about to throw caution to the
wind and challenge Gerry for him, on the other woman's
home ground, no less!

'Over there.' Sally nodded to the far side of the elegantly furnished room. 'Standing next to Gerry near the
window.'

Sally continued to give an exact description of the gorgeous man but Lilli was no longer listening to her, having
already located the intimately engrossed couple, feeling
the blood drain from her cheeks as she easily spotted the
man standing so arrogantly self-assured at Geraldine's
side.

No!

Not him. Not here. Not with *her*!

Oh, God...! How could he? How dared he?

'Isn't he just—? I say, Lilli, you've gone very pale all
of a sudden.' Sally looked at her concernedly.

Pale? She was surprised she hadn't gone grey, shocked
she was still standing on legs that seemed to be shaking
so badly her knees were knocking together, surprised she
wasn't screaming, *accusing*. What was *he* doing here?
And so obviously with Geraldine Simms, a woman with
the reputation of a man-eater.

'Are you feeling okay?' Sally touched her arm worriedly.

She wasn't feeling at all, seemed to have gone completely numb. It wasn't an emotion she was unfamiliar

with, but she had never thought he would be the one to deal her such a blow.

Oh, God, she had to get out of here, away from the noise, away from *them*!

'I'm fine, Sally,' she told her friend stiltedly, the smile she forced not quite managing to curve her lips. 'I—I think I've had enough for one night. It's my first time out for months,' she babbled. 'I'm obviously out of practice. I—I'll call you.' She put her champagne glass down on the nearest available table. 'We'll have lunch.'

Sally looked totally bewildered by Lilli's sudden urgency to be gone. 'But it's only eleven-thirty!'

And the party would go on until almost morning. In the past Lilli would probably have been among the last to leave. But not tonight. She had to get out of here now. She had to!

'I'll call you, Sally,' she promised distantly, turning to stumble across the room, muttering her apologies as she bumped into people on the way, blind to where she was going, just needing to escape.

She had a jacket somewhere, she remembered. It was in a room at the back of the house. And she didn't want to leave without it, didn't want to have to come back to this house again to collect it. She didn't want to ever have to see Geraldine Simms again. Not ever!

Where had they stored the coats? Every room she looked in appeared to be empty. One of them turned out not to be as empty as it at first appeared, a young couple in there taking advantage of the sofa to make love. But there were no coats.

She would just abandon her damn coat in a minute, would send someone over tomorrow for it, would just have to hope that it was still here.

She thrust open another door, deciding that if this room

proved as fruitless as the others she would quietly leave and find herself a taxi.

'Oh!' She gasped as she realised she had walked into what must be the main kitchen of the house. It wasn't empty. Not that there were any chefs rushing around preparing the food for the numerous guests. No, all the food, put out so deliciously on plates in the dining-room, had been provided by caterers.

A man sat at a long oak table in the middle of the room, his dark evening suit and snowy white shirt, with red bow-tie, tagging him as part of the elegant gathering in the main part of the house. Yet he sat alone in the kitchen, strong hands nursing what looked to be a glass of red wine, the open bottle on the table beside him, the only light in the room a single spotlight over the Aga.

But Lilli could see the man well enough, his dark, overlong hair with distinguished strands of grey at the temples, grey, enigmatic eyes in a face that might have been carved from granite, all sharp angles and hard-hewn features. From the way his long legs stretched out beneath the table, he was a very tall man, well over six feet, if Lilli had to guess. She would put his age in the late thirties.

She also knew, from that very first glance, that she had never seen him before!

She really was very much out of touch with the party scene! Once upon a time she would have known all the other guests at any occasion she went to, which was ultimately the reason they had become so boring to attend. But tonight there were at least two men present that she hadn't encountered at one of these parties before—one she didn't know at all, the other she most certainly did!

Her mouth tightened at her thoughts. 'I'm sorry to have disturbed you,' she told the man distractedly, turning to leave.

'Not at all,' the man drawled in a weary voice. 'It's quite pleasant to meet another refugee from that free-for-all out there!'

Lilli turned slowly back to him, dark brows raised. 'You aren't enjoying the party?'

His mouth quirked into a humourless smile, and he took a swallow of the wine before answering. 'Not particularly,' he dismissed disgustedly. 'If I had known—!' He picked up the bottle and refilled his glass, turning back to Lilli and raising the bottle in her direction. 'Can I offer you some wine? It's from Gerry's private stock,' he explained temptingly. 'Much preferable to that champagne being served out there.' He waved the bottle in the direction of the front of the house.

Gerry... Only Geraldine's really close friends shortened her name in that way. He also knew where Geraldine kept her cellar of wine.

Lilli looked at the man with new interest. He obviously was—or had been—a close friend of Geraldine Simms. And, while Geraldine might remain on good terms with her ex-lovers, she certainly didn't give them up to another woman easily...

Lilli entered the kitchen fully, aware of the man's gaze on her as she moved across the dimly lit room, able to tell by the cool assessment in those pale grey eyes that he liked what he saw. 'I would love some wine,' she accepted as she sat down at the table, not opposite him but next to him, pushing a long swathe of her dark hair over her shoulder as she did so, turning to look at him, green eyes dark, a smile curving lips coloured the same red as her dress. 'Thank you,' she added huskily.

'Good.' He nodded his satisfaction with her answer, standing up to get a second glass.

Now it was Lilli's turn to watch him. She had been

right about his height; he must be at least six feet four, the cut of his suit doing nothing to hide the powerfully muscled body beneath. It also did nothing to mask his obvious contempt for these elegant trappings of civilised company!

She had no doubt that Sally would also have described him as gorgeous!

Her smile faded somewhat as she vividly brought to mind that image of the other man Sally had called gorgeous tonight; her last vision had been of Geraldine Simms draped decoratively across him as the two of them talked softly together.

'Thank you,' she told the man as he sat down beside her to pour her wine, picking up the glass when it was filled to swallow a grateful gulp. She could instantly feel the warmth of the wine inside her, merging with the glasses of champagne she had already consumed.

'Patrick Devlin.' The man held out his hand.

'Lilli.' She shook his hand, liking its cool strength, his name meaning absolutely nothing to her.

He raised dark brows, still retaining his light hold on her hand. 'Just Lilli?'

Her gaze met his, seeing a wealth of experience in those grey depths. Some of that experience had been with Geraldine Simms, she felt sure. 'Just Lilli,' she nodded, sensing his interest in her. And she intended to keep that interest...

'Well, Just Lilli...' He slowly released her hand, although his gaze still easily held hers. 'As we're both bored with this party, what do you suggest we do with ourselves for the rest of the evening?' He quirked mocking lips.

She laughed softly, well versed in the art of seduction herself. 'What do you suggest we do?' she encouraged softly.

He turned back to sit with his elbows resting on the

table, sipping his wine. 'Well…we could count how many patterned tiles there are on the wall over there.' He nodded to the wall opposite.

Lilli didn't so much as glance at them. 'I have no interest in counting tiles, patterned or otherwise,' she returned dryly, drinking some of her own wine. He was right—this wine was much nicer than champagne. It was taking away the numbness she had felt earlier, too.

'No? Oh, well.' He shrugged at the playful shake of her head, refilling her glass. 'We could swap life stories?'

'Definitely not!' There was an edge of bitterness to her laugh this time.

He pursed his lips thoughtfully. 'You're probably right,' he said. 'We could bake a cake? We're certainly in the right place for it!' He looked about them.

'Can you cook?' Lilli prompted; he didn't look as if he knew one end of a cooker—or Aga!—from the other!

He grinned at her, showing very white and even teeth—and unlike most of the men here tonight, she would swear that he'd had none of them capped. 'No one has yet complained about my toast,' he drawled. 'And I've been told I pour a mean glass of orange juice!'

She nodded as he gave her the answer she had expected. 'And a mean glass of wine.' She raised her glass as if in a salute to him.

He poured the last of the wine into her glass. 'I'll open another bottle.' He stood up, moving confidently about the kitchen, walking to the cupboard at the back of the room, emerging triumphantly seconds later with a second bottle of the same wine.

Which he then proceeded to open deftly, refilling his own glass before sitting down next to Lilli once again. 'Your turn. To make some suggestions,' he elaborated huskily at her questioning look.

His words themselves were suggestive, but at this particular moment Lilli didn't care. She was actually enjoying herself, and after the shock she had received earlier this evening that was something in itself.

'Let me see...' She made a show of giving it some thought, happily playing along with the game. 'Do you play chess?'

'Tolerably,' he replied.

'Hmm. Draughts?'

'A champion,' he assured her confidently. 'That's the one with the black and white discs—'

'Not draughts, either,' Lilli laughed, green eyes glowing, her cheeks warm, whether from the effect of the wine and champagne, or their verbal flirtation, she wasn't really sure.

And she didn't care, either. This man was a special friend of Geraldine Simms', she was sure of it, and at this moment she had one hundred per cent of his attention. Wonderful!

'Snakes and ladders?' she suggested lightly.

'Yes...' he answered slowly. 'Although my sister always said I cheated when we played as children; I used to go up the snakes and down the ladders!'

Lilli laughed again. Either the man really was funny, or else the wine was taking effect; either way, this was the most fun she had had in a long time. 'I used to do that too,' she confided, lightly touching his arm, instantly feeling the steely strength beneath his jacket. 'And there's no way we can play if we both cheat!'

'True,' he agreed, suddenly very close, his face mere inches away from hers now. 'You know, Just Lilli, there's one game I have an idea we're both good at—and at which neither of us cheats!' His voice was mesmerisingly low now, his aftershave faintly elusive, but at the same time completely masculine. 'What do you say to the two of us—?'

'Patrick!' A feminine voice, slightly raised with impatience, interrupted him. 'Why aren't you at the party?'

He held Lilli's eyes for several seconds longer, a promise in his own, lightly squeezing her hand as it still rested on his arm, before turning to face the source of that feminine impatience. 'Because I prefer to be here,' he answered firmly. 'And, luckily for me, so does Lilli.'

'Lilli…?' The woman sounded startled now.

So much so that Lilli finally turned to look at her too. Geraldine Simms! She looked far from pleased to see the two of them sitting so close together, Patrick's hand still resting slightly possessively on Lilli's.

Lilli looked coldly at the other woman. 'Geraldine,' she greeted her hardly.

'I didn't realise you were here,' Geraldine said faintly.

She could easily have guessed that! 'Sally Walker telephoned me earlier and persuaded me to come with her.' Lilli finished abruptly, 'Wonderful party,' her sarcasm barely veiled.

'So wonderful Lilli and I were just about to leave.' Patrick stood up, lightly pulling Lilli to her feet beside him, his arm moving about the slenderness of her waist now. 'Weren't we,' he prompted.

As far as Lilli was aware—no, but it did seem like an excellent idea.

She turned her head slightly to give Geraldine a triumphant look. 'Yes, we were just about to leave,' she agreed brightly.

'But—' Geraldine looked flustered, not at all her usually confident self. 'Patrick, you can't leave!' She looked at him beseechingly, not at all certain of herself—or him.

His arm tightened about Lilli's waist. 'Watch me,' he stated determinedly.

'But—' Geraldine wrung her hands together. 'Patrick, I threw this party partly for you—'

'I hate parties, you know that.' There was a hard edge to his voice that hadn't been there when he'd flirted with Lilli. 'I'll come back tomorrow when all of this is over. In the meantime, I intend booking into a hotel for the night. Unless Lilli has any other ideas?' he added, looking at her with raised brows.

'Just Lilli' had realised, from the conversation between these two, that the original plan must have been for Patrick to spend the night here. And, considering Geraldine's intimacy with the man she had been draped over in the other room, that was no mean feat in itself; what did this woman do, line them up in relays? Whatever, Patrick had obviously decided he would rather spend the night with her, though the house she shared in Mayfair with her father was not the place for her to take him; she felt hurt and betrayed, but not *that* hurt and betrayed!

'A hotel sounds fine,' she accepted with bravado, green eyes challenging as she looked across the room at Geraldine.

The other woman's stare relaxed slightly as she met that challenge. 'Lilli, don't do something you'll regret,' she cautioned gently.

Geraldine knew she had seen the two of *them* together, knew why she was doing this! All the better; there was no satisfaction in revenge if the person targeted was unaware of it…!

Lilli turned slightly into Patrick's body, resting her head against the hardness of his chest. 'I'm sure Patrick will make sure I don't regret a thing,' she said huskily.

'Lilli—'

'Gerry, just butt out, will you?' Patrick told her impatiently. 'Go and find your ageing lover and leave Lilli and me to get on with our lives. I'm not a monster intent on seducing an innocent, and you aren't the girl's mother, for goodness' sake,' he added disgustedly.

Lilli looked at the other woman with pure venom in her eyes; she had never disliked anyone as much as she did Geraldine Simms at that moment. 'Yes, Geraldine,' she said flatly. 'Please go back to your lover; I'm sure he must be wondering where you are.'

'We'll go out the back way,' Patrick suggested lightly. 'Unless you want to fight your way out through the chaos?'

'No, the back way is fine.' Her coat didn't matter any more; no doubt it would be returned to her in time!

'Patrick!' Geraldine had crossed the room to stop them at the door, a restraining hand on Patrick's arm now. 'I realise you're angry with me right now, but please don't—'

'I'm not angry with you, Gerry,' he cut in contemptuously. 'No one has any ties on you; they never had!' His face was cold as he looked down at her.

'This isn't important just now,' the beautiful redhead dismissed impatiently. 'Anyone but Lilli, Patrick,' she groaned.

So the woman did have a conscience, after all! Unless, of course, she just didn't want Lilli, in particular, walking off with one of her men...? In the circumstances, that was probably closer to the truth.

'Please don't worry on my account, Geraldine.' Lilli deliberately used the other woman's full name. The two of them had never been particularly close in the past, although Lilli did usually call her Gerry; but after this evening she hoped they would never meet again. 'I know exactly what I'm doing,' she affirmed.

Geraldine looked at Lilli searchingly for several long seconds. 'I don't think you do.' She shook her head slowly. 'And I'm absolutely positive you don't, Patrick,' she added firmly. 'Lilli is—'

'Could we leave now, Patrick?' Lilli turned to him, open flirtation in the dark green of her eyes. 'Before I decide snakes and ladders is preferable!'

He looked at her admiringly. 'We're leaving, Gerry,' he told the other woman decisively. 'Now.'

'But—'

'Now, Gerry,' he insisted, opening the back door for Lilli to precede him. 'Enjoy your party,' he called over his shoulder, his arm once more about Lilli's waist as they stepped out into the cold December evening.

The blast of icy cold air was like a slap on the face, and Lilli could feel her head swimming from the amount of champagne and wine she had drunk during the evening. In fact, she suddenly felt decidedly light-headed.

'Steady.' Patrick's arm tightened about her waist as he held her beside him. 'My car is just over here. Don't you have a coat?' He frowned as she shivered from the cold while he unlocked the doors of his sleek black sports car.

She suddenly couldn't remember whether she had a coat or not. In fact, she was having trouble putting two thoughts together inside her head!

She gave a laugh as he opened the car door for her to get in, showing a long expanse of shapely leg as she dropped down into the low passenger seat. 'I'm sure you'll help me to get warm once we reach the hotel,' she told him seductively.

His mouth quirked. 'I'll do my best, Just Lilli,' he assured her, the promise in his voice unmistakable.

Lilli leant her head back against the seat as he closed her door to move around the car and get in behind the wheel. What was she doing here...? Oh, yes, she was getting away from Geraldine and him!

'Any preference on hotels?' Patrick glanced at her as he turned on the ignition.

Hotels? Why were they going to a hotel...? Oh, yes... this man was going to make love to her.

She shook her head, instantly wishing she hadn't as it began to spin once again. 'You choose,' she said weakly.

She wasn't actually going to be sick, was she?

God, she hoped not. Although she had no idea where they were going as Patrick turned the car out onto the road. And at that moment she didn't care either. Nothing mattered at the moment. Not her. Not him. Not Geraldine Simms!

'All right?' Patrick reached out to squeeze her hand reassuringly.

She didn't think she would ever be 'all right' again. She had felt as if her world had shattered three months ago; tonight it felt as if it had ended completely.

'Fine,' she answered as if from a long way away. 'Just take me somewhere private and make love to me.'

'Oh, I intend to, Just Lilli. I intend to.'

Lilli sat back with her eyes closed, wishing at that moment for total oblivion, not just a few hours in Patrick Devlin's arms...

CHAPTER TWO

'YOUR JACKET.' The garment was thrown over the back of a dining-room chair.

Lilli didn't move, didn't even raise her head. She wasn't sure that she could!

She had been sitting here at the dining-table for the last hour, just drinking strong, unsweetened black coffee; the smell of food on the serving plates sitting on the side board had made her feel nauseous, so she had asked for them to be taken away. There was no one else here to eat it, anyway. At least, there hadn't been...

'Did you hear what I said?'

'I heard you!' She winced as the sound of her own voice made the thumping in her head even louder. 'I heard you,' she repeated softly, her voice almost a whisper now. But it still sounded too loud for her sensitive ears!

'Well?'

He wasn't going to leave it at that. She should have known that he wouldn't. But all she really wanted to do, now that her head had at least stopped spinning, was to crawl into bed and sleep for twenty-four hours.

Fat chance!

'Lilli!' The impatience deepened in his voice.

At last she raised her head from where it had been resting in her hands as she stared down into her coffee cup, pushing back the dark thickness of her hair to look up at him with studied determination.

'My God, Lilli!' her father gasped disbelievingly. 'You look terrible!'

'Thank you!' Her smile was merely a caricature of one, even her facial muscles seeming to hurt.

She knew exactly how she looked, had recoiled from her own reflection in the mirror earlier this morning. Her eyes were a dull green, bruises from lack of sleep visible beneath them, her face chalk-white. Her tangled hair she had managed to smooth into some sort of order with her fingers, but the overall impression, she knew, was not good. It wasn't helped by the fact that she still had on the revealing red dress she had worn to the party the night before. A fact Grimes, the family butler, had definitely noted when she'd arrived back here by taxi an hour ago!

But if her father thought she looked bad now he should have seen her a couple of hours ago, when she'd first woken up; then she hadn't even been wearing the red dress! And the rich baritone voice of Patrick Devlin had been coming from the bathroom as he'd sung while he took a shower...!

Her father dropped down heavily into the chair opposite her. 'What were you thinking of, Lilli?' He looked at her searchingly. 'Or were you just not thinking at all?' he added with regret.

He knew; she could tell by the expression in his eyes that he did. Of course he knew; Geraldine would have told him!

Because her father had been the man at Geraldine Simms' side last night, the gorgeous man that Sally had referred to so interestedly, the man Geraldine had been draped over so intimately, her 'ageing lover', as Patrick had called him.

'Were *you*?' Lilli challenged insultingly. 'Yes, I saw
you last night,' she scorned as a guarded look came over
her father's handsome face. 'With Geraldine Simms,' she
continued accusingly, so angry she didn't care about the
pounding in her head at that moment. 'But I suppose *you*
call her Gerry.' Her top lip curled back contemptuously.
'All her *intimate* friends do!'

He drew in a harshly controlling breath. 'And is that
why you did what you did?' he asked flatly. 'Went off
with a man you had only just met? A man you obviously
spent the night with,' he added as he looked pointedly at
her dress.

'And what about you?' Lilli accused emotionally. 'I
don't need to ask where *you* spent the night. Or with
whom!' She was furiously angry, but at the same time
tears of pain glistened in her eyes.

Her father reached out to touch her hand, but she drew
back as if she had been burnt. 'You don't understand,
Lilli,' he told her in a hurt voice. 'You—'

'Oh, I understand only too well.' She stood up so suddenly, her chair fell over behind her with a loud clatter,
but neither of them took any notice of it as their green
eyes locked. 'You spent last night in the bed of a woman
everyone knows to be a man-eating flirt, a woman who
has been involved with numerous men since her brief
marriage—and equally quick divorce!—five years ago.
And with my mother, your wife, barely cold in her grave!'
She glared across the table at him, her breathing shallow
and erratic in her agitation, her hands clenched into fists
at her sides.

For that was what hurt the most about all this. After a
long illness, her mother had died three months ago—and
now her father was intimately involved with one of the
biggest flirts in London!

It was an insult to her mother's memory. It was—it was— God, the pain last night of seeing her father with another woman—with that woman in particular!—had been almost more than she could bear.

Her father looked as if she had physically hit him, his face as pale as her own, the likeness between them even more noticeable during those seconds. Lilli had always been so proud of her father, had adored him as a child, admired him as an adult, had always loved the fact that she looked so much like him, her hair as dark as his.

Now she wished she looked like anyone else but him— because at this particular moment she hated him!

'You're right, Father; I don't understand,' she told him coldly as she rose and walked away from him. 'But then, I don't think I particularly want to.'

'Lilli, did you spend the night with Patrick Devlin?'

She stopped at the door, her back still towards him. Then, swallowing hard, she turned to face him, her head held back defiantly. 'Yes, I did,' she told him starkly.

He frowned. 'You went to bed with him?'

Lilli stared at her parent woodenly. She had woken up in a hotel bedroom this morning, wearing only her lace panties, with Patrick Devlin singing in the adjoining bathroom as he took a shower, the other side of the double bed showing signs of someone having slept there, the pillow indented, the sheet tangled; so it was probably a fair assumption that she had been to bed with him!

But the real truth of the matter was she didn't actually remember, couldn't recall anything of the night before from the moment she had closed her eyes in the car— and even some of the events before that were a bit hazy!

Her mouth tightened stubbornly. 'What if I did? I'm over twenty-one.' Just! 'And a free agent.' Definitely that, since the end of her engagement. She had barely been out of the house during the last six months—which was the reason the champagne and wine she'd drunk last night had hit her so strongly, she was sure. At least, that was what she had told herself this morning when she'd finally managed to open her eyes and face the day. 'Who was I hurting?' she added challengingly.

Her father gave a weary sigh, shaking his head. 'Well, I believe the intention was to hurt me. But the person you've hurt the most is yourself. Lilli, do you have any idea who Patrick Devlin is?'

Why should she? As her father had already said, she had only met the man last night. And her nonsensical conversation with Patrick in the kitchen had told her nothing about him, except that he had a sense of humour. But then, she had told him nothing about herself either, was 'Just Lilli' as far as he was concerned. She never expected to see or hear from him again!

'I only wanted to go to bed with him, not hear his life story!' she scorned dismissively.

Her father drew a harsh breath. 'Perhaps if you had done the latter, and not the former, this conversation wouldn't be taking place. In fact, I'm sure it wouldn't,' he rasped abruptly. 'You really don't have any idea who he is?'

'Why do you keep harping on about the man?' She snapped her impatience. 'He isn't important—'

'Oh, but he is,' her father cut in softly.

'Not to me.' She gave a firm shake of her head, wincing as she did so.

She just wanted to forget about Patrick Devlin. Last night she had behaved completely out of character, mostly because, as her father had guessed, she wanted to hit out at him. But also at Geraldine Simms. Well, she had done that—more than done that if her father's reaction was anything to go by!—and now she just wanted to forget it had ever happened. She couldn't even remember half of last night's events, so it shouldn't be that hard to do!

'Oh, yes, Lilli, he is important to you too.' Her father nodded grimly. 'Patrick Devlin is the Chairman of Paradise Bank.'

She thought back to the man she had met last night in Geraldine Simms' kitchen—she couldn't count this morning; she had left the hotel before he'd stopped singing and emerged from the bathroom! She remembered a tall, handsome man, with slightly overlong dark hair, and laughter in his deep grey eyes. He hadn't looked anything like a banker.

She shrugged. 'So? Is he married, with a dozen children; is that the problem?' Although if he were he must have a very understanding wife, to have gone off to a party on his own and then have felt no compunction about staying out all night. No...somehow she didn't think he was married.

Her father gave a sigh at the mockery in her tone. 'Okay, let's leave that part alone for a while. Do you know what else he is, Lilli?'

'A Liberal Democrat,' she taunted.

'Oh, very funny!' Her father, a staunch Conservative voter, wasn't in the least amused at her continued levity.

'Look, Father, I don't—'

'And will you stop calling me "Father" in that judgemental tone?' he bit out tautly.

'I'm sorry, but you just don't seem like "Daddy" to me at the moment,' she told him in a pained voice, unable to look at him at that moment, too.

Her father had always been there for her in the past, she had always been 'Daddy's little girl', and now he suddenly seemed like a stranger...

'I'm really sorry you feel that way, Lilli.' He spoke gently. 'It wasn't meant to be this way.'

'I'm not even going to ask what you mean by that remark,' she said scathingly, turning towards the door once again.

'I haven't finished yet, Lilli—'

'But I have!' She swung round, eyes flashing deeply green. 'To be honest, I'm not sure I can listen to any more of this without being sick!' This time she did turn and walk out the door, her head held high.

'He's Geraldine's brother,' her father called after her. 'Patrick Devlin is Geraldine's older brother!'

She faltered only slightly, and then she just kept on walking, her legs moving automatically, that numbness she had known the night before thankfully creeping over her once again.

'Where are you going?' Her father now stood at the bottom of the stairs she had half ascended.

'To bed,' she told him flatly. 'To sleep.' For a million years, if she was lucky!

'This mess will still be here when you wake up, Lilli,' her father told her fiercely. '*I'll* still be here!'

She didn't answer him, didn't even glance at him, continuing up to her bedroom, closing the door firmly behind her, deliberately keeping her mind blank as she threw off the clothes she had worn last night, not even bothering to put on a nightgown before climbing in between the sheets of her bed, pulling the covers up over the top of her head, willing herself to go to sleep.

And when she woke up maybe she would find the last twelve hours had been a nightmare…!

Geraldine Simms' brother!

She didn't know what time it was, how long she had

slept, only that she had woken suddenly, sitting up in the bed, her eyes wide as that terrible truth pounded in her brain.

Patrick Devlin wasn't a past or present lover of Geraldine Simms, but her *brother*!

No wonder he had been so familiar with the house, with where the wine was kept. And he hadn't been going to spend the night there with Geraldine, but was obviously her guest at her house during his visit to London.

Lilli had thought she was being so clever, that she was walking away with a prize taken from under Geraldine's nose. But all the time Patrick was the woman's brother! No wonder Geraldine had tried to stop the two of them leaving together; considering her own involvement with Lilli's father, any relationship between Lilli and her brother was a complication she could well do without!

Lilli had been to bed with the enemy...!

But she wasn't involved with Patrick Devlin, had no 'relationship' with him; one night in bed together did not a relationship make!

One night in bed...

And she didn't even remember it, she inwardly groaned. But Patrick had been singing quite happily to himself in the shower this morning, so he obviously did!

With the exception of her ex-fiancé, she had spent the majority of the last four years ignoring the obvious advances of the 'beautiful men' she met at parties, not even aware of the less obvious ones. But in a single night she had wiped all of that out by going to bed with the one man she should have stayed well away from.

Her father was right—this was a mess!

She fell back against the pillows, her eyes closed. A million years of sleep couldn't undo what she had done last night.

Her only consolation—and it was a very slight one!—
was that she was sure Patrick had been involved in a conversation with his sister this morning very similar to the
one she'd had with her father. She wouldn't be 'Just Lilli'
to Patrick any more, but Elizabeth Bennett, daughter of
Richard Bennett, of Bennett International Hotels, the current man in Geraldine's life. No doubt her identity as the
daughter of his sister's 'ageing lover' had come as much
of a shock to him as it had to her to realise he was Geraldine's brother.

Lilli opened her eyes, her expression thoughtful now.
Patrick hadn't seemed any more pleased than she was at
his sister's choice of lover, which meant he wouldn't be
too eager ever to meet the lover's daughter again, either.
Which meant she could forget the whole sorry business.

End of mess.

Of course it was.

Now if she could just make her father see sense over
this ridiculous involvement with Geraldine Simms—She
turned towards the door as a knock sounded on it. She
hadn't left instructions that she wasn't to be disturbed,
but even so she was irritated at the intrusion. 'Yes?' she
prompted impatiently, getting out of bed to pull on her
robe.

'There's someone downstairs waiting to see you, Miss
Lilli, and—'

The young maid broke off in surprise as Lilli wrenched
open the door. 'There's someone to see you,' the maid repeated awkwardly.

'What time is it?' Lilli frowned, totally disoriented
after her daytime sleep.

'Three-thirty,' Emily provided, a girl not much younger
than Lilli herself. 'Would you like me to serve tea to you
and your visitor?'

She wasn't in the mood to receive visitors, let alone sit and have tea with them. 'I don't think so, thank you,' she replied distractedly. 'Who is it?' She frowned.

'A Mr Devlin,' Emily told her chattily. 'I asked him to wait in the small sitting-room—'

'Devlin!' Lilli repeated forcefully, causing the young maid to look alarmed all over again. 'Did you say a Mr Devlin, Emily?' Her thoughts raced.

Patrick was here? So much for her thinking he wouldn't ever want to see her again either once he realised who she was!

'Yes.' The young girl's face was alight with infatuation—all the evidence Lilli needed that indeed it was the handsome Patrick Devlin downstairs.

Thinking back to the way he had looked last night—tall, and so elegantly handsome—she found it easy to see how a woman's breath could be taken away just to look at him. And she had just spent the night with him!

Lilli drew in a sharp breath. 'Please tell him I'll be down in a few minutes.' Once she was dressed. His last memory of her must be of her wearing only cream lace panties; she intended the memory he took away of her today to be quite different!

It took more than the few minutes she had said to don a black sweater, fitted black trousers, apply a light make-up to hide the pallor of her face, and to braid her long hair into a loose plait down her spine. But at least when she looked in the mirror at her reflection she was satisfied with the result—cool and elegant.

Nevertheless, she took a deep breath before entering the room where Patrick Devlin waited for her. She had no idea what he was doing here—didn't a woman walking out on him without even a goodbye, after spending the night with him, tell him that she didn't want to see him again—ever? Obviously not, if his presence here was anything to go by...

He was standing in front of the window looking out at the winter garden when she entered, slowly turning to look at her as he became aware of her presence.

Lilli's breath caught in her throat. God, he was handsome!

She hadn't really registered that last night, but in the clear light of day he was incredibly attractive, ruggedly so, his hair so dark a brown it almost appeared black, with those distinguished wings of silver at his temples. His skin was lightly tanned, features so finely hewn they might have been carved from stone, his eyes a light, enigmatic grey.

He was dressed very similarly to her, except he wore a fine checked jacket over his black jumper. Which meant he had been back to Geraldine's house this morning—if only to change his clothes!

He moved forward in long, easy movements, looking her critically up and down. 'Well, well, well,' he finally drawled. 'If it isn't Just Lilli—alias Elizabeth Bennett.' His voice hardened over the latter.

'Mr Devlin.' She nodded coolly in acknowledgement, none of her inner turmoil—she hoped!—in evidence.

She had chosen to go with this man the evening before for two reasons: to hurt her father, and hit out at Geraldine Simms. And at this moment Patrick Devlin seemed very much aware of that!

His mouth twisted mockingly. 'Mr. Devlin...? Really, Lilli, it's a little late for formality between us, isn't it?' he taunted.

She moved pointedly away from him; his derisive manner was deliberately insulting. 'Why are you here?' She looked at him across the room with cool green eyes.

Dark brows rose at her tone. 'Well, I could say you left your bra behind and I've come to return it, but as you weren't wearing a bra last night...!'

'That's enough!' she snapped, two bright spots of embarrassed colour in her cheeks now.

'More than enough, I would say,' he agreed, his eyes glittering icily. 'Lilli, exactly what did you hope to achieve by going to bed with me?'

To hit out at her father, to hurt Geraldine Simms. Nothing more. But certainly nothing less. At the time she hadn't realised the man she had chosen to help her was actually the other woman's brother. She accepted it complicated things a little. Especially as he had come here today...

She deliberately gave a careless shrug. 'A good time.' It was half a question—because she couldn't remember whether or not they'd had a good time together!

He gave an acknowledging nod at her reply. 'And did you? Have a good time,' he persisted dryly at her puzzled expression.

She frowned. 'Didn't you?' she instantly returned. Two could play at this game!

His mouth quirked. 'Marks out of ten? Or do you have some other method of rating your lovers—?'

'There's no need to be insulting!' Lilli told him sharply.

'There's every need, damn you!' Patrick advanced towards her, his hand on her arm, fingers warm against her skin.

'Don't touch me!' she told him angrily, pulling away, and only succeeding in hurting herself. 'Let me go,' she ordered with every ounce of Bennett arrogance she possessed. This was her home, damn it, and he couldn't just come in here—uninvited!—and insult and manhandle her!

He thrust her away from him. 'I ought to break that beautiful neck of yours!' he ground out fiercely, eyes narrowed. 'You looked older last night... Exactly how old are you?' he bit out, his gaze sweeping over her scathingly.

She looked startled. 'What does my age have to do with anything?'

'Just answer the question, Lilli,' he rasped. 'And while you're at it explain to me exactly how the haughty Elizabeth Bennett ended up with a name like Lilli!'

Her own cheeks were flushed with anger now. 'Neither of those things is any of your business!'

'I'm making them so,' he told her levelly.

This man might be as good-looking as the devil, but he had the arrogance to match! Why hadn't she realised any of this the previous evening when she had met him? Because she hadn't been thinking straight, she acknowledged heavily, had been blinded by the fury she felt towards her father and the woman he was obviously involved with. This man's sister... She still had trouble connecting the two—they looked absolutely nothing alike!

'Well?' he prompted at her continued silence.

She glared at him resentfully, wanting him to leave but knowing he had no intention of doing so until he was good and ready—and he wasn't either of those things yet! 'I'm twenty-one,' she told him tautly.

'And?' He looked at her hardly.

'And three months,' she supplied challengingly, knowing it wasn't what he had been asking. But she had no intention of telling him that she had acquired the name Lilli because the baby brother she had adored, the baby brother who had died when he was only two years old, hadn't been able to manage the name Elizabeth. Just as she had no intention of telling him that she knew to the day exactly how old she was, because her mother, the mother she had also adored, had died on her twenty-first birthday... It was also the day her fiancée, her father's assistant, had walked out of her life...

He grimaced ruefully at her evasion. 'A mere child,' he ground out disgustedly. 'The sacrificial lamb!' He shook his head. 'I hate to tell you this, Lilli, but your efforts— enjoyable as they were!—were completely wasted.' His gaze hardened. 'If my own sister's pleadings failed to move me, you can be assured that a night of pleasure in your arms would have had even less effect!'

Lilli looked at him with haughty disdain. 'I don't have the least idea what you're talking about,' she snapped.

'No?' he queried sceptically.

'No,' she echoed tartly. 'I don't even know what you're doing here today. We were at a party, we decided to spend the night together—and that should have been the end of it. You came here, I didn't come to you,' she reminded him coldly.

'Actually, Lilli,' he drawled softly, 'I came to see your father, not you.'

Her head went back in astonishment. 'My father...?' she repeated in a puzzled voice.

Patrick nodded abruptly. 'Unfortunately, I was informed he isn't in,' he said grimly.

'So you asked to see me instead?' she realised incredulously.

'Correct,' he affirmed, with a slight inclination of his head. 'Sorry to disappoint you, Lilli,' he added.

She swallowed hard, quickly reassessing the situation. 'And just why did you want to see my father?'

Patrick looked at her with narrowed eyes. 'I'm sure you already know the answer to that question.'

'Because he's having a relationship with your sister?'

Lilli scorned. 'It must keep you very busy if you pay personal calls on all her lovers in this way!'

Anger flared briefly in the grey depths of his eyes, and then they became glacially enigmatic, that gaze sweeping over her with deliberate assessment. 'I'm sure you keep your father just as busy,' he drawled.

After her comment about Geraldine, she had probably deserved that remark. Unfortunately, both this man and his sister brought out the worst in her; she wasn't usually a bitchy person. But then, this whole situation was unusual!

'Perhaps he's paying a similar call on you at this very moment?' Lilli returned.

'I very much doubt it.' Patrick gave a smile. 'It hasn't been my impression, so far in our acquaintance, that your father has ever deliberately gone out of his way to meet me!'

Her eyes widened. 'The two of you have met?' If they had, her father hadn't mentioned that particular fact earlier!

'Several times,' Patrick confirmed enigmatically.

Exactly how long had her father been involved with Geraldine? Lilli had assumed it was a very recent thing, but if the two men had met 'several times'...

'Perhaps you could pass on a message to him that we will be meeting again, too. Very soon,' Patrick added grimly, walking to the door.

Lilli watched him frowningly. 'You're leaving...?' She hadn't meant her voice to sound wistful at all—and yet somehow it did. In the fifteen minutes Patrick had been here he had made insulting comments to her, enigmatic remarks about her father—but he hadn't really said anything. She wasn't really sure what she had expected him to say... But the two of them had spent the night together, and— He turned at the door, dark brows raised questioningly. 'Do we have anything else to say to each other?' he questioned in a bored voice.

No, of course they didn't. They had had nothing to say to each other from the beginning. It was just that—'Ten, Lilli,' he drawled softly. 'You were a ten,' he explained dryly as she gave him a puzzled look.

He laughed huskily as his meaning became clear and her cheeks suffused with heated colour.

She hadn't wanted to know—hadn't asked—'I'll let myself out, Lilli,' he volunteered, and did so, the door closing softly behind him.

Which was just as well—because Lilli had been rooted to the spot after that last statement.

Ten...

And she didn't remember a single moment of it...

CHAPTER THREE

'I WANT TO know exactly what is going on, Daddy,' Lilli told him firmly, having waited in the sitting-room for two hours before he came home, fortified by the tray of tea things Emily had brought in to her. After Patrick Devlin's departure, Lilli had felt in need of something, and whisky, at that hour of the day, had been out of the question. Although the man was enough to drive anyone to drink!

She had heard her father enter the house, accosting him in the hallway as he walked towards the wide staircase.

He turned at the sound of her voice, his expression grim. 'I was left in no doubt by you earlier that you didn't want to hear anything more about Geraldine.'

'I still don't,' Lilli told him impatiently. 'Her brother, however, is a different matter!'

'Patrick?' her father replied.

Her mouth twisted. 'Unless she has another brother—yes!'

Her father stiffened, striding forcefully across the hallway to join her as she went into the sitting-room, closing the door firmly behind him. 'What about him?' he said warily.

She gave an impatient sigh. 'That's what I just asked you!'

'You spent the night with him, Lilli,' her father reminded her. 'I would have thought you would know all there is to know about the man! We none of us have defences in bed. Or so I'm told...'

She bit back the reply she would have liked to make; that sort of conversation would take them absolutely nowhere, as it had this morning. 'I'm not talking about the man's prowess—or otherwise!—in the bedroom,' she snapped. 'He said the two of you know each other.'

'Did he?' her father returned with studied indifference.

'Daddy!' She glared at her father's back as he stood looking out of the window now—very much as Patrick had done earlier. He was trying to give the impression that the subject of the other man bored him, and yet, somehow, she knew that it didn't...

He sighed. 'I'm sorry. I just didn't realise the two of you had spent part of your night together discussing me—'

'We didn't,' Lilli cut in. 'He was here earlier.'

Her father froze, slowly turning to face her. 'Devlin came here?'

She wasn't wrong; she was sure she wasn't; she had never seen this emotion in her father before, but he actually looked slightly fearful. And it had something to do with Patrick Devlin...

'Yes, he was here,' she confirmed steadily. 'And he said some things—'

'He had no right, damn him!' her father told her fiercely, his hands clenched into fists at his sides.

'I'm your daughter—'

'And this is a business matter,' he barked tensely. 'If I had wanted to tell you about it then I would have done so.'

'Tell me now?' Lilli encouraged softly. Her father had mentioned this morning that Patrick Devlin was the chairman of Paradise Bank—could that have something to do with this 'business matter'? Although, as far as she was aware, her family had always banked with Cleveley...

'I told you, Patrick Devlin *is* Paradise Bank,' her father grated.

And she was none the wiser for his repeating the fact! 'Yes?'

'Don't you ever read the newspapers, Lilli?' her father said tersely. 'Or are you more like your mother than I realised, and only interested in what Bennett International Hotels can give you in terms of money and lifestyle?'

The accusation hung between them, everything suddenly seeming very quiet; even the air was still.

Lilli stared at her father, barely breathing, a tight pain in her chest.

Her father stared back at her, obviously mortified at what he had just said, his face very pale.

They never talked about her mother, or baby Robbie; they had, by tacit agreement, never talked about the loss of either.

Lilli drew in a deep breath. 'I know Mummy had her faults—'

'I'm sorry, Lilli—'

They had both begun talking at the same time, both coming to an abrupt halt, once again staring at each other, awkwardly this time. The last three months had been difficult; Lilli's grief at her mother's death was something she hadn't been able to share with anyone. Not even her father.

She had known that her father had his own pain to deal with. The years during which her mother's illness had deteriorated had been even more difficult for him than they had for Lilli, her mother's moods fluctuating between self-pity and anger. It had been hard to cope with, Lilli freely acknowledged. But she had had no idea how bitter her father had become...

'I shouldn't have said that.' Her father ran a weary hand through dark hair liberally peppered with grey. 'I'm sorry, Lilli.'

She wasn't sure whether he was apologising for the remarks about her mother, or for the fact that he felt the way he did...

'No, you shouldn't,' she agreed quietly. 'But a lot of things have been said and done in the last twenty-four hours that shouldn't have been.' She included her own behaviour with Patrick Devlin in that! 'Perhaps it would be better if we just forgot about them?' She certainly wanted to forget last night!

'I wish we could, Lilli.' Her father sat down heavily in one of the armchairs, shaking his head. 'But I don't think Devlin will let either of us do that.' He leant his head back against the chair, his eyes closed. 'What did he have to say when he came here earlier?' He opened his eyes to look at her frowningly.

Besides marking her as a ten...?

'Not a lot, Daddy.' She crossed the room to kneel on the carpet at his feet. 'Although he did say to tell you the two of you would be meeting again. Soon. Tell me what's going on, Daddy?' She looked up at him appealingly.

He reached out to smooth gently the loose tendrils of dark hair away from her cheeks. 'You're so young, Lilli.' He sounded pained. 'So very young,' he groaned. 'You give the outward impression of being so cool and self-possessed, and yet...'

'It's just an impression,' she acknowledged ruefully. 'How well you know me, Daddy.' She gave a wistful smile.

'I should do,' he said with gentle affection. 'I love you very much, Lilli. No matter what happens, I hope you never forget that.' He gave a heavy sigh.

Lilli once again felt that chill of foreboding down her

spine. What was going to happen? And what did Patrick Devlin have to do with it? Because she didn't doubt that he was at the root of her father's problem.

Her father straightened determinedly in his chair, that air of defeat instantly dispelled. 'Devlin and I are involved in some business that isn't going quite the way he wishes it would,' he explained briskly.

Lilli frowned, realising that, with this blunt statement, her father had decided not to tell her anything. 'He called me a sacrificial lamb,' she persisted.

'Did he, indeed?' her father rapped out harshly. 'What the hell does he think I am?' he cried angrily, rising forcefully to his feet. 'Devlin is right, Lilli—it's past time the two of us met again. Damn Gerry and her diplomatic approach—'

'About Geraldine Simms—'

'She's not for discussion, Lilli,' her father cut in defensively, those few minutes of father-daughter closeness definitely over.

Obviously Geraldine Simms was too important in his life to be discussed with her! It made Lilli question exactly how long this relationship with the other woman had been going on. Since her mother's death—or before that? The thought of her father having an affair with a woman like Geraldine Simms while her mother was still alive made Lilli feel ill. He couldn't have—could he...?

Lilli stood up too, eyes flashing deeply emerald. 'In that case,' she rebutted angrily, 'neither is the night I spent with her brother!'

'Lilli!' Her father stopped her as she was about to storm out of the room.

She turned slowly. 'Yes?' she said curtly.

'Stay away from Devlin,' he advised heavily. 'He's trouble.'

He might be, and until a short time ago she had been only too happy with the idea of never setting eyes on him again. But not any more. Patrick Devlin was the other half of this puzzle, and if her father wouldn't tell her what was going on perhaps Patrick would!

She met her father's gaze unblinkingly. 'Stay away from Geraldine Simms,' she mocked. 'She's trouble.'

Her father steadily met her rebellious gaze for several long seconds, and then he wearily shook his head. 'This is so much deeper than you can possibly realise. You're playing with fire where Devlin is concerned. He's a barracuda in a city suit,' he added bitterly.

'Sounds like a fascinating combination,' Lilli replied.

'More like deadly,' her father rasped, scowling darkly. 'Lilli, I'm ordering you to stay away from him!'

Her eyes widened in shock. This was much more serious than she had even imagined; she couldn't remember the last time her father had ordered her to do anything. If he ever had. But the fact that he did it now only made her all the more determined.

The real problem with that was she had no idea—yet!— how to even make contact with Patrick Devlin again, without it seeming as if she was doing exactly that. Because she had a feeling he would react exactly as her father was doing if she went to him and asked for answers to her questions: refuse to give any!

Well, she might be young, as both men had already stated quite clearly today, but she was the daughter of one man, and had spent the previous night in the arms of the other—she certainly wasn't a child, and she wasn't about to be treated like one. By either of them!

'Save that tone of voice for your employees, Father,' she told him coldly. 'Of which I—thankfully!—am not one!' She closed the door decisively behind her as she left the room.

It was only once she was safely outside in the hallway that she allowed some of her defiance to leave her. But she had meant every word she'd said in there, she would get to the bottom of this mystery. And she knew the very person to help her do that...

'Sally!' she said warmly a few minutes later when the other woman answered her call after the tenth ring. She had begun to think Sally must be out. And that didn't fit in with her plans at all. 'It's Lilli.'

'Wow, that was quick,' Sally returned lightly. 'I didn't expect to hear from you again for weeks.'

Lilli forced a bright laugh. 'I said I would call you,' she reminded her.

'It's a little late in the day for lunch,' Sally said dryly. 'Although to be honest,' she added confidingly, 'I've only just got out of bed. That was some party last night!'

Lilli wouldn't know. 'Any luck with that gorgeous man?' she said playfully—knowing full well there hadn't been; her father had spent the night with Geraldine Simms.

'None at all.' Sally sounded disappointed. 'But then, with Gerry on the hunt, I never expected it. She monopolised the man all night, and then—'

'Are you free for dinner this evening?' Lilli cut in sharply—she knew what came 'then'!

'Well...I was due to go to the Jameses' party this evening, but it will just be like every other party I've been to this month. Christmas-time is a bitch, isn't it? Everyone and his cousin throws a party—and invites exactly the same people to every one! In all honesty, I'm all partied out. And there's another ten days to go yet!' Sally groaned with feeling.

'Does that mean you're free for dinner?' Lilli prompted.

'Name the place!' The grin could be heard in Sally's voice.

Lilli did, choosing one of her own favourite restaurants, knowing the other woman would like it too. She also promised that it was her treat; Sally knew 'everyone and his cousin', and anything there was to know about them. Lilli didn't doubt she would know about Patrick Devlin too...

She wasn't disappointed in her choice of informant!

'Patrick!' Even the way Sally said his name spoke volumes. 'Now there *is* a gorgeous man. Tall, dark, handsome— He's Gerry's brother, you know—'

'I do know,' Lilli confirmed—she knew now!

'He's also intelligent, rich—oh yes, very rich.' Sally laughed softly.

'And single.' It was almost a question—because Lilli wasn't absolutely sure of his marital status. She had been to bed with the man, and she didn't even know whether he was married!

'He is now,' Sally nodded, nibbling on one of the prawns she had chosen to start her meal. 'Sanchia wasn't the faithful kind, and so he went through rather a messy divorce about five years ago. Sanchia took him for millions. Personally, I would rather have kept the man, but Sanchia settled for the cash and moved back to France, where she originally came from.'

Sanchia... Patrick had been married to a woman called Sanchia. A woman who had been unfaithful to him. She couldn't have known him very well if she had thought he would put up with that; Lilli had only known him twenty-four hours, but, even so, she knew he was a man who kept what he had. Exclusively.

But at least he wasn't married now, which was a relief to hear after last night. Although there was still so much Lilli wanted to know about him...

'What does he do?' Lilli frowned; chairman of a bank didn't tell her anything.

'I just told you.' Sally laughed. 'He makes millions.'

'And then gives them away to ex-wives,' Lilli scorned; that didn't sound very intelligent to her!

'One ex-wife,' Sally corrected her. 'And he didn't give it away. It was probably worth it to him to get that embarrassment out of his life. Sanchia liked men, and made no secret of the fact...'

'She sounds a lot like his sister,' Lilli said bitterly. How could her father have been so stupid as to have got mixed up with such a family?

'Gerry's okay,' Sally said grudgingly. 'Although Patrick is even better,' she added suggestively.

Lilli gave her a guarded look. 'Sally, you haven't— You and he haven't—'

'I should be so lucky!' Sally laughed again ruefully. 'But Patrick doesn't. Not any more. Not since Sanchia,' she amended wistfully.

Lilli hoped she succeeded in hiding the shock she felt at this last statement. Because Patrick most certainly did! At least, he had last night. With her...

Sally gave her a considering look. 'You do realise I'm going to have a few questions of my own at the end of this conversation?' she teased. 'And the first one is going to be, just when and where did you get to meet Patrick? As far as I'm aware, he's lived in New York for the last five years, and he's very rarely seen over here.'

Lilli kept her expression deliberately bland. 'Hey, I'm the one buying you dinner, remember,' she reminded her. She liked Sally very much, found her great fun to go out with, but she was also aware that her friend was the biggest gossip in London—that was the reason she had been the perfect choice for this conversation in the first place! 'Besides, just what makes you think I have met him?' She opened widely innocent eyes.

Sally gave a throaty chuckle, attracting the attention of several of the men at adjoining tables. Not that she seemed in the least concerned by this male interest; she was still looking thoughtfully at Lilli. 'Only a woman who had actually met Patrick would show this much interest in him; he's a presence to be reckoned with!'

Well, from all accounts—his account!—Lilli had met that challenge all too capably. 'I'm more interested in the business side of his life than his personal one.' Now that she had assured herself he wasn't married or seriously involved with anyone!

Sally shrugged. 'I've just told you he's based in New York. Chairman of Paradise Bank. Rich as Croesus. What else is there to know?'

His business connection to her father! 'English business interests?' she prompted skilfully.

'Oh, that one's easy,' the other woman returned. 'It was all in the newspapers a couple of months ago.' She smiled warmly at the waiter as he brought their main course.

Lilli barely stopped herself grinding her teeth together in frustration. What had been in the newspapers months ago? 'I was a little out of touch with things at the time,' she reminded Sally once they were alone again.

'I'm sorry, of course you were.' Sally at once looked contrite. 'Paradise Bank took over Cleveley Bank.'

Cleveley Bank... Her father's bank. But that still didn't make a lot of sense to Lilli. Bennett International Hotels had shown a profit since before she was born, so it couldn't possibly have anything to do with them.

'Personally, I thought it was wonderful news.' Sally grinned across at Lilli as she gave her a puzzled glance. 'It means Patrick will probably start spending more time in England. More chance for us eager women to make a play at being the second Mrs Patrick Devlin,' she explained. 'I could quite easily give up this round of parties and the bachelor-girl life if I had Patrick coming home to me every evening!'

'It wasn't enough for the first Mrs Devlin,' Lilli said sharply as she realised she was actually jealous of Sally's undoubted interest in Patrick. Ridiculous! The man was arrogant, insulting, dangerous. And she had spent last night in his arms...

'Sanchia was stupid,' Sally rejoined unhesitatingly. 'She thought Patrick was so besotted with her that he would forgive her little indiscretions with other men.' Sally shook her head disgustedly. 'What Patrick owns, he owns exclusively.'

Exactly what Lilli had thought earlier! 'Not even Patrick Devlin can own people,' she said quickly.

'You have met him!' Sally said speculatively.

She could feel the guilty colour in her cheeks. 'Perhaps,' she acknowledged grudgingly. Obviously Patrick hadn't spent any time at the party last night, otherwise Sally would have seen him there too...

'But you're not telling, hmm?' Sally said knowingly. 'Oh, don't worry, Lilli.' She lightly touched Lilli's arm. 'I wouldn't be telling anyone about it either if I had Patrick tucked away in my pocket. But you will invite me to the wedding, won't you?'

Lilli drew back in shocked revulsion at the very suggestion. 'I think you've misunderstood my interest, Sally—'

'Not in the least.' The other woman gave her a conspiratorial wink. 'And if you have him, Lilli, hang onto him.

There are dozens of women out there—including me!—who would snap him up given the chance!'

'But—'

'I won't tell a soul, Lilli,' Sally assured her softly. 'It will be our little secret.'

Perhaps her choice of informant hadn't been such a wise one, after all. Lilli had forgotten, in her need to know more about Patrick Devlin, just how much Sally loved what she considered a tasty piece of gossip—and how she loved sharing it with other people, despite what she might have just said to the contrary! The news of Lilli's interest in Patrick Devlin would be all over London by tomorrow if she didn't think of some way to avert it!

Her only hope seemed to be to give the other woman such a good time she wouldn't remember where they had spent the evening, let alone what they had talked about at the beginning of it—least of all Patrick Devlin.

A bottle of champagne later and Lilli wasn't sure what they had talked about either! Sally's suggestion that they go on to a club seemed an excellent idea. The restaurant staff seemed quite happy to see their last customers leave too, ordering a taxi to take them on to the club.

'I know I'm going to regret this some time tomorrow when I finally wake up,' Sally giggled as they got out of the taxi outside the club. 'But what the hell!'

Lilli's sentiments exactly. It seemed like years, not just months, since she had been out and enjoyed herself like this. Last night certainly didn't count!

She was enjoying herself, couldn't remember when she had had so much fun, dancing, chatting with friends she hadn't seen for such a long time, once again the life and soul of the party, as she always used to be.

'Well, if it isn't Just Lilli, come out to play once again,' drawled an all-too-familiar voice close behind her. 'It's our dance, I believe,' Patrick Devlin added forcefully—and before Lilli could so much as utter a protest she found herself on the dance floor with him.

And it wasn't one of the fast numbers she had danced to earlier, the evening was now mellowing out into early morning, and so was the music. Lilli found herself firmly moulded against Patrick's chest and thighs, his arms about her waist not ungentle, but unyielding nonetheless.

And Lilli knew, because she tried to move, pulling back to look up at him with furious green eyes. 'Let me go,' she ordered between gritted teeth.

God knew what Sally was going to make of this after their earlier conversation! Not that Lilli could be in the least responsible for this meeting; she hadn't even realised he was at the club, certainly hadn't seen him amongst the crowd of people here. But he had obviously seen her!

For all that she was tall herself, the high heels on her shoes making her even more so, she still had to tilt her head to look up into his face. 'I said—'

'I heard you,' he returned unconcernedly, continuing to move slowly in rhythm to the music, his warm breath stirring the loose tendrils of hair at her temples.

She glared up at him. 'I thought you didn't like parties,' she said accusingly. He had no right being here, spoiling her evening once again.

He glanced down at her. 'This isn't a party,' he dismissed easily. 'But you're right—I don't particularly like noisy clubs like this one. I came here to conclude a business deal.'

Business! She should have known he had a calculated reason for being here. 'Like last night,' she said waspishly.

His mouth tightened. 'Last night I expected a quiet dinner party with my sister, with perhaps a dozen or so other guests. Not including your father,' he bit out tersely.

'Or that madhouse I walked into—and as quickly walked out of again! To the kitchen, as it happens. Which was where I met you.'

Lilli stiffened in his arms. 'Earlier today you seemed to have the impression that *I* had deliberately found *you*,' she reminded him.

He shrugged unconcernedly. 'Earlier today I was talking to the haughty Elizabeth Bennett. Tonight you're Just Lilli again.' He looked down at her admiringly. 'I like your hair loose like this.' He ran one of his hands through her long, silky black tresses. 'And as for this dress...!' His eyes darkened in colour as he looked down at the figure-hugging black dress.

All Lilli could think of at that moment was that they were attracting too much attention. Obviously Patrick was well known by quite a lot of the people here, and the speculation in the room about the two of them was tangible. Especially as Sally was in the midst of one particular crowd, chatting away feverishly, Lilli sure their 'little secret' was no longer any such thing!

'I wouldn't worry about them if I were you,' Patrick followed her gaze—and, it seemed, her dismayed thoughts. 'Gossip, true or false, is what keeps most of them going. It's probably because they lead such boring lives themselves,' he added scornfully.

She knew he was right; it was one of the aspects of being part of a 'crowd' that she hadn't liked. But, even so, she wasn't sure she particularly liked being the subject—along with Patrick Devlin—of that gossip, either.

Patrick made no effort to leave the dance floor as one song ended and another began, continuing to guide her smoothly around. 'Forget about them, Lilli,' he suggested as she still frowned.

She would have liked to, but unfortunately she had a

feeling that by tomorrow half of London would believe she was involved in an affair with Patrick Devlin. And the other half wouldn't give a damn whom she was involved with—because they had never heard of her or Patrick!

'Lilli and Elizabeth Bennett are one and the same person.' She coldly answered his earlier remark.

'No, they aren't. Just Lilli is warm and giving, fun to be with. Elizabeth Bennett is as cold as ice.' He looked down at her with mocking grey eyes. 'I'm curious; which one were you with your ex-fiancé?'

How did he—? Not a single person she had met this evening had so much as mentioned Andy, let alone their broken engagement. Surely Patrick hadn't done the same as her—spent part of the day finding out more about her...?

If so, *why* had he?

'Don't bother to answer that, Lilli; I think I can guess.' Patrick grinned. 'If you had been Just Lilli with him then he would probably still be around—despite his other interests.'

Lilli deeply resented his even talking about her broken engagement. She had been deeply distressed by her mother's death, and then for Andy to walk out on her too...! It had seemed like a nightmare at the time.

She had just started to feel she was coming out of it when she had been plunged into another one—with the name of Patrick Devlin!

'Just Lilli is a pretty potent woman, you know.' Patrick's arms tightened about her as he moulded her even closer against his body, showing her all too forcibly just how 'potent' he found her! 'In fact, I haven't been able to get her out of my mind all day.'

She swallowed hard, not immune herself to the intimacy of the situation, her nipples firm and tingling, her thighs aching warmly. 'And Elizabeth Bennett?' she prompted huskily.

'A spoilt little rich girl who needs her bottom spanked,' he replied unhesitatingly.

Lilli gasped. How dared he—? Just who did he think he was, suddenly appearing in her life, and then proceeding to arrogantly—?

'And if I had been her fiancé that's exactly what I would have done,' he continued unconcernedly.

They were still dancing slowly to the music, the room still as noisy and crowded, and yet at the moment they could have been the only two people in the room, their gazes locked in silent battle, grey eyes calmly challenging, green eyes spitting fire.

Finally Lilli was the one to break that deadlock as she pulled away from him, ending the dance abruptly, the two of them simply standing on the dance floor now. 'I would never have agreed to marry you in the first place,' she told him insultingly.

Patrick shrugged, totally unmoved by her anger. 'But you will, Lilli,' he said softly. 'I guarantee that you will.'

'I—you— Never!' She spluttered her indignation. 'You're mad!' She shook her head incredulously.

'But not, thank God, about you,' he said calmly. 'I've been there, and done that. And I've realised that loving the person you marry is a recipe for disaster. I've found qualities in you that are infinitely more preferable.'

'Such as?' she challenged. She still couldn't believe they were having this conversation!

'Loyalty, for one. A true sense of family.' He shrugged. 'And, of course, I find you very desirable.' This last was added, it seemed, as an afterthought.

Loyalty? A sense of family! Desire! They weren't reasons for marrying someone— She was *not* going to marry Patrick Devlin!

He was mad. Completely. Utterly insane!

His mouth quirked with amusement as he saw those emotions flashing across her expressive face. 'A month, Lilli,' he told her softly. 'You will be my wife within the month.'

Lilli looked up at him frowningly; his gaze was enigmatic now. He sounded so sure of himself, so calmly certain…

She was not going to marry him.

She was not!

CHAPTER FOUR

'HE WHAT?' her father gasped as he once again sat across the breakfast table from her.

Lilli sighed, still slightly shell-shocked about last night herself. She had walked away from Patrick, and the club, after his ridiculous claim, still had trouble even now believing he could possibly have said what he did. But the bouquet of red roses, delivered early this morning, told her that Patrick had indeed stated last night that he intended marrying her.

Her father had been intrigued by the delivery of the roses when he'd joined her for breakfast, especially since there was no accompanying card with the flowers to say who they were from. But Lilli had no doubts who had sent them; only someone as arrogant as Patrick Devlin could have red roses delivered before the shops were even open!

'Your business associate, Mr Devlin, has decided he wants to marry me,' she repeated wearily, pushing her scrambled eggs distractedly about her plate. She couldn't possibly eat anything after the delivery of the roses!

Her father had lost interest in his bacon and eggs too now. 'What the hell did you do to him the other night?'

Lilli could feel the blush in her cheeks. She couldn't remember being with Patrick Devlin the night before last; she only wished she could. Well...part of her wished she could. The other part of her just wished it had never happened at all. Because Patrick wasn't going to let her forget it, that was for sure!

'I don't think his marriage proposal has anything to do with that,' she dismissed hurriedly.

Or did it? After all, he *had* said she was a ten...

Her father looked at her through narrowed lids. 'What does it have to do with, then?'

Lilli met his gaze steadily. 'You tell me?' She arched questioning brows.

'I have no idea.' Her father stood up, obviously having trouble coming to terms with this strange turn of events. *He* was having trouble coming to terms with it? *She* found it totally incredible.

'Why ever does he want to marry you?' Her father scowled darkly.

'Having already "had" me?' Lilli returned dryly.

'I didn't mean that at all!' Her father looked flustered. Dressed in a dark suit and formal tie and shirt, he was on his way to his office. Although he seemed in no hurry to get there... 'The two of you barely know— The two of you only met two days ago,' he hastily corrected as Lilli's expression clearly questioned his initial choice of words.

'Oh, don't imagine this proposal is based on love,' Lilli assured him. '"Loyalty" and "desire" were the words Patrick used.'

'Loyalty and—! Do you have "loyalty" and "desire" for him?' her father said incredulously.

She didn't even know the man!

Patrick Devlin was obviously a successful businessman, so she supposed he was to be admired for that, but whether or not he was an honest one was another matter. If her father's state of anxiety at being involved in business with him was anything to go by, then he probably wasn't.

As for desire… She supposed she must have wanted him the other night…

If she were honest, she had felt a stirring of that attraction towards him last night as well—'The whole thing is ridiculous!' She stood up abruptly too. 'The man has obviously tried marrying for love, and it was not a success, so now he seems to have decided to marry for totally different reasons.' Loyalty and desire…

Her father shook his head. 'Why does he want to marry at all?'

'It's time I provided the Devlin name with a couple of heirs,' drawled that all-too-familiar voice. The two of them turned to confront Patrick Devlin, a flustered Emily standing in the doorway behind him.

'I did ask Mr Devlin to wait, but—'

'Who knows?' Patrick continued softly. 'After the other night, perhaps Lilli is already pregnant with my child.'

Lilli gasped, her father went pale—and poor Emily looked as if she was about to faint!

Which wasn't surprising, in the circumstances. How dared Patrick Devlin just walk in here as if he owned the place? And make such outrageous remarks too!

Lilli turned dismissively to the young maid. 'That will be all, thank you, Emily.' She had no intention of giving the young girl any more information for gossip among the household staff.

'Perhaps you could bring us all a fresh pot of coffee?' Patrick Devlin smiled disarmingly at Emily before she could make good her escape. 'I'm sure we could all do with some,' he added dryly as he sat down—uninvited—at the dining-table.

Emily hesitated in the doorway, looking uncertainly at Lilli. Patrick Devlin might be behaving as if he owned the place, but Emily, at least, knew that he didn't!

'A pot of coffee will be fine, Emily,' Lilli said, waiting for the maid to leave and close the door behind her before turning to Patrick Devlin. 'What are you doing here?' she demanded, this man, with his arrogant behaviour, didn't deserve customary politeness!

He met her question unconcernedly. 'Waiting for fresh coffee to arrive,' he replied easily. 'Good morning, Richard. Has Lilli told you our good news?'

'If you're referring to that ridiculous marriage proposal,' her father blustered, 'then—'

'It isn't ridiculous, Richard,' Patrick cut in steadily. 'Ah, I see the roses arrived,' he said with satisfaction. 'I hope you like red roses?' He smiled across at Lilli.

There probably wasn't a woman alive who didn't, especially if you happened to be the lucky woman who received them. But in this case it depended who the sender was!

'You can't marry Lilli,' her father told the other man fiercely.

'Why not?' Patrick returned lightly. 'She isn't married already, is she?'

'No, of course not,' her father denied impatiently. 'But you—'

'I'm not married, either,' Patrick told him firmly. 'In which case, I can see no obstacle to our marrying each other.'

'But you don't know each other—'

'I know Lilli is beautiful. Popular—if last night is anything to go by. Well educated. And, as your daughter, an accomplished hostess. There's no doubting she's young, and she certainly seems healthy enough—'

'To provide you with those Devlin heirs you mentioned?' Lilli broke in disgustedly. 'You sound as if you're discussing buying a horse, or—or arranging a business contract, not considering taking a wife!'

'Marriage is a business, Lilli,' Patrick told her evenly, eyes coldly unmoving. 'And anyone who approaches it from any other angle is just asking for trouble. Not that it will be all business, of course,' he continued smoothly. 'I'm well aware of the fact that women like a little romance attached to things. I'm quite willing to play my role in that department too. If you think it necessary.' His derisive expression was indicative of his own feelings on the subject.

'Hence the sending of the roses,' Lilli guessed scornfully.

'Hence the roses.' He nodded in acknowledgement. 'Ah, coffee.' He turned to Emily as she came in carrying the steaming pot. 'Thank you.' He nodded to her, looking back at Lilli and her father once they were alone again. 'Shall I pour? Although you look as if you're on your way to your office, Richard, so perhaps you don't want another cup of coffee?' He quirked dark brows.

This man's arrogance was like nothing Lilli had ever encountered before; he had already taken over the staff, and now he appeared to be telling her father what to do too!

'Sit down and have some coffee, Daddy.' Lilli looked at Patrick pointedly as she resumed her own seat at the table—on the opposite side to him. 'I'm sure Patrick won't be staying very long.' She looked challengingly at the younger man.

'Oh, I'm in no hurry to leave,' Patrick replied, completely unperturbed by the fact that he obviously wasn't welcome here. 'I have nothing to do today until my business appointment with you this afternoon, Richard.' He looked across at the older man. 'You did ask my secretary for a three o'clock appointment, didn't you?' he queried pleasantly, pouring the three cups of coffee as he spoke.

Her father sat down abruptly. 'I did,' he confirmed gruffly.

'Good.' Patrick grinned his satisfaction. 'That means I'll have time to take Lilli to lunch first.'

'I—'

'You have to eat, Lilli.' Patrick gently forestalled her refusal.

'Not with you, I don't,' she told him heatedly; he wasn't being polite, so why should she be?

'What do you think, Richard?' He looked at Lilli's father. 'Don't you think Lilli would enjoy having lunch with me?'

Richard Bennett looked frustrated once again. 'I—'

'As my father won't be the one having lunch with you, his opinion on the subject is irrelevant!' Lilli snapped frostily.

Patrick raised dark brows at her vehemence. 'There speaks Miss Bennett,' he drawled, his expression innocent.

Too damned innocent! Lilli remembered all too well what his opinion of Elizabeth Bennett was!

'Mm, this is good coffee,' Patrick said appreciatively as he sipped the hot brew. 'I think I must have drunk too much champagne last night,' he opined ruefully.

Lilli glared at him. 'Is that your excuse for your outrageous announcement last night?' she said contemptuously.

'Do I take it you're referring to my marriage proposal?' He frowned.

'Of course.'

'Sorry for the confusion, but I don't consider it an "outrageous announcement",' he returned. 'Especially as I've made it again this morning. Several times,' he added in a bored voice.

'And I have dismissed it as ludicrous—several times!' Lilli told him with feeling.

'You know, Richard...' Patrick looked calmly across the table. 'You really should have taken Lilli in hand years ago—you've made the job of becoming her husband all the more difficult by not doing so!'

Lilli was so enraged by this last casually condemning remark about her independent nature that for a moment she couldn't even speak.

And her father laughed!

Considering he hadn't done so for some time, it was good to hear—but not at her expense! There was nothing in the least funny about this situation.

Her father looked a little shamefaced, sobering slowly. 'I'm sorry, Lilli.' He touched her hand in apology. 'It was just that—well—'

'He knows I'm right,' Patrick put in. 'Although I'm probably the first person brave enough to actually say as much.'

She had realised the first night she met him that he was very direct, but she hadn't known it was to the point of rudeness. What on earth had she been thinking of two nights ago, becoming involved with such a man? The trouble was, she hadn't been thinking at all, had just wanted to hit out and hurt, the way she had been hurt when she saw her father with Geraldine Simms.

How that had rebounded on her! Spending the night with Patrick had changed nothing—except that the man now seemed to think he was going to marry her! Oh, she had hurt her father, but he was still seeing Geraldine, and now she, it seemed, was stuck with the infuriating Patrick Devlin!

'Although I can quite easily see how it happened, Richard.' Patrick continued his conversation with her father. 'Lilli is the sort of woman you want to spoil.'

'Thank you.' Laughter still gleamed in her father's eyes. 'She was incredibly endearing as a little girl.'

'I can imagine.' Patrick nodded, turning back to Lilli. 'Make sure you stop me from spoiling our daughters, Lilli, because they're sure to look like you, and—'

'Daughters!' She gasped at the plural. 'How many children do you want?'

'You see, I knew you would come round.' Patrick grinned at her approvingly. 'I would like you to be mother to two sons and two daughters.'

Four children. 'You said "a couple of heirs" earlier,' she reminded him.

He shrugged. 'Four sounds a much better number. Besides, I'm sure you'll look even more beautiful when you're pregnant than you do now, so I'll—'

Her father stood up noisily, effectively cutting off the indignant reply he could see Lilli had been about to make. 'I'll leave the two of you to continue discussing this,' he said. 'And the outcome, as I've told you before—' he turned to Patrick with narrowed eyes '—will have no bearing whatsoever on our—business arrangement.'

'Agreed,' the other man conceded easily. 'Although, as your son-in-law, I could be more helpful to you…'

'I don't think so,' Lilli's father replied slowly, giving Lilli a considering look. 'As my son-in-law, you're likely to end up with a knife sticking in your back on your wedding night!'

Patrick's mouth twisted humorously. 'All the more reason for you to encourage the marriage, I would have thought,' he drawled.

'Ah, but then I would have to explain to Gerry how I let

this happen to the older brother she so obviously adores. And, as I know to my cost,' Richard dramatically added, 'an angry and upset Gerry is a force to be reckoned with!'

'But you have no personal objections to this marriage?' Patrick prompted.

'None at all-because it will never happen,' Lilli's father returned easily. 'I know my Lilli.' He kissed her lightly on the forehead in parting. 'I'll see you later, Devlin,' he said hardly before leaving the room.

Patrick turned back to Lilli with calm grey eyes. '*Does* he know you?' he asked. 'Did he really believe you could go off and spend the night with a man you had only just met?'

She could too easily recall the pained expression on her father's face yesterday morning. No, her father hadn't believed her capable of that. But then, neither had she!

Her head went back in haughty dismissal. 'No one has to spend a lifetime paying for the mistake of one night of stupidity any more.'

'Don't they?' Patrick said softly, standing up to move round the table to stand at her side. 'The other night wasn't stupid, Lilli,' he told her huskily as he pulled her easily to her feet to stand in front of him. 'I wouldn't still have it on my mind if it had been. You were warm and responsive, gave yourself—'

'Stop it!' she cut in desperately, not wanting to hear about what she couldn't even remember. Or did she...

Even as he spoke she had images flitting in and out of her head, of the two of them in bed together, of their bodies entwined, of Patrick's lips and hands on her body, of her own pleasure in those caresses—No! She didn't want to remember. It had been a mistake, and not one for which she intended paying for the rest of her life.

'But you were, Lilli,' Patrick told her, suddenly very close. 'And you did.'

He was too close! She could smell his aftershave, see black specks amongst the grey in his irises, feel the warmth of his breath on her cheek, knew—His mouth, as it claimed hers, was warm and gently caressing, his arms enfolding her against the hardness of his body, moulding her to each sinewed curve, deepening the kiss, desire and wanting suddenly taking over.

Lilli felt the same need, her body responding instinctively to the caress of his hands down her spine, shivers of delight coursing through her body, her mouth opening to the intimacy of his kiss, a feeling of hard possession sweeping over her.

It was the force of that feeling that made her at last struggle to be free of his arms. Yes, she responded to him. Yes, she could feel the heat in her body for him, for the need of him. But she didn't want to be possessed, by him or any other man. Especially not by Patrick Devlin!

Patrick felt her struggles and at once released her, his eyes dark with his own emotions as he looked at her. 'It would work between us, Lilli,' he whispered. 'What further proof do you want?'

Heated colour warmed her cheeks. 'Physically we—'

'Match completely,' he completed for her.

Lilli looked at him. 'We have a certain response to each other,' she allowed. 'But when you came here yesterday afternoon you believed I had spent the night with you for devious reasons of my own—reasons I'm still not fully sure of. Although I do know they involve my father, in some way.' She frowned. 'Last night when we met, your attitude towards me had changed yet again. For some reason you announced you wanted to marry me!' She shook her head, not acknowledging for the moment the fact that she had needed to see him again, anyway. His arrogant announcement about marrying her had made null and void any intention she might have had of asking him for the truth about his business dealings with her father. She would rather never know the truth about that than have to be nice to this man! 'You're inconsistent, as well as—'

'Not in the least, Lilli,' he interrupted smoothly, his eyes coolly grey once more. 'The things you just spoke of are the very reasons why I've realised you will make me an excellent wife.'

She became very still. 'I don't see how...'

'I'm under no illusions where you're concerned, Lilli,' he explained. 'I even respect the fact that you tried to help your father—'

'By—as you think—going to bed with you!' Her eyes glittered deeply green at the accusation.

He shrugged. 'By whatever means were at your disposal,' he countered. 'It shows loyalty to your father. And loyalty, if not love, is something to be admired in a wife. My wife,' he added softly.

That word again! She was not going to be his wife, no matter what warped logic he might have used to come to that decision. 'That's no guarantee I would be loyal to you,' she pointed out spiritedly. 'Why should I be? You're arrogant, domineering—'

'So are you,' he mocked in reply.

'And you seem to have some sort of hold over my father that no one will explain to me!' The last was said almost questioningly.

Patrick's mouth tightened. 'I agree with your father: business is business. Haven't I just explained that these two things are completely separate?'

'You don't "explain" things, Patrick,' she sighed. 'You simply make statements, and expect them to happen!'

He grinned. 'I think that's the first time you've called me Patrick. Plenty of other things, to my face, and otherwise, I suspect.' His grin widened to a smile. 'But never Patrick before.'

'It's your name. But you can be assured I'll never call you husband!' she said vehemently.

He seemed unconcerned. 'Never say never, Lilli. Stranger things have happened. I always said I would never marry again, but you see how wrong I was,' he reasoned patiently.

This man was so exasperating; she was going to scream in a minute! No wonder her father was having problems conducting business with him; he didn't listen to what anyone else had to say. About anything!

She gave an impatient shake of her head. 'Wasn't your first experience at marriage bad enough?' she challenged—and then wished she hadn't as his face darkened ominously. It was obviously still a sensitive subject... And it was also the reason he had no intention of marrying for love... She couldn't help wondering what the beautiful Sanchia had been like as a person, to have created such bitterness in a man as self-assured as Patrick...

'And what do you know of my first marriage?' he said softly—too softly. 'You would have been thirteen when I married, and sixteen when I divorced—in neither case old enough to be part of that scene.'

Lilli raised her eyebrows. 'You obviously continue to have gossip value, because people are still talking about it!'

'Indeed?' Patrick's voice became frostier. 'And what are these "people" saying about my marriage?'

She looked at him warily; obviously, despite his comment last night about the social gossips, he didn't like the thought that his own life might have been under discussion. 'Only that it didn't work out,' she answered evasively.

He met her gaze compellingly. 'And?'

'What else is there to say?' she said quickly, feeling decidedly uncomfortable now. She wished she had never mentioned his marriage! But she wouldn't have done so if he hadn't come out with that ridiculous statement about marrying her... 'A failed marriage, for whatever reason, is surely a good enough reason not to repeat the experience?'

Patrick gave an assenting nod of his head. 'As is a failed engagement,' he rejoined pointedly.

Lilli felt the heat of resentment in her cheeks. 'Now that isn't open for discussion,' she said sharply.

'Why not?' he taunted. 'The man was a fool. Given the same choices he was, I would have opted for the money *and* you. Although, for my own sake, I'm glad that he didn't.'

Lilli stared at him in frozen fascination. What was he talking about? She and Andy had been engaged for six months when he decided he no longer wanted to marry her, and that in the circumstances he couldn't continue to work for her father, either. It had been a terrible blow at the time, happening, as it did, at the same time as her mother's death. But she had got on with her life, hadn't even seen Andy since the day he broke their engagement. In fact, she had no idea where he was now. And she wasn't interested, either.

Although the comments Patrick had just made about him were rather curious...

'Would you?' she said. 'But then, you're rich in your own right.'

'True,' Patrick conceded dryly. 'Now isn't that a better prospect in a husband than a man who's only interested

in embezzling money from your father so that he can go
off with his male lover?'

Lilli's stare became even more fixed. He *was* talking
about Andy. She knew he was.

Could what he said possibly be true? Had Andy stolen money from her father? Before leaving with *another
man*...?

Andy had joined the company as her father's assistant two years ago, a tall blond Adonis, with a charm to
match—a charm Lilli, having become disenchanted with
the 'let's go to bed' attitude of the men in her social set,
had found very refreshing.

She had enjoyed his company too, often finding excuses to visit her father at his office, on the off chance
she might bump into Andy there. More often than not,
she had, although it had been a few months before he'd so
much as invited her to join him for lunch. Over that lunch
Lilli had found he was not only incredibly handsome, but
also very intelligent, enjoying the verbal challenge of him
as well as the physical one.

Looking back, she supposed she had done most of the
chasing, but she'd realised it must be awkward for him
as she was the boss's daughter. She had followed up that
initial lunch with an invitation of her own, so that she
might return the hospitality, suggesting the two of them
go out to dinner this time. Again Andy had been fun, a
witty conversationalist, and again he had behaved like
the perfect gentleman when it came time for them to part.

Lilli had been persistent in her interest in him, and after
that they'd had dinner together often. That her father ap-
proved of the relationship she hadn't doubted; in fact, he'd
seemed deeply relieved she was spending so much time
with his assistant and less time with her group of friends
who seemed to do nothing but party.

Lilli had been thrilled when Andy had asked her to marry him, and if she had been a little disappointed in his continued lack of ardour after their engagement she had accepted that it was out of respect for her, and could ultimately only bode well for their future marriage.

But now Patrick seemed to be saying something else completely, was implying that Andy's lack of physical interest in her hadn't stemmed from respect for her at all, but from the fact that his sexual inclinations lay elsewhere!

He also seemed to be saying that Andy's engagement to her had enabled him to steal from her father's company...

Admittedly, as her father's future son-in-law, Andy had been given more responsibility in the company, and as Lilli's mother's illness had deteriorated Andy had been left more and more in charge of things while her father spent time at home.

Had Andy used that trust in him to take the opportunity to steal from Bennett Hotels?

As she looked at Patrick, the certainty in his gaze, that contemptuous twist to his lips, she knew that was exactly what Andy had done. He had used her to cheat her father...!

The blackness was only on the outer edge of her consciousness at first, and then it seemed to fill her whole being. Darkness. No light. Her legs buckled beneath her as she crumpled to the carpeted floor.

CHAPTER FIVE

LILLIE COULDN'T FOCUS properly when she opened her eyes, but she did know enough to realise she was no longer on the floor of the dining-room, that someone—and that someone had to be Patrick Devlin!—had carried her through to the adjoining sitting-room and had laid her on the sofa there.

'My God, woman,' he rasped from nearby. 'Don't ever give me a scare like that again!'

He sounded angry—but then, he sounded like that a lot of the time!

What had she—? Why—?

Their conversation suddenly came flooding back in a sickening rush. Andy. Her father. The money...!

She moved to sit up, only to find herself pushed firmly back down once more.

'You aren't moving until I'm sure you aren't going to fall down again!' Patrick ordered as he bent over her, scowling darkly.

His expression alone was enough to make her want to shut her eyes and black out the world again, but even as she wished for that to happen she knew that the terrible truth would still be there when she was conscious again.

'Who else knows?' Her voice was barely audible. 'About Andy, I mean. The money. And—and the other man.' Her fiancé hadn't just walked out on her, which she had thought was bad enough—he had actually gone with another man!

Had the friends she'd spent the last two evenings with known about that? Had they all been laughing, or pitying her, behind her back? Had they all known that Andy's only reason for being with her at all was so that he had easier access to the Bennett funds? She didn't want to face any of them ever again if that were the case!

'I believe your father has managed to keep all of it in the family.' Patrick's mouth twisted wryly as he moved away from her. 'Besides, I'm more interested in the fact that you obviously didn't know. Not until I just told you. Did you?'

She drew in a shaky breath, sitting up, feeling at too much of a disadvantage lying supine on the sofa. She was at too much of a disadvantage with this man already! 'Obviously not,' she managed coolly. 'Who told you about—about Andy?'

'Gerry,' he said quietly. 'Yesterday. In an effort to warn me off you.'

'Which obviously didn't work,' Lilli returned, their conversation giving her the time she needed to collect her thoughts together—and God knew they had fragmented after Patrick's earlier revelation.

'Obviously not.' Patrick grinned. 'You didn't seem exactly heartbroken to me about the loss of your fiancé— even before you knew the truth about him!'

Too much had happened at that time for her to dwell on Andy's sudden disappearance from her life. Since her mother's death she had got through every day as it arrived; there had been no time to cry for her broken engagement. And now that she knew the truth she felt more like punching Andy on the nose than crying for him! How dared he used her in that way? How dared he abuse her father's trust in him?

She stood up, smoothing her pencil-slim black skirt down over her thighs, straightening her emerald-green cashmere sweater, before moving to stand before the mirror over the fireplace, tidying the wispy tendrils of her hair back into the neat plait that hung down her spine.

She could sense Patrick watching her as she smoothed her hair, could have seen his reflection in the mirror if she had chosen to turn her head slightly—but she didn't.

He and his sister were not 'family', even if her father was involved in an affair with Geraldine, even if Patrick did keep insisting he was going to marry her—and she hated the fact that her father seemed to have confided all of this to his mistress. She hated Geraldine Simms more than she had before because her father had confided in the other woman about Andy's betrayal and yet he hadn't told her!

Because now Patrick Devlin knew about it too...

'I'm afraid I'm busy for lunch today, Patrick.' She turned back to him casually.

His mouth quirked as he looked at her, his gaze mocking. 'And every other day, hmm?' he said knowingly.

Lilli calmly met his eyes. 'It is Christmas,' she shrugged.

But despite the numerous invitations she had received during the last few weeks she hadn't accepted any of them. She hadn't refused them either, had been too listless to bother with them. In view of what she had learned about Andy, she had no intention of accepting them now either. But Patrick Devlin didn't need to know that.

'I'm aware of what time of year it is,' Patrick replied. 'But I didn't think you were.' He looked around at the lack of any Christmas decorations in the room.

Neither she nor her father had felt like putting up a tree or their usual decorations this year. It would be their first Christmas without her mother, and so far neither of them had the heart for seasonal celebrations.

Although now that her father was involved with Geraldine Simms he might feel differently about that; the other woman's home had certainly been highly festooned with decorations at the party two days ago!

Lilli's mouth tightened, her eyes glacially green as she looked across at Patrick. 'We're still in mourning for my mother,' she stated flatly. Although she somehow didn't think her father was any more!

'Caroline.' Patrick nodded in acknowledgement of Lilli's mother. 'I met her several times. Before her illness curtailed her social life. She was a very beautiful woman. You look a lot like her,' he added softly.

Pain flickered in the depths of Lilli's eyes. Somehow it had never occurred to her that this man could have known her mother. Although, as he'd said, until her illness had incapacitated her a year before her death, her mother had been a familiar part of the social scene. Even her illness hadn't robbed her of her incredible beauty, the two of them often able to fool people into believing they were sisters rather than mother and daughter.

'I really do have to get on now, Patrick.' She gave a pointed look at her slender gold wristwatch.

To her chagrin he grinned across at her. 'Miss Bennett has spoken,' he taunted.

Angry colour darkened her cheeks at his continued insistence that she was two people. 'At least she's polite!' she snapped.

'To the point of coldness,' he acknowledged dryly. 'Why aren't you curious to know more about your ex-fiancée, Lilli?' His eyes were narrowed thoughtfully.

Because so much made sense now—Andy's initial reluctance to ask her out, his lack of ardour during their engagement. She didn't want to dwell on those things, felt humiliated enough already!

'My father will tell me anything I need to know,' she dismissed quickly.

Patrick gave a disgusted snort. 'He doesn't seem to have told you very much so far!'

She glared at him. 'My father is very protective of me.' She was positive that was the reason her father hadn't told her about Andy. She had been devastated by her mother's death, and to have learnt of Andy's complete betrayal at the same time would have been unbearable. In fact, the more she thought about it, the more she was sure Andy had chosen his timing for that very reason...! She had felt hurt before, but what she thought of Andy now wasn't even repeatable!

'To the point of stupidity, I now realise,' Patrick countered harshly. 'You simply have no idea.'

She swallowed hard at his accusing tone. She was beginning to realise, and she only loved her father all the more for trying to spare her further pain. Although it seemed to have caused him complications he could well have done without, including, she was sure, being at loggerheads with this man.

'The love of a parent for a child is all-forgiving,' she defended chokily, aware as she said so that it was time this 'child' stopped being cocooned and began to be of some help to her father. He had carried this heavy burden on his own for too long.

Possibly it was the reason he had become involved so quickly with someone so unsuitable as Geraldine Simms...?

In recent years, with her mother so ill, her father had

begun to confide in Lilli instead when it came to business matters, but she realised that for the last few months she had been too engrossed in her own pain to give him the attention he had so obviously needed. Which was why he had turned to someone outside the family for comfort.

'And the love of a child for the parent?' Patrick prompted softly.

Lilli gave him a sharp look. This man was too astute; he had guessed she was thinking of her father's involvement with his sister!

'Yes,' she answered unhesitating. She didn't like her father's involvement with Geraldine Simms, but after what she had just learnt of her father's recent worries she was no longer going to give him a hard time over it. She would just have to be around to help pick up the pieces when Geraldine tired of playing with him!

Patrick was still watching her closely. 'Do you like children, Lilli?'

She met his gaze defensively. 'Yes—did you think I wouldn't?' She and Andy had discussed the idea of having— She and Andy...! How ridiculous the idea of them having children seemed now!

Patrick shrugged. 'You didn't seem too keen earlier when I mentioned having four—'

'I like children, would dearly like some of my own,' Lilli interrupted firmly. 'I just don't intend for them to be yours!'

He looked totally unconcerned by her vehemence. 'But think of the social coup you will have made by getting me to the altar,' he mocked. 'I've made no secret of my contempt for the institution of marriage!'

As Sally had clearly told her last night. Certainly, walking off with the much coveted prize of Patrick Devlin as a husband would more than compensate for the humiliation of having had a fiancé who had left her for another man! But once all the excitement had died down she was the one who would be married to this man, and was a lifetime of his torment really worth that? At this moment in time, she didn't think so!

'Thank you for the offer—but no,' she said crisply.

He looked at her with assessing eyes. 'It won't be open for ever, you know,' he said.

She gave a wry smile. 'I never thought that it would.' She was still dazed he had asked her at all!

His mouth twisted mockingly. 'But the answer is still no?'

'Most definitely,' she agreed forcefully.

'For now,' he said.

Lilli looked at him suspiciously. She was still reeling from the shock of Andy's betrayal, couldn't even think straight yet. But she did know she didn't want to marry this man.

'I really do have things to do, Patrick,' she told him again firmly, wishing he would just leave now so that she could think.

He studied her for several seconds, and then he gave a brief nod. 'I have no doubts our paths will cross again,' he murmured huskily.

She didn't know how he could be so sure. They hadn't met at all in the previous five years. Admittedly, Patrick seemed to have lived in America for most of that time, but he had no doubt been in London on several occasions during those years, if only to see his sister, and Lilli had managed to avoid ever meeting him. The only connection she could scc between them now was the business he had with her father, and her father's relationship with his sister.

'Maybe,' she returned enigmatically.

He grinned again. 'But not if you can manage to avoid it!' he guessed.

'We've managed never to meet socially before, so perhaps it would be better if we left it that way,' she told him coolly.

'For whom?' he drawled. 'Having met you, Lilli, I'm in no hurry to lose you again.'

Was he never going to leave? She did have things to do—and going to see her father was top of that list. She intended speaking to him before his meeting with Patrick later this afternoon...

'And please don't say I've never had you to lose,' Patrick went on mockingly. 'You may have chosen to have a convenient memory lapse about the other night, but, believe me, I remember all of it!' he assured her.

She clearly, to her intense mortification, remembered waking up to the sound of him singing happily in the shower yesterday morning; he certainly hadn't sounded like a man dissatisfied with his night! But she hadn't 'chosen' to forget anything; she just didn't, apart from that brief memory flash earlier, remember what had happened between them that first night.

'I'm sure you do,' she dismissed briskly. 'But at the same time I doubt you ask every woman you go to bed with to marry you!'

He raised dark brows. 'In the last five years since my divorce?' he said thoughtfully. 'I think so—yes...' He nodded.

Lilli stared at him. Oh, Sally had said he didn't get involved, but— But Patrick couldn't really be saying she was the first woman he had been to bed with since his divorce. Could he...?

Patrick smiled at her stunned expression. 'It isn't exactly a secret, Lilli. Sanchia taught me never to trust anyone. Especially a woman,' he added hardly. 'And I never have,' he ground out harshly.

She drew in a sharp breath. 'I'm a woman,' she told him shakily.

'Undoubtedly so,' he agreed, touching her lightly on one creamy cheek. 'But I don't have to trust you to marry you. As I've already said, our marriage would be a business arrangement.'

She moved abruptly back from that caressing hand. 'No doubt with a suitable pre-nuptial agreement,' she derided scornfully.

He met her gaze steadily. 'That sort of agreement is only relevant if you intend divorcing each other at some later date. I have no wish to go through another divorce. The next time I marry it will be for life.'

She couldn't break her gaze away from his! She wanted to. Desperately wanted to. But she felt as if she was drowning in the depths of those dark grey eyes. And she knew he meant every word he said...!

She tilted her head back, flicking her plait back over her shoulder. 'No love, no divorce; is that the way it works?' she challenged, wishing she sounded a little more forceful. But she was seriously shaken by the determination of his gaze.

'Exactly.'

Lilli shook her head. 'I find that very sad, Patrick.' She frowned. 'Marriage should be for love.'

'Always?'

'Always,' she echoed firmly.

His mouth twisted. 'You can still say that, after the experience you've just gone through? With your parents' marriage as another shining example of marital bliss?' He shook his head. 'There's scepticism, and then there's stupidity, Lilli, and I'm very much afraid that you—'

'That is enough!' she cried, eyes as hard as emeralds now. 'Leave my parents out of this discussion. You know nothing about them or their marriage. All you know is that my father is now involved with your sister. But it won't last.' Her lips pursed disdainfully. 'Your sister's affairs never do.'

'And your father's affairs?' he taunted.

'My father doesn't have affairs!' Her cheeks were hot with indignation, her hands clenched angrily at her sides. 'Your sister has just caught him on the rebound from my mother's death. He wouldn't have looked at her twice while my mother was alive!' she added heatedly.

Patrick looked at her pityingly. 'Is everything this black and white for you, Lilli? No shades of grey at all?'

'My father brought me up never to accept less than the best,' she told him with passion. 'And so far I never have...!'

Patrick looked at her wordlessly for several long seconds, and then he slowly shook his head. 'And I hope—sincerely hope, Lilli—that you never do,' he murmured. 'And I mean that, Lilli. I really do.'

Somehow she believed him. 'Thank you,' she accepted.

His mouth quirked. 'Now go away?'

She gave a rueful smile. 'Yes.'

He laughed softly. 'I've enjoyed knowing you, Lilli. It's certainly never been boring. See me to the door?' he prompted throatily.

She had intended doing that anyway; as he had already said, she had been brought up to be a good hostess, and telling a guest to find his own way out, no matter who he was, was not polite! Besides, after trying to get him to leave for the last twenty minutes, she wanted to make sure he had actually gone!

'Certainly,' she agreed.

Patrick chuckled as the two of them walked down the hallway to the door, grinning as Lilli turned to him questioningly. 'You're very refreshing, Lilli; as far as I'm aware, you're the first woman who couldn't wait for me to go!' he explained self-derisively.

Not such a perfect hostess, after all! 'I—'

'Have things to do,' he finished for her. 'So you've already said.'

'Several times,' she reminded him playfully, relieved they had at last reached the door.

Patrick turned to her. 'Don't say goodbye, Lilli,' he murmured as she would have spoken. 'You may wish it were, but we both know it isn't.'

She knew no such thing! There was absolutely no reason—There was no time for further thought as Patrick bent down and kissed her!

And it wasn't a light kiss either, as he pulled her easily into his arms and moulded her body against his.

Lilli felt as if she was drowning, couldn't breathe, was aware of nothing but the possession of this man. And it was complete possession, of the mind, body, and senses.

She could only look up at him with dazed green eyes as he released her as suddenly as he had kissed her.

'No matter what you think to the contrary, neither of us can say goodbye to that, Lilli,' he told her gruffly in parting, the door closing softly behind him as he finally left.

Lilli didn't move, could hear the thunder of her own blood as it rushed around her body. She had been out with men before Andy, quite a few of them, but none of them, including Andy, had evoked the response that Patrick did. It was incredible. Unbelievable. Dangerous...! How could she respond to a man she didn't even like very much? For there was no denying the force of electricity that filled the air whenever they were together.

Well, despite what Patrick might have claimed to the contrary, she intended them not to be together again.

'Lilli...?' Her father stood up uncertainly from behind his desk, his eyes searching as he moved to kiss her lightly on the cheek in greeting. 'I didn't expect to see you again until this evening.' He looked at her a little warily, Lilli thought.

Which wasn't surprising, considering what she had learnt from Patrick earlier. Her father had carried that knowledge around with him for months now, and, on closer inspection, he looked grey with worry. Until today Lilli had put his gauntness down to the loss of her mother, but she now realised it was so much more than that. But she had no intention of letting him worry alone any longer.

She had been lucky when she'd arrived at his office a few minutes ago, his secretary able to happily inform her he was alone, and could see her immediately. Her father didn't look quite so pleased to see her!

Lilli looked at him with wide, unblinking eyes. 'Exactly how much money did Andy take?' she said evenly. 'And what are you doing about it?'

Her father staggered, as if she had actually hit him, sitting back down in the leather chair behind his desk, his face white now, eyes as green as her own gleaming brightly.

Her own legs felt slightly shaky, she had to admit, knowing from her father's reaction to those two simple questions that Patrick had told her the truth about Andy's disappearance. And, having told her the truth about the money, he no doubt had also told her the truth about whom Andy had gone away with...!

'Oh, Daddy!' She moved around the desk to hug him. 'You should have told me,' she said emotionally.

'No prizes for guessing exactly who did,' he muttered bitterly.

She moved back slightly to look down at him, her own eyes glittering with unshed tears. 'It's irrelevant who did the telling, Daddy. And to give Patrick his due,' she added grudgingly, 'he didn't realise I didn't already know.'

Her father's smile came out as more of a grimace. 'Did he survive the telling unbruised?'

Her mouth twisted at the memory of their conversation. 'Physically, yes. Verbally—probably not.' She shrugged. 'But I'm really not interested in Patrick Devlin's feelings just now; he isn't important.'

'I'm afraid he is, Lilli,' her father sighed. 'Very much so, in fact.'

She moved to sit on the edge of his desk. 'Tell me,' she invited.

It wasn't very pretty in the telling, and for the main part her father avoided meeting her gaze. It was more or less as Lilli had worked out in her own mind; Andy had used her father's preoccupation with his wife's illness to embezzle money from the company.

'How much?' she prompted softly.

'A lot—'

'How much Daddy?' she said forcefully.

He swallowed hard. 'Several million—'

'Several million!' Lilli repeated incredulously. 'Oh, my God…!' she groaned—this was so much worse than she had thought. Her eyes widened. 'That's why Patrick is involved in this, isn't it?' she realised weakly.

Her father scowled darkly. 'He had no right telling you that part,' he rasped harshly.

'He didn't,' she assured him shakily. 'I'm not completely stupid, Daddy; I can add two and two together and come up with the correct answer of four. Andy stole money from you, Patrick is a banker, you are now having difficult business discussions with Patrick; it isn't hard to work out that the two things are connected!'

'I wish to God they weren't!' Her father stood up abruptly, his expression grim. 'The money that Andy took was made through transactions at Cleveley Bank. It had been put in a separate account, ready to pay a loan we took out just over a year ago when we expanded into Australia. The loan was due for repayment two months ago. But when I accessed the account before that I found all the funds had been redirected out of the country,' he recalled heavily, even the memory of it, Lilli could see, bringing him out in a cold sweat.

'Into an account in Andy's name,' she easily guessed.

'Yes,' her father acknowledged dully.

'And Patrick now owns Cleveley Bank,' she said flatly. 'That's why the two of you have been locked in some sort of negotiation.'

Her father nodded. 'And Devlin won't give an inch.'

'But surely if you're prosecuting Andy Patrick can't just—'

'I'm not prosecuting Andy, Lilli,' her father told her.

'What?' she cried. 'But why on earth not? If you bring a case against Andy surely the bank can't— It's because of me, isn't it?' she suddenly realised, becoming very still. 'You haven't charged Andy because you don't want to involve me in this,' she groaned, realising this was what Patrick had meant earlier about the extent of her father's protectiveness of her. Well she knew now, and she had no intention of letting this situation continue. 'Daddy, I know all about Andy, about the money, about—about the other man.' She gave a pained grimace as he looked at her worriedly. 'And when you have your meeting with Patrick this afternoon I want you to tell him you are in the process of bringing a case against Andy. There's no way he can continue to hound you in this way if you're involved in a court case to try and retrieve the money.' Even as she spoke she wasn't sure of the truth of that statement.

She wasn't really sure how her father would stand legally even if he were prosecuting Andy over the theft of the money. And from what she had gathered from Patrick's comments the night she had met him—comments she now understood completely!—his sister's pleadings on behalf of her lover hadn't moved him, so perhaps this was going to make no difference to him either. After all, her father was the one who owed the money, and it probably wasn't the business of the bank if that money had been embezzled...

Her father sighed again wearily. 'Lilli, if I bring charges against Andy, then the whole story will come out.'

'I'm aware of that.'

'And you will end up looking totally ridiculous,' he continued gravely.

Her mouth twisted wryly. 'It won't be the first time!'

'I mean seriously humiliated, Lilli.' Her father shook his head. 'Andy's sexual inclinations are of no interest to anyone at this moment, but they will make headlines when put together with his engagement to you and his embezzling money from me. You would end up a laughing-stock, Lilli, and I won't have that,' he stated determinedly.

'At any price?' she prompted softly.

His mouth tightened stubbornly. 'At any price.'

Her expression softened lovingly, her smile a little shaky. 'I appreciate what you're saying Daddy. And I thank you for your loving protectiveness. But there's really no need,' she added brightly. 'You see, I won't end up a laughing-stock at all. Because I intend marrying Patrick Devlin!'

The answer to the problem was suddenly so simple. As Patrick had said, he was a good catch as a husband—and no one could possibly laugh at her, or pity her over her engagement to Andy, when she had managed to captivate such an eligible man as Patrick Devlin.

There was also the additional fact that, although Geraldine's pleadings on her lover's behalf might have fallen on stony ground, Patrick could hardly appear callous enough to the business world as to actually hound his own father-in-law.

Her marriage to Patrick was the answer to all their problems...

CHAPTER SIX

'LILLI!' GERALDINE SIMMS looked totally stunned as her maid showed Lilli into her sitting-room. She stood, very beautiful in slim-fitting black trousers and an even more fitted black jumper, her hair a tumble of deep red onto her shoulders and down her spine, her expression of surprise turning to one of wariness. 'What can I do for you?' she asked slowly.

Lilli steadily returned the other woman's stare, seeing Geraldine as men must see her—as her own father must see her! She was a self-assured woman of thirty-two, and there was no doubting Geraldine's beauty—almost as tall as Lilli, with that gorgeous abundance of red hair, eyes of deep blue, her face perfectly sculptured.

No wonder her father was smitten!

Lilli mouth tightened as she thought of Geraldine's relationship with her father. 'You can tell me where I might find Patrick,' she said abruptly. Contacting the man seemed to be her problem at the moment, and as her father had refused to tell her where Patrick's office was Lilli had had no choice but to come to Geraldine.

In fact, her father was proving altogether difficult at the moment where Patrick was concerned. Richard Bennett had been horrified by her announcement that she intended marrying Patrick, and had flatly refused to have any part of it when Lilli had proved stubbornly decided on the matter, to the point where he wouldn't even tell her where he was meeting with Patrick this afternoon. So, much as Lilli had wanted to avoid the other woman, Geraldine had seemed the obvious source—was sure to know, as he was a guest in her home, where her brother was.

'Patrick?' Geraldine looked even more startled. 'Why do you want to see Patrick?'

Lilli stiffened. She hadn't relished the idea of coming here at all, wished there were some other way of contacting Patrick; she certainly didn't intend to engage in a dialogue with Geraldine! 'I believe that's between Patrick and myself,' she returned coolly. The pluses of accepting Patrick's proposal far outweighed the minuses, but at the top of the minuses was definitely the fact that this woman was his sister!

Geraldine shook her head. 'Lilli—'

'I believe Lilli said it was private between the two of us, Gerry,' Patrick interjected as he strolled into the room, wearing a dark blue business suit and white shirt now, obviously dressed for the office. 'Did you decide to accept my lunch invitation, after all?' He turned enquiringly to Lilli.

'Yes,' she agreed thankfully. She hadn't actually expected him to be here, had no intention of accepting his marriage proposal in front of his sister. She had never been so pleased to see him!

'Fine.' He took a firm hold of Lilli's arm. 'See you later, Gerry,' he added dismissively, turning Lilli firmly toward the door.

'But—'

'Later, Gerry,' Patrick repeated hardly.

Lilli released her arm from Patrick's grip as soon as they were outside, silent as he unlocked his car before opening the door for her to get inside. She was silent, because at this moment she couldn't think of anything to say. Now that she was actually face to face with Patrick again, the enormity of what she was about to do was quite mind-boggling. How could she agree to be this man's wife, bear his children? But, by the same token, how could she not?

'Save it until we get to the restaurant.' Patrick reached out and briefly clasped her clenched hands as they lay in her lap, his eyes never wavering from the road ahead. 'I booked a table for one o'clock.'

She turned to him sharply. 'You booked...? You knew I would have lunch with you all the time?' Anger sharpened her voice.

'I—hoped that you would change your mind,' he answered carefully.

He had known she would have lunch with him after all. What else did he know...?'

Lilli gave him an assessing look before turning her head to stare rigidly out of the front windscreen. She felt as a mouse must do when being tormented by a cat—and she didn't like the feeling any more than the mouse did! This man always seemed to be one step ahead of her, and in a few short minutes she was going to agree to be his wife. What on earth was her life going to be like, married to him?

Even the restaurant he had chosen had been picked with privacy in mind, each table secluded in its own booth, the service quietly discreet as they were shown to one, Patrick obviously known here as he was greeted with obsequious politeness; Lilli, as his guest, was treated with that same solicitousness.

'Is it too early to order champagne?' Patrick asked her lightly as the waiter hovered for their drinks order.

Lilli's chin rose defiantly, she might be down, but she

wasn't defeated! 'As long as it's pink,' she told him haughtily. 'I never drink any other sort of champagne.'

Patrick's mouth twisted wryly. 'I'll try to remember that.' He turned to the waiter. 'A bottle of your best pink champagne,' he ordered.

'I don't think I've ever been here before.' Lilli gave a bored look round the room once they were alone again, noting how it was impossible, from the angle at which the booths were placed, to see any of the other people dining at the adjoining tables. 'It looks like the ideal place for a man to bring his mistress without fear of them being seen together,' she added scathingly.

Patrick smiled at her description. 'I wouldn't know,' he drawled, also looking casually about them. 'But you could be right.' He turned back to her. 'The food is excellent.' He indicated she should look at the menus they had been given.

Lilli looked at him for several long seconds, until she could withstand the laughter in his eyes no longer. 'The food,' she finally conceded, looking down at her menu.

'And the company,' Patrick added softly. 'Just Lilli,' he murmured huskily.

And she had been trying so hard to be Elizabeth Bennett. Damn him!

Her mouth tightened. 'Let's just get this over—'

'The champagne, Lilli,' he cut in softly, drawing her attention to the waiter waiting to pour their bubbling wine.

She drew in a ragged breath, sitting back in her seat while the champagne was poured into their glasses. She really did just want to get this over with now, and these constant interruptions weren't helping her at all.

Patrick raised his glass in a toast as soon as their glasses were full. 'To us, Lilli,' he stated firmly. 'Or am

I being a little premature?' he prompted as she made no move to pick up her own glass.

'How long have you known?' she said heavily. 'That I would marry you,' she explained as he raised questioning brows.

He shrugged. 'I told you last night as we danced, but I suppose I actually realised the merits of it after I had left you yesterday afternoon—'

'I mean, how long have you known I would marry you?' she cut in impatiently, glaring at him frustratedly.

'Oh, that.' He sipped his champagne before glancing down at his menu.

'Yes—that,' she bit out tautly. 'You really are the most arrogant, infuriating—'

'I love it when you talk to me like that.' He grinned. 'No one else does, you know. Except Gerry, and— I realise you don't even like the mention of her name.' He frowned and she flinched. 'But she is my sister, and as such will become your sister-in-law once we're married.'

Lilli met his remark coldly. 'Even so, I don't see that I have to have anything to do with her.'

'Lilli—'

'I mean it, Patrick,' she told him. 'I accept your marriage proposal—but it won't all be on your terms!'

'I never for a moment thought it would—'

'Oh, yes, you did.' Her eyes flashed deeply green. 'But you chose me because of the person I am, and that means the whole person; no matter what you think to the contrary, Lilli and Elizabeth Bennett are not two divisible people—and neither of them wants anything to do with your sister!'

'Hmm, this is difficult,' Patrick murmured thoughtfully.

'Not as difficult as trying to pretend the two of us will

ever accept each other! She's your sister. I will be your wife. The two of us—'

'I wasn't referring to that situation,' Patrick dismissed with a wave of his hand. 'I simply don't know whether to have the salmon or the pheasant for lunch.' He pursed his lips thoughtfully as he studied the menu once again.

Lilli stared at him incredulously. Did nothing trouble this man? Did he make a joke out of everything?

'No, Lilli, I don't,' he murmured softly as if reading her mind, reaching out to clasp one of her hands with his as it lay on the table-top. 'Close your mouth, my darling, and stop upsetting yourself,' he teased. 'The problem between you and Gerry will sort itself out in its own good time. You're both adult women. And I have no intention of interfering.'

Lilli wasn't incredulous any more, she was stunned. 'Darling'. He had called her his 'darling'... And as her husband he would have a perfect right to call her any endearment he pleased. He would have the right to do a lot more than that!

She hastily removed her hand from beneath his. 'I want a long engagement—'

'No,' he cut in calmly, to all intents and purposes still studying his menu.

Colour heightened her cheeks. 'I told you this isn't going to be all on your terms,' she reminded him tautly.

He gave a brief nod. 'And I agreed it wouldn't,' he said. 'But a long engagement is out of the question. With a special licence we can be married before Christmas.'

Lilli gasped. 'Before—! You can't be serious,' she protested, sitting forward. 'It's only nine days away; I can't possibly be ready to marry you between now and then!'

'Of course you can,' he assured her smoothly. 'Now I suggest we order our meal,' he added pleasantly as the waiter approached their table. 'I have a meeting at three o'clock,' he reminded her.

His meeting was with her father. They really didn't have the time before that meeting to sort this out properly. She couldn't decide on the rest of her life in an hour and a half!

'I haven't even had a chance to read the menu yet,' she told him dully; she had looked at it, but she hadn't actually read it.

'Another few minutes,' he told the waiter pleasantly.

Lilli shook her head. 'I'm really not hungry.'

Grey eyes looked compellingly into hers. 'You have to eat, Lilli.'

She swallowed hard. 'I really don't think I can—'

'Avocado salad and the salmon,' Patrick told the waiter decisively. 'For both of us.' He turned back to Lilli once they were alone again. 'I'll agree to any other terms you care to suggest, Lilli,' he offered. 'But the timing of our marriage is not for negotiation.' His mouth tightened. 'I have no intention of your father settling his problem with Andrew Brewster—and you breaking our engagement so fast you end up bruising yourself in your speed to get my ring off your finger!' His eyes glittered coldly as he looked at her between narrowed lids.

'A 'barracuda in a city suit' was how her father had described this man—and how right he was. Breaking off the engagement was exactly what she had been hoping to do! She really didn't want to be married to this man, had hoped—oh, God, she had hoped her father would be able to solve his financial problems without her actually having to go through with marriage to Patrick Devlin.

She should have known Patrick would see straight through any ideas like that!

Her head went back proudly, her eyes glittering

brightly. 'I suppose you've decided what I'm to wear for this wedding, too?'

'White, of course, Lilli.' He sipped his champagne, surveying her over the rim of his glass. 'Or are you telling me you don't have the right to wear that colour?' he challenged tauntingly.

'You can ask that, after the other night?' she scoffed.

'Our night together?'

'Of course our night together! Or doesn't it count if the bridegroom was the lover?'

Patrick looked at her thoughtfully for several long seconds. 'I think I should make one thing plain, Lilli,' he finally said. 'My first marriage, after the initial honeymoon period, was a battleground. It's not an experience I care to repeat!'

'Then why choose to marry someone you don't love and who doesn't even pretend to love you?' Lilli asked sceptically.

'Respect, Lilli. I have respect for you, for the love and loyalty you've shown towards your father—'

'A love that gives you the leverage to pressurise me into marrying you!' she accused heatedly.

His facial muscles tightened. 'I believe we both said we would keep my business with your father out of this?'

'You don't honestly think I would give marrying you a second thought if it weren't for that, do you?' She shook her head scathingly.

'It wasn't mentioned in the proposal. And I don't believe it was mentioned in the acceptance?' He raised dark brows pointedly.

'It may not have been mentioned, but—'

'Let's leave it that way, hmm?' His voice was dangerously soft now.

Lilli surveyed him mutinously, silenced by the coldness in his voice. But he couldn't seriously expect her to act as if she were in love with him? That would be asking the impossible!

She drew in a ragged breath. 'Patrick—'

'Our food, Lilli.' He sat back as the avocado was placed in front of them.

This was ridiculous. They couldn't possibly discuss something as important as the rest of their lives over lunch, with the constant interruptions that entailed. How on earth did he think—?

'Try the avocado, Lilli,' Patrick encouraged gently. 'I think we might both feel a little more—comfortable, once we've eaten something.'

She very much doubted this man knew what it was like to feel uncomfortable. But he was probably right about the food settling her ragged nerves; she hadn't eaten anything at all today. The only problem with that was that her stomach was churning so much she wasn't sure she would keep the food inside her if she ate it!

'Try it, Lilli.' Patrick held a forkful of his own avocado temptingly in front of her mouth.

She gave him a startled glance, slightly alarmed by his close proximity. But the determined look in his eyes told her he wasn't about to move away until she took the avocado from the fork he held out.

'This is ridiculous,' she muttered as she moved slightly forward to take the food into her mouth. 'Anyone would think we were a couple really in love,' she added irritably before moving back from him, picking up her own fork to eat her meal.

'Better?' He nodded his satisfaction with her compliance.

She had to admit, inwardly, that the food was indeed excellent, and it wasn't choking her as she had thought it might—but Patrick treating her as a recalcitrant child was! 'Don't treat me like a six-year-old, Patrick—'

'Then don't act like one,' he came back swiftly. 'I certainly don't want a temperamental child for a wife! Think, Lilli,' he continued hardly. 'Your father—does he know you've come to accept my proposal…?'

She swallowed. 'Yes.'

'And?'

'And what?' She frowned her tension.

Patrick's mouth twisted mockingly. 'And he's ecstatic at your choice of husband?' he taunted.

She gave a snort. 'Don't be ridiculous—'

'Exactly,' Patrick acknowledged dryly. 'As Gerry is going to be overjoyed at my choice of wife!'

Lilli stiffened. 'I'm really not interested in how your sister feels about me.'

'And your father's approval is of little importance to me, either,' he returned. 'But, if I'm correct in my assumption concerning your reasons for accepting my proposal, after all, then it's primarily to help your father, but also because once your father prosecutes Brewster the man's private life is bound to become public knowledge. But you will obviously have caught a much bigger fish on your marital hook, and so have no fear of becoming the object of the scorn or gossip that could ensue. Stop me if I'm wrong—'

'You know you aren't!' she snapped resentfully; did this man know everything? 'But exactly where is all this leading to?' she prompted impatiently.

'This is leading to the fact…' he deliberately held another morsel of avocado temptingly in front of her, leaning intimately forward as he did so '…that our engagement, and subsequent marriage, will be more believable to everyone, including your father and my sister, if it seems that we are genuinely in love with each other.'

Lilli stared at him as if he had gone insane—because at that moment it seemed he actually might be! No one could possibly believe the two of them really loved each other, least of all her father.

'Without that belief, Lilli,' Patrick continued, 'everyone will know the whole thing is a sham—and you will end up looking more foolish than if this whole thing had become public months ago!'

He was right... Once again he was right! Why hadn't she thought of that? Because she hadn't been thinking at all, only feeling, and this marriage to Patrick had seemed to solve everything.

She swallowed hard. 'What do you suggest?'

His mouth quirked. 'That you eat this avocado; it's in danger of falling off my fork!'

She was in danger of being at the centre of the biggest social farce to become public in years!

She ate the avocado, knowing as she did so exactly what she was committing herself to. The avocado, for all Patrick was making light of it, represented something so much more than a morsel of food. It took all of her willpower to chew it and actually swallow it down.

Patrick touched her cheek gently. 'I'm willing to give this a try if you are, Lilli.'

What choice did she have? She wanted her father to do something about the money that had been taken from his company, and for that to happen the whole thing had to become public. And it would only work if she and Patrick had a believable relationship.

She drew in a ragged breath. 'I'm not sure I can,' she told him honestly.

'I'll try and make it easy for you.' He leant forward

and brushed his lips against hers. 'There, that wasn't so difficult, was it?'

He was so close, his breath was lightly ruffling the hair at her temples. So close she could see the dark flecks of colour in his grey eyes. So close she could smell the elusiveness of his aftershave. So close she couldn't stop the slight trembling of her knees, the tight feeling in her chest, the disruption of her breathing.

'Not so difficult,' she admitted gruffly.

'And do you agree it will be better than people thinking we hardly know each other?' he teased.

That was the last thing she wanted! 'I agree.'

'The wedding will be next week—I thought a three out of three in the agreeing department was expecting a bit much!' He grinned as she looked panicked at the suggestion. 'It will fit in with the idea of a whirlwind romance,' he explained. 'Everyone loves a romance, Lilli—especially if it appears a love-match!'

Her stomach had given a sickening lurch at the very thought of being married to this man in only a matter of days. She swallowed hard. 'That sounds—reasonable.' What difference did it make? Patrick intended them to be married, had no intention of her dragging out their engagement in the hope she might never need to tie the knot. So she might as well get on with it!

He sat back so that their plates could be taken away— and allowed Lilli to breathe again!

This man was going to be her husband. They would live together. Patrick would come to know her body more intimately than she knew it herself. He— She was panicking again! Take each step as it comes! she told herself. If she looked at the whole thing she would become hysterical. Yes, that was it; she just had to take each day, each step, as it arrived. She would be fine. After all—'Make sure you have a white dress for the wedding, Lilli.' Patrick interrupted her thoughts. 'I'm aware you've been desperately trying to forget the night we spent together, but—'

'Please,' she hastily cut in. 'That night was completely out of character. I have never done anything like that before, and—'

'And you haven't done anything like that now, either, Lilli,' Patrick dismissed mockingly.

'How can you possibly say that?' She shook her head in self-disgust. 'I—'

'You were very beautiful that night, Lilli, very alluring, and I have to admit that, for the first time in years, I was physically interested. And I would probably have been only too happy to enjoy all the pleasure you were so obviously promising. Unfortunately—' he shook his head dramatically '—the champagne and wine took their toll on you, and you fell asleep on the bed in the hotel while I was in the bathroom.'

Lilli stared at him, not sure she was hearing him correctly.

He laughed softly at her stunned expression. 'I can see you're having trouble believing me. But I can assure you it's the truth.'

'But I—I was undressed,' she protested disbelievingly. She could clearly remember her embarrassment the next morning when she'd woken up to find she was only wearing her lace panties!

He nodded. 'You most certainly were. And you have a very beautiful body. But the only reason I know that, the reason you were undressed, is because I couldn't let you spoil that beautiful gown you were wearing. You looked lovely in it, and I'd like to see you in it again one day. You were asleep, so I simply took the dress off you and settled you more comfortably beneath the bedclothes.'

'And you—where did you sleep?' She was still reeling from the shock of realising she hadn't made love with this man at all.

But that memory flashback she had had...? She couldn't have dreamt being in his arms, being kissed by him, caressed by him—could she?

Patrick smiled. 'There was only the one double bed in the bedroom, Lilli, and I have to admit I'm not that much of a gentleman; I slept beside you, of course. And very cuddly you were too. In fact, you became quite charmingly friendly at about four o'clock in the morning,' he added wistfully. 'But there was no way I could make love to a woman who was too much asleep still to know where she was, let alone who she was with—'

'Stop it!' she cut in sharply. 'What you're saying is incredible.' She shook her head dazedly. 'How do I know you're telling the truth?' She frowned her uncertainty.

He gestured carelessly. 'What reason do I have to lie? It wouldn't do my reputation any good at all if it became public knowledge that I'd spent the whole night in bed with you and didn't even attempt to make love to you! Although, in retrospect, I can't say I'm disappointed by the fact. Unless I'm very much mistaken,' he continued at her questioning look, 'you have more right than most to wear white on your wedding day. And our wedding night will be the first time you've ever made love with any man. I feel very privileged that I'm going to be that man,' he added huskily.

This was incredible. Unbelievable...! But, as Patrick had so rightly pointed out, what reason could he possibly have for lying about it?

But until just now he had let her continue to think— Knew what she had believed had happened between them, and he hadn't disabused her of that belief.

She really had thought she had made love with this man two nights ago, had had no reason to think otherwise. And Patrick had perpetuated that belief with his remarks after that night, had known how she hated the idea of having gone to bed with him in that reckless way. He had continued to let her believe it…

Because it suited him to. Because he had enjoyed watching her discomfort over an incident she would rather forget had happened.

And she had just agreed to marry this man, to live with him, to bear his children. All four of them!

She had, she now realised, made a pact with the devil himself!

CHAPTER SEVEN

'I BELIEVE WE have guests coming to dinner this evening?' Lilli's father addressed her stiffly when he came in from his office a little after six; Lilli was in the day-room pretending to be interested in a magazine.

Pretending, because she couldn't really concentrate on anything at the moment!

How she had got through the rest of the lunch with Patrick, she had no idea. She vaguely remembered him talking about trivial things through the rest of their meal, seeming unconcerned with her monosyllabic answers, putting her in a taxi at two forty-five, so that he could go to his meeting with her father. His parting comment, she now remembered, had been something about them dining together this evening, so that her father could get used to the idea of him as a son-in-law.

But, however long his meeting with her father had taken, Patrick had somehow also found the time to call a prestigious newspaper and have notice of their forthcoming marriage put in the classifieds!

Lilli knew all about this because a reporter from the newspaper had telephoned her here just over an hour ago wanting further information on their whirlwind romance. Lilli's answer to this had been, 'No comment.' But not ten minutes later Sally had also telephoned to find out if it was true; it seemed a friend of a friend also worked on the newspaper, and, knowing Sally was a friend of Lilli's, had telephoned her for information. Which Sally couldn't give, thank goodness—because she didn't know any of the details of Lilli's relationship with Patrick!

There was no doubt that Patrick was going to give her no chance for second thoughts, was making this marriage a foregone conclusion by publicly announcing it.

Not that Lilli could have had second thoughts even if she had wanted to. But, Patrick being Patrick, he had made sure that she couldn't, not without causing even more publicity for herself.

She looked up at her father with dull green eyes, noting how strained he looked, matching her own dark mood of despair. 'Guest,' she corrected flatly.

'Guests,' her father insisted as he came further into the room, moving to the tray of drinks on the side table, pouring himself a liberal amount of whisky, swallowing half of the liquid down in one needy gulp. 'Patrick is bringing Gerry with him,' he told Lilli abruptly before swallowing the remaining contents of the glass he held.

This information brought Lilli out of her mood of despondency, her eyes now sparkling angrily. 'He is not bringing that woman to this house,' she stated furiously. 'I told him earlier exactly how I felt about his sister. He knows that I—'

'Lilli, Gerry isn't only Patrick's sister, she's the woman in my life,' her father cut in carefully. 'And while you might have strong feelings about that—in fact, I'm sure you do!—I would rather not hear them.'

'But—'

'I mean it, Lilli,' he told her in a voice that brooked no further argument. 'Now, as my banker, Patrick has advised that I go ahead with bringing a case against Andy for embezzlement,' he continued without a pause. 'He also told me the two of you are to be married before Christmas!'

Lilli's anger against Geraldine Simms left her so suddenly she felt like a deflated balloon. 'If that's what Patrick says, then it must be true,' she told him dryly.

'Lilli—'

'It's what I want, Daddy.' She stood up forcefully, moving restlessly about the room, tidying objects that didn't really need tidying.

'Do you also want to go and live in New York?' he asked.

'New York…?' Lilli stopped her restless movements, staring at her father. 'Did you say New York?'

Her father nodded. 'It's where Patrick is based. His business in England is almost concluded,' he added bitterly. 'He'll be returning to New York in the New Year. And, as his wife, you will go with him.'

She had to admit, she hadn't given much thought to where they would live after their wedding; she was still having trouble coming to terms with the idea of marrying Patrick at all! But New York…! She had completely forgotten he was based in America…

'Lilli, you haven't really thought this thing through at all,' her father sighed as he saw her confused expression. 'You don't even know anyone in New York.'

Except Patrick…

'You'll be all alone over there,' her father continued quietly.

Except for Patrick…

'There will be no one there to love and take care of you,' her father added in a wavering voice.

Except Patrick…!

This was turning out to be worse than she had realised.

Her father was right; she hadn't really thought it through at all, had just been looking for a solution to their immediate problems. The long term was something she hadn't really considered.

'Did Patrick tell you we would be going to New York?' she enquired.

'No, it was Gerry who thought of it—I called in to see her on my way home from the office,' he explained defensively as Lilli looked troubled.

Which explained why he was home later than usual. Geraldine had really got her claws into him, hadn't she?

'She's as worried as I am about your marriage to Patrick,' her father told her harshly.

Lilli stiffened. 'Well, thank her for her concern, but I'm quite capable of making my own decisions—and living with the consequences of them, even a move to New York.' She walked angrily to the door, wrenching it open. 'I think you underestimate my ability to adapt to living in New York. I'm sure I'll have a wonderful time. Now, if you'll excuse me, I have to go and change for dinner.' She closed the door firmly behind her.

How dared her father discuss her with that woman? How dared he?

'You look very beautiful,' Patrick told her huskily.

He had arrived at the house with his sister only minutes ago, the four of them in the sitting-room, Lilli's father busy with the dispensing of drinks, the beautiful Gerry already at his side. There was no doubt the other woman *was* beautiful, or that Lilli's father obviously thought so too—he seemed to have come quite boyishly alive in her company. Lilli hated even seeing the two of them together!

'Thank you.' She distantly accepted the compliment, very aware of the other couple in the room.

'As usual,' Patrick added softly.

Lilli turned to look at him, a contemptuous movement to her lips. 'You don't have to keep this up when it's just the two of us, Patrick!'

'But it isn't just the two of us.' He looked pointedly across the room at her father and his sister.

She drew in a ragged breath. 'My father would see straight through any effort on my part to pretend I'm in love with you.'

'Then I would advise you to try a little harder,' Patrick told her hardly. 'Unless you want to cause him even more grief! Andy Brewster was *your* fiancé, Lilli,' he callously reminded her.

As if to confirm Patrick's words, her father glanced worriedly across at the two of them, Lilli forcing a reassuring smile before turning back to Patrick. 'You don't play fair,' she told him in a muted voice.

'I don't "play" at all, Lilli,' he corrected her harshly. 'You should have realised that by now!'

Her eyes flashed her resentment. 'Is that the reason you've already sent the announcement of our marriage to that newspaper?'

Patrick didn't seem at all surprised at her accusation. 'I'm not even going to ask how you know about that; the London gossip grapevine must be one of the busiest in the world! But talking of our marriage...I have a present for you,' he tacked on gently.

She didn't want presents from him; she wished she didn't want anything at all from him!

'Don't look so alarmed, Lilli.' He pretended to chide her. 'This is perfectly in keeping with our new relationship. Ah, Richard, perfectly on cue with the champagne,' he greeted the other man as he held out the two glasses of bubbly pink liquid. 'I was just about to give Lilli her engagement ring.'

An engagement ring! There had been no mention of an engagement, only the wedding. She couldn't—'We can change it if you don't like it, Lilli,' Patrick assured her as he took the small blue ring-box from his jacket pocket, flicking open the lid to show her the contents.

If she didn't like it! How could any woman not like such a ring? It was beautiful, the hugest emerald Lilli had ever seen surrounded by twelve flawless small diamonds.

Lilli had never seen a ring like it before, let alone been offered such a beautiful piece of jewellery; the ring Andy had given her on their engagement, a ring she had discarded to the back of a drawer when their engagement had ended, had been a diamond solitaire, delicate, unobtrusive. Patrick was intent on making a statement with this magnificent emerald and diamond ring. Of ownership. 'Oh, Patrick,' Gerry breathed in an awestruck voice. 'It's absolutely beautiful!'

He replied ruefully, 'I believe that should be Lilli's line.'

Maybe it would be—if she could actually speak. But all she could do was stare at the ring. It was too much. Just too much. It must have cost a small fortune!

She had been brought up within a well-off family, could never remember being denied anything she had ever wanted, but this ring, and what it must have cost, had suddenly brought home to her exactly how wealthy Patrick was. Such wealth was, in its own way, quite frightening. And she was about to marry into it!

'You don't like it,' Patrick said, his gaze narrowed on the sudden paleness of her face.

She moistened dry lips. 'It isn't that...'

'Richard, you mentioned showing me the Turner you have in the dining-room?' Geraldine prompted.

Lilli looked sharply at the other woman, her mouth tightening at the obvious ease of the relationship between this handsome woman and her own father. 'There's no need to leave Patrick and I alone, Geraldine,' she announced. 'We aren't about to have an argument.'

She had to admit, for a few minutes she had been thrown totally by the ring Patrick had bought for her, but that one glance at how close Geraldine was standing to her father was enough to shake her out of that. Yes, the ring was beautiful. Yes, it had cost a small fortune. But then, Patrick Devlin wouldn't expect his future wife to wear anything but the best. The very best. The ring wasn't actually for her, it was for Patrick Devlin's fiancée—who just happened to be her. Once she had all that sorted out in her mind, there was no problem.

'Of course I like it, Patrick,' she assured him lightly. 'Any woman would,' she added with cool dismissal.

His eyes glittered dangerously. 'I'm not interested in "any woman's" opinion, Lilli,' he rasped. 'I wanted *you* to like it. I should obviously have let you choose it yourself.' He snapped the ring-box shut. 'We'll go out tomorrow and look at some others—'

'You chose this ring, Patrick.' She grasped his wrist to stop him putting the blue velvet box back in his pocket.

He looked down at the paleness of her slender fingers against his much darker skin, before slowly bringing his gaze back to her face.

Lilli withstood his probing assessment of her unflinchingly—although she couldn't say she wasn't relieved when he finally smiled. She couldn't have held his gaze for much longer, would have had to look away. 'The ring, Patrick,' she reminded him chokily.

'Only if you're sure it's what you want.' His smile had gone again now; that harshness was back in his face.

'I'm sure.' There was a challenge in her voice, and she slowly released his wrist, leaving the next move to him.

'Well, I'm not sure I am,' her father asserted. 'This whole thing is ridiculous—'

'The ring is absolutely gorgeous, Daddy.' Lilli smoothly stopped what she was sure was going to be her father's tirade.

'Lilli, you have no idea what you're doing,' he told her exasperatedly. 'You don't have to do—'

'Daddy!' She silenced him. 'Let's drink our champagne. After all, this is supposed to be a celebration.'

'I see nothing to celebrate!' Her father slammed down the glasses he had been holding for them. 'In fact—'

'Richard, I really would like to see that Turner.' Geraldine was the one to interrupt this time, taking a determined hold of his arm.

For long moments it looked as if Lilli's father would refuse, and then he acquiesced with an abrupt nod of his head, his back rigid as he and Geraldine left the room.

'I gather he doesn't approve of your choice of husband?' Patrick drawled softly as he watched the other man depart.

Lilli looked at him with flashing green eyes. 'Did you honestly expect him to?'

Patrick shrugged. 'I think he could be a little more understanding of what you're doing—'

'Understanding!' she echoed scathingly. 'I think he's too angry and upset at the moment to understand anything!'

'I did warn you he would need convincing this marriage was something you really want.'

'And just how am I supposed to do that?' she scorned.

'You can't be trusted, Patrick. You totally deceived me about that night we spent together—'

'That really rankles, doesn't it?' he mocked.

'Of course it rankles!' She had thought of little else since parting from him this afternoon. 'You—'

'Would you rather we had spent the whole night making mad, passionate love to each other?' he taunted.

'Of course not!' Her cheeks went hot with embarrassment just at the thought of it.

'Of course not,' he mimicked softly, suddenly very close. 'Lilli, your first time should be gentle and sensitive. Special. Not a night you don't even remember!'

She swallowed hard, moved, in spite of herself, by the seduction in his voice. 'You still lied to me—'

'When I said you were a ten?' he supplied.

Her blushed deepened. 'About the whole thing! You—'

'I never lied, Lilli,' he assured her. 'I never lie. Remember that,' he added. 'Because I expect the same honesty from the people I deal with.'

Especially wives! God, Sanchia had to have been incredibly brave—or incredibly stupid!—to have deceived this man.

'You're beautiful, Lilli.' He touched her cheek gently, his fingers trailing lightly down her throat to the milky softness of her slightly exposed breasts in the close-fitting black dress she wore. 'You respond to my lightest touch,' he murmured in satisfaction as she trembled. 'I know we're going to be physically compatible.'

Her skin felt on fire where his fingers had caressed. 'A ten...' she murmured weakly.

'Perfect,' he corrected her firmly. 'I only made that remark that day because I was damned angry with you and what I thought you had done. I don't give scores on sexual performance, Lilli. I'm sure I made it plain to you

there haven't been any women since I parted from Sanchia five years ago?'

'You said as much, yes...'

'If I said it, then it's the truth,' he bit out harshly.

'Patrick Devlin doesn't lie!'

'You know, Lilli,' he said with pleasant mildness, 'I'm
getting a little tired of having to deal with your temper—'

'I never knew I had one until I met you!' she returned
heatedly.

'You mean no one ever said no to you until me,' he
derided.

He was mocking her again now. And that just made
her more angry than ever!

She looked at him defiantly. 'I don't want to live in New
York after we're married,' she stated—and then wondered
where on earth it had come from. She hadn't meant to say
that in anger at all, had intended discussing it with him
calmly and reasonably. The problem with that was, she
never felt calm and reasonable when she was with him!

'I don't think it's right to discuss that now, Lilli,' he
dismissed predictably. 'Stop fighting me over everything,
woman,' he ordered as he pulled her into his arms. 'And
then maybe we can both start enjoying this!'

Enjoy being with this man? Enjoy being held by him?
Enjoy being kissed by him!

Because he was kissing her. Again. And, as on those
other occasions when he had kissed her, her body suddenly felt like liquid fire, her legs turning to jelly, so that
she clung to his shoulders as the kiss deepened, Patrick's
lips moving erotically against hers, his tongue moving
lightly over the sensitivity of her inner lip. Lilli moaned
low in her throat as he did so.

'Good God...!'

It was her father's shocked outburst that intruded into

the complete intimacy of the moment, and it was with some reluctance that Lilli dragged her mouth away from Patrick's, turning slowly to look dazedly in her father's direction.

'Don't look so shocked, Richard.' Patrick was the one to break the awkward silence. 'I realise you have some strange ideas about the reason Lilli and I are to be married, but as you've just witnessed—only too fully!—one of those reasons is that we are very attracted to each other. Haven't you ever heard of "love at first night"?'

Lilli ignored the pun, recovering her senses a lot slower than Patrick had. But with their return came the realisation that Patrick must have heard the other couple's impending return—and this show of passion had been all for their benefit, so that Geraldine and her father would believe the two of them were seriously in love!

If her father's nonplussed expression was anything to go by, it had succeeded! Why shouldn't it have done? Lilli was able to visualise all too easily—to her acute discomfort!—exactly the scene of intimacy her father and Geraldine had just walked in on. She had obviously been a more than willing recipient of Patrick's kisses and caresses!

'It happens this way sometimes, Richard,' Patrick continued, his arm like a steel band about Lilli's waist as he secured her to his side. 'Now that the two of you are back, we can put on Lilli's ring and drink the champagne.'

Lilli watched in a dreamlike state as Patrick slid the ring onto her finger, all the time having the feeling that, once it was on, her fate was sealed.

Who was she trying to fool? Her fate had been sealed from the moment she first met Patrick Devlin.

And as she watched the ring being put on her finger,

weighed down by the emerald and diamonds, she knew it was now too late to turn back.

Too late for all of them...

CHAPTER EIGHT

'HOLD STILL, LILLI, or we'll never get these flowers straight in your hair,' Sally chided lightly.

Lilli stared at her own reflection in the mirror. Hardly the picture of the ecstatic bride on her wedding day!

Oh, the trappings were all there—the white dress, her hair in long curls down her spine, the veil waiting on the back of the chair to be put over the flowers Sally was now entwining in her dark curls.

Sally, the friend she had chosen as her attendant. Sally, who had been absolutely astonished to discover the 'gorgeous man', from the night of Gerry Simms' party, was in fact Lilli's father.

If Lilli had been in the mood for humour, she would have found Sally's incredulity funny. It was definitely the first time she had seen her friend lost for words!

'There.' Sally stood back now to admire her handiwork. 'You look absolutely beautiful, Lilli. Breathtaking!'

She did. The white satin dress and long veil made her look like something from a fairy tale.

Except she wasn't marrying Prince Charming.

She was marrying Patrick Devlin.

Her heart still sank just at the thought of being his wife. It had not been an easy week; Patrick had been at the house constantly as hurried arrangements were made for their wedding. Lilli had given in over everything—the timing of the wedding, the white dress, the private reception later today for family and a few close friends, even the choosing of identical wedding rings.

The one thing she hadn't agreed to—though her father was her choice of witness and Gerry was Patrick's—was Gerry helping her get ready for the wedding. Her mother should have been the one here with her, and as her father's mistress Gerry Simms did not fit the bill! Hence Sally's presence instead.

Thirty more minutes and Lilli and Patrick would be husband and wife. She would be Mrs Patrick Devlin.

As far as Sally—and most of London, it seemed!—was concerned, she should be the happiest woman in the world at this moment.

Happy! She was far from being that. She was going to be married to Patrick, his to do with whatever and whenever he wished. Tonight, they would make love.

God, how she wished she could claim the shiver that ran down her spine at the mere thought of it was caused by revulsion, but she knew in her heart of hearts that it wasn't. The thought of making love with Patrick, of the two of them naked in bed together, entwined in each other's arms, certainly made her quiver—but with anticipation!

Because something else had been happening during the last few days, with Patrick constantly teasing her, bullying her a little, kissing her—oh, yes, the kissing hadn't stopped. In fact, he seemed to take delight in kissing her and touching her whenever the opportunity arose for him to do so. And there seemed to be all too many of those!

To her dismay, Lilli found she was falling in love with him... She had made a pact with the devil—and, to her horror, had found she was falling in love with him!

'What is it, Lilli?' Sally seemed concerned.

From a very long way away, it seemed, Lilli looked up at her dazedly.

'You've gone as white as those tea-roses in your hair,' Sally explained anxiously. 'Lilli, I— Please don't think I'm intruding,' she continued hurriedly, lightly touching Lilli's arm, 'but are you sure you aren't rushing this? I mean, you and Patrick haven't known each other that long, and— Well, he was so very much in love with Sanchia.' She shook her head, looking very good herself in a sleek red suit, blonde hair loose about her slender shoulders. 'I wouldn't want you to be hurt again,' she added worriedly. 'Andy was such a swine to walk out on you the way he did, and I—'

'I don't want to talk about Andy,' Lilli interjected; without Andy's involvement in her family, today wouldn't be happening at all! 'And I appreciate your concern, Sally,' she went on with a softening of her voice, genuinely fond of the other woman, despite the penchant she had for gossiping. 'But I can assure you I do know what I'm doing.'

How could she not know? Patrick had made it more than obvious that, while they would have a full marriage, and hopefully several children, love would never come into it.

That was what bothered her about this marriage. She was falling in love with a man who had told her quite bluntly he would never feel the same way about her. Courtesy of Sanchia. Well, he might have loved her very much, but the collapse of that marriage, in the way that it had, meant he would never love again. Legacy of Sanchia.

Lilli hated Patrick's first wife, and she had never even met her!

And how was she going to survive in a marriage without love, loving her husband, but never being loved by him in return?

Somehow this was worse than the completely loveless marriage she had initially anticipated.

So very much worse!

So, yes, she knew what she was doing, but she had no choice in the matter; the wedding was mere minutes away now instead of days—days that had flown by all too swiftly!—and, more importantly, her father's lawyers had already started work on bringing a case against Andy. In fact, he might already be aware of it!

Sally sat down, leaning forward conspiratorially. 'Well, Patrick is an absolutely—'

'Gorgeous man,' Lilli finished for her, smiling teasingly. 'I never realised before, Sally, the fascination you have for gorgeous men!' She stood up to pick up her veil, placing the circle of flowers on top of her shining hair, studying her reflection in the mirror. The 'sacrificial lamb' was well and truly ready for the altar!

'You're referring to your father, of course.' Sally ruefully accepted her teasing. 'I still can't believe he's the man from the party. When I arrived here the other day to find the two of you together in the sitting-room, I must admit that my first thought was you were being unfaithful to Patrick even before the wedding!' She gave a grimace. 'Do you think he's serious about Gerry? Or do I actually stand a chance where he's concerned?' She looked questioningly at Lilli.

'He isn't serious about Gerry,' Lilli replied defensively, her eyes flashing deeply green at the mere suggestion of it.

'So would you mind if I—?'

'Be my guest,' she invited, although the fact that her own father suddenly seemed very sought after, by beautiful young women, was still a rather strange concept for her to accept. Admittedly, he was only in his mid-forties, but she had somehow never thought of him in that light before. 'But for the record, Sally,' she went on, 'I don't intend ever to be unfaithful to Patrick—before or after the wedding!'

'Fine,' Sally accepted, grimacing at Lilli's vehemence.

'Sally...' Lilli remonstrated firmly.

Her friend held her hands up defensively. 'I believe you—okay?'

Lilli laughed. 'Time will tell. In the meantime, I think we have a wedding to go to!'

'Oh, gosh, yes.' Sally stood up hurriedly. 'It may be traditional for the bride to be late, but in this case I'm not so sure the groom wouldn't come looking for you! I'll get off now, and see you at the registry office.' She gave Lilli a reassuring hug before leaving.

Amazingly Lilli's conversation with Sally had lifted her feelings somewhat, and she was smiling as she descended the wide staircase, her smile widening warmly as she saw her father standing at the bottom waiting for her, looking especially handsome today in his grey morning suit.

'Daddy, you look magnificent,' she praised glowingly as she reached him.

'*I* look—!' There were tears in his eyes as he looked down at her. 'Lilli, you look beautiful. So like your mother did at this age. I wish she could have been here to see you—'

'Not now, Daddy,' she dismissed briskly; talking about her mother was the one thing she couldn't cope with today, of all days. It was going to be difficult enough to get through anyway, without thoughts of her mother. Besides, she very much doubted this marriage was what her mother would have wished for her. It wouldn't do to dwell on that thought… 'Patrick will be becoming impatient,' she said brightly.

'Talking of Patrick…' Her father frowned, turning to the table that stood in the centre of the reception area, picking up a flat blue velvet box. 'He sent this for you earlier.' Her father snapped open the lid of the box, the two of them gasping as he revealed the most amazing necklace Lilli had ever seen. The emerald and diamond droplet in the centre of the delicate gold chain was an exact match for the engagement ring Lilli had transferred to her right hand for the marriage ceremony…

Her hand trembled slightly as she picked up the card that lay in the circle of gold, recognising the large scrawling handwriting as Patrick's before she even read the words written there. His cryptic sense of humour was all too apparent in the message.

Something new, Lilli—and if your eyes had been blue instead of green it could have been something blue too! Please wear it for me today.

Yours, Patrick.

'Lilli…!' her father breathed dazedly, still staring at the perfection of the necklace.

She swallowed hard, carefully replacing the card in the box before releasing the necklace and holding it out to her father. 'Would you help me put it on, Daddy?' She turned around, carefully lifting up her hair so that he could secure the catch. 'We'll have to hurry, Daddy,' she encouraged as he made no effort to do so. 'The car is waiting outside.'

'I still can't believe—Lilli, you're my little girl, and—'

'Please, Daddy.' Her own voice quivered with emotion. 'Put the necklace on and let's just go!' Before she totally destroyed the work of the last hour and began to cry.

He did so with slightly shaking fingers, careful not to ruffle her hair. 'Absolutely incredible,' her father said huskily as he stepped back to look at her.

Lilli gave a tight smile, not bothering to glance in the hall mirror as they walked out to the car. 'Only the best for Patrick. He would hardly give his future wife anything less.'

'I was referring to you, not the necklace,' her father gently rebuked. 'But then, you are the best; those jewels only enhance what is already perfection.'

She laughed. 'I think you may be slightly biased, Daddy!'

'I think Patrick Devlin is a very lucky man,' he stated. 'Take a deep breath before we go outside, Lilli,' he warned as he held her arm. 'I think half the world's press is gathered outside to snap a photograph of Patrick Devlin's bride!'

Which certainly wasn't an understatement!

A barrage of flashing cameras and intrusive microphones were pointed at the two of them as soon as they stepped outside into what was a crisply cold but bright, sunny December day. Questions were flung at them thick and fast, questions Lilli chose to ignore as she and her father hurried to the waiting car. The press had been hounding her continuously since the announcement of the wedding had appeared in the newspaper, and the wedding day itself had been sure to engender this excess of interest.

It was all so ridiculous to Lilli. Didn't these people have a war or something to write about and fill their newspapers with? This interest in what was, after all, just another society wedding, albeit with one of the principal players possibly being one of the richest men in England, seemed rather obscene to Lilli, and — She was half in the car and half out of it when, her face paling, she caught sight of a familiar face amongst the crowd.

Andy...

She shook her head in denial of her imaginings. It couldn't have been Andy. Not here; this was the last place he would ever be seen. The only place she *wanted* to see him was in a courtroom, in the dock!

'Lilli...? Her father was waiting to get into the car beside her. 'What is it?' He saw her ashen cheeks.

'Nothing.' She turned to give him a glowing smile, the cameras clicking anew at what she supposed must look like the blushing bride on her way to her wedding. 'We'll be late if we don't go now,' she encouraged.

Her father looked as if he was about to add something to that, but at her determined expression he seemed to change his mind.

She had made her decision last week; there would be no last-minute nerves, no change of plan. That glimpse of someone she had thought looked a little like Andy had shaken her a little, but that was all...

'If I don't have the chance to tell you so again, you look absolutely beautiful,' Patrick whispered to her as they awaited the arrival of their guests to the private reception her father had organised at the Bennett Hotel.

Lilli barely glanced at him. She was almost afraid to. Half an hour ago she had married this man, was now his wife—and she had never been so scared of anything in her life before! In fact, she couldn't ever remember feeling scared before at all.

But Patrick had seemed like a remote stranger when they'd met at the registry office, making Lilli all too aware that that was exactly what he was!

Brides who had known their groom for years, and were

secure in mutually expressed love, still had wedding-day nerves over the rightness of what they were doing; how much deeper, in the circumstances, was her own trepidation?

Just looking at the man who was now her husband was part of her panic. How on earth had she ever thought she could spend the rest of her life with this man? He was as good-looking as the devil, cool as ice, didn't love her, and had assured her he never would. God, this was—'Gerry, when our guests arrive, greet them for us and assure them we will be with them shortly.' Patrick spoke quietly to his sister even as he grasped Lilli's arm.

Lilli's father frowned at him; the four of them had been the first to arrive at the reception room. 'Where are the two of you going?'

Patrick's hand was firm on Lilli's elbow as he led her away. 'Upstairs to our suite so that I can kiss my bride in private,' he told the other man grimly.

'But—'

'Let them go, Richard,' Gerry advised, her hand resting gently on his arm.

Lilli was shaking so badly now she could barely walk, the thought of actually being alone with Patrick sending her into a complete panic. This was real. Far, far too real, as the warmth of Patrick's guiding hand on her arm told her all too forcefully. It had seemed such a simple decision to make—the only decision she could make in the circumstances!—but the reality of it was all too much. She wanted to scream. Run away. To shout—'Not here,' Patrick said suddenly, moving swiftly to swing her up into his arms.

Much to the interest of all the other hotel guests who stood watching them, he strode purposefully through the lobby to the lifts, several indulgent smiles directed their way as people observed their hurried departure. It didn't need two guesses to know what these people were thinking. But they were wrong! So very wrong...

Patrick, literally kicked open the door to the suite he had arranged for them to stay in tonight, setting Lilli down once they were safely inside. She looked up at him with widely apprehensive eyes.

'*Now* you can scream,' he encouraged indulgently.

Her breath left her with a shaky sigh. 'It was that obvious?'

'Only to me,' he assured her. 'I'm only surprised this didn't happen earlier. You've been too controlled this last week—'

'But I am controlled.' She swung impatiently away from him, angry with herself because she didn't seem able to stop shaking. 'I'm just being very stupid now,' she confessed self-disgustedly.

'You're being a twenty-one-year-old young lady who just made probably the biggest decision of her entire life.' Patrick's hands gently squeezed her shoulders as he turned her to face him. 'But I promise you I'll treat you well. That I'll try to curb this urge I have to dominate. I will honour and cherish you,' he added gruffly.

But he wouldn't love her; that omission was all too apparent to Lilli.

'But it isn't that, is it...?' Patrick said slowly, studying her closely. 'Tell me what it is, Lilli?'

She couldn't possibly tell him how she felt, that as she'd looked at him earlier as they'd made their wedding vows to each other she had known that she, at least, meant every word. She wasn't falling in love with him—she had already done so!

There was absolutely no doubt in her mind that she loved Patrick. It was nothing like what she had felt for

Andy, was so much more intense, so— Oh, God, Andy...
Had it been him she had seen earlier, or just someone that
looked very like him?

Patrick shook her gently as she frowned. 'What is it,
Lilli?' There was an edge of urgency to his voice now.

'I thought— You're going to think I'm imagining
things now. But I—I thought I saw Andy outside the house
earlier.' She frowned again up at Patrick as he released
her abruptly, his expression serious now. 'I told you it
was stupid—'

'Not at all,' Patrick barked. 'I have it on good author-
ity that Brewster is back in London.'

She swallowed hard. 'He is?' She suddenly felt very
sick. After what Andy had done to her father, and to her,
she had no wish for him ever to come near her again. But
with Patrick's confirmation that he was in London she
was even more convinced that it had been Andy she'd
seen outside the house...

Why? What had he been doing there? What had he
hoped to achieve by being outside her father's house on
her wedding day to another man?

'It's a little late for second thoughts, Lilli.' Patrick was
watching her closely. 'You're my wife now.'

With all that entailed. He owned her now; it was there
in every arrogant inch of his tensely held body. Minutes
ago, his gentleness and understanding drawing her close
to him, she had almost been tempted to tell him how stupid she had been, that she was in love with him! Thank
God she hadn't. She was a Devlin possession, a beautiful trophy to display on his arm, a wife with none of the
complications of love involved.

She nodded in cool agreement. 'Our guests will have
arrived downstairs.'

'You feel up to meeting them now?'

'Don't worry, Patrick, I won't embarrass you. My nerves simply got the better of me for a moment. It won't happen again.'

'No,' Patrick finally said slowly. 'I don't believe it will.'

Regret...? Or perhaps she had just imagined that particular emotion in his voice; the last thing he wanted was an emotional child for a wife. Her loss of control wouldn't happen again. After all, he had just assured her he would treat her well! He couldn't possibly realise that, loving him as she did, there were cruel things he could do to her...

And he must never know!

'We made a bargain, Patrick,' she told him distantly. 'And, like you, I never break my word once it's given.'

His expression hardened. 'I'm glad to hear it. Now, as you've already pointed out, our guests will be waiting.' He indicated she should precede him out of the suite, walking this time; the two of them were physically apart as well as emotionally.

That moment of gentleness and understanding was well and truly over, and for the next three hours Lilli didn't have the time even to think, concentrating on their guests, portraying the image that she and Patrick were a golden couple. There was no doubting they succeeded; family and friends smiled at them indulgently every time Lilli glanced around the large table where they all sat eating their meal. No doubt the few members of her family present thought she was very fortunate to have married someone as eligible as Patrick, especially after the 'Andy incident', as most of them referred to her previous engagement. Once the embezzlement story hit the headlines, perhaps some of them would draw their own conclusions, but for the moment everyone was obviously enjoying themselves.

Except, Lilli noticed, the late arrival standing in the

doorway looking at the gathering with contemptuous blue eyes...

She didn't recognise the woman, so she could only assume she was a guest of Patrick's. A very beautiful guest, Lilli acknowledged with a stab of jealousy. Tall and blonde, with ice-blue eyes, she stood almost six feet tall, with the slender elegance of a model about to make an entrance onto the catwalk.

That icy blue gaze met Lilli's puzzled one, the woman's red pouting mouth twisting contemptuously as her hard eyes swept critically over Lilli—and obviously found her wanting—before passing on to Patrick. Now the blue eyes weren't so icy; in fact, they became positively heated, seeming to devour him at a glance!

Lilli felt herself bridle indignantly. How dared this woman—whoever she was—come here and look at her husband in that way? Patrick had told her, several times, that there had been no women in his life since his marriage ended, but the way this woman was looking at him seemed to tell a very different story!

Lilli's indignation rose. If she belonged to Patrick now, then he also belonged to her, and women from his past had no place at their wedding reception.

She turned to him sharply. 'Patrick—'

'My God...!' he exclaimed even as she spoke, the intensity of the blonde woman's stare somehow seeming to have made him aware of her presence in the doorway, his face set grimly, a nerve pulsing in his jaw. 'What the hell...?' he ground out disbelievingly.

Lilli blinked at him, unsure of his mood. She had seen him mocking, contemptuous, coldly angry, passionately aroused, even gently teasing, but she had no idea what emotion he was feeling as he took in the woman in the doorway. Every muscle in his body seemed to be tensed, and his fingers looked in danger of snapping the slender stem of the champagne glass he held.

'Patrick…?' Lilli prompted uncertainly now.

His glass landed with a thump on the table-top as he stood up abruptly, unseeing as he looked down at her. 'I'll be back in a few minutes,' he grated, turning to leave.

Lilli didn't need to be told he was going to the woman across the room, a woman he obviously knew very well if that blaze of awareness in the woman's eyes as she looked at him had been anything to go by! He couldn't do this to her, not at their wedding reception!

'Let him go, Lilli,' his sister advised quietly as Lilli would have reached out and stopped his departure. Gerry was looking across the room at the blond woman too now.

Lilli's mouth tightened resentfully, both at Gerry's intervention and Patrick's powerful strides across the room towards the beautiful woman. Her eyes flashed deeply green as she turned to the woman who was now her sister-in-law. 'You know that woman?' she asked.

'Oh, yes.' Gerry's mouth twisted contemptuously, although her gaze was soft as she looked at Lilli. 'I'm hardly likely to forget the woman who made Patrick into the hardened cynic he is today!'

Sanchia!

The beautiful woman in the doorway, the woman who had looked at Patrick so possessively, was his ex-wife? Here? Now?

Lilli turned sharply, just in time to see Sanchia smile seductively up at Patrick, before he took a firm hold of her arm and forcefully escorted her from the room.

CHAPTER NINE

'GERRY…? WHAT THE hell is she doing here?' Lilli's father hissed agitatedly.

Lilli turned to him. 'You know Patrick's ex-wife too?'

'Of course. Your mother and I were part of that crowd five years ago,' he reminded her.

Before her mother's illness became such that it was impossible for her to go anywhere…

'Where are you going, Lilli?' Her father's hand on her arm restrained her as she stood up.

Her expression was calm, a smile curving her lips—even if the green of her eyes spat fire. 'I'm going to join my bridegroom,' she told him, releasing her arm. 'Don't worry, Daddy.' Her smile was wry now at his expression of panic. 'I can assure you, I intend it to be a civilised meeting.'

Gerry grimaced. 'Sanchia isn't known for her civility!'

Lilli gave a genuinely warm smile as she bent down to answer the other woman. 'I'll let you into a secret, Gerry,' she murmured. 'Neither am I when I'm pushed into a corner!' She straightened, looking towards the door through which Patrick had left so hastily minutes earlier. 'And I've just been pushed,' she muttered as she turned to move determinedly towards that door.

Gerry touched her arm lightly as she passed her. 'Just watch out for the claws,' she warned.

Lilli nodded her thanks. 'I'll do that.'

It wasn't difficult to locate Patrick and Sanchia once she was out in the corridor; the sound of raised voices came from a room a little further down the hallway, Patrick's icily calm, the female voice—Sanchia's—raised to the point of hysteria.

The claws Gerry had warned Lilli about were raised in the direction of Patrick's face as Lilli silently entered the room, Patrick's hands on the other woman's wrists to prevent her nails actually making contact with his cheeks.

'Dear, dear, dear,' Lilli murmured mockingly as she closed the door firmly behind her. 'Do I take it this isn't a happy reunion?'

The two people already in the room were frozen as if in a tableau. Both turned to face Lilli as she calmly stood looking at them, dark brows raised questioningly. Patrick looked far from pleased at the interruption, but Sanchia slowly lowered her hands, her icy blue eyes suddenly speculative as she looked Lilli up and down.

'The bride,' she drawled derisively.

Lilli steadily met the other woman's contemptuous glare. 'And the ex-bride,' she returned just as scathingly, knowing she had scored a direct hit as Sanchia's mouth tightened furiously. 'Patrick, our guests are waiting,' Lilli reminded him lightly.

Sanchia released her arms from Patrick's steely grip, eyes blazing. 'Unless he's changed a great deal—which I very much doubt!—Patrick doesn't respond well to orders!' The accent to her English was slightly more noticeable in this longer speech.

Green eyes met icy blue. 'Patrick hasn't changed. In

any way,' Lilli added pointedly. 'Darling?' she prompted again.

He couldn't let her down now. He just couldn't! If he did, their marriage was over before it had even begun. No matter what his feelings towards Sanchia—and Lilli really had no idea what they were, or indeed about the other woman's towards him; Sanchia had obviously felt strongly enough about something, possibly Patrick, to have turned up here today!—it was Lilli he was married to now. And she had married him. For better or for worse.

To her relief Patrick walked determinedly to her side, his expression grim as his arm moved possessively about her waist. 'As I've told you, Sanchia—' he looked at his former wife resolutely '—there's no place for you here.'

'This—this child—' Sanchia looked at Lilli scornfully '—could never take my place in your life! You need a real woman, Patrick—and I was always that.'

Lilli stiffened at this mention of intimacy between the two, although her outward expression remained calm. She didn't particularly want to hear about Patrick's marriage to Sanchia. And Patrick, his arm still about her waist, must have felt her reaction.

'Patrick likes them a little younger nowadays,' Lilli told Sanchia wryly, knowing by the angry flush that appeared in the other woman's cheeks that her barb had hit its mark. Sanchia was probably only ten years older than her, but she obviously felt those years...

'Inexperienced, you mean,' Sanchia returned bitchily. 'Patrick bores easily too,' she warned.

Lilli smiled. 'I'm sure you would know that better than I.' She felt the tightening of Patrick's hand on her waist, but chose to ignore it; she knew she was playing with fire, but at this particular moment she didn't mind getting her fingers burnt.

Sanchia gave a snort before turning to Patrick. 'I give this marriage a matter of months, darling,' she drawled, picking her bag up from the table. 'And I'll still be around when it's over. In fact, I'm thinking of moving to New York.'

'Really? I'm sure you'll enjoy the life over there.' Patrick was the one to answer her. 'Frankly—' his arm settled more comfortably about Lilli's waist '—I'm tired of it. Lilli and I will be living in London.'

That was news to Lilli! They hadn't so much as mentioned where they would live after their marriage since the night Patrick had given her the engagement ring, and she had behaved so stupidly about moving to New York. Now, it seemed, they weren't going to live there at all...

'I don't believe it,' Sanchia gasped. 'You've always loved New York.'

He gave an acknowledging nod. 'And now I love Lilli—and her family and friends are all in London.'

Two bright spots of angry colour appeared in Sanchia's cheeks. 'My family and friends were in Paris, but you refused to live there!' she accused heatedly, turning to Lilli with furious blue eyes. 'Enjoy his indulgence while you can,' she advised. 'I can assure you, it doesn't last for long!'

Considering one of this woman's indulgences had been other men, that wasn't so surprising!

Lilli met her gaze unflinchingly. 'I wouldn't hold your breath,' she said.

Sanchia gave a hard smile. 'Or you yours! Take care, Patrick.' She reached out to run a caressing hand down his cheek lightly. 'And remember, I'm still here.'

This last, Lilli knew, was said for her benefit. And while a visit from an ex-wife was enough to chill the heart of any new one—no matter what the circumstances of the divorce had been, the previous wife having an intimate knowledge of the man, of his likes and dislikes, that was totally intrusive—at that moment Lilli didn't feel in the least threatened by the other woman, had seen the look of absolute loathing in Patrick's face for Sanchia when she'd entered this room a few minutes ago. Patrick disliked his ex-wife intensely.

'Excuse us,' Patrick told Sanchia coldly. 'We have a wedding reception to attend.' His hand was firm against Lilli's back as he guided her to the door, neither of them looking back as they left. '"Patrick likes them younger nowadays"?' he repeated as soon as the two of them were out of earshot in the hallway.

Lilli glanced up at him from beneath lowered lashes, knowing by the curve to his mouth that he wasn't in the least angry at her remark. 'I believe I said "a *little* younger",' she returned, grinning up at him mischievously.

Patrick looked down at her, shaking his head incredulously. 'You weren't in the least thrown by her appearance here, were you?'

She wouldn't go quite so far as to say that, but if it was what Patrick believed...

She shrugged, the two of them standing outside the reception room now. 'Should I have been?'

'Not at all,' he returned easily. 'The part of my life that contained Sanchia is dead and buried as far as I'm concerned.' His expression was grim.

'That's what I thought.' Lilli accepted—gratefully, inside!—putting her hand in the crook of his arm. 'Let's join our guests; you still have a speech to give!'

'Oh, God, yes,' he groaned. 'I'm not quite sure what to say about my bride any more,' he added dryly.

Lilli grinned. 'Beautiful. Intelligent. Undemanding—'

'Sometimes wise beyond her years,' he put in. 'And full of surprises. I was sure you would give me hell over Sanchia turning up here, today of all days. Full of surprises...'

She shook her head. 'You can't be held responsible for the actions of a vindictive woman. She wanted to cause trouble between us, unnerve you, and upset me—I vote we don't give her the satisfaction!'

'I stopped caring years ago about anything that Sanchia does,' Patrick revealed. 'I was more worried about you and how you would feel about it.'

And she could see that he had been, his concern still in the deep grey of his eyes. 'Don't be,' she told him brightly, needing no further assurances from him concerning his ex-wife. 'And as for being full of surprises—when did *we* decide to live in London?' She quirked dark brows again.

He frowned in thought. 'I believe it was the night we became engaged.'

'No.' Lilli shook her head. 'You refused to even discuss it then.'

'Because at the time I was intent on kissing you, if I remember correctly.' He grinned as she blushed at the memory. 'But your wish not to live in New York was duly noted, and—'

'Acted upon.' Lilli frowned. 'I can see I'll have to be more careful about what I say in future. Or was Sanchia right about your indulgence?' she added teasingly. 'Won't it last?'

Patrick's arms moved smoothly about her waist. 'It isn't a question of indulging you, Lilli. You said you didn't want to live in New York, and, as I have no feelings either way, it seems obvious that we live here. I want you to be happy in our marriage,' he added gruffly. 'And if living in London is going to help do that, then this is where we'll live. I thought, with your agreement, that we could go house-hunting in the new year?'

He probably couldn't see it—and, in the circumstances, Lilli had no intention of pointing it out to him, either, because living in London suited her fine!—but the fact that he had made this decision on his own, without any consultation with her, was an act of arrogance in itself.

'Fine,' she nodded.

'Do you mind staying here in the hotel until we find a house? I somehow don't think we should move in with either your father or my sister.'

Lilli grimaced. 'Certainly not!'

Patrick grinned. 'Ditto.'

She blinked up at him. 'That's amazing, Patrick; do you realise that's three things we've agreed on in the last five minutes?'

'Three things...?' He looked serious as he thought back over their conversation.

She nodded. 'To live in London. And that your ex-wife is a bitch! She even chose to wear a white suit to come here today.' Lilli had duly noted the deliberate ploy of Sanchia to upstage the bride; the beautiful silk suit obviously had a designer label, and white was usually the colour reserved for the bride on her wedding day. She didn't doubt that Sanchia had been reminding her that she had been Patrick's bride first!

He grimaced. 'But the jacket, if I remember correctly, was edged with black. And Sanchia is more black than white!'

There was so much pain behind that stark comment. Lilli could only hope that one day he would feel comfortable enough in their relationship to talk to her about the marriage that had ended so disastrously.

For the first time that she could remember in their acquaintance Lilli was the one to reach up and initiate a kiss between them.

Patrick seemed as surprised as she was to start with, and then he kissed her back.

It hadn't been premeditated on her part; Lilli could have had no idea Sanchia would choose that particular moment to storm out of the reception room further down the hallway. But that was exactly what she did, her eyes narrowing glacially as she took in the scene of intimacy. With one last furious glare in their direction, she turned on her heel and walked away.

For good, Lilli hoped.

'Good timing,' Patrick told her dryly as he grasped her elbow to take her back to their guests.

He believed she had kissed him at that moment deliberately, so that Sanchia would see them!

And perhaps it was better if he continued to think that, Lilli decided as they moved around the huge dining-room chatting to each of their guests. Patrick had clearly stated he did not want a wife who loved him, only one that would be faithful and loyal.

Loving him as she did, those two things would be quite easy to be, and it was best to leave it at that...

'Thank goodness that's over!' Patrick pulled off his bow-tie with some relief, discarding his jacket onto a chair too, unbuttoning the top button of his shirt. 'I thought your father and Gerry were never going to leave.'

Lilli smiled at the memory of her father dithering about downstairs, drinking two glasses of champagne that he really didn't want, simply because now the time had come for him to leave Lilli alone with her husband and he was reluctant to do so.

She shook her head. 'And I thought the bride was the

one that was nervous; you would have thought it was Daddy's wedding night the way he kept so obviously delaying our departure upstairs!' She smiled affectionately, sitting in one of the armchairs in the sitting-room of their suite, her veil discarded hours ago, the tea-roses still entwined in the flowing darkness of her hair.

Patrick looked across at her with dark grey eyes. 'And are you?' he said gruffly. 'Nervous,' he explained softly at her frown.

She swallowed hard. 'A little,' she acknowledged huskily.

He came down on his haunches beside her chair. 'You don't have to be, you know.' He smoothed the hair back from her cheeks. 'It's been a pretty eventful day, one way or another. And now it's very late, and we're both tired, and we have the rest of our lives together. I suggest we both take a shower and then get some sleep.' He straightened. 'There are two bathrooms in this suite; you take one and I'll take the other.'

Lilli looked at him dazedly as he picked up his jacket. He didn't want her!

'Lilli?'

She focused on him with effort. He was so tall and masculine, so devastatingly attractive. And he was her husband.

Damn it, she wanted to make love with him! This was their wedding night. And a part of her—the part that wasn't nervous!—had been anticipating the two of them making love. And now he had decided they weren't going to, after all...

He gave an impatient sigh. 'Stop looking at me as if I've just hit you! I'm not a monster, Lilli, and I can see how tired you are. A shower and then sleep will be the best thing for you at the moment.'

The exhaustion she had felt on their way up here had suddenly vanished. Patrick didn't want to make love to her! Was this the way it was when you didn't marry for love? Or was he more affected by Sanchia's visit than he had admitted? Had seeing the other woman again made him realise he had made a mistake? What—?

'You're letting your imagination run away with you now,' he rasped suddenly, looking at her assessingly. 'Asking yourself questions that, in the clear light of day, you will recognise as nonsensical. I'm trying to be a gentleman, Lilli,' he explained. 'But if it makes you feel better I could always throw you down on the carpet right now and—'

'No!' she cut in forcefully, getting to her feet, avoiding looking at him as she did so. 'I'll go and take that shower.'

He nodded abruptly. 'I'll see you shortly.'

Lilli went through to the bedroom; her clothes had been brought here the day before and unpacked into the drawers. She took out the white silk nightgown before going through to the adjoining bathroom, thankfully closing the door behind her.

She had made a fool of herself just now, and it wasn't a feeling she was comfortable with. Patrick wasn't an eager bridegroom, in love with his new wife, desperate to make love with her. There was no urgency to consummate their marriage. They had plenty of time for that...

Patrick was already in bed when she came through from the bathroom half an hour later, the sheet resting about his waist, his chest bare, the hair there dark and curling, his skin lightly tanned. His hair was still damp from his shower, and he looked—Lilli quickly looked away as he turned towards her, knowing the flare of desire she felt at the sight of him would be evident in her eyes. 'I'm sorry I took so long.' She moved about the room, hanging up her wedding dress and veil. 'It took me ages to get the flowers out of my hair and then pull a brush through it.' She held up a hand to her long vibrant hair. 'And then I—'

'Lilli, just leave all that and get into bed,' he interrupted wearily. 'You're wearing me out just watching you! It isn't as if it matters whether or not the dress gets creased; you won't be wearing it again.'

She thrust the dress on its hanger into the back of the wardrobe, as if it had burnt her. No, she wouldn't be wearing it again. Because she would always be married to Patrick. And look how disastrous it was turning out to be!

'Don't make me come and get you, Lilli,' Patrick urged as she still made no effort to get into the bed beside him. 'I never wear anything in bed, and I have a feeling you're the one that would end up feeling embarrassed if I were to get up right now!'

She scrambled into the bed beside him so quickly that her foot became entangled in the sheet and threatened to pull the damn thing off him anyway!

How stupidly she was behaving; she inwardly sighed once she had finally settled onto her own side of the wide double bed. Not at all like the normally composed Lilli. And as for Elizabeth Bennett…!

Patrick reached out to switch off the light, lying back in the darkness.

Lilli lay stiffly on her side of the bed, her eyes adjusting to the small amount of light shining into the room through the curtains at the window. She was never going to be able to sleep, couldn't possibly—'If it's not too much to ask—' Patrick spoke softly beside her '—*I* would like to give my wife a cuddle before we go to sleep.'

She swallowed hard as he propped himself up on one elbow to look down at her, his individual features not discernible to her, although she could make out the shadows of his face. And he looked as if he was smiling!

'*Is* it too much to ask?' he prompted huskily.

'Of course not.' She moved in the darkness, putting her head on his shoulder as he lay back against the pillow, his arm curved around her, his hand resting possessively on her hip, the warmth of his body—his naked body!—instantly warming her too.

He gave a sigh of contentment, turning to kiss her temple lightly. 'This is worth all of the hectic circus today has been.' He relaxed against her.

Lilli still felt unsure of herself. Through the ridiculousness of his marriage proposal, her reluctant acceptance of it, the hectic activity during the week that followed, she had never doubted that Patrick desired her. In fact, he had seemed to have great difficulty keeping his hands off her! But now they were married, alone together at last, he didn't seem—'You're letting your imagination run away with you again. Lilli, has it ever occurred to you that maybe *I'm* a little nervous?'

'You?' She turned to him, raising her head in surprise.

'Yes. Me,' he confirmed, pushing her head back down onto his shoulder. 'I told you, it's a long time since I did this. Maybe I've forgotten how to do it. Maybe I won't be able to please you.' He gave a deep sigh. 'God knows, the last time I attempted to make love to a woman, she fell asleep before we even got started! I'm talking about *you*, Lilli,' he explained as he felt her stiffen defensively in his arms. 'Five minutes earlier you had been full of sensual promise, and then—nothing.'

She buried her face in his shoulder at the memory. 'I had too much to drink. It had nothing to do with—with—'

'Well, it did absolutely nothing for my ego,' he assured her. 'Now will you accept that and just leave this for tonight?'

When he put it that way—of course she would! She had never imagined that Patrick had moments of uncertainty too. He was so damned arrogant most of the time, it was difficult to imagine him being nervous about anything. Certainly not about making love to her!

'Of course I will.' She snuggled closer to him in the darkness, her hand resting lightly on his chest. 'Mm, this is nice,' she murmured contentedly.

'Go to sleep, Lilli,' he muttered.

She slept. Not because Patrick had ordered her to, but because, as he'd said, she was truly exhausted.

Quite what woke her she had no idea, but as she slowly came awake she realised it was probably because she had subconsciously registered that she was alone in the bed, the lean length of Patrick no longer beside her.

She looked sleepily around the bedroom, realising by the fact that it was still dark in the room that it must be quite early. She finally located Patrick sitting in the chair by the window, a dark robe pulled on over his nakedness.

She moved up onto her elbows, blinking sleepily across at him. 'Patrick…?'

'Who the hell is Robbie?' he returned harshly.

CHAPTER TEN

LILLIE WAS DAZED, not really awake yet, totally thrown by
the savagely accusing question.

Patrick surged forcefully to his feet, crossing the room
to sit down on the side of the bed, instantly tightening
the bedclothes above her, holding her pinned to the mat-
tress. He placed his hands on the pillow at either side
of her head, glaring down at her in the semi-darkness.
'I want to know who Robbie is,' he repeated in a harsh,
controlled voice.

Lilli pushed her tousled hair back from her forehead.
'I don't— What—?'

'Imagine my surprise,' Patrick ground out, 'when my
bride of a few hours starts calling for another man—a
man I've never heard of!—in her sleep!'

She swallowed hard, moistening her lips. She didn't
remember dreaming at all, certainly not of Robbie. But
Patrick said she had called out his name…? 'I did that?'
She frowned her confusion.

Patrick's mouth twisted. 'It's hardly something I'm
likely to have made up, is it?' he grated.

No, of course it wasn't. She just couldn't imagine why
she had done such a thing…

'Lilli, I'm not going to ask you again.' He grasped her
shoulders. 'Who the hell is he?'

She turned away from the livid anger in his face. '*Was* he,' she corrected him chokily. 'He's dead.'

Patrick released her abruptly, sitting back now, no longer leaning over her so oppressively. 'You loved him,' he stated flatly.

'Very much,' she confirmed shakily.

He stood up to pace the room. 'I don't believe this! Now I have a damned ghost to contend with as well as an ex-fiancé...!' He shook his head disgustedly. 'No one has ever mentioned someone in your life called Robbie.' He glared at her.

'There was no need for them to do so,' she said heavily, painful memories assailing her anew. 'He's been dead a long time.' She sighed. 'Patrick, Robbie was—'

'I can guess,' he cut in savagely. 'He was the reason you settled for someone like Andy Brewster. The reason you're now married to me. He was—'

'The person that gave me the name Lilli,' she told him, her voice very small. 'Remember you once asked me about my name? Actually, it was Lillibet originally,' she recalled sadly. 'But over the years it's been shortened to Lilli.'

'Lillibet?' Patrick repeated. 'It sounds like something a child might say. What sort of—?'

'It *was* something a child might say—a very young child,' she told him slowly, no longer looking at him, her vision all inwards, on the past, on memories of Robbie. 'Robbie couldn't get his tongue around the name Elizabeth, and so his version came out as Lillibet.' She smiled at the memory, that smile fading as quickly as it appeared. 'He was only two when he died of meningitis.' She looked at Patrick with dull eyes. 'He was my brother.'

Patrick paled. 'He— But— I—'

Patrick at a loss for words would have been funny

under any other circumstances. But at the moment it was lost on her.

'I was eleven when he died. One day he was here, giggling and fun, and the next he had— I—I—' She fought the control she always lost when talking of her brother. 'I loved him from the day he was born. Perhaps the difference in our ages helped with that; I don't know.' She shook her head. 'But I could never accept—I didn't understand. In some ways I still don't. He was beautiful.' She looked at Patrick with tear-wet eyes. 'I loved him so much,' she added brokenly. 'I have no idea why I called for him last night. I don't remember. I just—'

'Hey, it's all right.' Patrick sank down beside her on the bed, his arms moving about her as he held her close against him. 'I had no idea, Lilli. I'm so sorry. I do vaguely remember something—God, I'm just making this worse.' He angrily berated himself. 'I shouldn't "vaguely remember" anything! Robbie was your brother—'

'But you didn't know him. You didn't know us.' Her voice was muffled against his chest. 'Robbie was special to me; I still can't think of him without crying. I'm sorry.' She began to cry in earnest now.

'Lilli, please don't cry,' Patrick groaned. 'I do know what it's like to lose someone you love. I was seven when my mother gave birth to Gerry. Gerry was born, and my mother died. I was left with that same bewilderment you obviously were. And my father and I were left with the onerous task of bringing up a new-born baby. For fifteen years we managed to do exactly that, and then my father died, and it was left completely to me.'

As he spoke of his mother and father, his childhood with Gerry, his voice somehow lost its smoothness, acquiring a slightly Irish lilt to it. And Lilli could only guess, from the emotion in his voice, just how difficult it had been for him to lose his mother—and be presented with a totally helpless baby.

His statements had been starkly made, telling her about none of the trauma he and his father must have felt in surviving such sorrow. Or how difficult it must have been for him, at only twenty-two, to have the sole charge of a fifteen-year-old girl. And yet he had done it and, from the success he had made of his business life and the closeness between himself and Gerry, all too capably.

Lilli shook her head. 'I didn't know—'

'Why should you?' He lightly touched her hair. 'We have the rest of our lives to get to know about each other, both past and present.'

Lilli hoped that would include speaking about his marriage to Sanchia. As she looked up into the gentleness of his face, she thought it would...

'I didn't mean to make you cry just now,' he continued. 'I only—I just— I was jealous,' he admitted. 'I thought he was a man you had cared for.'

She looked up at him with puzzled, tear-wet eyes. If he had felt jealousy, did that mean he cared for her, after all? Even as her heart leapt at the thought, she realised it wasn't that at all; what Patrick possessed, he possessed exclusively. Didn't he despise Sanchia because she hadn't been exclusively his?

She shook her head. 'You need have no worries like that concerning me. Andy was my one and only venture into commitment—and look how disastrously that turned out!'

Patrick settled himself on the bed beside her. 'Well, you're totally committed now,' he told her with satisfaction. 'How does it feel?'

'Not a lot different than before.'

He looked at her with teasing eyes. 'Do I detect a note of disappointment in your voice?'

Did he? Possibly. There couldn't be too many virgin brides who had built themselves up to being made love to on their wedding night—only to be told by their bridegroom that he was too tired! Although that wasn't strictly true... He had said they were both too tired. And the proof of her own tiredness was that she couldn't even remember falling asleep, although she must have done so almost immediately she shut her eyes.

But she wasn't sleepy now; in fact, she was wide awake...and suddenly very aware of Patrick as he lay beside her wearing only a robe to hide his nakedness.

Patrick gently raised her chin, smoky grey eyes looking straight into candid green. 'I know what you were thinking last night, Lilli,' he said gruffly. 'Oh, yes, I do,' he insisted as she would have protested. 'But the truth of the matter is, I want you too much, want us to enjoy each other too much, to have it spoilt in any way.'

She swallowed hard, the desire he spoke of evident in the burning intensity of his gaze. 'We're not tired now,' she pointed out shyly.

He laughed. 'No, we're not. And we are going to make love, Lilli.' He bent his head, his mouth claiming hers, lips moving erotically against hers, the tip of his tongue lightly caressing the inner moisture of her mouth.

Her arms curved up about his neck as she held him close to her, heart pounding, his hair feeling soft and silky beneath her fingertips, shoulders and back firmly muscled.

Lilli relaxed against the pillows, pulling Patrick with her, his robe and her nightgown easily disposed of as flesh met flesh, Lilli's softness against Patrick's hardness, the dark hair on his chest tickling the sensitive tips of her breasts now.

And then Patrick's lips were teasing those sensitive tips, Lilli's head back as she gasped at the liquid fire that coursed through her body, groaning low in her throat as she felt the moist warmth of his tongue flicking over her hardened nipples.

His lips and hands caressed every part of her body during the timeless hours before dawn, encouraging her to touch him in return, to discover how he liked to be caressed too, to be kissed. But she seemed to know that instinctively, revelling in the response her lips and hands evoked, until his tender ministrations reached the most intimate part of her body and she could no longer think straight as heat such as she had never known before consumed her in flames.

And then Patrick was once more kissing her on the lips, his hands on her breasts as he slowly raised her to fulfilment once again. And again. And again.

And when his body finally joined with hers there was no pain, only pleasure of another kind, his slow, caressing movements deep inside her taking her to another plateau completely. A plateau Patrick joined her on, his own groans of pleasure merging with hers, before they lay damply together, their bodies merged, their breathing deep and ragged.

'I don't think you could have forgotten a thing,' Lilli finally said when she at last found the strength to talk.

Patrick laughed. 'I hope not—any more than that and I could die of a heart attack!'

She lay on top of him, moving slightly so that she could look into his face, unconcerned with her nakedness now; there wasn't an inch of her body that Patrick didn't now know intimately. 'You weren't nervous at all last night, were you?' she realised shakily.

'You needed time to get used to me.'

'Used to' him; she was totally possessed by him at this moment! 'But you weren't really nervous, were you?' she persisted.

'Lilli.' He smoothed the tangled hair back over her shoulders, revealing the pertness of her breasts. 'If you only knew the ways I've imagined making love to you!'

He still hadn't answered her question. Or perhaps he had... He had been thinking of her last night, giving her time to become accustomed to their new relationship.

'I think I just experienced them,' she recalled breathlessly.

'Oh, no, Lilli. We've barely touched the surface,' he assured her with promise.

She quivered in anticipation, only able to imagine the delights yet to come.

'But not right now,' Patrick soothed, settling her head comfortably against his shoulder. 'Now we're going to have a nap.'

She swallowed hard. 'Like this?'

'Exactly like this,' he said with satisfaction. 'I like having you as part of me. And vice versa, I hope.' He quirked dark eyebrows.

'Oh, yes,' she admitted shyly, very much aware of the way in which he was still 'part of' her! 'But it must be late.' Daylight was visible now through the curtains at the window. 'Shouldn't we—?'

'This is the morning after our wedding, Lilli,' he teased. 'No one, least of all the hotel staff, will expect to hear from us for hours yet. At which time we will order breakfast—even if it's two o'clock in the afternoon. This is a Bennett hotel; I'm sure they will accommodate us!'

Lilli was sure they would too. But whether or not she would ever, as the owner's daughter, be able to face any of the hotel staff again after her honeymoon was another matter!

But for the moment she didn't care, was content in Patrick's arms, being with him like this. And as she drifted off into sleep she had a feeling she always would be...

'What the hell—?'

Lilli woke suddenly, to the sound of Patrick's swearing, and the reason for it—a loud knocking on the outer door of their hotel suite.

She sat up groggily, just in time to see Patrick pulling on his robe and tying the belt tightly about his waist. 'I thought you said no one would disturb us today?' she giggled, pulling the sheet up to her chin as she watched him.

'I didn't think anyone would dare to!' He scowled darkly, glaring in the direction of the loud banging. 'It had better be for a good reason!'

As he strode out of the bedroom to the suite door Lilli couldn't help but feel sorry for the person who was standing on the other side of it, although she had to admit she was a little annoyed at the intrusion herself. Patrick's words, before they'd both fallen asleep, had promised so much more...

He didn't return immediately, as she had expected he would, and finally her lethargy turned to curiosity; it must be something important to keep Patrick away this long. She could hear the murmur of male voices in the sitting-room...

She pulled on her white silk robe over her nakedness, belting it securely before running a brush lightly through her hair; she might have just spent several hours of pleasure in her husband's arms, but she didn't want everyone to realise that just by looking at her!

'Daddy!' She gasped her surprise as she saw he was the man talking to Patrick. 'Good grief, Daddy, what on earth are you doing here?' She shook her head dazedly.

'Would you believe he came to make sure I hadn't strangled you on our wedding night?' Patrick drawled derisively. 'Or you hadn't stuck that knife in my back that he once suggested!'

Lilli looked at the two men, her father flushed and agitated, Patrick calm and controlled. 'Actually—no,' she answered firmly. 'So, why are you really here, Daddy?' she prompted.

'You certainly didn't raise a fool, Richard,' Patrick said appreciatively.

The older man gave him an exasperated glare before turning back to Lilli. 'Good afternoon, Lilli,' he greeted her. 'I'm sorry to interrupt—I mean, I realise I shouldn't have—' He broke off awkwardly, the way they were both dressed—or undressed!—telling its own story. 'Gerry told me I shouldn't come here...'

'You should have listened to her,' Patrick bit out tersely. 'I, for one, do not appreciate the interruption.'

Lilli had stilled at the mention of the other woman's name. Then she remembered how kind Gerry had been to her yesterday when Sanchia had appeared so inappropriately at the wedding. Although she still resented the other woman's place in her father's life, some of what Patrick had told her earlier about his sister made her realise that, as her own father was to her, Gerry was all the family Patrick had. And, as such, Lilli couldn't continue to alienate her.

'Perhaps you *should* have listened to her,' she told her father quietly.

Her father's eyes widened, but he didn't comment on the lack of the usual resentment in her voice when she spoke of the other woman. 'Maybe I should,' he agreed. 'But I thought this was important.'

Lilli returned his gaze frowningly; he must have done to risk Patrick's wrath by intruding on their honeymoon in this way. And he had obviously got more than he bargained for by finding them so obviously still in bed! 'How important?' she said slowly.

'Very,' he insisted firmly.

'I disagree,' Patrick put in hardly.

Lilli's father shot him a questioning glance. 'I think that's for Lilli to decide, don't you...?'

Patrick's head went back arrogantly. 'As it happens, no. I don't think this concerns Lilli at all. Not any more.'

She was intrigued by the mystery of her father's visit. Obviously, whatever it was about, Patrick didn't want her involved in it.

She moved to sit on one of the armchairs. 'Tell me,' she prompted her father.

He glanced uncertainly at the younger man, obviously far from reassured by Patrick's stony expression.

'Daddy!' Lilli encouraged impatiently.

He no longer met her gaze. 'Perhaps Patrick is right; this can wait until after your honeymoon—'

'We've had our honeymoon,' she assured him firmly. 'Have you forgotten we're joining you tomorrow for Christmas.' She didn't even look at Patrick now, knowing she would see disapproval in his face. But she was not a child, and she refused to be treated like one, by either man.

Her father slumped down into another of the armchairs. 'I'd completely forgotten it's Christmas...!' he groaned.

'Don't let Gerry hear you say that,' Patrick warned

mockingly. 'She loves Christmas. I suggest you make sure you have something suitable for her by tomorrow!'

'Stop trying to change the subject, Patrick.' Again Lilli didn't so much as look at him. 'I'm not so easily deterred.'

'Does that mean you've already bought my Christmas present?' he returned tauntingly.

She had, as a matter of fact—a beautiful watch, already wrapped and ready to give him on Christmas morning. But that wasn't important just now.

'It means,' she said with slow determination, 'that I'm not going to be sidetracked. Daddy!' She was even more forceful this time.

'She gets her stubbornness from me, I'm afraid,' he told the younger man ruefully.

'It's irrelevant where she gets it from,' Patrick dismissed tersely. 'This is none of her business.'

'I'll be the judge of that,' she snapped. She had been kept in the dark too much already by these two men; it wasn't going to continue.

'You aren't Elizabeth Bennett any more, Lilli,' Patrick rasped. 'You're Mrs Lilli Devlin. And *Mr* Devlin has already decided this does not concern you!'

She stood up angrily. '*Mr* Devlin doesn't own me,' she returned furiously. 'Maybe someone should have told you: women aren't chattels any more! Now, either one of you tells me what's going on, or I'll go and ask someone who will tell me,' she added challengingly.

Patrick looked at her scathingly. 'Such as who?'

'Such as Gerry!' she announced triumphantly, knowing by the stunned look on both the men's faces that this hadn't even occurred to them as a possibility. Lilli wasn't so sure it was either; she might feel less antagonistic towards the other woman, but she wasn't sure she would be able to go to her about this! But hopefully neither of these two men would realise that… 'Well?' she prompted hardly when her announcement didn't produce the result she wanted, looking from one man to the other, her father looking decidedly uncomfortable, Patrick stubbornly unmoved. 'Fine,' she finally snapped, walking towards the bedroom, her clear intention to go and dress before leaving. 'Gerry it is!'

'Lilli, I forbid you to go anywhere near Gerry!' Patrick thundered autocratically.

She halted in her tracks, turning slowly, looking at him with cool incredulity.

'Uh-oh,' her father muttered warily. 'You've done it now, Patrick. The last time I forbade Lilli from going near someone she ended up *marrying* you!'

Patrick's mouth quirked. 'That hardly applies in this case, does it? Besides, it's because Lilli is married to me that I—'

'Think you can tell me what to do,' she finished scathingly, shaking her head. 'I don't think so,' she bit out coldly. 'Daddy?' she prompted in a voice that brooked no further argument.

He sighed, giving a regretful glance in Patrick's direction before turning back to Lilli. 'Andy telephoned me this morning,' he stated without flourish.

She gasped in shock. Whatever she had been expecting, it wasn't this!

She froze momentarily. 'Andy did…?'

Her father nodded. 'He wants to see you, Lilli,' he told her softly.

She hadn't been mistaken yesterday; it had been Andy standing outside in the crowd as she went to the wedding. But why did he want to see her…?

CHAPTER ELEVEN

'YOU JUST AREN'T thinking this through at all, Lilli,' Patrick said as he sat watching her dress. 'Brewster believes that by talking to you, appealing to your softer nature, he may be able to stop your father's legal proceedings against him!'

She didn't look at him, hadn't done so since he'd followed her into the bedroom a few minutes ago. They had made love in this room, knew each other intimately, and yet she still felt slightly self-conscious at having Patrick watch her, thankfully pulling up the side zip to olive-green trousers before pulling on a matching sweater.

She was still stunned by Andy's contact with her father, couldn't imagine what had made him do such a thing. She certainly didn't agree with Patrick's last comment; she had every reason to hate Andy, and he must be well aware of that fact. Where Andy was concerned, she had no 'softer nature' to appeal to!

'And just how do you think he hopes to achieve that?' she replied, still smarting from Patrick's earlier attempt to tell her what she could and couldn't do. Marriage was a partnership—particularly this marriage!—and she was not about to be told whom she could or couldn't see.

'You were engaged to the man—'

'And he used that engagement to cheat my father,' she reminded him forcefully.

'You loved him—'

'I thought I did,' she corrected him; loving Patrick as she now did, she knew damn well she had never really loved Andy at all!

'You were going to marry him—'

'And now I'm married to you.' She looked at him challengingly. 'A fact I'm unlikely to forget!'

Patrick returned her gaze. 'We made a bargain, Lilli—'

'And I won't renege on that,' she returned sharply. 'But being married to you does not make me your prisoner. I have no idea why Andy wants to talk to me,' she added as his face darkened ominously, 'but I honestly don't see that it can cause any harm.' Her father was right; telling her not to do something was a sure way of ensuring that she did!

Patrick stood up, throwing off his robe, completely unconcerned by his own nakedness as he took underwear from a drawer. 'I'm coming with you,' he informed her as he dressed.

'No!'

He halted in the action of buttoning up his shirt. 'What do you mean...no?' he said slowly.

'I mean no, Patrick,' she repeated firmly, outwardly undaunted by his fury—inwardly quaking. Patrick was again the coldly resilient man who had come to her home the day after their initial night together, a man who seemed like a stranger to her. But she wouldn't allow Patrick to see any of her inner apprehension. 'Andy asked to see me—'

'And I'm now your husband—'

'We aren't joined at the hip, Patrick!' she snapped impatiently. 'And I really don't have the time for this,' she added after glancing at her wristwatch. 'The sooner I see Andy, the sooner we'll all know what's going on.'

'I've already told you what's going on: the man believes he can use emotional pressure, or possibly blackmail—'

'Strangely, I would rather hear all this from Andy himself.' Her eyes flashed deeply green.

Patrick looked at her between narrowed lids. 'You still care for the man…!'

'Rubbish!' Her cheeks were flushed with anger at the very suggestion of it.

In truth, she had come to realise in the last week exactly how shallow her feelings for Andy had been… And it was because she loved Patrick, loved him in a totally different way, completely, intensely, in every way there was to love a man—even his anger!

Andy had been a challenge to her, she had realised, a man who didn't respond to the way she looked as other men always had—for reasons she understood only too well now! But his lack of interest had only piqued her own interest in him a year ago, and it was only since loving Patrick, when every nerve-ending, every part of her, was live to his presence, that she had realised how lukewarm her desire for Andy had been.

To have married him, she now knew, would have been a complete disaster. But she couldn't explain that to Patrick without admitting how she had come to realise that fact. And she couldn't, at this moment, admit to Patrick that he was the very reason she could now see Andy without fear of emotional pressure, of any kind, having any effect whatsoever. Loving Patrick consumed all of her emotions; there was no room for anyone else.

But it was almost as if Patrick's tenderness last night, and again this morning, might never have happened as he continued to glare at her accusingly. Lilli didn't have time to deal with his temper just now, wanted to get this meeting with Andy over and done with.

'Daddy's waiting,' she told Patrick briskly. 'We can talk when I get back—'

'I won't be here, Lilli,' Patrick said flatly.

She gave him a startled look. 'What do you mean…?'

He shrugged. 'By your own words, our honeymoon is over. In which case, I may as well go to my office for a couple of hours.'

For a moment she had thought—! Ridiculous—she and Patrick were married, for life, by his own decree. And, both being determined people, she didn't doubt they would have many disagreements in the future, but that didn't mean either of them intended giving up on their marriage. As Patrick had said earlier, they had made a bargain. For all they knew, she could already have conceived the first of those four children…

Patrick nodded abruptly. 'I'll see you later, Lilli.' He strode out of the room.

No parting kiss, not even a second glance; he just went. And it was with a heavy heart that Lilli joined her father in the suite lounge where he had sat waiting for her.

He looked up, frowning at her. 'Patrick looks—' He hesitated over his choice of description.

'Furious,' she finished for him. 'That's probably because he is.' She slipped on her jacket.

'Actually, I was going to use a much more basic word to describe how he looked,' her father returned ruefully.

She gave a warn smile. 'He doesn't want me to see Andy.'

'I think he made that more than obvious earlier.' Her father grimaced. 'And for once I have to agree with him.'

Her eyes widened accusingly. 'I wouldn't even know Andy wanted to talk to me if you hadn't come here and told me!'

'I know,' he said wearily. 'And I think now I was probably wrong to do so.'

She laughed dismissively. 'Let's go, Daddy—before you start proving as stubborn as Patrick!' She took a firm hold of his arm and led him out of the suite, locking the door behind them; Patrick had his own key if he returned before them. 'I believe you said Andy wants me to meet him at—' She named a very exclusive hotel as they entered the lift. 'He's staying there on your money, I suppose!' she added scornfully.

Her father raised his eyebrows. 'Who knows? I'm at a complete loss as to what's going on. All he would say when he telephoned earlier was that he had to talk to you—'

'I thought you said he telephoned *you*?' she reminded him.

'I had to say that.' He grimaced. 'How do you think Patrick would have reacted to being told it was you your ex-fiancé wanted—insisted!—on talking to all the time?'

Exactly as he had reacted now—he had walked away!

But she still didn't understand; why did Andy want to talk to her? He had to know how she felt about him now, had to realise that what they had once shared had been over the moment he decided to cheat her father. And used her to do it!

She gave a heavy sigh. 'Maybe we had better not speculate any of this until we see Andy—'

'*You* see him,' her father corrected her. 'He had the damned nerve to tell me he doesn't want to speak to me. Although, to be honest, now that I'm involved in legal proceedings against him, I don't want to speak to him either. I think if I saw him, after the heartache he's caused, I would probably just hit him and think about the consequences of that action later—which wouldn't help anyone! I'll wait outside the hotel for you. But make sure he realises, exactly as I told him on the telephone this morning, that whatever he has to say to you will make no difference to the legal proceedings being brought against him.'

Now she was even more puzzled by this meeting between Andy and herself. He didn't want to see her father... She didn't know what she had been expecting—perhaps a plea from Andy, or even the blackmail that Patrick had suggested. Now she wasn't so sure...

Andy sat alone at one of the tables in the huge reception area, a pot of coffee in front of him. Lilli had time to study him before he was aware of her presence. The last three months hadn't been kind to him either; his handsome face was ravaged and tired-looking, his suit fitting him loosely, as if he had lost weight too.

Lilli hardened her heart to the way he looked; he was the cause of everyone's unhappiness, including his own, from the look of him!

She walked to the table, standing beside it looking down at him wordlessly as she waited for him to say something.

He stood up. 'At least sit down, Lilli,' he said, holding back the chair for her. 'You're looking well,' he told her as he resumed his own seat opposite her.

'What do you want, Andy?'

'I suppose it is a little late for social politeness between us,' he conceded. 'Could I just say, I never meant to hurt you, Lilli—?'

'Didn't you?' she interrupted.

He gave a sad sigh. 'No...'

'You hurt me because of what you did to my father, but on a more personal level...?' She shook her head, her eyes flashing her pain. If she had been hurt in any way

by the end of their engagement then it had been her pride
that had taken the blow—and, as Patrick had already assured her all too clearly, she had more than enough of that!

Andy looked at her closely for several seconds, and
then he slowly nodded. 'I'm glad about that. I thought
by the announcement of your marriage to Devlin that I
couldn't have done you too much harm—'

'I haven't come here to discuss the harm—or otherwise!—that you did to me,' Lilli cut in. 'My father is the
one— What on earth is that?' She stopped as Andy pro-
duced a small flat package from his jacket pocket, the
paper brightly coloured, decorated with a silver bow and
ribbon. 'I realise it's Christmas tomorrow, Andy—' her
mouth twisted contemptuously as she looked at the present '—but I—'

'It isn't a Christmas present, Lilli, it's a wedding gift,'
Andy told her, holding out the small present to her.

Her eyes widened, her hands tightly locked together in
her lap. 'I don't want anything from you!' And she knew,
without even consulting him, that Patrick wouldn't want
it either!

'You'll want this.' Andy continued to hold out the gaily
wrapped gift, but when she still didn't take it he put it
down on the table between them, standing up. 'Please tell
your father I'm sorry.'

'Where are you going?' she said incredulously as he
would have walked away; she still had so much to say
to him!

He gave a little smile. 'I'm not going anywhere, Lilli;
I'm staying exactly where I am. The last three months
have been a nightmare—'

'You think they've been a nightmare for *you*?' she demanded disbelievingly. 'What do you think it's been like
for my father? He—'

'I know,' Andy acknowledged heavily, coming down on his haunches beside her chair, reaching out to clasp both her hands in his. 'I do know, Lilli. That's why I'll understand if, after opening your present, your father still wants to prosecute me.' He shook his head sadly. 'It was all so tempting, Lilli, too much so in the circumstances.' He looked at her pleadingly. 'I was involved in a relationship that—well, I was in over my head. I thought if I had some money of my own—'

'I know about your—relationship, Andy,' she told him hardly. 'It's the reason I know you could never really have cared for me!'

He closed his eyes briefly, those eyes slightly over-bright when he raised his lids to look at her once again. 'I did—do—care for you, Lilli. You're a wonderful woman—'

'Please, Andy.' She instantly shook her head. 'Don't take me for a complete fool!'

He let out a deep breath. 'I know how it must seem to you, but I— If things had been different—'

'Don't you mean, if *you* had been different?' she countered, pulling her hands away from his.

'Yes,' he acknowledged. 'But you really are an exceptional woman, Lilli—a caring, beautiful woman. And you deserved so much better than me—'

'She got it!' interrupted a harsh voice.

Lilli and Andy turned sharply in the direction of that voice, Lilli troubled, Andy guarded, slowly straightening to face the other man. Lilli couldn't even begin to imagine what Andy thought of Patrick's presence here—she was too busy wondering about that herself!

Patrick's mouth showed his contempt as he looked at the younger man. The two were in such stark contrast to each other, Patrick so dark where Andy was golden, Patrick's face masculine, Andy's, seen against such stark masculinity, appearing much softer, his features so regular and handsome he appeared almost beautiful.

As the two men continued to stare at each other, Lilli couldn't help wondering if Patrick had entered the hotel in time to see Andy holding her hands...!

Whatever he had or hadn't seen, his cold anger of earlier this afternoon certainly hadn't diminished; he still looked furious!

'Lilli and I were married yesterday,' he informed Andy icily, pulling Lilli to her feet so that she stood at his side, holding her there firmly, his arm like a steel band about her waist.

Andy nodded. 'I realise that.'

'Then you must also realise that you have intruded on our honeymoon,' Patrick barked. 'An unwelcome intrusion.'

'I realise that too,' Andy acknowledged ruefully. 'But I had something I had to give to Lilli.' He bent down and picked up the gaily wrapped present before handing it to Lilli. 'I hope the two of you will be very happy together,' he added lightly, although he seemed to frown as he glanced at Patrick's harshly set face, his expression softening as he turned to Lilli. 'You're a very lucky man to have Lilli for your wife.' Even as he spoke to Patrick he bent forward and lightly kissed Lilli on the cheek. 'Take care, love. And be happy.' He turned and walked away.

There was complete silence as Andy left the hotel, Lilli still clutching the small present he had given her, Patrick silent at her side. She didn't need two guesses as to why; he was absolutely furious—at her for seeing Andy at all, but also at the fact that the man had dared to kiss her, albeit on the cheek!

'For goodness' sake, stop brooding, Patrick!' she told

him spiritedly as she moved out of his grasp. 'I don't re-call that I behaved this way yesterday when your ex-wife decided to turn up at our wedding!' In fact, that subject hadn't been mentioned, by either of them, since.

He looked blank, as if the memory was something he had completely forgotten about. And perhaps it was; San-chia didn't appear to be someone he wanted to remember. But that didn't change the fact that his reaction to Andy now was completely unfair to her.

Patrick relaxed suddenly. 'Let's sit down for a while. Your father has gone home, so he isn't going to be wait-ing outside. I spoke to him on my way in,' he supplied at her questioning look. 'I couldn't see the point in both of us waiting for you.' The two of them sat at the table Andy had recently vacated.

Of course not. And, of course, her father would also have seen the sense of that—with a little help from Pat-rick...!

'Open the damned present,' Patrick instructed tersely. 'Although I still think, given the circumstances, that Brewster had a damned nerve wanting to see you at all, let alone give you a present!'

Lilli wasn't really listening to him, was staring down at the gift she had just unwrapped, the silver ribbon and bow hanging limply from her hand now.

'What is it?' Patrick prompted sharply. 'Lilli!'

She looked across at him, her eyes unfocusing, her face pale. She couldn't think, let alone speak!

'For God's sake...!' Patrick stood up to come round the table and take the package roughly out of her hand, looking quickly at the contents. 'My God...!' he finally breathed dazedly.

Lilli knew exactly what had caused his astonishment. The same thing that had caused her own... Andy's gift to her was a bank account, made out in her name. For the amount of five million pounds!

The amount he had taken from her father…?

She looked up at Patrick. 'Is that what he owed?'

His expression was grim now. 'More or less,' he grated.

She frowned. 'How much less?'

He shrugged. 'Probably the interest that should have been earned in the last three to four months. Brewster has probably needed that for his living expenses. I doubt your father will mind that, as long as he gets the capital returned to him.'

Lilli was still totally fazed, couldn't believe what had just happened. 'Why do you think Andy did it? Gave it back, I mean.' It was almost like a dream, and if it weren't for that bank account—for five million!—Lilli would have had trouble believing Andy had been here at all.

Patrick threw the bank book and account statement down onto the table, sitting in the chair opposite hers once again. 'I did some checking during the short time I had before coming here. Brewster's relationship has apparently foundered, probably because of the pending court case; his lover is apparently the type who doesn't care to be associated with criminals! So maybe Brewster just decided to try and salvage at least part of his life and try to walk away. I have a feeling your father will let him do that.'

So did she, once she had spoken to her father. 'He's certainly going to be ecstatic at the return of this.' She touched the statement as if she still couldn't believe the money was actually there, within her father's grasp.

Patrick said, 'He's gone back to Gerry's house, if you want to take it to him.'

This time Lilli didn't feel that sickening lurch in her stomach at the mention of the relationship between his sister and her father. Maybe she was getting used to the idea...

'And you?' Patrick suddenly asked her. 'How do you feel about it?'

She gave a glowing smile. 'Wonderful! Daddy has his money back, and it looks as if all the publicity a court case would have engendered can be avoided as well. It's— But you don't look too pleased, Patrick.' She suddenly realised he looked grimmer than ever. 'Do you think there's something wrong with the return of the money?' She looked down at the bank statement. 'Is Andy playing some sort of cruel joke on us all? Do you—?'

'Relax,' Patrick advised. 'The money is in a bank account in your name. It's yours. But it means the two of us have some serious talking to do once you've seen your father,' he added firmly.

Lilli looked startled. 'We do...?'

'One day, Lilli,' he bit out. 'Do you realise that if Brewster had returned that money to you just one day earlier you wouldn't now be my wife?' He looked at her intently. 'Would you?'

All the colour drained from her face as the force of his words hit her. One day... If Andy had come to see her the day before her marriage to Patrick, then he was right— there would have been no wedding. She wouldn't now be Patrick's wife. Never would have been!

She couldn't speak as this sickening realisation hit her.

'Exactly,' he grated, standing up. 'I really do have some things to do at the moment, Lilli. But we'll talk about this later at the hotel.'

Lilli sat and watched him go, her eyes dark green pools. Exactly what were they going to talk about? Not divorce? Did Patrick realise, with the return of this money, that

they should never have been married at all? Did none of
last night and this morning matter to him? Did he want
to end their marriage before it had even begun?

CHAPTER TWELVE

'BUT THIS IS wonderful!' Her father's delight was obvious as he smiled broadly. 'Absolutely marvellous!'

'But is it?' Gerry said slowly, looking at Lilli. 'Lilli doesn't look too happy.'

Her father turned to her too now, noticing the paleness of her face. 'Lilli?' he said warily. 'Brewster didn't say or do anything to upset you, did he?'

'No,' she dismissed with a shaky laugh.

'There aren't any hidden conditions attached to the return of this money, are there?'

She had come in a taxi straight to Gerry's house, knew she had to put her father's mind at rest as soon as possible. But inside she was still in shock from Patrick's enigmatic comments before he'd left her, couldn't actually remember the taxi journey here.

'No hidden conditions,' she assured her father wryly. 'I think Andy was quite relieved to get rid of it; a life of crime doesn't seem to have brought him too much happiness!'

'Then—'

'Where is Patrick, Lilli?' Gerry interjected. 'Richard said he came to join you at the hotel...?'

'He did.' She avoided the other woman's gaze. Gerry

saw far too much! 'But he had some business to attend to,' she added brightly.

'Did he?' Gerry returned sceptically.

Lilli still didn't meet her sister-in-law's eyes. 'He said he did, yes.'

'But...?'

'Really, Gerry.' Lilli gave a light laugh, although no humour reached the dull pain in her eyes. 'You know Patrick—if he says he has something else to do, then he has something else to do.'

'I do know Patrick,' his sister acknowledged softly. 'We've always been very close. He more or less brought me up, you know.'

'Yes, he told me about that,' Lilli replied, those moments of intimacy between them seeming a lifetime away.

'Did he?' Gerry nodded her satisfaction with that. 'Then you must realise that the two of us know each other rather better than most brothers and sisters, that we've always had an emotional closeness?'

Lilli gave the other woman a puzzled glance. 'I don't understand where all this is leading to—'

'It's leading to the fact that Patrick is in love with you,' Gerry told her impatiently. 'And I have a feeling—a terrible feeling!—that because of this—' she held up the bank book and statement '—Patrick is going to do something incredibly stupid!'

Lilli was quick to protest, 'Patrick isn't in love with me, and—'

'Oh, yes, he is,' the other woman assured her with certainty.

'—he never does anything "incredibly stupid",' Lilli finished determinedly. 'Unless you count marrying me in the first place,' she added bitterly.

'Lilli, exactly what has Patrick said to you?' Gerry probed.

Lilli stood up and turned away from both her father and the other woman. 'Apart from more or less saying we should start talking about a divorce?' she said fiercely. 'Not a lot!'

'A divorce?' her father echoed incredulously. 'But you were only married yesterday! He can't be serious—'

'They were married yesterday, Richard,' Gerry cut in gently. 'But today the reason for Lilli marrying Patrick— that money—' she gestured in the direction of the bank book '—was made null and void. That is the reason Patrick believes you married him, isn't it, Lilli?'

She was starting to resent Gerry again; this was none of her business, even if she was Patrick's sister! '*It is* the reason I married him,' Lilli came back; she didn't believe either of these two could seriously have ever been fooled into believing otherwise!

'So you're going to agree to a divorce?' Gerry watched her shrewdly.

Lilli felt ill just at the thought of it, knowing she must have once again gone pale. 'If that's what Patrick's wants, yes.'

'And what do *you* want?' the other woman persisted.

'You know Patrick; I don't think I'll have a lot of say in this one way or the other!'

'Lilli, your father told me Patrick said he hadn't raised a fool.' Gerry spoke plainly. 'But at this moment you're being extremely foolish!' she added caustically.

'I don't think I asked for your opinion!' Lilli felt deep resentment.

'And now you're being very rude,' her father said sternly, moving forward to put his arms about Gerry's shoulders. 'Gerry is trying to help you—'

'I don't need—or want!—her help,' Lilli told him forcefully, her hands clenched at her sides at this show of solidarity from the couple. The last thing she needed at this moment was to have their relationship pushed in her face. She felt as if her whole world was falling apart already, without that!

'Calm down, Richard.' Gerry put a soothing hand against his chest as he would have exploded angrily. 'Lilli is hurt and upset—and God knows we all do stupid things when we feel like that! I think it's time, Richard,' she opined slowly, 'that Lilli heard about some of the stupid things I did in the past—don't you?'

He looked down at her uncertainly. 'I—'

'It's time, Richard,' Gerry repeated firmly. 'Unless you want Lilli to make the same mistake I did? Because, believe me, these two are even more stubborn than we are, and at this moment, basically because she's here and Patrick isn't, I think Lilli is more open to reason.'

Lilli's father glanced across at his daughter uncertainly, Lilli steadily returning his gaze. She had no idea what all this was about, and she wasn't sure she wanted to know either. But she did know that when she got back to the hotel Patrick was going to talk about their future— or lack of it!—and anything that delayed that happening was acceptable!

'Very well.' Her father finally gave his agreement. 'But listen carefully, Lilli. And try not to judge,' he added almost pleadingly.

'Do I need to sit down for this?'

'Yes,' her father confirmed, going to the drinks tray on the side dresser. 'You're also going to need this.' He handed her a glass of brandy. 'We all are!' He handed another glass to Gerry, and kept one for himself.

Lilli sat, although she made no move to drink the

brandy, putting the glass down on the table beside her chair, looking up expectantly at Gerry.

The other woman looked apprehensive at her sceptical expression. 'Your father is right, Lilli—you aren't going to like what you hear,' she said. 'But please try to understand; this isn't being done to hurt; I'm doing this for an altogether different reason.'

'I'll try,' Lilli conceded dryly.

'Lilli—'

'Leave it, Richard,' the other woman told him lightly. 'Lilli makes no pretence of doing anything other than disliking me, and at least it's honest. It isn't what I would like, but it's honest.' She walked over to the blazing fire, suddenly seeming to need its warmth. 'Six years ago I met a man I fell very much in love with,' she began. 'Unfortunately, the man was married— We haven't all led neatly packaged lives, Lilli,' she added at Lilli's derisive expression. 'The man was married. Unhappily—I know, aren't they all?' she acknowledged self-deprecatingly. 'But in this case it was true. I had seen the two of them together, knew that the wife was involved with someone else. And I—I fell in love with the husband. And he loved me in return.'

'But your marriage only lasted a couple of months,' Lilli pointed out. 'Hardly the love of a lifetime!' she said scathingly, wondering why she was being told all this.

'Because I didn't marry the man I loved!' Gerry returned curtly. 'There were complications. The man had a child. At fifteen, not a very young child, I'll admit, but a child the father loved very much. And there were reasons why—why this man couldn't leave his wife and child.'

'Once again, there always are,' Lilli returned without interest, this was an all-too-familiar story, surely...?

Gerry drew in a harsh breath. 'But in this case the wife

threatened to completely alienate the child from the father if he dared to leave her—'

'But I thought you said she was involved in an affair, too?'

'She was,' Gerry rasped. 'And if things had been—different she had intended leaving her husband! But the woman became ill, seriously so, and her—lover decided he didn't want to tie himself to a woman dying of cancer.'

Lilli had become suddenly still, her eyes wide now as she stared at Gerry. 'Go on...'

'Your father and I were deeply in love, Lilli,' Gerry told her emotionally. 'We had intended being together. But he—he left it too late to agree to giving your mother a divorce. She had been diagnosed as terminally ill, her lover left her, and suddenly all she was left with was a broken marriage. And her daughter.' Gerry swallowed hard. 'She was determined to hang onto both of them—at any cost.'

Lilli could hardly breathe, felt suddenly numb.

'Your parents' marriage began to deteriorate after your brother died, Lilli,' the other woman continued huskily. 'Your father buried himself in his work—and loving you. And your mother went from one affair to another. And the love they had once felt for each other turned to a tolerant contempt. By the time I met your father four years later they were living completely separate lives, with you as their only common ground.'

Lilli looked at her father with pained eyes, couldn't believe she could have been so blind to her parents' loveless marriage. Or perhaps she hadn't... She had known they spent little time together, that her mother could be verbally vicious to her father when she chose to be, but she had always put that down to the pain of her illness. Now she could see that perhaps it had been that they simply didn't love each other any more...

'Daddy...?' She looked at him emotionally now.

'I'm sorry, Lilli. So sorry.' He gripped her hands tightly. 'But it's all true. In fact, there's so much more. Your mother had asked me for a divorce before she found out about her illness, was going off with this other man—'

'Richard...!' Gerry looked at him uncertainly.

He shook his head, his gaze still on Lilli. 'It's time it all came out, Gerry. Your mother was leaving us, Lilli. She had told me she was going, asked me for a divorce—on her terms, of course. She wanted a huge settlement of money, and in return she would leave you with me. The man she was involved with was ten years younger than her, and he didn't want Caroline's fifteen-year-old daughter cluttering up their lives.'

'Mummy was leaving me behind,' Lilli said dazedly.

'Yes,' he replied. 'And I was happy to give her the money if I could keep you. Then she found out she had cancer...' His expression darkened. 'And everything changed!'

'Lilli!' Gerry came to her side as she swayed where she sat. 'No more of that, Richard,' she said briskly. 'I only wanted to try to explain a little...'

'I've misjudged you,' Lilli realised flatly, reaching out blindly to clasp the other woman's hand—blindly because her eyes were full of tears. 'Patrick knows all of this, doesn't he?' She realised only too well now what he had meant when he'd said her father had been protective of her to the point of stupidity! She looked up at her father now. 'You gave up your chance of happiness because you didn't want to lose me,' she said brokenly.

'You had already been through so much when we lost Robbie—'

'You gave up the woman you loved—Gerry—' she looked at the other woman as the tears began to fall down her cheeks '—so that Mummy wouldn't destroy all our lives. And you…' She tightly squeezed Gerry's hand. 'You married someone else on the rebound.' She recalled her father's words… 'An angry and upset Gerry is a force to be reckoned with!'

'Oh, Lilli!' Gerry moved to hug her. 'Don't make the same mistake. Please!'

She pulled back slightly. 'You mean Patrick?'

'I mean my stubborn, arrogant brother,' Gerry confirmed. 'It runs in the family, I'm afraid. Your father went out of my life five years ago because I was too stubborn to listen to him. I married—disastrously—to spite him. I loved him, wanted to be with him, and although I understood what he was doing it was impossible for me to stay in his life. My marriage was a mess, and within a couple of months I had to admit I had made a terrible mistake.' She grimaced at the memory. 'Don't do something stupid like I did, Lilli. I know Patrick; he would never have married you if he didn't love you.'

'When he asked me to marry him it was because he said I had the qualities he wanted in his wife, in the mother of his children—'

'He probably believed it when he said it too.' Gerry shook her head with affectionate exasperation. 'But it's all nonsense. Patrick is in love with you— Yes, he is, Lilli,' she insisted firmly even as Lilli opened her mouth to deny it. 'Do you love him? The truth, Lilli. It's the day for the truth,' she went on throatily.

Lilli took a deep breath. 'I— Yes!' The word was virtually forced out of her. It was one thing to admit to herself how she felt, quite another thing to admit it to someone else. Even someone she realised she had completely misjudged… God, Gerry should have been the one resenting her all this time, not the other way around. So many years wasted... And what Gerry was saying to her now was, did she want to waste as many by giving up on Patrick without a fight? But Gerry had known Richard loved her, whereas Patrick didn't love Lilli at all...

'Then what do you have to lose by telling him so?' Gerry sat back, her expression encouraging. 'Your pride? Oh, Lilli!' She held her hand out towards the man she loved, straightening to stand at his side. 'My pride, after I made such a mess of things, cost me years I could have spent with your father. Long, lonely years, when I went out with lots of men who meant nothing to me, men who, because of their own male pride, would never admit to anyone that those relationships were never physical. I've been so lonely, for so long, without your father, Lilli; but thank God he came back and claimed me once he was free to do so!'

'And—thank God—she let me!' Lilli's father added with feeling.

Lilli smiled shakily up at the two of them. 'So when are the two of you getting married?'

'As soon as you and Patrick agree to be our witnesses,' her father told her.

Patrick... A shadow passed over her face, her smile, emotional as it was, fading.

'I'm ordering you to stay away from him, Lilli,' her father told her expectantly.

Her smile returned, a little wanly, but it did return. 'That won't work this time, Daddy. I—' She broke off as the telephone began to ring, Gerry going to answer it.

'Good afternoon, Patrick,' she greeted once he had identified himself as the caller. 'Richard is ecstatic over the news, and— Yes, Lilli is still here.' She glanced across the room at a now tense Lilli. 'Well, we're all just about to sit down and enjoy a celebratory glass of cham-

pagne— Yes, I know it's your honeymoon,' she answered
him smoothly. 'But it's Christmas too. And we all have
something to celebrate—why don't you come and join
us—?' Gerry suddenly held the receiver away from her
ear, wincing as the loudness of Patrick's voice down the
receiver could now be heard by all of them, although the
words themselves were indistinct. 'Well, it's your choice,
of course. Lilli will be back later.' Gerry looked down at
the receiver, shrugging before placing it back on its cradle.
'I'll give him twenty minutes.' She grinned.

'For what?' Lilli frowned, having been frozen in her
seat since she realised it was Patrick on the telephone, her
hands still shaking slightly.

'For him to get here.' Gerry grinned her satisfaction.
'And you doubted he loves you! Patrick never shouts, Lilli.
He's never needed to. The softer he talks, the more anxious people are to do what he wants. But he's shouting
now, Lilli—and it's because I deliberately gave him the
impression you wouldn't be going back to the hotel until
later this evening.' She laughed, glancing at her wristwatch. 'Eighteen minutes, and counting!'

Lilli was sure the other woman was wrong. As his
sister, she might know Patrick very well, but she had no
knowledge of him as a husband. There was no way Patrick would come to her...

And she wasn't going to him yet either, wasn't ready
for that, readily falling in with her father's suggestion
that they have the champagne after all. Anything to delay
going back to the hotel. And discussing their divorce...

'To the two of you.' She toasted her father and Gerry
with pink champagne. 'May you be happy together at last.'
She owed them this much, owed them so much more than
she had ever realised.

Her marriage to Patrick meant she was no longer a

child, and she was learning all too forcefully what Patrick had said all along: things were never just black and white. No one was to blame for the triangle that had evolved six years ago, not even her mother. Maybe it wasn't emotionally fair, but, faced with a sure slow death, her mother had clung to the things that she still could, and that included her husband and daughter. Given the same circumstances, Lilli wasn't sure she would have done the same thing, but it was what had happened, and it was over now. It was time to shut the door on that, and start again.

For all of them, it seemed...

She swallowed down her feelings of apprehension with the champagne. Time enough to face all that later; right now was the time to let her father celebrate. And for him and Gerry to be allowed to be happy with each other at long last.

'Hmm, three minutes early,' Gerry suddenly murmured after another glance at her watch. 'He must have broken several speed limits to get here this fast at this time of the day—and on Christmas Eve!' She smiled across at Lilli. 'I just heard Patrick's car in the driveway.' She listened again. 'Patrick entering the house,' she added ruefully as the front door could be heard slamming loudly shut. 'Patrick entering the room,' she announced before turning to face him, a glowing smile lighting up her face. 'Patrick, what a surprise!' she greeted warmly. 'You decided to join us, after all.'

He didn't even glance at his sister, all his attention focused on Lilli as she stood near the fire. 'I thought you were coming back to the hotel once you had spoken to your father,' he grated accusingly.

Her hand trembled slightly as she held onto her champagne glass. 'We were celebrating,' she said with soft dismissal.

'Richard and I were just going off in search of another bottle of champagne,' Gerry said lightly. 'Weren't we, darling?' she prompted pointedly.

'Er—yes. We were,' he agreed somewhat disjointedly, frowning at Lilli and Patrick.

Patrick returned his gaze coldly. 'Pink, of course,' he said. 'It's Lilli's favourite.'

'How well you know your wife,' Gerry drawled, lightly touching his cheek as she passed him on her way to the door. 'We shouldn't be too long,' she assured Lilli gently in passing.

The room suddenly seemed very quiet once the other couple had left, closing the door softly behind them, even the ticking of the clock on the fireplace suddenly audible.

Lilli could only stare at Patrick. Dear God, he looked grim. Her hands began to shake again as she tightly gripped the glass.

'But not for much longer, hmm, Lilli?' he suddenly exclaimed as he strode further into the room, dark and overpowering in black denims and a black sweater. 'Will I know you as my wife?' he added at her puzzled frown.

Something seemed to snap inside her at that moment, a return of the old Lilli through the fog of uncertainty, pain, truth—so much truth, it was still difficult to take it all in!—and she faced Patrick unflinchingly as she carefully placed her glass down on the table behind her. 'I thought we had an agreement that our marriage was for life,' she reminded him haughtily—every inch Elizabeth Bennett at that moment. But she was neither Just Lilli nor Elizabeth Bennett any more, she was Lilli Devlin—and she was about to fight for what she wanted! 'The agreement—verbal though it might have been—was binding on both sides. You can't just opt out of it when it suits you, Patrick.' She still didn't believe that Patrick loved her—it would be too much to hope for!—but if she could remain his wife, who knew what might happen in the future...?

'When it suits me—!' he exploded furiously, a nerve pulsing erratically in the hardness of his cheek. 'It doesn't *suit* me at all to have my wife walk out on me the day after our wedding! Even Sanchia waited a little longer than that.'

'Forget Sanchia,' Lilli returned. 'I am not her, am nothing like her. And I'm not walking out on you.'

'I have just spent most of the day, the day following our wedding, at the hotel on my own,' he bit out. 'I would say that's walking out!'

'Rubbish,' she snapped back. 'I spent all of the morning and part of the afternoon, at the hotel with you,' she reminded him, a blush to her cheeks as she remembered those hours of intimacy. 'We've been apart maybe three hours at the most—'

'And look what happened in those three hours!' he said disgustedly.

'What, Patrick? What happened during that time?' she challenged. 'My father had his money returned to him. What does that have to do with us, with our marriage? You told me last week that it wasn't mentioned during the proposal or the acceptance; so what bearing does this afternoon's events have on our marriage? Well?' she pressed after several seconds of tense silence.

He gave a snort. 'Everything!'

She became suddenly still, looking at him carefully. 'Why?'

'Oh, for God's sake, Lilli.' He paced about the room. 'It may not have been mentioned, but we both know how relevant Brewster giving the money back is to us; you admitted as much yourself earlier this afternoon when I asked you!'

She thought back to their conversation after Andy had left, to what Patrick had said, because she hadn't said anything! 'And just how did I admit it, Patrick?' she asked softly. 'I don't believe *I* said anything.'

'You didn't have to,' he groaned. 'The look on your face when you realised how close you had come to not marrying me spoke for itself; you went white!'

She drew in a deep breath. Pride, Gerry had told her, had cost her six years of happiness with the man she loved...

'Are you interested in why I went white, Patrick?' she said.

'I know why you went white,' he ground out, glaring at her. 'You missed keeping your freedom by twenty-four hours!'

Lilli steadily met his tempestuous gaze, unmoved by the fierceness of his expression. 'You're partly right—' She ignored his second snort of disgust in as many minutes, choosing her words carefully. 'I realised,' she said slowly, 'how narrowing I had avoided not marrying you—'

'Then we don't have a problem, do we, because—?'

'Be quiet, Patrick, and let me finish what I'm saying!' She glared at him. 'And listen, damn it! I said "how narrowly I had avoided *not* marrying you"—because if Andy had come back into our lives two days ago *you* would have been the one to call off the wedding. Wouldn't you?' she persisted.

'I—'

'Not me, Patrick,' she continued unwaveringly. 'I wouldn't have called it off, because I *wanted* to marry you!' The last came out in a rush, Lilli holding her breath now as she waited for his reaction.

He continued to look at her, but some of the fierceness went out of his expression, uncertainty taking its place.

And uncertainty wasn't an emotion Lilli had ever associated with Patrick before...

'Why?' he said bluntly.

She swallowed hard. Could she really just tell him—? Pride, Gerry had called it. And look what it had cost the other woman in terms of real happiness...!

She drew in a deeply controlling breath. 'Because I love you!' Once again the words came out in a rush, and it was her turn to look uncertain now. 'I know you don't love me,' she continued hurriedly at Patrick's stunned expression. 'That you decided never to love again after Sanchia—'

'As you said earlier—forget Sanchia,' he dismissed harshly. 'As far as I'm concerned she ceased to exist the day she decided to destroy our child because she believed pregnancy would ruin her figure—'

'Patrick, no!' Lilli gasped disbelievingly. How could anyone destroy another human life for such selfish reasons? The life of Patrick's child... Which was why he had asked her if she wanted children... Why he had made such a point of telling her she would look beautiful when she was pregnant...! 'Oh, Patrick...!' Her voice broke emotionally as she went to him, her arms going about his waist as she rested her head against his chest.

'You said you loved me...?' he said quietly.

He stood a little apart from her, his own arms loose at his sides, his expression distant as she looked up at him. 'Not the past tense, Patrick.' She shook her head firmly. 'I do love you. Very much. And I do not want a divorce,' she added determinedly. 'I told you before, you aren't going to have everything your own way—'

'I don't want a divorce either!' His voice rose agitatedly, moving at last, his arms coming tightly about her waist. 'I thought you did. I thought— Lilli, I know what I said to you when I asked you to marry me.' He looked intently down at her. 'I was trying to protect myself, trying—' He shook his head in self-disgust. 'I lied, Lilli. I—'

'You don't tell lies, Patrick,' she reminded him softly, hope starting to blossom somewhere deep inside her, too deep down yet to actually flower, but it was there nonetheless...

'Lilli. Just Lilli. *My* Lilli.' His hands cupped either side of her face as he raised it to his. 'That first night at the hotel, as you lay sleeping in the bed— Don't look like that, Lilli,' he admonished gently. 'You were beautiful that night. I lay beside you for hours just watching you.' He smiled as she looked startled. 'You were—are—so beautiful, and yet as you slept you looked so vulnerable. By the time morning came I had decided I wanted to spend the rest of my life waking up with you beside me. I didn't recognise those feelings as love then, but—'

'Love?' she echoed huskily, that hope starting to flower now, to grow and grow, until it filled her.

'Love, Lilli. I fell in love with you that night. Although I certainly didn't recognise it as such.' He grimaced. 'Only that I wanted you with me for the rest of my life. But when I came out of the bathroom that morning you had gone...'

'I felt so embarrassed by what I had done.'

'I realise that,' he nodded. 'It was the shock of my life, only a matter of hours after that, to discover you were actually Richard Bennett's daughter. With all the complications that entailed—'

'I know about my mother, Patrick,' she interrupted. 'And about Gerry and my father. I— We've all made our peace.'

'Have you? I'm glad. Gerry's life was such a mess five

years ago, and for years I harboured very strong feelings against your father for causing that unhappiness. And then two months ago Gerry took him back into her life, and I— I didn't take the news too well initially. Maybe I was a bit over-zealous—businesswise—where your father was concerned, because of that. Part of me wanted him destroyed in the way he had destroyed my sister's life,' he admitted heavily.

'And you hated me because I was his daughter,' Lilli said knowingly.

'I didn't hate you.' His arms tightened about her once again. 'I could never hate you. I was not—pleased to discover you were his daughter.'

'You believed I had slept with you deliberately,' she reminded him teasingly.

'Only for a matter of a few hours. I was so damned angry when I found out who you really were that it seemed the only explanation for the way you had left the party with me—'

'I had just seen my father with Gerry,' she told him. 'I was angry and upset, and although I didn't know you were Gerry's brother the two of you seemed close, and so I—I decided to go with you to spite her. Not very nice, I'll grant you, but at the time I just wasn't thinking straight. I got the shock of my life when I woke up that morning in a hotel bedroom and heard you singing in the adjoining bathroom!'

'Well, of course I was singing,' he grinned. 'I had just found the woman I wanted to spend the rest of my life with!'

'And I thought I had spent the night making love with you and couldn't even remember it!' she recalled with a groan.

'I know, love,' he said. 'That was obvious when I came to your house later that day.'

'And you let me carry on believing it!' she reproved exasperatedly.

'Don't be too angry with me, Lilli.' He kissed her gently on the lips. 'It was the fact that we hadn't made love that made me realise I had made a mistake about that. When I sat and thought about it later, if you really had set out to trick me that night, you would never have allowed yourself to go to sleep in the way that you did, and you certainly wouldn't have left the hotel so abruptly. I also realised, as I sat angrily churning all this through my mind, that our night together actually made things less complicated rather than more so. It enabled me to ask you to marry me,' he explained at her questioning look, 'to point out all the advantages of such a marriage, without ever having to admit how I felt about you. I didn't want to love anyone, Lilli, but— What I feel for you is like nothing I have ever known before. I want to be with you all the time. To make love with you. To argue with you—we do them both so well!' He smiled. 'I've never felt like this before, Lilli,' he told her intently. 'I love you so very much.'

She believed him! Patrick loved her. And she loved him.

And if either of them needed any further proof of that then the kiss they shared was enough, full of love and aching passion—enough to last a lifetime.

Lilli's eyes glowed, her cheeks were flushed, her lips bare of gloss, when she looked up at him some time later. 'Would you really have let me go?' she prompted huskily.

He frowned. 'If it was what you wanted,' he said slowly.

No, he wouldn't. She knew him too well already to actually believe that. 'Without a fight?' she teased.

'No,' he admitted dryly.

She laughed softly, hugging him tightly. 'I'm so glad you said that—because I wouldn't have gone without kicking and screaming either!'

His answering laugh was full of indulgent joy. 'We're never going to part, Lilli. I'll do everything in my power to make you happy.'

'Just continue to love me,' she told him. 'It will be enough. I—'

'Can we come back in yet?' Gerry looked cautiously around the door she had just opened. 'Only the champagne is getting warm!'

'Do come in.' Lilli held her hand out towards the other woman. 'Let's drink the champagne and make a toast.' She smiled glowingly at her father as he came in carrying the tray with the champagne bottle—pink, of course!— and another glass. 'To a wonderful Christmas and New Year for all of us,' she announced as they all held up their glasses, sure in her heart that every year was going to be a happy one from now on. For all of them.

'How could you do this to me?' Patrick groaned tragically. 'I'll never survive!'

Lilli laughed at his comical expression, very tired, but filled with a glow that shone from deep inside her. 'You'll survive only too well,' she said knowingly. 'Now there will be three of us to love and spoil you.'

'Twins!' Patrick looked down into the cribs that stood next to the hospital bed, gazing in wonder at the identical beauty of the babies that slept within them. 'And both girls,' he added achingly. 'I'm going to end up spoiling all of *you*!'

Lilli smiled at him indulgently. Their daughters had been born fifty-five and fifty-one minutes ago, respectively, and Patrick had been at her side the whole time she had been in labour. As he had been at her side during the whole of the last year...

Lilli had been right; this past year had been the happiest of her life. And she knew it had been the same for Patrick, that the birth of their beautiful daughters on New Year's Eve had made it all complete.

'Think how poor Daddy felt.' She gave a happy laugh. 'James Robert was born on Christmas Day!' No one, it seemed, could have been more surprised than her father when Gerry had presented him with a son a week ago.

It was probably the celebrating that had been going on ever since the birth that had brought on Lilli's own slightly premature labour. But it hadn't been a difficult birth, and their darling little girls were worth any pain she might have felt.

'Now all we have to do is think of names for them both,' Patrick said a little dazedly.

He was right. They hadn't even known she was expecting twins, and because they had been absolutely convinced the baby she carried was a boy they hadn't chosen any girls' names at all.

'Is there room for three more in there?' Her father stood in the doorway, his baby son in his arms, Gerry at his side. 'Or are the Devlins taking over?' he added teasingly.

Lilli's family was complete as her father, Gerry and her new little brother came into the room.

Since she and Patrick had admitted their love for each other, Lilli had been convinced that every new day was the happiest of her life. But as she looked at all her family gathered there together, all so happy, she knew this was definitely their happiest day. Yet...

* * * * *

A Yuletide Seduction

CAROLE MORTIMER

CHAPTER ONE

GOLD.

Bright, shiny, *tarnished* gold.

She didn't want to touch it any more than she needed to, didn't want it touching her either, the metal seeming to burn her flesh where it nestled on her left hand.

She pulled the gold from her finger. It wasn't difficult to do. She was so much slimmer than when the ring had first been placed on her finger. In fact, the ring had become so loose that it had spun loosely against her skin, only her knuckles stopping it from falling off by itself.

How she wished it had fallen off, fallen to the ground, never to be seen again. She should have pulled it off, wrenched it from her finger, weeks ago, months ago, but she had been consumed with other things. This tiny scrap of gold lying in the palm of her hand hadn't seemed important then.

But it was important now. It was the only physical reminder she had that she had ever—ever—

Her fingers closed around the small ring of metal, so tightly that her nails dug into her flesh, breaking through the skin. But she was immune to the pain. She even welcomed it. Because that slight stinging sensation in her hand, the show of blood, told her that she, at least, was still real. Everything around her seemed to have crumbled and fallen apart, until there was nothing left. She was the only reality, it seemed.

And this ring.

She unclenched her fingers, staring down at the ring, fighting back the memories just the sight of it evoked. Lies. All lies! And now he was dead, as dead as their marriage had been.

Oh, God, no! She wouldn't cry. Never that. Not again. Not ever again!

She quickly blinked back those tears before they could fall. Remember. She had to remember, to keep on remembering, before she would be allowed to forget! If she ever did...

But first she had to get rid of this ring. She never wanted it near her again, never wanted to set eyes on it again, or for anyone else to do so either.

Her fingers curled around it again, but lightly this time, and she lifted up her arm, swung it back as far as it would go, before launching it forward again. And as she did so she threw the ring as far as it would go, as far away from her as she could make it fly, watching as it spun through the air in what seemed like slow motion, making hardly a ripple in the water as it was swallowed up by the swiftly running river in front of her, falling down, to be sucked in by the mud and slime at the bottom of the river.

It took her several breath-holding seconds to realise it had gone. Finally. Irrevocably. And with its falling came release, freedom, a freedom she hadn't known for such a long, long time.

But freedom to do what...?

CHAPTER TWO

"TAKE the cups through to—" Jane abruptly broke off her calm instruction as one of those cups landed with a crash on the kitchen floor, its delicate china breaking into a dozen pieces. The three women in the room stared down at it, with the one who had dropped it looking absolutely horrified at what she had done.

"Oh, Jane, I'm so sorry." Paula groaned her dismay. "I don't know what happened. I'll pay for it, of course. I—"

"Don't be silly, Paula," Jane dismissed, still calmly.

Once upon a time—and not so long ago—an accident like this would have sent Jane into a panic, the money she would have to pay for the replacement cup cutting deeply into the profit she would make from catering a private dinner party. But those days were gone now, thank goodness. Now she could afford the odd loss without considering it a disaster. Besides, if this evening was the success Felicity Warner hoped it would be, then Jane doubted the other woman would be too concerned that one of the coffee cups in her twelve-place-setting dinner service had met with an accident.

"Take the cups through." Jane replaced the broken cup, putting it carefully beside the other seven already on the tray. "Rosemary will bring the coffee. I'll clear away the broken cup." She gave Paula's arm a reassuring squeeze before the two women left the high-tech kitchen to serve coffee to the Warners and their six dinner guests.

Jane almost laughed at herself as she bent down, dust-pan and brush in her hand. In the last two years since she'd first begun this exclusive catering service to the rich and influential, she had moved from a one-woman band to being able to employ people like Paula and Rose-mary to help with the serving, at least. But, nonetheless, she was back down on her hands and knees sweeping up! Some things just never changed!

"My dear Jane, I just had to— Darling…?" Felicity Warner herself had come out to the kitchen, coming to an abrupt halt as she spotted Jane on the floor behind the breakfast-bar. "What on earth—?"

Jane straightened, holding out the dustpan containing the broken cup. "You'll be reimbursed, of course—"

"Don't give it another thought, darling," her employer for the evening dismissed uninterestedly, the affectation sounding perfectly natural coming from this elegantly beautiful woman, slim in her short, figure-hugging dress, long red hair loose about her shoulders, beautiful face alight with pleasure. "After this evening I'm hoping to be able to buy a whole new dinner service and throw this old thing away!"

"This old thing" was a delicate china dinner service that would have cost thousands to buy rather than hundreds! "It's been a success, then?" Jane queried politely as she disposed of the broken cup, her movements as measured and controlled as they usually were.

"A success!" Felicity laughed happily, clapping her hands together in pleasure. "My dear Jane, after the wonderful meal you've served us this evening, Richard is likely to divorce me and marry you!"

Jane's professional smile didn't waver for a second, although inwardly the mere thought of being married to anyone, even someone as nice as Richard Warner appeared to be, filled her with revulsion. Although she knew Felicity was only joking; her husband obviously adored her and their two young daughters.

But she was pleased the evening seemed to be working out for this friendly couple. Cooking this evening's meal for the Warners had been a last-minute arrangement, aided by the fact that Jane had had a cancellation in her busy diary. And, from what Felicity had told her this afternoon, the last few months had been difficult ones for her husband's business. The couple could certainly do with a little good luck for a change!

Although it was the first time Jane had actually cooked for Felicity, she had found the other woman warm and friendly; in fact, the other woman had been chattering away to her all afternoon. Some of it through nervousness concerning the success of this evening, Jane was sure, and so she had just let Felicity talk as she continued to work.

Every morsel of food that had appeared on the table this evening had been personally prepared by Jane herself, even down to the chocolates now being served with the coffee, meaning that she'd spent a considerable time at her client's home before the meal was due to begin. Felicity, aware of how important this evening was—to her husband, to the whole family—had followed Jane about the kitchen most of the afternoon, talking endlessly. So much so that Jane now felt she knew the family—and their problems—intimately. Felicity obviously felt the same way!

"Nothing has actually been said, of course," Felicity

continued excitedly. "But Gabe has asked to meet Richard at his office tomorrow morning, so that they can "talk." She smiled her pleasure at this development. "A vast improvement on just buying Richard out and to hell with him! And I'm sure it's your wonderful meal that's mellowed him and tipped the balance!" She grinned conspiratorially. "He told me he doesn't usually eat dessert, but I persuaded him to just try a little of your wonderful white chocolate mousse—and there wasn't a word out of him while he ate every mouthful! He was so relaxed by the time he had eaten it that he readily agreed to talk with Richard in the morning!" she concluded gleefully.

So it wasn't the other man who had actually asked for the meeting, but Richard Warner who had instigated it. Oh, well, a little poetic licence was allowed on the other woman's part in the circumstances. Felicity's husband ran and owned an ailing computer company, and, from what Felicity had told Jane, this man Gabe was a shark: a great white, who ate up his own species as well as other fish, without thought or conscience for the devastation he left behind him. The fact that he had agreed to have dinner with them at all had, according to Felicity, been more than she had ever hoped for.

The man sounded like a first-class bastard to Jane, not a man anyone would particularly want to do business with. But the Warners didn't seem to have any choice in the matter!

"I'm really pleased for you, Felicity," she told the other woman warmly. "But shouldn't you be returning to your guests…?" And then Jane could begin the unenviable task of clearing away. She never left a home without first doing this; it was part of the service that none of the mess from her catering would be left for the client to clean up. Paula and Rosemary would leave as soon as they had served coffee, but Jane would be here until the end of the evening.

But she didn't mind that. She would work an eighteen-hour day, as she had done a lot at the beginning, as long as she was independent. Free...

"Heavens, yes." Felicity giggled now at her own social gaffe. "I was just so thrilled, I had to come and tell you. I'll talk to you again later." She gave Jane's arm a grateful squeeze before hurrying back to rejoin her guests in the dining-room, leaving a trail of the aroma of her expensive perfume behind her.

Jane shook her head ruefully, turning her attention to the dessert dishes. Under other circumstances, she and Felicity might have become friends. As it was, no matter how friendly they might have become today, Jane knew she would leave here this evening and not see Felicity again until—or if—the other woman needed her professional services again.

She readily admitted that it was a strange life she had chosen for herself. Her refined speech and obvious education—an education that had included, thank goodness, a Cordon Bleu cookery course—set her apart from many people, and yet the fact that she was an employee of Felicity's, despite being the owner of the business, meant she didn't "belong" in that set of people, either.

A strange life, yes, but it was one that gave her great satisfaction. Although occasionally it was a lonely life.

"—really is an absolute treasure," Felicity could be heard gushing out in the hallway. "I don't know why she doesn't open up her own restaurant; there's no doubting it would be all the rage." Her voice became louder as she entered the kitchen. "Jane, I've brought someone to meet you," she announced happily, a thread of excitement underlying her voice. "I think he's fallen in love with your cooking," she added flirtatiously.

There was no warning. No sign. No alarm bells. Nothing to tell Jane that her life was about to be turned upside down for the second time in three years!

She picked up the towel to dry her hands before turning, fixing a smile on her lips as she did so, only to have that smile freeze into place as she looked at the man Felicity had brought into the kitchen to meet her.

No!

Not him!

It couldn't be!

She was successful. Independent. *Free.*

It couldn't be him. She couldn't bear it. Not when she had worked so hard.

"This is Gabriel Vaughan, Jane." Felicity introduced him innocently. "Gabe, our wonderful cook for the evening, Jane Smith." She beamed at the two of them.

The Gabe Felicity had been chattering on about all afternoon had been Gabriel Vaughan? *The* Gabriel Vaughan?

Of course it was—he was standing across the kitchen from where Jane stood as if she had been turned to stone. He was older, of course—but then, so was she!—but the granite-like features of his face still looked as if they had been hewn from solid rock, despite the fact that he was smiling at her.

Smiling at her? It was the last thing he would be doing if he had recognised her in return!

"Jane Smith," he greeted in a voice that perfectly matched the unyielding hardness of him.

He would be thirty-nine now. His dark hair was slightly overlong, easily brushing the collar of his dinner jacket, and he had a firmly set jaw, sculptured lips, a long, aristocratic nose jutting out arrogantly beneath the only redeeming feature in that hard face—eyes so blue they were almost aquamarine, like the clear, warm sea Jane had once swum in off the Bahamas, long, long ago.

"Or may I call you Jane?" he added charmingly, his American accent softening that harshness.

The black evening suit and snowy white shirt that Gabriel Vaughan wore with such disregard for their elegance did little to hide the power of the body beneath. His wide shoulders rippled with muscle; his height, at least six feet four inches, meant that he would easily tower over most men he would meet. At only five feet two inches tall herself, Jane had to bend her neck backwards to look up into that harshly carved face, a face that seemed to have become grimmer in the last few years, despite the fact that he was directing a charming smile in her direction at this moment.

Oh, Paul, Jane cried inwardly, how could you ever have thought to come up against this man and win?

But then, Paul hadn't won, had he? she acknowledged dully. No one ever had against Gabe, if the past newspaper reports about this man were to be believed. In fact, now that she knew who Felicity and Richard Warner were dealing with, she believed Felicity might be rather premature in her earlier feelings of celebration!

"Jane will be fine," she answered him in the soft, calm voice she had learnt to use in every contingency over the last three years—although she was inwardly surprised she had managed to do so on this occasion!

This was Gabriel Vaughan she was talking to, the man who had ripped through the fabric of her life as if he were a tornado. She was damn sure he had never looked back to see what destruction he had left behind him!

"I'm pleased you enjoyed your meal, Mr Vaughan," she added dismissively, hoping he would now return to the dining-room with his hostess. Outwardly she might appear calm, but her legs were already starting to shake, and it was only a matter of time before they would no longer support her!

He gave an inclination of his head, the overhead light making his dark hair almost appear black, although there were touches of grey now visible amongst that darkness. "Your husband is a very lucky man," he drawled softly.

Questioningly, it seemed to Jane. She resisted the impulse to glance down at her now bare left hand, knowing that not even an indentation now remained to show she had once worn a gold band there. "I'm not married, Mr Vaughan," she returned distantly.

He looked at her steadily for long, timeless seconds, taking in everything about her as he did so. And Jane was aware of everything he would see: nondescript brown hair restrained from her face with a black velvet band at her nape, pale, make-up-less features dominated by huge brown eyes, her figure obviously slender, but her businesslike cream blouse and black skirt doing nothing to emphasise her shapeliness.

What Jane didn't see when she looked at her own reflection in the mirror—and would have been horrified if she had!—were the red highlights in the abundance of the shoulder-length hair she was at such pains to keep confined, or the stark contrast between that dark curling hair and the pale magnolia of her face, those huge brown eyes often taking on the same deep sherry colour of her hair. Her nose was small, her mouth having a sensual fullness she could do little to hide—despite not wearing lipgloss. In fact, she deliberately wore no make-up, but her face was peaches and cream anyway, adding to the hugeness of her captivating brown eyes. And, for all she believed her clothes to be businesslike, the cream blouse was a perfect foil for her colouring, and the knee-length of her skirt could do little to hide the curvaceousness of her long, silky legs.

"May I say," Gabriel Vaughan murmured huskily, his bright blue gaze easily holding hers, "that fact is to one poor man's detriment—and every other man's delight?"

"My dear Gabe," Felicity teased, "I do believe you're flirting with Jane." She was obviously deeply amused by the fact.

He gave the other woman a mocking glance. "My dear Felicity," he drawled dryly, "I do believe I am!" He turned back challengingly to Jane.

Flirting? With her? Impossible. If only he knew—

But he didn't know. He didn't recognise her. There was no way he would be looking at her with such warm admiration if he did!

Was she so changed? Facially, more mature, yes. But the main change, she readily accepted, was in her hair. Deliberately so. Once her hair had reached down to her waist, a straight curtain the golden colour of ripe corn—a stark contrast to the shoulder-length chestnut-brown it now was. She had been amazed herself at the differ-ence the change of colour and style made to her whole appearance, seeming to change even the shape of her face. And eyes she had always believed were just brown had taken on the rich colour of her hair, the pale skin that was natural to her blonde hair becoming magnolia against the rich chestnut.

Yes, she had changed, and deliberately so, but until this moment, with Gabriel Vaughan looking at her with a complete lack of recognition, she hadn't realised just how successful she had been in effecting that change!

"Mr Vaughan…" She finally found her voice to answer him, her shocked surprise under control, if not eliminated. She was Jane Smith, personal chef to the beautiful and affluent, and this man was just another guest at one of those dinner parties she catered for. He shouldn't even be out here in the kitchen! "I do believe—" she spoke slowly but firmly "—that you're wasting your time!"

His smile didn't waver for a second, but that brilliant blue gaze sharpened with interest. "My dear Jane—" he lingered over the deliberate use of her first name, well aware of her own formality "—I make a point of never doing that."

Outwardly she again remained calm, but inwardly she felt a shiver of apprehension down her spine. And it was a feeling she hadn't known for three years…

"Now, Gabe," Felicity cut in laughingly, linking her arm through his, "I can't have you upsetting Jane," she scolded lightly. "Let's go back to the dining-room and have a liqueur, and let's leave poor Jane in peace." She slanted an apologetic smile towards Jane. "I'm sure she would like to get home some time before morning. Come on, Gabe," she encouraged firmly as he still made no effort to move. "Or Richard will think we've run away together!"

Gabriel Vaughan didn't join in her throaty laughter. "Richard need have no worries like that on my account. You're a beautiful woman, Felicity," he added to take the sting out of his initial remark, "but other men's wives have never held any appeal for me."

Jane drew in a sharp breath, swallowing hard. Because she knew the reason "other men's wives never held any appeal" for Gabriel Vaughan. Oh, yes, she knew only too well.

"I'm sure Richard will be pleased to hear that," Jane dismissed with a calmness that had now become second nature to her. "But Felicity is quite right; I do still have a lot to do. And your coffee will be going cold." She turned to smile at Paula and Rosemary as they returned from serving coffee and liqueurs. Their timing couldn't have been more perfect!

She willed Gabriel Vaughan to leave the kitchen now, before her calm shattered and her legs collapsed beneath her.

She had believed she had succeeded in pushing the past to the back of her mind, but at this moment she had a vivid image of three years ago when her own photograph had appeared side by side with this man's for days on end in all the national newspapers.

She had wanted to run away and hide then, and to all intents and purposes she had done so. And although he wasn't aware of it—and she hoped he never would be—the man who had once haunted her every nightmare, waking as well as asleep, had finally caught up with her!

He was still watching her, that intent blue gaze unwavering, despite the urgings of his hostess to return to the dining-room. His behaviour, Jane knew, was bordering on rudeness, but, as she was also aware, he was very conscious of the fact that he had the upper hand here this evening. In the process of buying out Richard Warner's ailing company, backed up by the millions of pounds that was his own personal fortune, he had no reason to do any other than what he pleased. And at this particular moment he wanted to look at Jane...!

Finally—when Jane was on the point of wondering just how much longer she could withstand that stare!—he visibly relaxed, smiling that lazily charming smile, his eyes once more that brilliant shining aqua. "It was a pleasure meeting you, Jane Smith," he murmured huskily, holding out his hand to her in parting.

Paula and Rosemary, after one wide-eyed glance in her direction at finding their hostess and one of her guests in the kitchen chatting away to Jane, had busied themselves washing up the dessert dishes Jane hadn't been able to deal with because of the interruption. And Felicity was smiling happily, still filled with what she considered the success of the evening. Only Jane, it seemed, was aware that she viewed that hand being held out to her—a long, ringless hand, filled with strength—as if it were a viper about to strike!

"Thank you," she returned coolly, not about to return the pleasantry. If there were any "pleasure" attached to this meeting then it was definitely all on his side!

But she knew she had no choice but to shake the hand held out to her. Not to do so would be inexplicable. At least, to everyone else in the room. She knew exactly why she didn't want to touch this man—his hand or any other part of him. And if he knew, if he realised, he wouldn't be holding out that hand of friendship either!

His hand was cool and dry, his grip firm. Not that Jane gave him much chance to do the latter, her hand against his only fleetingly.

Those startling blue eyes narrowed once again, his hand falling lightly to his side. "Perhaps we'll meet again," he said huskily.

"Perhaps," she nodded noncommittally.

And perhaps they wouldn't! She had managed to get through three years without bumping into this man, and if she had her way it would be another three years— or longer!—before it happened again. And as Gabriel Vaughan spent most of his time in his native America, with only the occasional swim into English waters in his search for fresh prey, that shouldn't be too difficult to achieve!

"I should be in England for several months." He seemed to read at least some of her thoughts, instantly squashing them. "In fact," he added softly, "I've rented an apartment for three months; I can't stand the impersonality of hotels."

Three months! They could be as long, or short, as he made them!

"I hope you enjoy your stay," she returned dismissively, turning away now, no longer able to even look at him. She needed to sit down, her legs shaking very badly now. Why didn't he just go?

She moved to put the clean dessert dishes back on the pine dresser across the room, and by the time she turned back again, he had gone.

Jane swayed weakly on her feet, moving to sit heavily on one of the pine chairs that stood around the kitchen table. In reality, Gabriel Vaughan could only have been in the kitchen a matter of minutes—it just seemed much, much longer!

"Gosh, he was handsome, wasn't he?" Rosemary sighed longingly as she finished drying her hands, seeming unaware of Jane's distress.

Handsome? She supposed he was. She just had more reason to fear him—fear him realising who she was—than she had to find him attractive. Although it was obvious from Paula's appreciative grin that she too had found Gabriel Vaughan "handsome".

"Looks are only skin-deep," Jane dismissed sharply, feeling her strength slowly returning. "And underneath those trappings of civilisation—" there was no denying how dazzlingly attractive Gabriel Vaughan had looked in his dinner suit, or the charm of his manner "—Gabriel Vaughan is a piranha!"

Paula made a face at her vehemence. "He seemed rather taken with you," she said speculatively.

Jane gave a derisive smile. "Men like him are not 'taken' with the hired help! Now, it's time you two went off home to your husbands," she added teasingly as she stood up. "I can deal with what's left here."

In fact, she was glad of the time alone once the two women had left for home. She could almost convince herself, as she pottered about the kitchen putting dishes away, that everything was once again back to normal, that the encounter with Gabriel Vaughan had never happened. Almost...

But there was absolutely no reason for their paths to cross again. Lightning really didn't strike twice in the same place, did it? Of course it didn't! Just as having Gabriel Vaughan enter her life once again wouldn't happen...

EVERYTHING was cleared away, the last guest having taken their leave, when Felicity came back into the kitchen half an hour later. And she looked so happy, so vastly different from the worried woman Jane had spent the afternoon with, that Jane didn't have the heart to tell her of her earlier misgivings about the evening having been quite the success Felicity obviously considered it had been. The other woman would no doubt find that out for herself soon enough. After Gabriel Vaughan's meeting with Richard, no doubt!

"I can't thank you enough, Jane." She smiled, looking tired, the evening obviously having been more of a strain than it had earlier appeared. "I don't know how I would have managed without you."

"You would have been just fine," Jane said with certainty; Richard Warner obviously had a treasure in his young wife.

"I'm not so sure." The other woman grimaced. "But tomorrow will tell if it was all worth it!"

It certainly would! And Jane really hoped this nice couple weren't in for a deep disappointment. Although, given what she knew of Gabriel Vaughan, it didn't auger well...

Felicity yawned tiredly. "I think I'll go up to bed. Richard's just bringing through the last of the glasses. But leave them, Jane," she insisted firmly. "You must be much more tired than I am—and I'm staggering!" She walked to the kitchen door. "Please go home, Jane," she added with another yawn, turning before leaving the room. "By the way, you made a definite hit this evening." She raised auburn brows pointedly. "Gabe was very interested."

Jane forced herself to once again remain outwardly

composed, revealing none of her inner panic. "How interested?" she drawled lightly.

"Very." Felicity smiled knowingly. "I shouldn't be at all surprised if you and he meet again."

She drew her breath in sharply. "And what makes you think that?" she prompted tautly, still managing to keep a tight control over her nerves. Although it was becoming increasingly difficult to do so, the longer they discussed Gabriel Vaughan!

Surely he hadn't continued to be curious about her once he and Felicity had returned to the dinner party? There had been two other couples present, and Richard's recently divorced sister had been included to make up the eight; and Jane certainly didn't think any of them would have been interested in listening to a conversation about the caterer!

"Well, he— Ah, Richard," Felicity moved aside so that her husband could enter the kitchen to put down the glasses. "I was just telling Jane that I'm sure she and Gabe are going to meet again," she said archly.

Richard shot an affectionate smile at his wife. He was in his early thirties, tall and blond, with young Robert Redford good looks, and had a perfect partner in his vivacious wife. "Stop your matchmaking, darling. I'm sure Jane and Gabe are more than capable of making their own arrangements. If necessary," he added with a rueful glance at Jane.

"It never hurts to give these things a helping hand." Felicity gave another tired yawn.

"Will you please go to bed, Fliss?" her husband said firmly. "I'll just see Jane out, and then I'll join you," he promised.

And Jane wanted to leave; of that there was no doubt.

But she had felt a chill inside her at Felicity's last statement. What had the other woman done to give a "helping hand"?

"Okay," Felicity concurred sleepily. "And I do thank you so much for doing this for us at such short notice, Jane. You've been wonderful!"

"My pleasure," she dismissed lightly. "But I can't help but feel curious as to why you should think Mr Vaughan and myself will meet again," she persisted.

"Because he asked for your business card, darling," the other woman supplied happily. "He said it was so that he could call you when he gave his next dinner party, but I have a feeling you'll hear from him much sooner than that! Don't be too long, darling." She smiled glowingly at her husband before finally going upstairs to their bedroom.

"I'm sorry about all that nonsense, Jane," Richard said distractedly, running agitated fingers through the thickness of his blond hair. "Fliss has been so worried these last few weeks, and that isn't good for her in early pregnancy. But take it from me: Gabe Vaughan is the last man you should become involved with," he added grimly. "He would gobble you up and spit you out again before you had a chance to say no!"

Gabriel Vaughan was the last man she ever *would* become involved with!

She had been frozen into immobility since Felicity's announcement of having given Gabriel Vaughan her business card, but she moved now, hurriedly putting on her jacket. "I didn't realise Felicity was pregnant," she said slowly. The other woman was so slim and elegant, the pregnancy certainly couldn't be very far along yet, and Felicity hadn't mentioned it. She had no doubt this happily married couple were pleased about the baby, but at the same time she realised it had probably happened at a bad time for them, what with the uncertainty about Richard's business.

"Only just." Richard gave what looked like a strained smile. "Felicity is longing to give me a son. Although at this rate there will be no business for him to grow up and take over!" he added bleakly. He shook his head self-derisively. "Much as I also appreciate all that you've done this evening, Jane, unlike Felicity I think it's going to take a little more than an exceptional meal to convince Gabriel Vaughan that my company is worth saving rather than being gathered up into his vast, faceless business pool!"

Jane was inclined to agree with him. From what she knew of the ruthless American, he wasn't into "saving" companies, only taking them over completely!

She certainly didn't envy Richard Warner his meeting with the older man tomorrow!

She reached out to squeeze his arm understandingly. "I'll keep my fingers crossed for you," she told him softly before straightening. "Now I have to be on my way— and I think you should go upstairs and give your lovely wife a hug! There's a lot to be said for having a loyal wife and a beautiful family like you have, you know," she added gently, having no doubts that Felicity would stand by her husband, no matter what the outcome of his meeting with Gabriel Vaughan.

Richard looked at her blankly for several seconds, and then he laughed softly. "How right you are, Jane," he agreed lightly. "How right you are!"

She was well aware that it sometimes took someone outside the situation to remind one of how fortunate one was. And, no matter what happened tomorrow, this man would still have his beautiful wife and daughters, and their unborn child. And that was certainly a lot more than very many other people had.

And sometimes, Jane remembered bleakly as she left the house, all the positive things you thought you had in your life could be wiped out or simply taken away from you.

And a prime example of that had been this evening when Gabriel Vaughan had turned out to be the guest of honour at the Warners' dinner party! She had worked so hard to build up this business, to build something for herself—she would not allow it all to be wiped out a second time!

It had not been a good evening for Jane. First that broken cup—which she would replace, despite Felicity's protests that it wasn't necessary—then Gabriel Vaughan coming into the kitchen: the very last man she'd ever wanted to see again! Ever! And Felicity, poor romantic Felicity, had given him Jane's business card!

What else could possibly go wrong tonight?

She found that out a few minutes later—when her van wouldn't start!

CHAPTER THREE

JANE almost choked over her morning mug of coffee!
As it was, her hand shook so badly that she spilt some
of that coffee onto the newspaper that lay open on the
breakfast-bar in front of her, the liquid splashing onto the
smiling countenance of the man's face that had caused
her to choke in the first place!

Gabriel Vaughan!

But then, nothing seemed to have gone right for her
since meeting the man the evening before. It had been
past one o'clock in the morning when she'd discovered
her van wouldn't start, and a glance towards the Warners' house had shown her that it was in darkness. And,
in the circumstances, Jane had been loath to disturb the
already troubled couple. Besides, she had decided, if
Richard Warner had any sense, he would be making
love to his wife at this very moment—and she certainly
had no inclination to interrupt that!

But it had been too late to contact a garage, and there
had been no taxis cruising by in the exclusive suburb,
and finding a public telephone to call for a taxi hadn't
proved all that easy to do, either. And when she'd come
to leave the call box after making the call it was to find
it had begun to rain. Not gentle, barely discernible rain,
but torrents of it, as if the sky itself had opened up and
dropped the deluge.

Tired, wet and extremely disgruntled, she had finally arrived back at her apartment at almost two-thirty in the morning. And opening her newspapers at nine o'clock the following morning, and being confronted by a photograph of a smiling Gabriel Vaughan, was positively the last thing she needed!

This was the time of day when she allowed herself a few hours' relaxation. First she would go for her morning run, collecting her newspaper, and freshly baked croissants from her favourite patisserie on the way back. She had made a career out of cooking for other people, but she wasn't averse to sampling—and enjoying—other people's cooking in the privacy of her own home. And François's croissants, liberally spread with butter and honey, melted in the mouth.

But not this morning. She hadn't even got as far as taking her first mouthful, and now she had totally lost her appetite. And all because of Gabriel Vaughan!

She would never see him again, she had assured herself in the park earlier as her feet pounded on the pathway as she ran, slender in her running shorts and sweatshirt, her hair tied back with a black ribbon. As far as she was aware, the man had only paid brief visits to England over the last three years, and just because he had rented an apartment for three months that didn't mean he would actually stay that long. Once his business with Richard Warner had reached a suitable conclusion— to Gabriel Vaughan's benefit, of course!—he would no doubt be returning to America. And staying there, Jane hoped!

But this photograph in this morning's newspaper—of Gabriel with a dazzling blonde clinging to his arm—had been taken while at a weekend party given by a popular politician. It seemed to imply that his rare visits to this country in recent years had in no way affected his social popularity when he was here.

Jane stood up impatiently, her relaxation totally ruined for this morning. Damn the man! He had helped ruin her life once—she couldn't allow him to do it again, not when she had worked so hard to make a life and career for Jane Smith.

Jane Smith.

Yes, that was who she was now.

She drew in a deeply controlling breath, forcing back the panic and anger, bringing back the calm that had become such a necessary part of her for the last few years, reaching out as she did so to close the newspaper, not taking so much as another glance at the photograph that had so disturbed her minutes ago.

She had a job to do, another dinner party to arrange for this evening, and the first thing on her list of things to do was to check with the garage she had called earlier, and see if they had had any luck in starting her van. If it wasn't yet fixed she would have to hire alternative transport for the next few days.

Yes, she had a business to run, and she intended running it!

Despite Gabriel Vaughan.

Or in spite of him!

"HELL, I hate these damned things! If you're there, Jane Smith, pick up the damned receiver!"

Jane reached out with trembling fingers and switched off the recorded messages on her answer machine, quickly, as if the machine itself were capable of doing her harm. Which, of course, it wasn't. But the recorded message of that impatient male voice—even though the man hadn't given his name but had slammed the receiver down when he received no reply to his impatience—was easily recognisable as being that of Gabriel Vaughan.

She had telephoned the garage before taking her shower, had been informed that it would be ready for collection in half an hours' time, once they had replaced the old and worn battery. Then she'd showered quickly before switching on her answer machine as she usually did when she had to go out.

She had only been out of her apartment for an hour, but the flashing light on the answer machine had told her she had five messages. The first two had been innocuous enough—enquiries about bookings, which she would deal with before she went out to collect her supplies for this evening's dinner party. But the third call—! He didn't even need to say who it was—she could recognise that transatlantic drawl anywhere!

It wasn't even twelve hours since she had left the Warners' home; the damned man had left no time at all before trying to contact her again!

What did he want?

Whatever it was, she wasn't interested. Not on a personal or professional level. On a personal level, he was the last man she wanted anything to do with, and the same applied on a professional level. For the same reason. The less contact she had with Gabriel Vaughan—on any level—the better she would like it.

That decision made, she decided to totally ignore the call, pretend it never happened. After all, he hadn't left a name or contact number, just those few words of angry impatience.

Having so decided, she reached out to switch the machine back on. After all, she had a business to run.

"Jane! Oh, Jane…!" There was a short pause in the fourth message, before the woman continued. "It's Felicity Warner here. Give me a call as soon as you come in. Please!" Felicity had sounded tearful enough at the beginning of the message, but that last word sounded like a pleading sob!

And Jane didn't need two guesses as to why the other woman had sounded so different on the recording from the happily excited one she had left the evening before; no doubt Richard had been to his meeting with Gabriel Vaughan!

Maybe she should have tried to warn the other woman last night, after all, once she had realised who Richard was dealing with? But if she had done that Felicity would only have wanted to know how she knew so much about the man. And it had taken her almost three years to shake off the how and why she had ever known a man like Gabriel Vaughan.

But Felicity sounded desperately upset, so unhappy. Which really couldn't be good for her in her condition—

"Don't you ever switch this damned thing off, Jane Smith?" The fifth message began to play, Gabriel Vaughan's voice sounding mockingly amused this time—and just as instantly recognisable to Jane as on the previous message. "Well, I refuse to talk to a machine," he continued dismissively. "I'll try you again later." He rang off abruptly, again without actually saying who the caller had been.

But Jane was in no doubt whatsoever who the caller had been, remembered all too well from last night when he had called her "Jane Smith" in that mocking drawl. Two calls in a hour! What did the man want?

Some time in the last hour—if Felicity's cry for help was anything to go by—he had also spoken to Richard Warner!

The man was a machine. An automaton. He bought and sold, ruined people's lives, without a thought for the consequences. And the consequences, in this case, could be Felicity's pregnancy...!

Once again Jane switched off the answer machine. She didn't want to get involved in this, not from any angle. And if she returned Felicity's call she would become involved. If she wasn't already!

She didn't really know the Warners that well. She understood they had been guests at several other dinner parties she had catered for, which was why Felicity had telephoned her for the booking last night.

Over the years Jane had made a point of not getting too close to clients; she was employed by them, and so she never, ever made the mistake of thinking she was anything else. But somehow yesterday had been different. Felicity had obviously been deeply worried, had desperately needed someone she could talk to. And she had chosen Jane as that confidante, probably because she realised, with the delicacy of Jane's position working in other people's homes, that she had to be discreet, that the things Felicity talked to her about would go no further.

Jane never had been a gossip, but now there was a very good reason why what Felicity had told her would go no further: she simply had no one she could possibly tell!

Her life was a busy one, and she met lots of people

in the course of her work, but friends, good friends, were something she had necessarily moved away from in recent years. It was an unspoken part of her contract that she never discussed the people she worked for, and Jane guarded her own privacy even more jealously!

Her life had taken a dramatic turn three years ago, but determination and hard work meant she now ran her own life, and her own business. Successfully.

That success meant she could afford to rent this apartment; it was completely open-plan, with polished wood floors, scatter rugs, antique furniture, and no television, because not only did she not have the time to watch it, but she didn't like it either, her relaxation time spent listening to her extensive music collection, and reading the library of books that took up the whole of one wall. It was all completely, uniquely her own, and her idea of heaven on an evening off wasn't to go out partying as she would once have done, but to sit and listen to one of her favourite classical music tapes while rereading one of her many books.

But somehow those last three messages on her answer machine seemed even to have invaded the peace and tranquillity of her home...

Much as she liked Felicity and felt sorry for the other woman, she simply couldn't return that beseeching telephone call.

She just couldn't...!

SHE was tired by the time she returned to her apartment at one o'clock the following morning. The dinner party had been a success, but the reason for her weariness was the disturbance in her personal life over the last twenty-four hours.

The answer machine was flashing repeatedly—one, two, three, four, five, six, she counted warily. How many of those calls would be from Gabriel Vaughan?

Or was she becoming paranoid? The man she had met the evening before did not look as if he had to chase after any woman, least of all one who cooked for other people for a living! And yet on the second of those last recorded messages he had said he would "try again later"!

Jane sighed. She was tired. It was late. And she wanted to go to bed. But would she be able to sleep, knowing that there were six messages on her machine that hadn't been listened to?

Probably not, she conceded with impatient anger. She didn't like this. Not one little bit. She deeply resented Gabriel Vaughan's intrusion, but at the same time she was annoyed at her own reaction to it. She was not about to live in fear ever again. This was her home, damn it, her space, and Gabriel Vaughan was not welcome in it. He certainly wasn't going to invade it.

She reached out and firmly pushed the "play" button on the answermachine.

"Hello, Jane, Richard Warner here. Felicity wanted me to call you. She's been taken into hospital. The doctor thinks she may lose the baby. I—she— Thank you for all your help last night." The message came to an abrupt end, Richard Warner obviously not knowing what else to say.

Because there was nothing else to say, Jane realised numbly. What had Gabriel Vaughan said to Richard, what had he done, to have created such—?

No!

She couldn't become involved. She dared not risk— dared not risk— She just didn't darc!

But Felicity had called her earlier today, feeling that in some way she needed Jane. And, from Richard's call just now, the other woman had been proved right! Could Jane now just ignore this call for help? Or was it already too late…?

She couldn't change anything even if she did return Richard's call. What could she do? She would be the last person Gabriel Vaughan would listen to—even if she reversed her own decision about never wanting to speak to him again.

But what about Felicity…?

It was almost one-thirty in the morning now—too late to call either Richard or the hospital; she doubted the nurses on duty at the latter would volunteer any information about Felicity, anyway. She would go to bed, get a good night's sleep, and try calling Richard in the morning. Maybe Felicity's condition would be a little more positive by then.

Or maybe it wouldn't.

She absently listened to the rest of her messages, curious now about the other five calls.

They were all business calls, not a single one in the transatlantic drawl she had quickly come to recognise—and dread—as being that of Gabriel Vaughan. And after those two calls this morning within an hour of each other his silence this evening did not reassure her. It unnerved her!

"She's—stable—that's how the doctor described her condition to me this morning," Richard Warner told Jane in answer to her early morning telephone query about Felicity. "Whatever that means," he added disgustedly.

"What happened, Richard?" Jane prompted abruptly.

This call was against her better judgement; it came completely from the softness of emotions that she must never allow to rule her a second time. But she couldn't, she had decided in the clear light of day, simply ignore Felicity's and Richard's telephone calls.

"What do you think? Gabriel Vaughan is what happened!" Richard told her bitterly—and predictably!

Gabriel Vaughan seemed to just sail through life, sweeping away anything and anyone who should happen to stand in his way. And at the moment Richard Warner was in his way. Tomorrow, next week, next month, it would be someone else completely, any consequences that might follow Gabe's actions either ignored or simply unknown to him.

"I would really rather not talk about it, Jane," Richard added agitatedly. "At the moment my company is in chaos, my wife is in hospital—and just talking about Gabriel Vaughan makes my blood-pressure rise! I'll tell Felicity you rang," he added wearily. "And once again, thank you for all your help." He rang off.

And a lot of good her help had done them, Jane sighed as she replaced her own receiver. Gabriel Vaughan had happened—who else...? What else? He was a man totally without—

Jane almost fell off her chair as the telephone beside her began to ring. Eight-fifteen. It was only eight-fifteen in the morning; she had deliberately telephoned Richard Warner this early so that she could speak to him before he either left for the office or the hospital. But she wasn't even dressed yet herself, let alone taken her run; who on earth—?

Suddenly she knew exactly who. And, after her recent calls from the Warners, and her conversation with

Richard just now, she was in exactly the right frame of mind to talk to him!

She snatched up the receiver. "Yes?" she snapped, all of her impatience evident in that single word.

"I didn't get you out of bed, did I, Jane Smith?" Gabriel Vaughan returned in his mocking drawl.

Her hand tightened about the receiver. She had known it was him—it couldn't have been anyone else, in the circumstances!—but even so she couldn't help her instant recoil just at the sound of his voice.

She drew in a steadying breath. "No, Mr Vaughan," she answered calmly, "you didn't get me out of bed." And, remembering what she had once been told about this man, she knew that he had probably already been up for hours, that he only needed three or four hours' sleep a night.

"I didn't—interrupt anything, did I?" he continued derisively.

"Only my first coffee of the morning," she bit out tersely.

"How do you take it?"

"My coffee?" she returned, frowning.

"Your coffee," he confirmed, laughter evident in his voice now.

"Black, no sugar," she came back tautly—and then wished she hadn't. In retrospect, she could think of only one reason why he would be interested in how she liked her first cup of coffee of the morning!

"I'll make sure I remember that," Gabriel Vaughan assured her huskily.

"I'm sure you didn't call me to find out how I take my coffee," Jane snapped, sure that he remembered most things.

Except that other her, it seemed.

But how long would that last? Three years on, and not only did she look different, she *was* different, but Gabriel Vaughan had a very good reason for remembering everything that had happened three years ago, leading her to believe that his memory lapse where she was concerned would not continue. She had no doubt there would be no flirtatious early morning telephone calls then!

"You're wrong there, Jane Smith," he murmured throatily now. "You see, I want to know everything about you that there is to know—including how you take your coffee!"

Jane's breath left her in a shaky sigh, her hand tightening painfully about the receiver. "I'm an extremely boring individual, I can assure you, Mr Vaughan," she told him abruptly.

"Gabe," he put in smoothly. "And I very much doubt *that*, Jane," he added teasingly.

She didn't care what he doubted. She worked, she went to bed, she ran, she shopped, she read, she worked, she went to bed Her life was structured, deliberately so. Routine, safe, uncomplicated. This man threatened complications she didn't even want to think about!

"Are you aware that Felicity Warner is in hospital, in danger of losing her baby?" she attacked accusingly.

There was a slight pause on the other end of the telephone line. Very short, only a second or two, but Jane picked up on it anyway. To her surprise. Three years ago nothing had deterred this man. And she couldn't really believe that had changed in any way.

"I wasn't aware that Felicity was pregnant," he finally rasped harshly.

"Would it have made any difference if you had

known?" Jane scorned disgustedly, already knowing the answer to that question. Nothing distracted this man away from his purpose. And she couldn't help feeling that he had been playing with the Warners by accepting their dinner invitation two evenings ago…!

"Any difference to what?" he returned in a silkily soft voice.

"Let's not play games, Mr Vaughan." She continued to be deliberately formal, despite his earlier invitation for her not to be. "You have business with Richard Warner, and that business appears to be affecting his wife's health. And that of their unborn child," she added shakily. "Don't you think—?"

"I'm not sure you would like to hear what I think, Jane Smith," Gabriel Vaughan bit out coldly.

"You're right—I don't," she snapped tersely. "But I think it's way past time someone told you about your lack of thought for the people lives you walk into and instantly dismantle! Your method of dealing with people leaves a lot to be desired, and—" She broke off abruptly, feeling the icy silence at the other end of the telephone line as it blasted its way in her direction. And at the same time she realised she had said too much…

"And just what do you know about my 'method of dealing with people', Jane Smith?" he prompted mildly— too mildly for comfort!

Too much. She had said too much! "You're a public figure, Mr Vaughan." She attempted to cover up her lapse.

"Not in England," he rasped. "Not for several years," he added harshly, all his previous lazy charm obliterated in cold anger.

"Strange; I'm sure I saw your photograph in my daily

newspaper yesterday morning…" she came back pointedly; she had to try and salvage this conversation as best
she could; she'd already been far too outspoken.

The last thing she wanted to do was increase this
man's interest in her! Ideally, she would like him to
forget he had ever met someone called Jane Smith, but
she would settle for disinterest—which wasn't going to
be achieved if she kept challenging him!

"Of course, that was a social thing," she added lightly.
"You were a guest at a party."

"I'm a sociable person, Jane," he drawled dryly.
"Which was actually the reason for this call…"

He was going to ask her to cater a dinner party for
him! There was no way she could work for or with this
man. Absolutely no way!

"I'm very heavily booked at this time of year, Mr
Vaughan," she told him stiffly: Christmas was now only
two weeks away. "My diary has been full for weeks,
some of those bookings made months ago. However, I
could recommend another catering firm who I'm sure
would be only too pleased to—"

Gabriel Vaughan's husky laugh cut in on her businesslike refusal. "You misunderstood me, Jane," he murmured, that laugh still evident in his voice. "I was asking
you to have dinner with me, not trying to book your
services as a cook—impressive as they might be!"

Now it was Jane's turn to fall silent. Not because she
was angry, as Gabriel Vaughan had been minutes ago—
where had that anger gone…? No, she was stunned. Gabriel Vaughan was asking her for a date. Impossible. He
just didn't realise how impossible that was.

"No," she said abruptly.

"Just—no?" he said slowly, musingly. "You don't even want a little time to think about it?"

She doubted too many women had to do that where this man was concerned; he was handsome, single, undoubtedly rich, sophisticated, witty—what more could any woman want?

All Jane knew was that she did not want Gabriel Vaughan!

"No," she repeated sharply.

"Then I take it I was right earlier in assuming there's someone else in your life," he dismissed hardly, a chill edging his tone.

Jane frowned. When earlier in this conversation had he assumed there was already someone else in her life? They hadn't even touched on the subject.

"I have no idea what you're talking about," she snapped.

"It's occurred to me, Jane, that you have an unhealthy interest—as far as Felicity goes—in Richard Warner's affairs. And I don't just mean his business ones!" he added harshly.

"You're disgusting, Mr Vaughan," Jane told him angrily. "Other women's husbands have never held any appeal for me, either!" She deliberately threw his words to Felicity two evenings ago back in his face, then slammed down the receiver, immediately switching on the answer machine.

She didn't think Gabriel Vaughan was the sort of man to ring a woman back when she had angrily terminated their telephone conversation, but on the off chance that he just might she had no intention of answering that call herself.

He had just implied she was having an affair with Richard Warner!

How dared he?

CHAPTER FOUR

"WE MEET again, my dear Jane Smith."

Jane froze in the act of placing the freshly baked meringues onto the cooling tray, closing her eyes briefly, hoping this was only a nightmare. One that she would wake up from at any second!

But closing her eyes achieved nothing, because she could smell his aftershave now, and knew that when she turned Gabriel Vaughan was going to be standing only feet behind her. Could it only be coincidence that this was the second dinner party in a week that she had catered for where Gabriel Vaughan was a guest…?

She opened her eyes, straightening her shoulders before turning sharply to face him, her heart missing a beat as the total masculinity of him suddenly dominated the kitchen in which she had worked so harmoniously for the last four hours.

She was realising that he was a man who wore a black evening suit and white shirt with a nonchalance that totally belied the exclusive cut of the expensive material. He was vibrantly attractive, in a way that stated he didn't give a damn how he looked, that he was totally confident of his own masculinity, the challenging glitter of those aqua-blue eyes daring anyone to question it.

To her dismay, Jane realised that was probably exactly

what she had done two days ago when she had turned down his invitation to dinner!

She gave a cool inclination of her head. "You mentioned that you're a sociable person," she dismissed coldly.

"And you," Gabe returned mockingly, "mentioned how busy you were for the next few weeks." He shrugged. "The mountain came to Mohammed!"

Her eyes narrowed warily. Could this man possibly have—? No, she couldn't believe he would go to the extreme of having himself invited to a dinner party she was catering simply so that he— Couldn't she…? Hadn't the hostess this evening telephoned her earlier this morning and apologetically explained that, if it wasn't going to be too much of a problem for her, there would be two extra guests for dinner this evening. Was Gabriel Vaughan one of those guests…?

"I see," she murmured noncommittally. "I hope you're enjoying the meal, Mr Vaughan," she added dismissively.

But Gabe wasn't to be dismissed, leaning back against one of the kitchen units, totally relaxed—at least, on the surface; he must have been as aware as she was that the last time the two of them had spoken she had slammed the telephone down on him!

"I am now," he assured her huskily, looking at her admiringly. "That's quite a temper you have there, Jane Smith." There was an edge of admiration in his mocking tone as he too recalled the abrupt end of their telephone conversation two days ago.

Jane returned his gaze unblinkingly. "That was quite an accusation you made—Gabriel Vaughan," she returned, undaunted.

He smiled. More of a grin really, deep grooves beside his mouth, teeth white against his tanned skin. "Richard wasn't too happy about it, either," he murmured with amusement.

Her eyes widened, the colour of rich sherry. "You repeated that—that ridiculous accusation to him?" she gasped disbelievingly.

"Mmm," Gabe acknowledged ruefully, his gaze lightly mocking. "Tell me," he continued consideringly, "what *do* you do for exercise?"

She shook her head, totally amazed at this man's insulting conversation; he didn't even try to be polite!

"I run, Mr Vaughan," she snapped angrily. "And I really can't believe you were so insensitive as to have repeated such an accusation to Richard, at a time like this—"

"Felicity is out of hospital, you know." Gabe straightened, not as relaxed as he had been; in fact he looked slightly defensive, the challenging look back in his eyes.

As it happened, Jane did know—but she was surprised he did. She hadn't actually gone in to see Felicity when she was in hospital, but she had telephoned the hospital to pass on her well wishes, and she had called Richard every day to check on his wife's condition, relieved when she'd spoken to him this morning and heard that the doctor considered Felicity well enough to go home, the miscarriage in abeyance. For the moment. But surely if this man continued his hounding of Richard—and throwing out obscene accusations—that may not last...!

"How long for?" Jane scorned. "When do you intend making your next assault on Richard's company?" she added disgustedly.

"I don't assault, Jane," Gabe drawled derisively. "I acquire companies—"

"By going for the jugular of the owner!" she accused heatedly. "Look for the weakness, and then go for it!"

Gabe looked completely unmoved by her accusation. But those aqua-blue eyes had narrowed and a pulse was beating in his clenched jaw. Maybe he wasn't as completely lacking in compassion as she had believed...

No, she couldn't believe that. Three years ago he had been completely ruthless, totally without compassion. It had been his behaviour then that had turned an unbearable situation into a living hell. It was the very reason she had reacted so strongly to Felicity and Richard's situation. For all the good that had done her—Gabriel Vaughan had taken her emotional response and immediately jumped to the conclusion that she must be having an affair with Richard!

"Every company has its weak spot, Jane," Gabe mocked now. "But I only acquire the ones that are of interest to me." He pursed his lips thoughtfully. "I don't wish to alarm you, Jane, but there appears to be smoke coming from—"

Her second batch of meringues!

Ruined. Burned, she discovered as she quickly opened the oven door and black smoke belched out into the kitchen.

"Don't be a fool!" Gabe rasped harshly, pushing her none too gently out of the way as she would have pulled the tray from inside the oven. "You open the kitchen door, and I'll throw the tray out into the garden." He took the oven-glove from her unresisting fingers. "The door, Jane," he prompted again firmly as she still didn't move.

Damn the man, she muttered to herself as she finally went to open the door. She couldn't remember the last time she had burnt anything, let alone in the middle of a dinner party. But this man had disturbed her so badly that he had achieved it quite easily. She was losing it, damn it. Damn him!

"Out of my way, Jane," Gabe instructed grimly, going past her to throw the blackened meringues, and the tray, out into the garden.

Jane watched wordlessly as the burnt mess landed outside in the snow. Yes, snow. Somewhere, in the midst of what was turning out to be a terrible evening—the second in a week—it had begun to snow, a layer of white already dusting everything, the overheated tray sizzling and crackling in the coldness.

"Where do you run?"

She turned back to look at Gabriel Vaughan, dismayed at how close he was to her as they both stood in the open doorway, blinking up at him dazedly, the coldness of their breath intertwining. "The park near my apartment. Why?" She frowned her sudden suspicion at the question.

His gaze remained unblinkingly on her own. "Just curious."

She shook her head, outwardly unmoved by his closeness, but inwardly…! But if she moved away he would merely realise how disturbing she found it to be standing this close to him. And as far as she was concerned he already had enough of an advantage—even if he wasn't aware of it!

And he could keep his damned curiosity to himself! Not that it really mattered; he had no idea where she lived, and so consequently he wouldn't know which park it was, either!

"By the look of this snow—" she looked up into a sky that seemed full of the heavy whiteness "—I won't be running anywhere tomorrow morning." Her morning run in the nearby park cleared her head and set the tone for the rest of her day, and finding Gabriel Vaughan there, accidentally or otherwise, would totally nullify the exercise!

"A fair-weather runner, hmm?" Gabe drawled derisively.

Her brows rose indignantly over wide sherry-brown eyes. "I don't—"

"Ah, Gabriel, this is where you've been hiding yourself," murmured a husky female voice. "What on earth is that dreadful smell?" Celia Barnaby, the hostess of the evening, a tall, elegant blonde, wrinkled her nose at the smell of the burnt meringues that still lingered in the kitchen.

Gabe looked down at Jane, winking conspiratorially before turning to stroll across the kitchen to join his hostess. "I believe it was dessert, Celia," he drawled laughingly, taking a light hold of her arm as he guided her back out of the kitchen. "I think we should leave Jane alone so that she can do her best to salvage it in peace!"

"But—"

"I believe you were going to tell me about the skiing holiday you're taking in the New Year?" Gabe prompted lightly, continuing to steer the obviously reluctant Celia away from the disaster area. "Aspen, wasn't it?" He glanced back at Jane over the top of the other woman's head, his smile one of intimate collusion.

"Damn the man," Jane muttered to herself as she set about "salvaging"; and she didn't have a lot of time to do it. Her two helpers for the evening were now returning with the empty vegetable dishes, as the main course had just been served.

By the time she had finished arranging the meringues and fruit on the plates, lightly covering the latter with a raspberry sauce, no one would ever have guessed that there should actually have been two meringues on each plate.

Except Gabriel Vaughan, of course. But then, he was the reason for the omission; if she hadn't been busy fending off his questions then this disaster wouldn't have happened. She was just too professional, too organised, for this to happen under normal circumstances. But with Gabriel Vaughan once again present it was far from normal!

In fact, she was slightly on edge for the rest of the evening, kept half expecting Gabriel Vaughan to stroll back into the kitchen unannounced; it just didn't seem to occur to him that the dinner guests weren't supposed to just stroll about the homes of their host or hostess, let alone go into the kitchen and chat to the hired help! That was his inborn arrogance, Jane decided derisively; Gabriel Vaughan would go where he wanted, when he wanted.

And he would also say exactly what he pleased, even if it was insulting!

She couldn't even imagine what Richard Warner must be thinking about the other man's accusations concerning the two of them. It was so ludicrous it would be laughable in other circumstances. As it was, she could imagine that Gabe's words that Richard "wasn't too happy" about it were definitely an understatement where Richard was concerned!

It was extremely late by the time she had tidied away the last of the dishes from the meal, and she had to admit she was exhausted. But not from physical work; it was due entirely to tension. Unfortunately, she didn't manage to make her escape before Celia Barnaby came through to the kitchen, the last of her guests having finally left.

And it was unfortunate, because Celia wasn't one of Jane's favourite people. She was a beautiful divorcee, who had obviously only married her weak husband for the millions she had been able to take off him as part of their divorce settlement. Jane found her brittle and condescending, altogether too jaded.

Nevertheless she smiled politely at the other woman; she didn't have to like the people she worked for; it certainly wasn't conditional to her supplying the superb food she was known for. If that condition had applied two years ago, when she'd first begun this exclusive service, then she would have been out of work within a month!

Celia arched shaped brows. "Have you and Gabriel known each other long?" she enquired lightly.

Jane gave her a startled look. This woman certainly didn't believe in the "lead up to" approach! "Known each other long...?" she repeated dazedly. The two of them didn't know each other at all!

"Mmm," Celia drawled. "Gabriel explained to me that the two of you are old friends."

"He—!" Jane broke off, swallowing hard. "He said that?" She frowned darkly.

"Don't be so coy, Jane." The other woman gave her a knowing smile. "I always thought you were a bit of a dark horse, anyway. And I've never understood why you became a brunette; did no one ever tell you blondes have more fun?" she drawled suggestively, looking disparagingly at Jane's hair.

Jane was totally stunned. By all that this woman had just said. For one thing, she was surprised this woman had ever spared her a second thought. And she was rendered speechless by that comment about blondes.

The change of colour and style to her hair, she had felt two and a half years ago, had been an important part of the new her. It wasn't only Gabriel Vaughan she didn't want recognising her; it wouldn't do for any of the people she worked for to realise she had once led a similar lifestyle to their own, either, and so the change in her appearance had served a double purpose. Until this moment she had thought the disguise worked, always took care to have her hair coloured once a month. Before now no one had ever told her they knew she was really a blonde!

On top of that Gabriel Vaughan's claim that the two of them were "old friends" was just too much. Almost a week's acquaintance did not make them old friends— and she wouldn't term them as friends anyway!

Unless Gabriel Vaughan did remember her from three years ago, after all, and he was just playing with her...?

"Not very long, no." She woodenly answered Celia's original question.

"Pity." Celia grimaced her disappointment at her answer. "I wondered what his wife had been like. You did know he's been married, didn't you?" She looked at Jane fron beneath lowered lashes.

Oh, yes, she knew he had been married, Jane acknowledged with an inward shiver. The death of Gabriel

Vaughan's wife had only added to the spiralling out of control of her own life!

"Yes," Jane confirmed abruptly. "And surely you saw her photograph in the newspapers at the time of the accident?" She seemed to be having trouble articulating; her lips felt stiff and unmoving. It was so long since anyone had talked about these things...!

"Didn't everyone? Such a scandal, my dear," Celia said with obvious relish. "Jennifer Vaughan was so beautiful it made every other woman want to weep!" she added disgustedly. "No, I know what she looked like, Jane; I just wondered what she was really like. I never actually met her, you see; I didn't know Gabriel in those days."

Jane had never met Jennifer Vaughan either. But she had come to fear her, and the effect of her beauty.

"I can't be of any help to you there, I'm afraid, Celia," she dismissed coolly, wanting to make good her escape now, and it had little to do with the lateness of the hour. All this talk of Jennifer Vaughan; it was unnerving! "I've only met Gabriel since the death of his wife, too." She was deliberately economical with the facts.

For herself she didn't care if Celia knew she and Gabriel Vaughan had only spoken for the first time a few days ago, but to tell the other woman that, in the face of Gabe's contradictory claim, would only arouse the other woman's curiosity even more. And that she didn't want!

"Oh, well." Celia straightened, obviously realising she wasn't going to get much information out of Jane. "It was a marvellous meal this evening, Jane," she added offhandedly. "You'll send your bill through, as usual?"

"Of course," she nodded, and, as usual, Celia would

delay paying it for as long as possible; for a woman with millions, she was very loath to pay her bills.

In fact, Jane had thought long and hard before agreeing to cater this dinner party. Celia could be extremely difficult to work for, and with the added problem of her reluctance to pay...

In view of the fact that Gabriel Vaughan had turned out to be one of the guests, she wished she had followed her instincts and said no, Jane told herself as she left the house, a blast of icy snow hitting her in the face. It was—

"Here, let me take that for you." The box of personal utensils was plucked out of her hands, Gabriel Vaughan grinning at her unconcernedly over the top of it. "Hurry up, Jane," he encouraged as she stood rooted to the spot, stunned into immobility by his presence. "It's still snowing!" he pointed out dryly, his mouth twisting derisively as he stated the obvious.

In actual fact, it was snowing heavier than ever, everywhere covered with it now, although luckily the roads looked to be clear. But it wasn't the snow or the conditions of the road that bothered her. What was Gabriel Vaughan still doing here? She'd thought he'd left some time ago.

She hoped Celia, inside the brightly lit house, didn't see the two of them outside together! Although, having spoken to Jane, and realising how little she actually knew about Gabriel Vaughan, the other woman had seemed to lose interest. Jane just hoped that Celia hadn't questioned Gabe in the way she had her—or mentioned the curious fact of Jane's dyed hair!

"Come on, Jane," he urged impatiently, both of them

having snowflakes in their hair now. "Open up your van, where it's at least dry!"

She moved automatically to unlock the door and climbed inside, only to turn and find Gabe sitting in the passenger seat beside her. And looking very pleased with himself, too, his smile one of satisfaction now.

"What are you doing here?" Jane snapped irritably; she really had had enough for one night.

His mouth twisted derisively. "That's a pretty blunt question, Jane," he drawled.

"I'm a pretty blunt person—Mr Vaughan," she bit out caustically. "You see, I thought we had said all we have to say to each other earlier."

He leant his head back against the seat as he gave her a considering look. The snow had melted on his hair, making it look darker than ever in the light blazing out from the house. "What have I ever done to you, Jane, to provoke such animosity? Oh, I'll accept you don't like my business practices," he continued unhurriedly before she could make a reply. "But you said yourself—and Richard confirmed it—that you aren't involved with him, and Felicity didn't give me the impression the two of you are big buddies either, so what is the problem you have concerning my business dealings with Richard? You don't give the impression of someone who takes up a campaign against injustice on someone else's part—in fact, just the opposite!" He looked at her through narrowed lids.

Jane stiffened at this last statement. "Meaning?" she prompted tautly.

He shrugged. "Meaning you don't seem to me to be a person that likes to draw attention to yourself. That, like me, you prefer to shun the limelight."

Her mouth twisted at the latter description. "That sounds a little odd coming from someone whose photograph recently appeared in the daily newspapers!" There had been yet another mention of him yesterday after he'd attended a charity dinner. Thankfully, she hadn't reacted to it in the way she had the other morning, and she had managed not to spill any of her coffee, either! "But then, you did mention that you're a sociable person!" she added mockingly.

Again he gave her that considering look, very still as he sat beside her. "Believe it or not, Jane, I hate parties," he finally drawled. "And dinner parties are even more boring; whoever your dinner companion for the evening turns out to be, you're stuck with them! And this evening I was stuck between Celia and a woman old enough to be my grandmother!"

In fact, Jane knew, the elderly lady he was referring to was actually Celia's grandmother, a titled lady that Celia considered of social value. But as she was aged in her seventies, and slightly deaf, it was only too easy to guess why Celia had seated Gabe as she had; given the choice between talking to an elderly, slightly deaf lady and the beautiful Celia, Gabe would be sure to spend the majority of the evening talking to Celia herself. Except for those ten minutes or so when Gabe had joined Jane in the kitchen.

"You hide your aversion to dinner parties very well," Jane told him dryly.

"You know exactly why I was at Richard and Felicity's that evening," Gabe rasped. "Would you like to hear why I was here tonight?" He quirked dark brows challengingly.

She looked at him, recognising that challenge, and

suddenly she knew, in view of Celia's call this morning concerning two extra guests, that Gabe's reason for being here tonight was the last thing she wanted to hear!

"It's late, Mr Vaughan." She straightened in her seat, putting the key in the ignition in preparation for leaving. "And I would very much like to go home now," she added pointedly.

Gabe nodded. "And exactly where is home?" he prompted softly.

She glanced at him sharply. "London, of course," she answered warily.

Gabe's mouth twisted wryly. "It's a big place," he drawled. "Close to one of the parks, I imagine— Your running, Jane," he explained at her sharp look. "But couldn't you be a little more specific?" he coaxed softly.

No, she couldn't; her privacy was something she guarded with the ferocity of a lioness over her den! And her apartment was her final point of refuge.

"You're a very difficult woman to pin down, Jane Smith," he murmured at her continued silence. "No one I've spoken to about you seems to have any idea where you live. Clients contact you by telephone, bills are paid to a post office box number, there's none of the usual advertising on the side of your van—in fact, it's unmarked." He shook his head. "Why all the secrecy, Jane?"

Jane stared at him with wide sherry-coloured eyes. He had talked to people about her? Tried to find out where she lived? Why?

"Why?" he repeated questioningly—making her aware that she had spoken the word out loud. "Do you have any idea how beautiful you are, Jane Smith?" he asked her huskily, suddenly much closer in the confines of the van. "And your damned elusiveness only makes you all the more intriguing!" He was so close now, the warmth of his breath stirred the wispy strands of her fringe.

She couldn't move, was held mesmerised by the intensity of those aqua-blue eyes, was transfixed by the sudden intimacy that had sprung up between them.

"Jane—"

"I don't think so, Mr Vaughan." She flinched away from the caressing hand he laid against the nerve pulsing in her throat, straightening again in her seat, moving away from him as she did so. "Now, would you please get out of my van?" she said angrily—not sure if that anger was directed at him or herself.

Had she really almost felt tempted to let him kiss her, as his warm gaze had promised he wanted to do as he'd moved closer to her? That would have been madness. Not only for her personally, but it would have threatened every vestige of peace she had built for herself over the last two years.

Gabe didn't move, frowning across at her. "Was I wrong, and you are involved with someone? Is that why you protect your privacy so fiercely?" he rasped.

And why she flinched away from letting him kiss her? He didn't say the words, but the question was there anyway. Jane realised that, to him, a man used to getting what he wanted, and having any woman he wanted, her aversion to him had to have some explanation. Whereas the real reason for her aversion to him would probably send him into shock—before another emotion entirely took over!

"No," she assured him dryly.

Blue eyes narrowed. "No man," he mused. "How

about a woman?" he added as if the thought had just occurred to him.

Jane gave a slight laugh. "Or woman," she added, with a derisive shake of her head.

He shrugged. "You never can tell." He excused his own grasping at straws. "Look, Jane, I've been completely open with you from the first. I like you. I was drawn to you from the moment—"

"Please don't go on," she cut in coldly. "You're only going to embarrass me—as well as yourself!"

Anger flashed briefly across his face, his jaw hardening, and then he had himself under control again, relaxing as he smiled that slow, charming smile. "I'm rarely embarrassed, Jane. And you don't get anywhere without asking," he added huskily.

She shot him a chilling look. "Most men would be gracious enough to accept what is definitely no for an answer!"

"Most men," Gabe nodded. "But I've invariably found that it's the things worth persisting for that are worth having," he teased lightly, before glancing out of the van window. "The snow appears to be getting heavier, so perhaps you should be getting home." He reached for the door handle. "Take care driving home, won't you?" came his parting shot.

She always took care, in everything that she did. And one of the biggest things she had taken care over was avoiding any possibility of meeting this man over the last three years. But now what she had always dreaded had happened; he had found her. And, for some inexplicable reason, he believed he was attracted to her!

He had tried to find her three years ago. He had pursued her until she had felt she couldn't run any longer, when the only answer had seemed to be to shake off all that she was, all that she had been. And with those changes—her name, her appearance—she had finally been able to make the life for herself that she had been searching for. How ironic, after all that had happened, that she should have Gabriel Vaughan to thank for making that possible!

But how long would it be, Jane wondered with a sinking heart as she drove home through the treacherous snow conditions, before Gabe saw through what was, after all, only a superficial disguise, and that attraction he believed he felt towards her turned into something much more ugly...?

CHAPTER FIVE

"I HAVE no idea what you said to him, Jane," Felicity announced happily, "but whatever it was I thank you for it!"

Jane had called in to see Felicity two days after Celia Barnaby's dinner party, having no bookings for that day and, having decided long ago that, no matter how good it was for business to have so many bookings in the run up to Christmas, she also needed a certain amount of time off. It would do business absolutely no good whatsoever if she should collapse under the strain.

There were plenty of other things she could have done with her day off, but she was very conscious of the fact that she hadn't actually visited the other woman since her discharge from hospital, and so she had called in after lunch.

But she couldn't actually say she liked the turn the conversation had taken once the two women were sitting down with a cup of tea. "I'm sorry, Felicity." She shook her head. "I have no idea what you're talking about." She gave a vaguely dismissive smile, appearing outwardly puzzled—she hoped. Inwardly she had an idea she knew exactly who "him" was, even if she wasn't too sure what Gabriel Vaughan had done now. The one thing she was absolutely sure of was that whatever it was, she didn't come into it!

Felicity gave her a teasing smile, still taking things

easy after the scare earlier in the week, although she certainly looked glowing enough this afternoon. "From what Richard told me," Felicity grinned, "I got the impression you had told Gabe exactly what you thought of him!"

Jane could feel the warm colour in her cheeks. "Only from a business point of view," she confirmed reluctantly.

Felicity raised auburn brows. "Is there another point of view?"

"Not as far as I'm concerned, no," Jane told the other woman flatly.

"Whatever," Felicity accepted, giving Jane's arm an understanding squeeze. "I'm not going to pry," she assured her huskily. "All I know is that instead of buying Richard out, and basically taking over the company, Gabe has agreed to financially back Richard until the company is back on its feet again."

"Why?" Jane frowned; it sounded too good to be true to her. There had to be something in it for Gabriel Vaughan.

"Richard asked him the same question." The other woman nodded knowingly. "And do you know what his answer was?"

She couldn't even begin to guess. Didn't really want to know. But she had a feeling Felicity was going to tell her anyway!

"I have no idea," she shrugged.

The other woman smiled. "Gabe said it was because of something someone had said to him. And the only 'someone' we could think of was you!"

Jane didn't believe that anything she could have said to Gabriel Vaughan could possibly have made any difference to his sudden change of plans where Richard's company was concerned. There had to be another reason for it. Although she very much doubted Gabe would decide to let any of them in on what it actually was. Until he was ready to, of course!

"I don't think so, Felicity," she said dryly. "Although I'm glad, for both your sakes, that he's decided to back off." And she sincerely hoped, for Felicity's sake, that he didn't as quickly change his mind back again! "But if I were Richard I would make the agreement legally binding as soon as possible," she added derisively.

"Already done," the other woman assured her happily. "Gabe has his own legal team, and between them and Richard's lawyer they tied the deal up very neatly yesterday afternoon. I can't tell you how much better I feel, Jane." Felicity sighed contentedly.

Jane could see how much more relaxed the other woman was; she just wished she felt the same way!

Unfortunately she didn't. As she drove back to her own apartment she was filled with disquieting feelings. Why had Gabriel Vaughan, when he had seemed so set on taking over Richard Warner's company, suddenly done an about-face and come to a much less aggressive agreement with the other man?

Jane refused point-blank to believe it had anything to do with what she had said to him! The man was simply too hardened, too ruthless to be swayed by such things as human frailty in Felicity's case, and emotional accusations in hers. She should know!

So it wasn't the best time in the world, with her thoughts confused and worried, for her to arrive back outside her apartment, her arms full of the food shopping

she had done on the way home, to find a huge bouquet
of flowers lying outside her apartment front door!

For one thing the flowers, whoever they were from—
and she had an uneasy feeling she knew exactly who
that might be!—were completely unwelcome. She had
made a decision, after the pain and disillusionment she
had suffered three years ago, that no man, apparently
nice or otherwise, would ever get close enough to her
again to cause the complete destruction of her life that
she had known then.

For a second thing, how had the flowers got all the
way up here to her apartment in the first place? This
was supposed to be a secure building, and her apartment
on the fourth floor—laughingly called the penthouse
apartment—could only be reached by the lift and fire-
stairs. In which case, any flowers that had been delivered
to the building should have been left downstairs in the
vestibule between the outside door and the security door,
a door that could only be unlocked by one of the four
residents.

So just how had this bouquet of flowers arrived up
here outside her door...?

"The lady in apartment number three let me in."
Gabriel Vaughan rose to his feet from the shadows of
the hallway where he had obviously been sitting on the
carpeted floor, walking slowly towards her. "A very
romantic lady," he explained as he drew level with an
open-mouthed Jane, dressed casually in denims and a
black shirt, the latter worn beneath a grey jacket. "She
was only too happy to let me in when I explained I was
your fiancée from America, and that I had come over to
surprise you!"

Jane was still stunned at actually seeing him standing

here in the hallway, let alone able to take in what he was actually saying.

But the words finally did penetrate her numbed brain, and with that comprehension came anger at the way he'd managed to trick his way in. And she was already angry enough that he was here at all! This was her home, her private sanctuary, and no one invaded it. And certainly not Gabriel Vaughan.

Never Gabriel Vaughan...!

She looked at him with coldly glittering eyes. "Take your flowers, Mr Vaughan," she bit out in a heavily controlled voice, "and—"

"I hope you aren't about to say something rude, Jane," he cut in mockingly.

"And yourself," she finished hardly, breathing deeply in her agitation, two spots of angry colour in her cheeks. "And leave. Before I call the police and have you thrown out!" she added warningly as he would have spoken. "I have no idea how you found out where I actually live, but—"

"I've hired a car for my stay over here; the weather was so bad the other evening, I decided to follow you home, to make sure you got back okay," he explained softly, his eyes narrowed on her as he saw all too easily how angry and upset she was.

He might be able to see it, but he was also going to hear it! "Your behaviour, Mr Vaughan, is bordering on harassment," she bit out tartly. "And if it continues I certainly will make a complaint to the police." Even as she repeated that threat, she knew that she would do no such thing.

The police had been involved three years ago, calling at her home, poking and prying into her personal life, into Paul's life— There was no way she would willingly open herself up to that sort of turmoil again, and certainly not with Gabriel Vaughan once again at its centre!

Gabe gave a pained grimace. "I only wanted to make sure you got home safely in that awful weather," he excused challengingly.

Jane glared at him. "I don't believe you! And after I've explained your other behaviour I don't think the police would either!"

"Aren't you taking this all a little too seriously, Jane?" He attempted to cajole her, shaking his head teasingly.

He had followed her home the other evening so that he knew where she lived, had tricked his way into her apartment building today on the pretext of bringing her flowers but actually so that he could be here waiting for her when she got home; no, she didn't think she was overreacting at all!

"Evie—the lady in the apartment below," she explained impatiently at his puzzled look, "may have found your actions romantic, Mr Vaughan…" The other woman had been trying to find out from Jane for months if there was a man in her life; Evie was involved with a married man herself, which was how she was able to live in the apartment she did. "I, on the other hand," Jane added hardly, "find them completely intrusive. If I had wanted you to know where I lived then I would have told you!"

His mouth twisted ruefully. "Don't you have any sympathy at all for a lone male in a foreign country?"

Jane gave him a disgusted look. "Not when that 'lone male' could have women queuing up outside his door to keep him company!"

He raised dark brows. "I prefer to choose my own female company," he drawled.

"Me?" Jane sighed scathingly.

"In a word—yes," Gabe nodded. "Jane, you're bright, funny, independent, run your own very successful business, and you're very, very beautiful," he added huskily.

She swallowed hard. It was so long since any man had spoken to her like this, had told her she was beautiful. It had been her decision, she accepted that, but why, oh, why did that man now have to be Gabriel Vaughan?

"As opposed to?" she prompted dryly, sure she couldn't be that unique in his acquaintance.

He grimaced. "Oh, undoubtedly beautiful," he conceded. "But also vacuous, self-oriented, self-centred, and usually having no other thought in their head other than marrying a rich man. So that they can continue to be vacuous, self-oriented, et cetera, et cetera," he concluded harshly.

He had just, from what little Jane knew of the other woman, exactly described the woman who had been his wife—Jennifer Vaughan, she'd been tall, beautiful, elegant—and totally selfish!

Jane sighed, closing her eyes briefly before looking at him once again. "Gabe—"

"That's the first time you've dropped the Mr Vaughan." He pounced, sensing some sort of victory. "Do you have the makings of dinner in here?" He took the two bags of shopping out of her arms before she could stop him, looking in at the contents. "Spaghetti bolognese," he guessed accurately seconds later. "I could make the sauce while you see to the pasta," he offered lightly.

"You—"

"Let someone else cook for you for a change, Jane," he prompted determinedly. "I make a mean bolognese sauce," he promised her.

She did a mental inventory of her apartment as she had left it a couple of hours ago: tidy, comfortably so, but also impersonal, no incriminating photographs, absolutely nothing to show the woman she had once been...

And then she brought herself up with a start. She wasn't seriously contemplating taking Gabriel Vaughan into her home, was she?

That was exactly what she was thinking!

What magic had this man worked on her that she could even be considering such an idea? Perhaps it was that "lone male" remark, after all...? She, of all people, knew just how miserable, how desolate loneliness could be...

"No standing around just watching me work once we're inside," she warned as she picked up the flowers before unlocking the door and going inside.

She strode through, giving him little time to look around her open-plan lounge. The large kitchen was wood-panelled, with herbs and spices hanging from the ceiling, pots and pans shining brightly as they hung from hooks placed over the table in the centre of the room—an old oak table that she had bought in an auction at a manor house, its years of constant use meaning it was scored with cuts and scratches, some of which Jane had added herself in the last year.

"Exactly as I imagined it," Gabe said slowly as he looked around admiringly.

How he had "imagined it"...? Since when had he started imagining what her home looked like?

"Since that first night at Felicity and Richard's." He lightly answered the accusing question in her eyes. "You can tell a lot about a person from their home."

Which was probably the reason why she never brought anyone here! She didn't want anyone to be able to "tell" anything about her—

"This is the kitchen of a chef," Gabe announced happily, starting to unpack the shopping bags. "Everything you could possibly need to cook." He indicated the numerous pots and pans. "The knives all sharp." He pulled one neatly from the kniferack. "And a bottle of red wine—room temperature, of course!—to sip and enjoy while we cook." He looked at her enquiringly as he held up the bottle that already stood on the table.

He was right; she had left the wine out so that it would be exactly the right temperature for drinking when she returned home to prepare her meal. But this to "enjoy while we cook" sounded a little too—cosy, intimate. Everything she was hoping to avoid where this man was concerned.

"Lighten up, Jane," Gabe advised laughingly as he read the indecision in her expression, deftly removing the cork from the bottle of wine as Jane busied herself putting the flowers in water. "I was suggesting we share a bottle of wine—not a bed!" He slipped off his jacket, placing it on the back of one of the kitchen chairs.

Jane put the vase of flowers down on the window-ledge with a thump. "You'll find the glasses in the cupboard over there." She nodded abruptly across the kitchen.

Share a bed, indeed! She hadn't shared a bed with

any man since— She shuddered just at the thought of having once shared a bed with Paul!

Luckily she was concentrating on preparing the pasta by the time Gabe came back with the wine glasses, her shudder of revulsion unseen by him. Otherwise he might have wanted to know just why a woman of twenty-eight, obviously healthy, and not unattractive, should shudder at the mere thought of such intimacy...!

Gabe sliced up the onion with one of her sharp knives, and Jane couldn't help but admire the way he diced it into small pieces, ready for sautéing in the butter he had gently melting in a frying pan on top of the Aga. And he was obviously enjoying himself too, perfectly relaxed, humming softly to himself as he worked.

Strange; she had always thought of Gabriel Vaughan as an over-tall man, powerfully built, his face set into grimly angry lines. And this man, grinning to himself as he fried onions, didn't fit into that picture at all...!

He turned to take a sip from the nearest of the two glasses of wine he had poured out for them. "This is fun, isn't it?" He smiled widely at her.

Jane's smile was much more cautious; she had a feeling a little like having been swept over by a tornado, not even sure how the two of them had come to be in her kitchen cooking a meal together. He was the very last man she would have thought she would spend any time with!

"Jane?" he prompted softly at her silence, no longer smiling, frowning at her lack of response.

It was the disappearance of that smile that affected her the most; it had been a completely natural smile, without cynicism or innuendo. He really had been enjoying himself a moment ago as he'd cooked the onions!

And now she felt guilty for upsetting his pleasure...

"You dealt with that onion very professionally," she told him lightly, taking a break to sip her own wine. "At a guess, I would say it's something you've done before!" she added teasingly.

"Dozens of times," he nodded, that light note back in his voice as he turned to toss the onions in the butter. "I've always liked to cook at home," he shrugged. "Although I have to admit I haven't done so for some time." He frowned at the realisation. "Jennifer—my wife— didn't think it was worth bothering to eat at all if there was no one to see her doing it," he added ruefully.

His wife. Jennifer. How the very sound of that name had once hurt her! But now she'd heard it, from the man who had been her husband, and she felt nothing, not even the numbness that had once been so necessary to her.

"There was you," she told Gabe dismissively, suddenly busy with the pasta once again.

"There was me," he echoed self-derisively, tipping in the minced steak to cook with the onions. "Unfortunately, Jennifer was the type of woman who was more interested in what other women's husbands thought of her rather than what interested her own husband!"

Jane hadn't even been aware of holding the knife in her hand, let alone how she came to slice her finger with it, but suddenly there was blood on the work surface in front of her, and, she realised belatedly, a stinging pain on the index finger of her left hand.

How ironic, she thought even through the pain, that it should be her left hand that she had cut. The hand that had once worn her wedding ring...

"It was something I— Hell, Jane!" Gabe suddenly saw the blood too, taking the frying-pan off the heat before rushing over to her side, pressing her finger to stop the flow of blood. "What the hell happened?" He barked his concern. "Do you think it's bad enough to need stitches? Perhaps I should call—"

"Gabe," Jane cut in soothingly—she was the one with the cut finger, but he was definitely the one who was panicking! "It's only a tiny cut. A hazard of the trade," she added lightly, deliberately playing down the problem this cut would give her over the next busy few weeks. Preparing food, having her hands constantly in and out of water—this cut, even though it really wasn't very serious, would cause her deep discomfort for some time to come.

Damn; she couldn't remember the last time she had done anything this silly. Of course, it had been Gabe's comments about his wife that had caused her lapse in concentration...

"You'll find some plasters in the cupboard over the dishwasher," she told him abruptly, moving to wash the cut under cold water as he went to get the plasters, the stinging pain in her hand helping to relieve some of the shock she had felt at hearing him discuss his wife so casually.

Gabe deftly applied the plaster once her finger had been dried. "I don't have a wife any more, Jane," he told her softly, his gaze searching as he looked down into her face.

He believed it was the thought of having dinner with a potentially married man that had caused her to have this accident! Perhaps it was better that he should continue to think that was the reason...

"I'm glad to hear it," she dismissed lightly. "Because if you did," she added as she saw the light of triumph in his eyes, "Evie—the woman downstairs—" she reminded him who had let him into the building—and why "—would be devastated. It would blow all her romantic illusions out of the window!"

"I see," he sighed, nodding abruptly, before turning his attention back to his bolognese sauce. "My wife died," he rasped harshly, no longer looking at Jane.

Because the memory of Jennifer's death must still be a painful one for him, Jane acknowledged. She should know, better than most people, that a person didn't necessarily have to be nice to have someone fall in love with them.

And Jennifer Vaughan had not been a nice woman: tall, beautiful, vivacious, and ultimately dangerous, with a need inside her to bewitch every man she came into contact with, while at the same time eluding any ownership of herself. Only one man had succeeded in taming her even a little. Gabriel Vaughan. And from the little he had so far said about Jennifer, and from what Jane already knew from her own experience, that ownership had been bitter-sweet—and probably more bitter than sweet!

But there could be no doubting that, despite all her faults, Gabe had loved his wife—

"Jennifer was a bitch," he bit out suddenly, those aqua-blue eyes piercing in their intensity now as he turned back to hold Jane's gaze. "Beautiful, immoral, whose only pleasure in life seemed to be to destroy what others had built," he told Jane grimly. "Like a child with a pile of building bricks another child may have taken time and care to put in place; Jennifer would knock it all down, with an impish grin and a flash of her wicked green eyes!"

Jane swallowed hard. She didn't want to hear any of this! "Gabe—"

"Don't worry, Jane," he bit out derisively. "The only reason I'm telling you this is so that you know I'm not about to launch into some sorrowful tale about how wonderful my marriage was—"

"But you loved her—"

"Of course I loved her!" he rasped, reaching out to grasp the tops of Jane's arms, his gaze burning with intensity now. "I married her. Maybe that was my mistake, I don't know." He shook his head impotently. "The excitement was all in the chase to Jennifer." His mouth twisted. "A loving captive was not what she wanted!"

"Gabe, I really—"

"Don't want to hear?" He easily guessed her cry of protest. "Well, that's just too bad, because I intend telling you whether you want to know or not!" he told her savagely.

"But why?" Jane choked, looking up at him imploringly, her face pale, eyes dark brown. "I've asked you for nothing, want nothing from you. I don't want anyone—"

"You don't want anyone disturbing the life you've made for yourself in your ivory tower," he acknowledged grimly. "Oh, I'll grant you, it's comfortable enough, Jane." He looked about him appreciatively. "But, nevertheless, it's still an ivory tower. And I'm giving you notice that I intend knocking down the walls—"

"Doesn't that make you as destructive as you just described your wife?" Jane cut in scornfully, her whole body rigid now, standing as far away from him as his grasp on her arms would allow.

Because those fingers were like steel bands on her

flesh, not hurting, but at the same time totally unmove-
able. The only way to distance herself from him was
verbally, to hurt him as his words were hurting her.

"Late wife, Jane," he corrected her harshly. "Past
tense. And no, it doesn't make me like Jennifer at all.
I'm not out to destroy for destruction's sake. I want to
build—"

"For the couple of months or so you claim you're
going to be in England?" she came back disgustedly,
shaking her head. "I don't think so, thank you, Gabe.
Why don't you try Celia Barnaby?" she scorned. "I'm
sure she would be more than happy to—"

Her words were cut off abruptly as Gabe's mouth
came crashing down on hers, pulling her into the hardness of his body, knocking the breath from her lungs as
he did so, rendering her momentarily helpless.

And Gabe took full advantage of that helplessness,
his mouth plundering, taking what he wanted, sipping,
tasting the nectar to be found there. And then finally
the onslaught ceased, Gabe having sensed her lack of
response.

He began to kiss her gently now, his hands moving to
cradle either side of her face as his lips moved caress-
ingly against her own, that gentleness Jane's undoing.

She began to respond…!

Something deep, deep inside her began to break free
at the softly caressing movement of Gabe's lips against
hers, a yearning for something she had denied herself for
the last three years, a warming to an emotion she hadn't
allowed in her life for three years.

But Gabe didn't love her. And she certainly didn't
love him. And anything else they might be able to give

each other would be totally destroyed the moment he discovered who she really was...!

Gabe raised his head slightly, his hands still cradling each side of her face, his eyes glittering down into hers, but not with anger now—with another emotion entirely. "I'm not interested in Celia Barnaby, Jane," he told her huskily. "In any way. The only reason I was anywhere near her home at all the other evening was because I knew you would be there," he admitted self-derisively.

It was as she had guessed, but hoped wasn't true. Gabe had to have been one of those extra guests Celia had telephoned her about—and it had been by his own design.

"I want you, Jane—"

She pulled sharply away from him, breathing easier once she was free. "You can't have me, Gabe," she told him dully. "Because I don't want you," she added as he would have protested, his expression grim now. "I realise it must be difficult for the eligible Gabriel Vaughan to accept that a woman may not want him, but—"

"Cut the insults, Jane," he put in scathingly. "I heard what you said the first time around! What is it about you, Jane?" he added with a shake of his head as he took in her appearance from head to toe, her hair slightly di-shevelled now from his caressing fingers, her eyes twin pools of sherry-brown in the paleness of her face. "I've wanted you since the moment I first set eyes on you! Not only that," he continued harshly, "but I've found myself thinking more—and now talking, too—about the wife I've tried to put from my mind for three years. Why is that, do you think, Jane?" His eyes glittered with anger once again, but it was impossible to tell whether that anger was directed at Jane or himself.

She knew exactly why she had thought more of the past, of Paul, her own dead husband, this last week. Gabriel Vaughan, with his own involvement in that death, had brought back all the unwanted memories she had mainly succeeded in pushing to the very back of her mind. And part of Gabe, Jane was beginning to realise—although it was only subconsciously in him at the moment—recognised something in her, evoking his own thoughts and memories of the past.

How long before those subconscious memories became full awareness...?

"I really have no interest in learning why, Gabe," she told him dismissively. "And that's something I do know the answer to—I'm not interested in you!" She looked across at him with cold challenge, her heart pounding loudly in her chest as she waited for his reaction.

He predictably met that challenge, his gaze unwavering. "You know damn well that isn't true—and so do I!" he bit out harshly. "Whoever he was, Jane—" he shook his head "—he certainly isn't worth hiding yourself away—"

"In my ivory tower?" she finished scornfully, angry with herself and him—for the tell-tale colour that had appeared in her cheeks when he had challenged her denial of being interested in him. Because he had breached the barriers she had erected around her emotions, no matter how briefly... "Was Jennifer worth it?" she returned pointedly.

His brows arched, his mouth twisting ruefully. "Neatly turned, Jane," he drawled admiringly. "But completely ineffective; Jennifer, and anything she may have done while she was alive, lost the power to hurt me long ago," he assured her disgustedly.

"How about the pain she caused when she died?" Jane returned harshly.

And then wished she hadn't as she saw Gabe's gaze narrow speculatively. She was becoming careless in her own agitation with this situation...!

"She died in a car accident, Jane," Gabe said softly. "And there's nothing more final than death," he added harshly. "Dead people can't hurt you."

"Can't they?" she breathed huskily.

He gave a firm shake of his head. "If Jennifer hadn't died when she did, I think I would one day have ended up strangling her myself! So you see," he added scathingly, "the only thing Jennifer did when she died was save me the trouble of doing the job myself!"

It wasn't. Jane knew it wasn't. And, no matter how bitter he might now have become about his wife's past behaviour, so did Gabe. Because three years ago, after the car accident in which Jennifer died, Gabe had been like a man demented, had needed to blame someone, and with the death of the only person he could blame he had turned his anger and humiliation onto the only person left in the whole sorry mess that he could still reach...!

Gabe was right when he guessed a man was responsible for her living in an emotional fortress, what he chose to call her "ivory tower".

It was the same man who was partly responsible for her becoming plain Jane Smith.

The same man she had been hiding her real self away from for the past three years.

And that man was Gabriel Vaughan himself!

CHAPTER SIX

"DON'T look so worried, Jane," he taunted now. "Those murderous feelings were only directed towards my wife; I actually abhor violence!"

So did she. Oh, God, so did she. But, nevertheless, she was no stranger to it...

"It's said there's a very fine line between love and hate," she said dully.

And she knew that too. She had been so in love with Paul when she'd married him, but at the end of four years she had hated him. For what he had done to her family. And for what he had taken from her.

But she also knew, no matter how difficult to live with, how selfish Jennifer had been, that Gabe had loved his wife. That he had loved her enough to seek out the people he felt were involved in her death...

"Shouldn't we finish cooking this meal?" Gabe suddenly suggested with bright efficiency, placing the frying-pan back on top of the Aga.

Jane continued to look at him dazedly for several long seconds. She had no interest in cooking the meal, let alone eating it, not after what had been said. Or the way Gabe had kissed her minutes ago... She wasn't even sure she could eat after that!

"Come on, Jane," Gabe said briskly. "The food will do us both good." He turned away again, as if what he had just said settled the matter; they would eat dinner together.

Because he was a man used to giving orders. And having them carried out.

But Jane didn't finish cooking the spaghetti for either of those reasons. Quite simply, when she cooked, created, she could forget all that was going on around her. And, after thinking of her marriage to Paul, it was very necessary that she do that at this moment.

"Excellent!" Gabe pronounced with satisfaction a short time later, having almost finished eating the spaghetti bolognese on his plate. The two of them were seated at the huge oak dining table, their glasses replenished with the red wine, the remaining food still steaming hot on their plates. "Maybe the two of us should go into business together," he added in a challengingly soft voice.

Jane gave him a sharp look, knowing by the teasing glitter in his eyes that he was looking for a reaction from her. "I don't think so," she came back dismissively. "Somehow I don't see you working for anyone!"

Dark brows rose. "I was thinking more along the lines of a partnership," he drawled.

She gave an acknowledging inclination of her head— she was well aware of exactly what he had meant! "And I was thinking more along the lines of the clients I work for!"

Gabe laughed softly, forking up some more of his food. "Why a personal chef, Jane, as opposed to the restaurant Felicity suggested the other evening?" he asked interestedly. "Surely a restaurant would mean more customers, more—"

"Overheads," she finished for him. "More people

working for me. Just more complications altogether," she shrugged dismissively.

Although she had to admit that, at the time she'd begun her business it hadn't been for those reasons that she had chosen to go alone. There had been no money to invest in such a risky venture as opening up her own restaurant. Three years ago she had been left with only one commodity she could use—herself. And her talent at cooking had seemed by far the best course for her to take! Even then it had been a painful year of indecision before that option had occurred to her.

"And you're a person that likes to avoid complications, aren't you?" Gabe said shrewdly.

She returned his narrow-eyed gaze unblinkingly. "With only myself to rely on, I felt I stood a better chance of success." She deliberately didn't answer his question.

"But what about now?" Gabe continued conversationally. "You've already effectively built up your clientele; it wouldn't take too much to—"

"Not everyone is as ambitious as you are, Gabe," she cut in firmly. "Three years ago I didn't even have my business—"

"What happened three years ago?" he interrupted softly. "Just curiosity, Jane," he assured her as she gave him a startled look. "Maybe I phrased the question badly," he conceded ruefully as she still didn't answer. "Perhaps I should have asked what it was you did *before* three years ago?"

Until the age of eighteen she had been at school. And at eighteen, instead of going to university, she had chosen to go to France, where she had taken an advanced cookery course. At twenty, a few months after her return home, she had met Paul and they'd become engaged. At twenty-one she was married. And at twenty-five she was widowed. The details of those four years as Paul's wife she preferred not to think about!

And she intended telling Gabriel Vaughan none of those things, wished now that she hadn't mentioned "three years ago" at all. Because it was exactly that length of time since his wife had died...

"I kept busy." She was deliberately noncommittal, studiously avoiding that searching aqua-blue gaze. "But I had always wanted to run my own business." Instead of living in someone else's shadow, always having to tell them how wonderful they were, how successful, how— How *deceitful*!

"And now you have it," Gabe acknowledged lightly. "Is it as much fun as you thought it would be?"

Fun? She hadn't ever expected it to be "fun". She had wanted independence, freedom, hadn't looked for anything else. And her business had certainly given her those things; she answered to no one!

"There's more to life than success, Jane," Gabe added at her lack of reply.

"Such as?" she challenged scornfully; he wasn't exactly unsuccessful himself, so how could he be a judge of that?

He shrugged. "Love," he suggested huskily.

Jane gave a derisive laugh. "I don't see how you can possibly say that when you obviously had a love/hate relationship with your own wife!"

His mouth tightened. "Jennifer did not make me happy," he conceded. "But I thought I'd found the perfect woman," he rasped, his thoughts all inwards now. "And then she just evaporated, disappeared before my eyes."

He looked across at Jane with pained eyes. "I haven't been able to look at another woman since without seeing her image imprinted there. At least," he added gruffly, "I hadn't. Until six days ago."

"What happened—? Oh, no, Gabe," she dismissed scathingly as she realised he was talking of his initial meeting with her. "Does this chat-up line usually work?" she added disgustedly.

"It isn't a chat-up line," he told her steadily. "You know that. And so do I," he added evenly, keeping his gaze fixed on hers.

It was that steady gaze that made her realise he meant every word he was saying!

"You're being ridiculous, Gabe," she bit out agitatedly. "You can't be attracted to me!"

He tilted his head thoughtfully to one side. "That's a very interesting way of putting it."

Again she realised her mistake too late; it was an "interesting way of putting it". And she knew exactly why she had said it that way. But the last thing she wanted was for Gabe to know that reason!

"I'm just not your type," she said impatiently.

Those dark brows rose again. "Do I have a type?" he drawled in amusement.

Jane sighed. "Of course you do," she snapped irritably. "You've always been attracted to tall, elegant blondes. You married a tall, elegant blonde! Whereas I—" She broke off, having realised by the widening of his eyes that she had once again said too much.

She just couldn't seem to help it where this man was concerned. She simply wasn't any good at playing the sophisticated games that people like Gabe—and Paul— liked to play. It was one of the reasons Paul had become so bored with her; he had been sure that the doting daughter and equally doting fiancée were an act, had been furious after their marriage to learn that that was exactly what she was. Her shyness annoyed him, her total love irritated him, and as for the doting daughter—!

It had become a marriage made in hell, her shyness turning to coldness as a way of protecting herself from Paul's taunts; her total love had deteriorated to pity that he obviously wasn't able to feel such emotion himself. And the "doting daughter" had kept all her pain and misery to herself, in an effort to spare her parents the heartache of knowing she had made a terrible mistake in marrying Paul!

"You're a short brunette," Gabe conceded dryly. "Which makes a mockery of the tall blonde." His eyes narrowed. "How did you know my wife was blonde? I'm sure I didn't mention it…"

There was an underlying edge of steel to his tone that hadn't been there before, and Jane realised that a lot depended on her next answer. "Celia Barnaby insisted on talking to me about you the other evening," she told him truthfully, relieved to see some of the tension ease out of his stiffly held shoulders. And it was the truth—except Celia hadn't told her his wife was a blonde either! But if what he had told her about Celia was true, then he was never likely to find that out from the other woman, was he? "I believe the implication was that, being tall and blonde herself, she was worthy of your interest," Jane added mockingly.

He shrugged, relaxed once more. "I seem to have lost my appetite for tall blondes," he returned dryly.

Then it was a pity her hair wasn't its natural honey-blonde; it would have nullified her attraction on one count, at least! But if her hair had still been blonde Gabe would probably have instantly recognised her, anyway. And that would never do!

"Celia assures me that blondes have more fun," Jane derided, having no intention of explaining to him the circumstances under which the other woman had made that remark! She was still unnerved herself at the other woman's realisation of her real hair colour...

"If you like that sort of fun." Gabe's mouth twisted scornfully. "I don't. How old are you, Jane?" He abruptly changed the subject.

She blinked, seeming to have averted one catastrophe—but unsure whether or not she was heading for another one! "Twenty-eight," she supplied with a frown.

He nodded, as if it was about what he had already guessed. "And I'm thirty-nine."

She shook her head. "I don't see—"

"Because I hadn't finished," he told her with mild rebuke. "I'm thirty-nine years old, was married, and now I'm not. I'm a wealthy man, can do what I like, when I like—pretty much as you can, I imagine," he acknowledged ruefully. "The difference being," he continued as she would have spoken, "that for me it isn't enough. When my wife died three years ago— Strange that your life seems to have changed around that time too...?" he added thoughtfully.

Jane held her breath as she waited for him to continue. If he did. Oh, please, God, don't let him pursue that subject!

He shrugged, as if it was something he would go back to another time; right now he was talking about something completely different. "When Jennifer died all my illusions died along with her," he continued harshly. "And that illusion of perfection disappeared too."

Not surprising, in the circumstances! He must have really loved Jennifer to have ever thought she was perfect! But then, hadn't Jane made the same mistake about Paul...? Love, it appeared, made fools of them all!

"Or so it seemed," Gabe added softly, looking pointedly at Jane.

He didn't seem the type of man who fell victim to infatuations, and yet the way he was looking at her...! Maybe she had formed completely the wrong impression of this man, because at this moment that was exactly how he was behaving!

"I can assure you, I'm far from perfect," she told him firmly, standing up to clear away her plate, the food only half eaten, but the evening over as far as she was concerned. "I wish you luck in your search for this perfection, Gabe," she added dismissively. "But count me out. I don't meet the criteria, and, even more important, I happen to like my life exactly the way it is." Her eyes flashed a warning.

Because she did like her life the way it was. She was her own boss, both privately and professionally, could pick and choose now what she would and wouldn't do. And she had deliberately planned for it to be that way. And it was how she intended it to stay.

Gabe clearly saw that warning in her eyes, standing up too. "Don't you ever long for anything different, Jane? Marriage? Children?" he persisted.

Jane felt the pain only briefly, bringing a shutter down over her emotions, her gaze impenetrable as she looked at him coldly. "Like you, Gabe, I've tried the former," she bit out between stiff lips. "And I also know it isn't necessary for the latter," she added flatly. "And no, I don't long for either of those things." Not again. Not ever again. She belonged to herself, would never be owned by anyone ever again.

Gabe looked at her through narrowed lids. "You've been married?"

Once again this man had provoked her into saying too much. Far, far too much. She seemed to head him off from one direction, only to find he was going in another one that was just as intrusive.

"Hasn't everyone?" she dismissed with deliberate carelessness. "With the divorce rate as high as it is, surely it's inevitable!" she added scathingly.

That aqua-blue gaze remained narrowed on her thoughtfully. And Jane hadn't missed that glance he had briefly given her left hand. But he would find no tell-tale signs of a ring having been worn there, no indentation, no paler skin from a summer tan; her ring had been consigned to a river long ago. Along with all the painful memories that went with it.

"You're divorced?" Gabe probed softly now.

Oh, no, he wasn't going to get any more information out of her that way!

"My father told me you should try everything once," she answered mockingly. "And if you don't like it the first time then don't repeat the experience!" Once again she didn't actually answer his question, and she knew by the rueful expression on his face that he was well aware of the fact, that it was yet another subject he would store away for the moment to be returned to on another occasion.

And he would be wasting his time, now and in the

future; she had no intention of answering any of his questions about her marriage!

"Do your parents live in London?"

She drew in a gasping breath—this man just didn't give up, did he!

"No," she answered unhelpfully. "Do yours live in America?"

His mouth twisted in acknowledgement of her having turned the question back to him. "They do," he drawled dryly, the two of them having cleared the table now. "In Washington DC. My dad was in politics, but he's retired now."

If he thought that by appearing open about his own family she would return the compliment, then he was mistaken! "Do politicians ever retire?"

"Not really." Gabe smiled at the question. "But it's what he likes to tell people. He and Mom have been married for forty years."

And her own parents had been married for thirty. In fact, tomorrow was their wedding anniversary, and she intended going to see them for a few hours on Saturday. Sadly a few hours was all she could bear nowadays.

It used to be so different, her parents doting on their only child. But what Paul had done three years ago had affected them all, and now her father was a mere shadow of his former self, and her mother desperately tried to keep up a pretence for Jane's benefit that everything was normal whenever she went to see them. But Jane wasn't fooled for a minute, and her visits, few and far between nowadays, were as much of a strain for her as they were for her parents.

"Someone should give them a medal," she told

Gabe cynically. "A lasting marriage seems to be a dying art!"

"That isn't true," he defended. "There are lots of happily married couples. Look at Felicity and Richard," he pointed out triumphantly.

"You didn't," Jane reminded him dryly. "You accused me of having an affair with Richard!"

Gabe grimaced. "A natural mistake, in the circumstances."

Jane gave him a look of exasperation. "And just what 'circumstances' would they be?"

He shrugged uncomfortably. "You were very strong in your defence of him."

Because of her past knowledge of Gabe, not because she was actually close to the other couple. Although she did like Felicity and Richard, admired their happy marriage and beautiful daughters. And it had been the destruction she knew this man could wreak that had made her defend them so fiercely. It seemed that defence had succeeded in arousing Gabe's suspicions, but in completely the wrong direction—thank goodness!

"It's an English trait," she answered dryly. "We always root for the underdog," she explained at Gabe's puzzled expression.

His mouth twisted ruefully. "I doubt Felicity and Richard think of themselves as such!"

"I visited Felicity today." Jane looked at him pointedly.

He gave that mocking inclination of his head. "And she told you about my business deal with Richard," he guessed wryly. "And now part of you—a very big part if I know anything about you at all—is wondering what I'm up to now! Will it make any difference if I tell you nothing; it's a straightforward business arrangement, with no hidden agenda?"

Jane still looked at him sceptically. "And what's in it for you?" Because from what Felicity had told her about that deal, he had gained absolutely nothing. And that didn't sound like the Gabriel Vaughan she knew at all!

"It means I can sleep nights," he muttered harshly.

Her eyes widened. "Don't tell me you have a conscience, Gabe?" she said disbelievingly.

"Is that so hard to believe?" he rasped.

She shrugged; three years ago she wouldn't have believed he had a conscience to bother—and she didn't want to start changing her opinion of him now! "I find it so, yes," she answered truthfully.

"Oh, it's there, I can assure you," he bit out. "And I've just realised you very neatly changed the subject again a few minutes ago," he added mockingly.

Jane looked at him with innocently wide sherry-brown eyes. She wasn't actually sure which subject he meant; there seemed to be so many of them that she didn't wish to discuss with this man!

Gabe threw back his head and laughed. "Does that innocent-little-girl expression usually work?" he finally sobered enough to ask.

"Usually—yes." Jane grinned back at him in spite of herself.

"God, Jane, you're beautiful when you smile!" he said with husky admiration. "You're also trying to change the subject—again!" he added chidingly.

She arched her brows. "Am I?"

"Oh, yes," he acknowledged without rancour. "Tell me, do you play bridge?"

"As a matter of fact, I do," she admitted dryly.

"And chess?"

She smiled again, knowing exactly what he was getting at. "Yes," she confirmed wryly.

"Unfortunately—for you—so do I!" Gabe drawled teasingly. "Tell me, Jane, do you believe in love at first sight?" he added softly, his gaze suddenly intense once again.

"No," she answered without hesitation. "Not at second, third, or fourth, either!" she bit out tautly.

He frowned at her answer. "Was your marriage that awful?"

"In its own way. Wasn't yours?" she challenged, once again avoiding talking about her marriage to Paul. "Awful" didn't even begin to describe it! "Even loving your wife as you did?"

He sighed heavily. "Let me tell you about my feelings for Jennifer—"

"Gabe, I don't want to know about your marriage or your wife," Jane cut in agitatedly; she already knew all she needed to know about both those things. "If you're still having trouble coming to terms with what happened, and need someone to talk to about it, then I suggest you try a marriage guidance counsellor—or a priest!" she added insultingly, eyes gleaming darkly.

He drew in a sharp breath. "What the hell do you mean by that?"

"I have no idea," she sighed wearily. "But that's my whole point really, Gabe; I have no idea because I don't want to know. How many times do I have to keep saying that?" she added with deliberate scorn.

"I'm obviously a slow learner," he murmured thoughtfully, picking up his jacket from the back of the chair. "I thought you were different, Jane." He frowned. "I still think that," he added firmly. "I also don't think you're as indifferent to me as you would like to think you are." He shrugged into his jacket. "Thanks for the meal, Jane. And the conversation. Believe it or not, I enjoyed both!"

She did find that hard to believe. Oh, parts of the evening—very small parts!—had been pleasant, but his kisses had had a devastating effect on the emotional barriers she had succeeded in putting up over the last three years, and the conversation about his wife was something she hadn't enjoyed at all, and she couldn't believe Gabe had enjoyed talking about Jennifer either. And Jane certainly regretted having revealed so much about her own life...

"Thank you for the flowers," she said stiffly. "But please don't try and use Evie again to get in here," she added hardly, eyes glittering warningly. "She may be a romantic—but I'm not!"

"And you intend putting her straight about your American fiancée," Gabe guessed easily. "Next time I come here, Jane, it will be at your invitation," he promised.

That day would never come, she inwardly assured herself as she walked him to the door.

Gabe turned in the doorway, gently touching one of her pale cheeks. "I really mean you no harm, Jane," he told her huskily.

He might not mean to harm her, but he had already shaken the foundations of her new life. "I wouldn't allow you to," she assured him firmly.

He gave a wry smile. "Look after yourself, Jane Smith," he told her softly. "Because I very much doubt you would allow anyone else to do so!" came his parting shot.

Jane closed and locked the door before he had even walked down the carpeted hallway to the lift, leaning back against it with a sigh, closing her eyes wearily.

But the action had little effect in closing out the image of Gabe in her apartment, of Gabe kissing her until she responded...

CHAPTER SEVEN

THE house looked the same as it always had as Jane drove down the long driveway. There was snow still on the grass verge and trees, but it had mainly melted on the gravel driveway—evidence that one or both of her parents had driven down it in the last few days.

Jane had always loved this house set in the Berkshire countryside. She'd grown up here from child to teenager in the surrounding grounds and woods. This was her parents' home, where she had only ever known love and the closeness of a happy family.

Although she felt none of that warmth now as she parked her van outside the house. It was no longer the grand house it had once been; the paintwork outside was in need of redoing, and inside only the main parts of the house were kept in liveable order now. The once gracious wings on either side of this were closed up now, being too expensive to heat, let alone keep clean and tidy. There was only Mrs Weaver in the kitchen now to cook and tend the house, a young girl from the village coming in at weekends to help with the heavy housework. Once the house had had a full-time staff of five, and three gardeners to tend the grounds. But not any more. Not for three years now...

Jane got out of her van, taking with her the cake she had made for her parents' anniversary and the bunch of flowers she had bought to signify the occasion. She let herself in through the oak front door, knowing Mrs Weaver had enough to keep her busy without having to answer the door to the daughter of the house.

Jane paused in the grand hallway, putting down the box containing the cake on the round table there, before looking up at the wide sweep of the staircase, briefly recalling the ball that had been held here for her eighteenth birthday—her walking down that staircase in the beautiful black gown her mother had helped her to choose, with her honey-coloured waist-length hair swinging loosely down her slender back.

At the time it had seemed to Jane she had the whole world at her feet, little dreaming that ten years later her perfect world would have been totally destroyed. And as for her youthful dreams that night of Mr Right and happy-ever-after...! As she had told Gabriel Vaughan two evenings ago, she no longer believed in them, either!

Gabriel Vaughan...

She had tried not to think of him for the last two days, and as she had been particularly busy, catering for a lunch as well as a dinner yesterday, she had managed to do that quite successfully. Although she had to admit she had felt slightly apprehensive about the dinner party the evening before, in case Gabe should once again be one of the guests!

But it had been a trouble-free evening. As the last two days had been Gabriel Vaughan-free. And strangely enough, after his initial bombardment of her privacy and emotions, she found his complete silence now almost as unnerving. What was he up to now...?

"Janette, darling!" her mother greeted warmly as Jane entered the comfortable sitting-room, a fire blazing in the hearth—the only form of heating they had in the house now that central heating was an unaffordable luxury. Fires were lit each day in this sitting-room and in the master bedroom.

Her mother looked as elegantly beautiful as ever as she rose to kiss Jane, tall and stately, blonde hair perfectly styled, make-up enhancing the beauty of her face. And despite her fifty-one years, and the birth of her daughter, Daphne Smythe-Roberts was still as gracefully thin as she had been in her youth.

It took Jane a little longer to turn and greet her father, schooling her features not to reveal the shock she felt whenever she looked at his now stooped and dispirited body. Ten years older than her mother, her father looked much older than that, no longer the vibrantly fit man he had once been, a force to be reckoned with in business.

Jane forced a bright smile to her face as he too rose to kiss and hug her, over six feet in height, but his stooped shoulders somehow making him appear shorter, the thickness of his hair no longer salt-and-pepper but completely salt, his handsome face also lined with age.

Guilt.

Jane felt overwhelmed with it every time she visited her parents nowadays. If she hadn't fallen in love with Paul, if she hadn't married him, if her father hadn't decided to groom his son-in-law to take over the business from him one day, handing more and more of the responsibility for the day-to-day running of the company to the younger man, at the same time trusting Paul more and more on the financial side of things too… If only. If only!

Because it had been a trust Paul had abused. And as

his wife, as his widow, Jane could only feel guilt and despair for the duplicity on Paul's part that had robbed her parents of the comfortable retirement years they had expected to enjoy together.

"You're looking wonderful, darling." Her father held her at arm's length as he looked at her proudly with eyes as brown as her own.

"So are you," she answered, more with affection than truth.

Her father had lost more than his business three years ago, he had also lost the self-respect that had made his electronics company into one of the largest privately owned companies in the country. And at fifty-eight he had felt too old—too defeated!—to want to start all over again. And so her parents lived out their years in genteel poverty, instead of travelling the world together as they had once planned to do when her father finally retired.

Guilt.

God, yes, Jane felt guilty!

"I think you're looking a little pale, Janette," her mother put in concernedly. "You aren't working too hard, are you, darling?"

Guilt.

Yes, her parents felt that guilt too, but for a different reason. The life Jane had now, catering for other peoples' dinner parties, was not the one they had envisaged for their only and much beloved child. But none of them had been in a financial position three years ago to do more than offer each other emotional support.

Things were slightly better for Jane now, and she did what she could, without their knowledge, to help them in the ways that she was able. Before she left later this afternoon she would deliver to the kitchen such things as the smoked salmon that her mother loved, several bottles of her father's favourite Scotch, and many other things that simply could not be bought in the normal budget of the household as it now was. Her mother, Jane felt, probably was aware of the extras that Jane supplied them with—after all, her mother had always managed the household budget—but by tacit agreement neither of them ever mentioned the luxuries that would appear after one of Jane's visits.

"Not at all, Mummy," Janette Smythe-Roberts assured her mother. She'd once been Janette Granger, before she'd thrown that life away along with her wedding ring—Jane Smith, personal chef, taking her place. "The business is doing marvellously," she told her. "It's just a busy time of year. But I'm not here to talk about me." She smiled, holding out the flowers to her mother. "Happy Anniversary!"

"Oh, darling, how lovely!" Her mother blinked back the tears as she looked at her favourite lilies and orchids that Jane had picked out for her.

"And this is for you, Daddy." She handed her father a bottle of the whisky that she wouldn't have to sneak to Mrs Weaver in the kitchen later, her eyes widening appreciatively as she saw for the first time the display of roses on the table in the bay window. "My goodness, Daddy," she said admiringly, the deep yellow and white roses absolutely beautiful. "Did you grow these in your greenhouse?" Rose-growing had become her father's hobby in the last few years, and whenever he couldn't be found in the house he was out in the greenhouse tending his beloved roses.

In years gone by, the house would have been full of flowers, a huge display on the table in the hallway, smaller vases in the sitting-room and dining-room, posies of scented flowers in the bedrooms. But not any more; there were no gardeners now to tend the numerous blooms her mother had needed to make such colourful arrangements.

"I'm afraid not." Her father grimaced ruefully. "Would that I had. Beautiful specimens, aren't they?" he said admiringly.

Beautiful. But if her father hadn't grown them, where had they come from...?

Her parents' circle of friends had narrowed down to several couples they had known from when they were first married, and Jane couldn't imagine any of them had sent these wonderful roses either. There were at least fifty blooms there, and they must have cost a small fortune to buy.

Her parents' sudden change of financial circumstances had had a strange effect on the majority of people they had been friendly with three years ago, most of them suddenly avoiding the other couple, almost as if they were frightened the collapse and financial take-over of David Smythe-Roberts' company might be catching!

So who had given them the roses?

"We had a visitor yesterday, darling." Her mother's tone was light, but her gaze avoided actually meeting Jane's suddenly sharp one. "Of course, he didn't realise it was our anniversary yesterday." Daphne laughed dismissively. "But the roses are absolutely lovely, aren't they?" she continued brightly.

He? A sense of foreboding began to spread through Jane. He! Which he?

Her hands began to shake, and she suddenly felt short of breath, sure she could actually feel the blood starting to drain out of her cheeks as she continued to stare at her mother.

"Oh, Janette, don't look like that!" Her mother moved forward, clasping both of Jane's hands in her own. "It was perfectly all right," she assured her. "Mr Vaughan didn't stay very long—well, just long enough for a cup of tea," she admitted awkwardly. "Talking of tea," she added desperately as Jane looked even more distressed, "I think I'll ring for Mrs Weaver to bring us all—"

"No!" Jane at last found her voice again.

Mr Vaughan! Her worst fear had come true; it was Gabe who had come here, to her parents' home, bringing those beautiful roses with him.

Why? It was three years ago now; why couldn't he just leave them all alone? Or had he come here to see the results of what he and Paul, between them if not together, had done to her family?

The man she had spent time with this last week didn't seem to be that cruel, and his actions towards Felicity and Richard Warner didn't imply deliberate cruelty either. But if it wasn't for that reason, why had he come here...?

"I'll take these flowers through to the kitchen and put them in a vase," she told her parents desperately. "And I'll ask Mrs Weaver for the tea at the same time." She had to escape for a few minutes, had to try and make some sense out of what was happening. And she needed to be away from her parents to be able to do that.

"Janie—"

"I won't be long, Daddy," she assured him quickly, his use of his childhood name for her making her want to sit down and cry. Instead she fled from the sitting-room, much to the dismay of her parents, but necessarily for her own well-being.

She drew a deep breath into her lungs once she was out in the hallway, desperately trying to come to terms with what her mother had just said.

Gabe had been here! To her family home. In the house where she had spent her childhood and teenage years.

Why? she inwardly cried again.

She could hear the concerned murmur of her parents' voices in the room behind her, knew that her reaction had disturbed them. Ordinarily she kept her feelings to herself, felt her parents already had enough to cope with. But hearing of Gabe's visit here had just been too much of a shock, so completely unexpected that this time it had been impossible to hide her emotions from her parents.

But she had to calm herself now, put the flowers in a vase, ask Mrs Weaver to serve tea, and take in to her parents the cake that she had made to celebrate their anniversary. She had to keep everything as normal as possible. After all, her parents had no idea she had met "Mr Vaughan" again too...

The housekeeper was, as usual, pleased to see Jane, having worked in the house since Jane was a child. The two of them chatted amiably together as Jane arranged the orchids and lilies in the vase, the very normality of it helping her to put things into perspective. Her family would have their tea and cake, and then they could return to the disturbing subject of Gabriel Vaughan; she felt she had to know what Gabe had found to talk to her parents about during his visit. More to the point, she needed to know what her parents had talked to him about!

Her parents seemed relieved at her relaxed mood

when she rejoined them, thrilled with the cake she had made them, all of them having a slice of it with the tea the housekeeper brought in a few minutes later.

But they were all just biding their time, Jane knew; she could feel her parents' tension as well as her own.

"You'll stay and have dinner with us, of course, darling?" her mother prompted expectantly a short time later.

Jane grimaced her regret. "I'm afraid I won't be able to," she said.

"Another dinner party, Janie?" her father guessed mildly, the regret in his eyes saying she should be attending the dinner party, not cooking it for other people.

"It's almost Christmas, Daddy," she reminded him, looking pointedly at the festive decorations they had already put up. "It's my busiest time."

He sighed heavily. "You'll never meet anyone stuck in other people's kitchens!"

She didn't want to meet anyone! Besides, she had met someone. She had met Gabriel Vaughan...

"Always the bridesmaid, never the bride, that's me," she dismissed teasingly. "But tell me," she added lightly, "besides bringing you the roses, what did Gabriel Vaughan come here for?"

Jane had taken a good look around the sitting-room when she'd returned from the kitchen, looking for any incriminating photographs. There were no recent ones of her in here, only ones of her when she was very young, and then at gymkhanas as she went up to collect one of the rosettes she'd often won. And in those she was a round-faced teenager, with long blonde hair, smiling widely into the camera, a brace on her teeth that she had worn until shortly before her sixteenth birthday.

No, there was nothing in this room to indicate that Jane Smith had once been Janette Smythe-Roberts. And not a single thing in the house, she knew, to say she had ever been Janette Granger, Paul Granger's wife. As Jane had done herself, her parents had destroyed anything that would remind them she had ever been married to Paul Granger, and that included disposing of any photographs of them together. Including their wedding photographs.

"I really couldn't say, dear," her mother answered vaguely. "He didn't really seem to want anything, did he, David?" She looked at her husband for support.

"No, he didn't." Jane's father seemed to answer a little too readily for Jane's comfort. "He just spent a rather pleasant hour here, chatting about this and that, and then he left again." He shrugged his shoulders.

From the little she had come to know about Gabe, he didn't have "pleasant hours" to waste chatting! "Daddy, the man sat back and watched as your company floundered and almost fell, and then he stepped in with an offer you couldn't refuse—literally!" she said exasperatedly. "How on earth could you have just sat there and taken tea with the man?"

"What happened in the past was business, Janette," her father answered firmly, showing some of his old spirit. "And you have to give the man some credit for keeping on most of the original staff and turning the company around."

She didn't have to give Gabriel Vaughan credit for anything! But then, her parents had no idea of the way the man had tried so relentlessly to hound her down three years ago. Oh, Gabe had asked her parents for her whereabouts too, and in the circumstances her parents had decided she had already been through enough heartache, and had refused to tell him where she was.

That was when the lies had begun, on Jane's part, her guilt taking on the form of protectiveness from any more emotional pain for her parents. They had already suffered enough.

And so her parents simply had no idea of how Gabe had gone to each of her friends in turn with the same question, how for three months she hadn't been able to contact anyone she knew for fear Gabriel Vaughan would get to hear about it and somehow manage to find her.

Her parents weren't even aware that Gabe was part of the reason she had chosen to open her business under the name Jane Smith. They'd believed her when she'd told them it was because she would prefer it that no one realised she had once been Janette Smythe-Roberts. They'd been through too many humiliations themselves concerning their change of financial circumstances not to believe her!

But now Gabe had been here, to their home, and there was just no way that Jane, having come to know him a little better this last week, believed he had simply come here for tea and a pleasant chat!

"You could have done all that yourself if he had backed you financially rather than taken over the company," she reasoned tautly. He had just done that for Richard Warner; he could have done the same for her father three years ago!

Her father shook his head, smiling sadly. "Gabriel Vaughan is not a charitable institution, Janette, he's a businessman. Besides, I was almost sixty then—far too old to dredge up the youthful enthusiasm needed to turn the company around."

Jane bit back her angry retort, knowing that in a way her father was right about Gabe; he hadn't been the one responsible for breaking her father's spirit. The person who had done that was dead, and beyond anyone's retribution.

Paul, her own husband, was responsible for what had happened to her father's company, for all that had happened three years ago.

And now she was back full circle to those feelings of guilt that always assailed her whenever she visited her parents.

"I still think it's very odd for Gabriel Vaughan to have come here," she muttered.

It was so odd, she decided later on the slow drive home, that she intended, at the first opportunity, to find out exactly what he had thought he was doing by going to see Daphne and David Smythe-Roberts!

"JANE!" Felicity greeted her warmly as she recognised her voice on the other end of the telephone line. "How marvellous! I was just about to call you."

"You were?" Jane prompted warily.

It had taken her twenty-four hours of thought, of trying to sit back from the problem, to try and work out how best to approach solving it. And her problem was Gabriel Vaughan. Wasn't it always?

But the problem this time wasn't how to avoid him, but how to meet him again without it appearing as if she had deliberately set out to do so. Not knowing where his rented apartment was, or where he had set up his office for his stay in England, she had been left with only one line of attack: Felicity and Richard Warner.

She had telephoned the other woman with the intention

of calling in to see her, and at the same time casually bringing the conversation round to Gabriel Vaughan.

"I was." Felicity laughed happily. "I'm feeling so much better now, and Richard and I did so much want to say thank you for all your help—"

"There's no need—"

"So you've already said," the other woman dismissed lightly. "We happen to disagree with you. I suggested we invite you out to dinner, but Richard said that was like taking coals to Newcastle! But being a woman I don't think that's the case at all; I know just how nice it is to let someone else do the cooking for a change!"

Felicity was right, of course. Because Jane cooked for a living, most people seemed to think she just threw meals together for herself like the ones she served to them. She didn't, of course, and one of the few luxuries she allowed herself was to occasionally order a take-out pizza!

"It's a lovely thought, Felicity." She answered the other woman politely. "But there really is no need. And I have no wish to play gooseberry—"

"Oh, but you won't be; we're going to invite Gabe to make up the foursome!" Felicity announced triumphantly.

Jane wanted to see Gabe, needed to see him—wasn't that the reason for her call in the first place?—but did she really want to sit down and have dinner with the man?

The answer to that was definitely no; the last time the two of them had had dinner together Gabe had kissed her until her legs felt weak! But the other side of the argument was that they wouldn't be alone this time, so there would be no occasion for him to take such liberties.

Another positive thing about accepting this invitation was that she wouldn't have organised meeting Gabe again; Felicity and Richard would be their hosts for the evening...

"Jane?" Felicity prompted uncertainly at her continued silence.

She quickly flicked through her business diary that always sat beside the telephone. With only a week to go to Christmas, she really was heavily booked. But she also appreciated she wasn't going to find a better opportunity for meeting Gabe on more neutral ground than this.

Not that she had any idea how she was possibly going to broach the subject of his visit to her parents— or, rather, the Smythe-Robertses—all she could hope was that an opportunity would present itself some time during the evening.

"I only have a cocktail party to cater for on Tuesday evening," she told Felicity thoughtfully. "I just may be able to make dinner for eight-thirty that evening, if that's any good for you and Richard...?" And, of course, Gabriel Vaughan. Because if he wasn't there, the whole evening would, as far as she was concerned, be a complete waste of time.

It wasn't that she didn't appreciate the Warners' invitation, or the reason behind it; it was just that ordinarily there were so many other things she could have done on Tuesday evening—like taking a rest for a few hours.

"Lovely." Felicity accepted instantly. "We'll book Antonio's. Shall we call for you? Or perhaps Gabe would—"

"I'll meet you all at the restaurant," Jane put in quickly, well acquainted with the popular Italian restaurant. "I can't leave until the people at the cocktail party have gone on to the theatre, so I can't guarantee it will be exactly eight-thirty when I get there."

She had no intention—no matter how Felicity might still think she was trying to matchmake!—of going to the dinner party as Gabe's partner for the evening, and she didn't want to give that impression by arriving at the restaurant with him.

"As long as you get there eventually," Felicity said lightly. "See you Tuesday." She rang off.

Jane replaced her own receiver much more slowly. She had her wish—she was going to see Gabriel Vaughan again...

She had never thought a time would come when she would willingly place herself in his company!

She only hoped she didn't live to regret it!

CHAPTER EIGHT

"JANE!" Antonio himself came out of his kitchen to greet her when she arrived at the restaurant shortly after eight-thirty on Tuesday evening.

She wasn't deliberately late: she'd been delayed clearing up from the cocktail party. And then she'd had to change before coming here. Luckily she had taken her black dress and shoes with her, and had been able to drive straight to the resturant once she had finished tidying up.

She and Antonio were old friends. Pasta hadn't been something she was too familiar with preparing two years ago, and so she had gone to the expert so that she might learn before opening up her own business. She had spent a month here at the restaurant working in the kitchen at Antonio's side, and despite what she had heard about temperamental Italian chefs—and Antonio was definitely an example of that!—her month here had been highly enjoyable, and by the end of that time she and Antonio were firm friends.

They kissed each other on both cheeks in greeting, Jane grinning up at the handsome Italian. "I'm meeting Mr and Mrs Warner," she explained.

Dark brows rose over teasing brown eyes. "And Mr Gabriel Vaughan," he added pointedly.

Gabe was here! She hadn't spoken to either Felicity or Richard since the telephone call on Sunday, so she'd had no idea whether or not Gabe had accepted their invitation. Antonio's speculative teasing assured her that not only had he accepted, but he was obviously already here!

"And Mr Gabriel Vaughan." She dryly echoed Antonio's words. "Stop grinning like that, Antonio; this is business." Which wasn't strictly true, but it certainly wasn't pleasure either, not in the way Antonio thought it was!

"Always business with you, Jane." He held up his hands exasperatedly. "Although you never came to work in my kitchen dressed like that!" He looked at her admiringly, the black fitted dress showing the slender perfection of her figure, its short length revealing long, shapely legs. She had brushed her hair loosely about her shoulders, having applied some light make-up, and a peach gloss to her lips.

No, she had to admit, she had never come to work in Antonio's kitchen dressed like this...!

And she had delayed going to the table long enough! "Point me in the right direction, Antonio," she requested.

"I will do better than that." He took a firm hold of her elbow. "Tonight you are the customer, Jane; I will personally show you to your table."

Having the extremely tall, incredibly handsome proprietor of the restaurant guide her through the dining-room to her table wasn't conducive to the low-profile life she liked to lead, with all eyes turning in their direction. And Jane couldn't even bring herself to look at the three people already seated at the table he took her to, aware that the two men stood up when Antonio pulled back her chair with a flourish for her to sit down.

Antonio paused to pick up one of her hands, bending to kiss the back of it lightly. "It's wonderful to see you again, Jane," he told her huskily, devilment gleaming in those dark brown eyes before he turned and walked arrogantly back to his kitchen.

Devil just about described him, Jane decided with affectionate irritation, her cheeks burning with embarrassment. Antonio had deliberately—

"Mutual admiration society?" rasped an all-too-familiar voice.

Jane turned calmly to meet the hard mockery in those aqua-blue eyes, hopefully revealing none of the nervousness she felt at meeting this man again. Nervous, because the last time they had met he had kissed her. And, worse than that, this man had visited her family home, had talked with her parents, and she still had no idea why, or what he had learnt by going there.

"As it happens, Gabe, yes," she answered him lightly. "I admire Antonio as a chef immensely. And I believe he respects my ability too," she added challengingly.

Heavens, Gabe looked so handsome in his black evening suit and snowy white shirt, the dark thickness of his hair lightly brushing the shirt collar. Jane's breath caught in her throat as she returned the steadiness of his gaze.

She had to thrust her trembling hands beneath the table, on the pretext of placing her napkin across her knees, but in reality so that he shouldn't see that shaking of her hands, and speculate as to the reason for it.

Meeting Gabe again, she decided, under any circumstances, was a mistake!

"Good evening, Felicity, Richard." She turned warmly to the other couple. "And once again thank you for inviting me."

"Our pleasure," Richard assured her warmly, much more relaxed than when Jane had last seen him.

"I had no idea you knew Antonio?" Felicity teased interestedly.

Jane ruefully returned the other woman's smile. But even as she did so she could feel that aqua-blue gaze still on her. Had no one ever told Gabe it was rude to stare? Probably, she acknowledged ruefully, but, as she knew only too well, Gabe was a law unto himself, and would do exactly as he pleased. And at the moment, despite how uncomfortable it might make her feel, it pleased him to stare at her!

"I worked here for a while," she explained to Felicity; what was the point in doing anything other than telling the truth? She worked for a living, and, no matter how much her parents might hate the fact that she had to do so, it was an irreversible fact! "It was where I learnt to avoid the flying kitchen utensils," she recalled ruefully; Antonio's patience was non-existent when it came to his cooking staff!

"Temperamental, is he?" Gabe drawled dismissively.

Once again she calmly returned his gaze. "Most men are, I've found," she told him softly.

"You meant in the kitchen, of course," Gabe returned challengingly.

She gave a slight inclination of her head. "Of course," she agreed dryly.

Gabe chuckled, shaking his head. "You meant no such thing," he acknowledged, visibly relaxing as he sat forward, elbows resting on the table-top. "It's good to see you again, Jane Smith," he told her huskily.

She wasn't quite sure how she felt about seeing him again! Her pulse rate had definitely quickened at how handsome he looked in his evening suit, so powerfully male. And yet deep inside her was still that fear of what he might, or might not, have learnt on his visit to her parents' home. And at the moment she wasn't sure which emotion was the dominant one!

"How are the flowers?" he prompted softly at her continued silence. "Or did you give them away to the first person you saw after I left the other evening?" he added self-derisively.

Jane gave Felicity and Richard a self-conscious glance, but they both gave every impression of being engrossed in their menus. Although Jane was sure that Felicity, for one, romantic that she was, was listening avidly to their exchange.

As for the flowers, Jane hadn't been sure initially whether he meant the flowers he had given her or the roses he had given to her parents! Thankfully, his second question had clarified that for her.

"That would have been the height of bad manners, Gabe," she returned coolly. "Especially considering all the trouble you went to to give them to me," she added pointedly.

"Oh, it was no trouble at all, Jane," Gabe returned huskily, eyes glowing with laughter—at her expense. "And you did give me dinner afterwards."

Devil!

She had thought she was meeting him challenge for

challenge, but from the grin Felicity shot her way she knew Gabe had definitely won this particular round. "As I recall," she said derisively, "you had to help cook it!"

"It's such fun cooking together, isn't it?" The effervescent Felicity simply couldn't stay out of the conversation any longer. "We used to do it all the time, didn't we, Richard?" She turned warmly to her handsome husband.

Richard looked up from his menu. "We still do, if your condition is anything to go by!" he drawled teasingly.

Felicity blushed prettily. "I was actually talking about cooking together, darling," she rebuked laughingly.

Jane couldn't help but admire the obvious happiness of this married couple. Felicity was the same age as her, and yet the other woman had a marvellous husband who obviously adored her, two lovely daughters, and a third child on the way.

Jane had longed for those things too once; for a while she'd even thought that she actually had them. Her expression was wistful now as she realised how fleeting that dream had been.

Then she realised Gabe was watching her, dark brows raised questioningly as he saw the different emotions flitting across her face!

She deliberately schooled her features into their usual inscrutable expression. "Time to order, I think," she murmured pointedly, smiling up at Vincenzo as he gave her a friendly wink of recognition.

But her own smile wavered and faded as she turned back and found Gabe was still watching her, the harsh expression on his face saying he didn't appreciate her friendly exchange with the waiter one little bit.

Well, what had he expected? She was twenty-eight

years old, and just because she was disillusioned with the opposite sex that did not mean that men didn't still flirt with her! Besides, hadn't Gabe himself been doing that since the moment the two of them were introduced?

His scowling expression seemed to say it was okay for him to do it, but not any other man!

Which wasn't very realistic on his part; most men liked to flirt, but that didn't mean they wanted it to go any further than that. And Vincenzo was a prime example of that. Jane knew for a fact that he adored his wife. Besides which, Anna would probably beat her husband to a pulp if he went any further than flirting with another woman!

Gabe's scowl lightened slightly as he saw that Vincenzo spoke to Felicity with the same warmth he had to Jane seconds earlier, Gabe's expression becoming rueful as he turned and saw Jane's mocking one. He shrugged, as if to say, Okay, my mistake.

It wasn't the only mistake he had made, Jane decided irritably. He had no right to feel jealous of the other man in the first place! One bunch of flowers and a home-cooked meal did not give him any rights where she was concerned!

But as the evening progressed, with Felicity and Richard's presence ensuring that it went smoothly, it became more and more obvious to Jane that she still had no idea how to introduce the subject of his visit to her parents. It was impossible to introduce such a delicate subject casually into the conversation. Even Felicity's questions to Gabe on how his work in England was going only elicited a dismissive reply that he was keeping himself busy.

By the end of the evening Jane felt thoroughly

frustrated at not being able to find out what she really wanted to know: why Gabe had visited her parents on Friday!

"Did you drive here, Gabe?" Richard asked as they prepared to leave the restaurant. "Or can Felicity and I offer you a lift home?"

"I was hoping Jane might offer to drive me." Gabe answered the younger man, but his aqua-blue gaze was fixed compellingly on Jane at she looked up at him sharply. "I noticed you only drank half a glass of wine with your meal," he drawled. "So I guessed you must have driven here yourself." He added, "I came by cab."

With satisfaction, it seemed to Jane. And he noticed too damn much!

But if she did drive him home maybe then she would find the opportunity—? Who was she kidding? There was no way that she could think of to casually introduce the subject of his visit to the Smythe-Robertses' home!

"I'll drive you home," she offered flatly. After all, with the other couple present, what choice did she have? "Thank you both for dinner." She turned to Felicity and Richard. "I've enjoyed it."

And she had. The food had been superb, as usual, and with the other couple present the conversation had flowed smoothly too. Even Gabe's annoying presence hadn't jarred too much as, after his initial terseness, he seemed set to be charming for the rest of the evening. And so Jane's only irritation with the evening was that question regarding her parents. And the way things stood she might just have to let that go. If it wasn't repeated, then perhaps it wasn't a problem…?

"Jane!" Antonio left his kitchen for the second time that evening as he came out to hug her goodnight, smiling down at her as he still held her in his arms. "I have two wonderful new recipes that you would love," he told her huskily. "Come in and see me when you have the time, hmm?"

She answered Antonio positively, explaining that it would have to wait until after the New Year now, as she was so busy, all the time aware that Gabe was listening to their conversation with a sceptical glitter in his eyes and a mocking twist to those firm lips.

"Sorry about that," she apologised dismissively as they walked out to her van, having parted from the other couple, Gabe's hand light on her elbow. "Antonio and I are old friends."

"So you explained earlier." He nodded tersely as she unlocked the doors. "'Come and try my recipes' is certainly a twist on 'etchings'!"

Jane turned to give him a cold look once they were seated inside her van. "Antonio is a married man!" she told him disgustedly.

"And you have no interest in other women's husbands," Gabe remembered dryly.

"None whatsoever," she acknowledged stiffly as she turned on the ignition, warming the engine, as well as themselves. The weather outside was still icy cold, although the snow of last week had now disappeared. "I would never cause another woman that sort of pain!"

Gabe sat back, perfectly relaxed. "Then it's as well I'm not still married, isn't it?" he said with satisfaction.

Jane made no reply, not quite sure what he meant by that remark—and not sure she wanted to be, either! This man had so many other minuses against her ever becoming involved with him that his being married would have come last on her list of dislikes where he was concerned!

"Perhaps you would care to tell me where I'm to drive you?" she prompted distantly.

"Mayfair."

Where else? Only the best for this man. After all, he didn't like hotels, did he? Too impersonal—

"I telephoned you over the weekend."

Jane glanced sharply across at Gabe before instantly returning her attention to the road. She had received no call from him, no more cryptic messages left on her machine from him, either. But then, as she very well knew, he hated those "damned things"!

She shrugged. "I did tell you I was very busy in this time leading up to Christmas."

"It was Saturday afternoon," he told her evenly. "I decided that if I waited for you to contact me I would be dead in my coffin and you might—only might, you understand!—turn up for my funeral!" he bit out disgustedly.

A long shot, concerning his funeral, she had to agree!

And Saturday afternoon she had been visiting her parents...

"I was out of town," she told him lightly, her heart once again thudding in her chest. But it was probably the only chance she was ever going to have... "A thirtieth wedding anniversary," she told him truthfully. "In Berkshire. A couple called Smythe-Roberts." The last was added breathlessly.

Ordinarily she would never have dreamt of talking of her clients to a third party, but as her parents weren't actually clients… This was too good an opportunity to be missed!

"I've met them," he nodded dismissively. "Working on a Saturday afternoon, too." He shook his head. "You do keep busy," he teased. "Turn left here," he advised softly. "It's the apartment block on the right."

Was that it—"I've met them"? She had finally got around to the subject she was really interested in, and he'd dismissed it with just three words!

And it wasn't true that he had only "met them". He had visited them only the day before she had, had taken them roses; wasn't the coincidence of that worth mentioning?

Jane was so agitated by his casual dismissal that she only narrowly avoided hitting a Jaguar coming the other way as she drove the van over to the other side of the road and parked outside the building Gabe had indicated.

Well, she wasn't going to give up now, not when they had come so close. "What a coincidence," she said lightly.

Gabe's expression was completely blank in the light given off by the street lamp outside. "My renting an apartment in Mayfair?" He frowned. "Do you know someone else who lives here?"

Hardly! Maybe once upon a time her friends might have moved in these sorts of circles, as she had herself, but, as with her parents' friends, most of her own had drifted away too with her own change of circumstances.

Besides, was this man being deliberately obtuse? Probably not, she conceded grudgingly as she saw he still looked baffled by her remark.

"I meant that you know the Smythe-Robertses' too," she explained patiently.

"I think 'know' them is probably putting it too strongly," Gabe dismissed uninterestedly. "I knew their daughter much better!"

Jane stared at him, her whole body stiffening in reaction. They hadn't even met three years ago, so how on earth could he claim to have known her?

"Daughter?" She forced herself to sound only casually interested—although it was definitely a strain on her nerves. "I didn't see their daughter when I was there on Saturday." Well, she hadn't looked in any of the mirrors there, had she?

She was a person who hated lies—being told them and telling them herself—but she was aware she was stretching the truth now, no matter what she might tell herself to the contrary!

"That doesn't surprise me," Gabe said disgustedly, glancing up at his apartment building. "Would you like to come in for a nightcap?"

Would she? Not really. And yet if she wanted to continue this conversation with him...

"Just a coffee would be nice," she accepted. She got out, and locked the van behind them before following Gabe into the building, the man in the lobby ensuring there could be no incidents like the one where Gabe had tricked Evie into letting him go up to her own apartment.

She didn't really want the coffee, found that it kept her awake if she drank it last thing at night. But she wanted to know why Gabe wasn't surprised that Janette Smythe-Roberts hadn't been present at her own parents' thirtieth wedding anniversary...

"Decaffeinated?" Gabe questioned as they entered the plush apartment, switching on the soft glow of lights as he made his way over to the kitchen.

"Thanks," Jane accepted vaguely, following slowly.

The apartment was gorgeous, with antique furnishings, the brocade paper on the walls looking genuine too. Only the best, Jane thought again.

"Do I take it that you had an involvement with the Smythe-Robertses' daughter?" she prompted teasingly as she joined Gabe in the ultra-modern kitchen.

She knew damn well he hadn't been involved with Janette Smythe-Roberts, but she needed to keep on this subject if she were to get anywhere at all.

"Hardly." Gabe barely glanced at her as he moved economically about the kitchen, preparing the coffee. "Spoilt little rich girls have never appealed to me, either!"

Spoilt little—! Jane glared across the room at the powerful width of his back. She might have been over-indulged by her loving parents when she was younger, but marriage to Paul had obliterated any of that. And there was no money now for her to be "spoilt" with!

And this man, after his visit to her parents' home last week, must be aware of that…

"The Smythe-Robertses didn't appear overly wealthy to me." She spoke lightly as Gabe joined her at the break-fast-bar with the coffee.

"Nor me," he acknowledged tightly. "But there was plenty of money there three years ago—and I should know, because I bought David Smythe-Roberts's company from him!—so I can only assume the daughter has it all!"

Jane stared at him. Was that really what he thought?

That she would have gone off with the money and left her parents living in what was, in comparison to how they had once lived, near poverty?

Didn't this man know of the debts there had been to pay three years ago, of Paul Granger's gambling, of the way he had siphoned money out of the company to supplement his habit?

But even that hadn't been enough for Paul in the end, and he had begun to sign IOUs he hadn't a hope of paying. IOUs that on his death had passed on to his widow. IOUs that, because of Janette's own ill health at the time, her father had paid out of the money he had received for his much depleted company, her parents having decided she had already suffered enough at Paul Granger's hands.

By the time Jane had felt well enough to deal with any of it, it was already too late; her father had already sorted it all out.

Only Gabriel Vaughan's need for vengeance had survived that sorry mess, and the only person left alive to answer that need had been Janette Granger, Paul Granger's widow. So Janette had been the one to come under his vengeful gaze.

Because, at the time of her death, Gabe's wife, Jennifer, had been leaving him. And the man she had been leaving him for had been Paul Granger, Jane/Janette's own husband...!

CHAPTER NINE

JANE licked suddenly dry lips, frowning darkly. "You mean that the daughter—"

"Janette Smythe-Roberts, or rather Janette Granger—her married name," Gabe supplied scornfully.

"Are you saying her parents gave her all their money and left themselves—left themselves—?" How to describe her parents' present financial position? Genteel poverty probably best described it. But "spoilt little rich girl" did not best describe her!

"Almost penniless, from what I saw last week," Gabe said much more bluntly. "According to the parents their daughter now lives abroad." The disgust was back in his voice. "Admittedly, she was beautiful—the most beautiful woman I've ever seen—present company excepted, of course—"

"Please, Gabe," Jane protested weakly in rebuke, still totally stunned by his summing-up of Janette Smythe-Roberts. As for living "abroad", there was more than one meaning to that word, and she lived in freedom now, not in another country, as Gabe believed!

And beauty was no good, no good at all, if the person who possessed that beauty was as unhappy as she had been married to Paul. Gabe didn't know, couldn't even begin to guess at the hell her marriage had been. Or the pain that had quickly followed his death...

Gabe grinned now in acknowledgement of her rebuke. "Okay, I'll cut the compliments. But Janette Smythe-Roberts had the perfect face, the perfect body, the most glorious golden hair I've ever set eyes on," he told her grimly. "And all that perfection only acted as a shield to the selfishness within. Do you have any idea what she did three years ago, after her husband died, and her father's company was in trouble? No, of course you don't." He shook his head as he scathingly answered his own question. "There was simply no sign of the grieving widow, the supportive daughter, because Janette disappeared. Just disappeared!" he repeated disbelievingly.

Jane stared at him, taken aback by the interpretation he had obviously put on that disappearance.

But there had been a very good reason why she hadn't been on show, why she couldn't face the barrage of publicity that accompanied the death of her husband in the company of Gabe's wife; why her parents had shielded her from the worst of their financial ruin.

For, like Felicity Warner now, with her husband Richard in difficulties with his own company, Janette had been pregnant three years ago. And upon learning of Paul's duplicity, of how he had taken money from her father's company to back up his gambling, of his intention of walking out on her, and leaving her father's business in ruins and herself pregnant with their child, she had lost the baby that she had so wanted, her own life also hanging in the balance.

Was that the selfishness of Janette Smythe-Roberts that Gabe referred to...?

Because she hadn't "disappeared" at all. She'd been in a private nursing home, under the protection of her parents and doctor, until the danger had passed and she had been well enough to go home—not to the home she had shared with Paul, or even her parents' home, but a rented cottage in Devon, far away from prying eyes.

Gabe had simply chosen to put his own interpretation on how he perceived her disappearance... But he was wrong, so very wrong.

Jane looked at him now. "Is it still possible to disappear in this day and age?" she derided lightly.

"Thousands do it every year, so I'm told." Gabe shrugged dismissively. "And Janette Smythe-Roberts did it so well, no one seems to have seen her since!"

She shook her head. "I find that hard to believe."

He shrugged again. "Nevertheless, that appears to be the case."

"Appears to be" was certainly correct! "Has anyone ever tried to find her?" Jane asked.

Gabe grimaced. "I had some sort of mistaken idea of helping her myself three years ago—"

"You did?" Her surprise wasn't in the least feigned. Help? Gabe hadn't come bearing gifts three years ago, but something else completely! "I thought you said you weren't involved with her?" She tried to sound teasing, but somehow it came out accusingly...

"I wasn't." Gabe grimaced again, his gaze warm now as he reached out and lightly touched her hand. "Do I detect a note of jealousy in your voice, Jane?"

How could she possibly be jealous of herself?

She snatched her hand away as if he had burnt her. "Don't be ridiculous," she snapped, standing up. "I think it's time I was going—"

"I was only teasing you, Jane." Gabe laughed softly as he too stood up. "For some reason that's beyond me, we seem to have spent the latter part of this evening discussing a woman you don't even know—and who I haven't set eyes on for three years!" He frowned. "And we were doing so well until then, too!" he added cajolingly.

That was his interpretation of the evening; until these last few minutes she hadn't even been able to approach the subject that really interested her!

But in a way he was right; talking of Janette Smythe-Roberts and her parents had certainly caused friction in what had, until then, been a lightly enjoyable evening. Surprisingly so, Jane realised. But then, Felicity and Richard had been understandably relaxed after the end of their recent worries, and Gabe had been charming to all of them.

But as she looked up at Gabe now and saw the teasing light in his gaze turn to something much more dangerous she knew it was definitely time she left...

She knew, as Gabe's head lowered and his mouth claimed hers, that she had left it far too late to reach that conclusion...

She wrenched her mouth away from his. "No, Gabe—"

"Yes, Jane!" he groaned, cradling either side of her face with his hands as he kissed her gently—first her eyes, then her nose, then her cheeks, and finally her mouth again.

It was that gentleness that was her undoing. If he had been demanding, or even passionate, she would have resisted, but he just kissed her again and again with those gently caressing lips.

"That wasn't so bad, was it?" he finally murmured, resting his forehead against hers.

"No..." she confirmed huskily. "Not bad." In fact, it

had felt too good. And yet she wished he would kiss her again!

He smiled at her, aqua-blue eyes so close to her own as he gazed into those sherry-brown depths. "How long did you think you could go on hiding, Jane?" he murmured affectionately.

Every alarm bell she possessed went off inside her at the same time, her eyes widening, her breath catching in her throat, every muscle and sinew in her body seeming to stiffen into immobility. "I wasn't hiding from you," she snapped angrily, moving sharply away from him.

Gabe gave her a deeply considering look. "I didn't say you were hiding from me," he pointed out softly.

Jane swallowed hard, thinking back to what he had said. No, he hadn't said that exactly, but— "Or from anyone else, either!" she bit out tautly, glaring at him accusingly.

He shook his head in gentle rebuke. "You've misunderstood me totally."

Had she? Minutes ago he had been telling her about Janette Smythe-Roberts, about the fact that she had disappeared three years ago without apparent trace, and now he was asking her how long she'd expected to go on hiding! What conclusion was she supposed to draw from that?

With her own knowledge that she was Janette Smythe-Roberts—his supposed "perfect" woman he had once seen—there could only be one conclusion to draw. But as Gabe had given no indication, either now or in the past, that he realised she was Janette, perhaps she had jumped to the wrong conclusion...?

She swallowed hard, looking at him with narrowed

eyes. "Kindly explain what you did mean," she invited stiffly.

He shrugged, a smile playing about those sensuous lips. "I was referring to your role in the kitchen—always keeping in the background."

"Always the bridesmaid, never the bride." She came back with the same comment she had made to her father at the weekend, warning bells still ringing inside her, but a little more quietly now.

"Exactly," Gabe nodded, grinning openly now. "While you hide away in other women's kitchens, you're never likely to have one of your own."

His reply was much like her father's had been too!

"But I already have a kitchen of my own," she reminded him mockingly. "You've seen it for yourself."

"You're being deliberately obtuse now," he drawled impatiently. "I meant—"

"I know what you meant, Gabe," she cut in with dismissive derision. "And your remarks are presupposing that I want a kitchen of my own." She shuddered at the thought of it, her experience of marriage definitely not a happy one. "I'm happy the way I am, Gabe," she assured him lightly, picking up her evening bag. "Thank you for the coffee," she added with finality.

"And goodbye. Again," he added wryly.

Jane glanced back at him, not unmoved by how ruggedly handsome he was, or that teasing light in his eyes as he looked across at her with raised brows. But he was dangerous—very much so.

"Exactly." She ruefully acknowledged his last remark. "That word doesn't seem to have worked too well on you so far!"

"Are you sure you really want it to?" he prompted softly.

"Of course I want it to!" she replied sharply. "You—"

"Jane, I have a confession to make..." he cut in reluctantly.

She looked at him warily; he already seemed to have said so much tonight! "Such as?" she challenged brittlely.

He sighed. "Well, I'm not sure just how close you and Felicity are—"

"I've already told you, I'm not especially close to either of the Warners! I just don't like to see injustice." She looked at him pointedly.

He gave a mocking inclination of his head. "Your views were duly noted on that subject," he drawled self-derisively. "But I think you should know—just in case Felicity feels duty-bound to mention it at some stage—that I—well, I sort of mentioned to Richard at the weekend that it might be nice if the four of us had dinner together some time!" he admitted, with a pained wince for what her reaction to that was going to be.

Ordinarily she would have been furious at the machinations behind this evening's dinner invitation, but in the circumstances it was difficult to stop herself smiling. There she had been, racking her brain trying to think of some way of seeing him again, albeit so that she could question him about his visit to her parents, and all the time he had been nefariously arranging such a meeting himself!

But Gabe wasn't to know that!

"You really are a man that likes his own way, aren't you?" she said disgustedly. "So okay, Gabe, we've all had dinner—but I still have to go now," she added firmly.

"Could we say goodnight rather than goodbye?" he prompted huskily. "Goodbye is so final, and goodnight leaves a little hope—for me—that we'll meet again."

Jane couldn't help herself; she did laugh this time, shaking her head ruefully. This man really was impossible.

"Goodnight, Gabe," she told him dryly.

"There, that wasn't so difficult, was it?" he said with light satisfaction as he walked with her to the door, his arm resting lightly about her shoulders. "Drive home carefully," he told her softly.

And, unlike Jane when he had visited her at her apartment last week, Gabe watched her as she walked over to the lift and stepped inside, pressing the button for the ground floor, Gabe still standing in the doorway to his apartment as the lift doors closed.

Gabe had had no need to tell her to drive carefully; she never drove any other way. She was all too aware of how fragile metal and glass could be, the glass smashing, the metal twisting out of all recognition. As fragile as the people inside the vehicle...

She hadn't been the one to go and identify Paul after the accident three years ago; that onerous task had fallen to her father. Jane had been admitted to a private nursing home almost as soon as she'd learnt of the accident, delirious with pain as she lost the baby she had only carried for nine weeks.

It was a time in her life she tried very hard not to think about—Paul's death, his betrayal nothing in comparison with the loss of her baby.

The pregnancy couldn't have happened at a worse time in their marriage: Paul was rarely at home any more, and Jane was no longer bothered by his long absences; in fact she felt relieved by them.

But when she'd found out about the pregnancy she had known that she wanted her baby, wanted it very much, and had thought that perhaps there was something to be salvaged from their marriage after all. But Paul had easily disabuscd her of that fairy tale, laughingly informing her that he was leaving her to be with Jennifer Vaughan.

Which was what he had been doing at the time of the accident...

The scandal that had followed the two of them being killed together in Paul's BMW had been too much for Jane on top of what she had already suffered. The newspapers had been full of it, her own photograph, as Paul's wife, and that of Gabriel Vaughan, as Jennifer's husband, appearing side by side together in a stream of speculation that had gone on for days on end.

Jane had been too emotionally broken to deal with any of it, and it had been weeks before she was even aware enough to realise that Gabriel Vaughan was looking for her. And as far as she was concerned there had been only one conclusion to draw from his search: somehow he blamed her for the fact that her husband had been involved in an affair with his wife!

That was when she had decided Janette Granger had to disappear, not just for the months she had already been secluded away because of her ill health, but for always if she were ever to make a life for herself.

And so she had disappeared.

But her fear of Gabriel Vaughan had not! Oh, not the Gabe who teased and kissed her; that Gabe was all too easy to like. But the Gabe who had been to visit

Daphne and David Smythe-Roberts last week, the Gabe who could still talk so contemptuously of his believed selfishness of Janette Granger; he was definitely a man still to be feared!

And, while Janette Granger might have been able to disappear without apparent trace, Jane Smith knew better than not to heed that fear...

"GOOD MORNING, Jane. Lovely morning for a run, isn't it," Gabe said conversationally as he fell into stride beside her.

Jane faltered only slightly at the unexpected appearance of her running companion, continuing her measured pace.

And Gabe was right about the morning being lovely; it was one of those crisp, clear days so often to be found in England in mid-December, and with the snow now melted it was perfect for her early morning run. Although its perfection had now been marred somewhat by the advent of Gabe at her side! Gabe was the last person she had expected to see running in *her* park at seven o'clock in the morning...!

They ran on in silence, Jane determined not to have her routine disrupted. She enjoyed these early morning runs, putting her brain in neutral, just concentrating on the physical exercise, unhindered by cares or worries.

And this morning was no different as she continued her run round the park. Gabe, at her side, seemed to have no trouble at all keeping pace with her, for all that he must spend most of his time sitting behind a desk.

"I run too when I'm at home." He seemed to read her thoughts. "And when I'm not at home I usually find a gym where I can work out."

She should have known, by the width of his shoulders and the hard muscles of his stomach and legs. "I'm honoured," she shot back dryly, looking to neither right nor left as she continued her run.

She didn't believe for a moment that his presence here, at this time, was a coincidence. She had told him last week that she ran in the park near her apartment, and now that he knew the location of that apartment it couldn't have been too difficult for him to work out where it was that she ran. It was the fact that he was here, obviously waiting for her, at seven o'clock in the morning, that had surprised her. And still did.

Gabe glanced sideways noting her concentrated expression. "I've had some very strange looks while I've been waiting for you!" Again he seemed able to read her thoughts.

Jane could well imagine he had! The only people here at this time of the morning were the homeless who had managed to find—and keep—one of the benches on which to spend the night, and other dedicated runners like herself, exercising before they prepared to go to work. Gabe, in his expensive, obviously new trainers, designer-logo shorts and sweatshirt top, did not fit into either of those categories.

"I'm not surprised," she drawled, continuing her pounding on the tarmacked pathway.

It was beautiful here at this time of the morning. The birds were singing in the treetops, the sounds of the early morning traffic muted. Ordinarily Jane enjoyed this time of day, but with Gabe for a companion her enjoyment was as muted as the traffic noise!

She stopped once she reached the gate through which she had made her entrance earlier, having worked up a healthy sheen of perspiration, her breasts heaving slightly beneath her white vest-top. Gabe's breathing was much heavier, his chest moving as he took in long gulps of air. Not so untroubled by the exercise as she had assumed!

He looked up at her with a rueful frown. "Okay, so I haven't managed to find a gym since I arrived two weeks ago; I've been too busy chasing after the most elusive woman I've ever known!" he said irritably as there was no change in her mockingly knowing expression.

Jane stiffened. "Janette Granger?" she said warily.

"You!" he corrected impatiently. "Give me a break, Jane. Haven't I proved to you yet that I'm not as ruthless as you initially thought I was?"

Her eyes narrowed, still slightly shaken by his earlier remark. "Is that what it was all about? Your change of heart where Richard Warner's company was concerned," she explained scathingly. "Was it done to impress me?"

Gabe became suddenly still, aqua-blue eyes narrowed angrily. "You know something, you really are the most—" He broke off abruptly, his mouth a thin, straight line. "Do you mean to be insulting, Jane, or does it just come naturally to you?" he grated harshly.

She had been thrown by what she had thought was a reference to her past self, and in retrospect she had just been incredibly insulting. After all, it had been three years; she had changed, so why shouldn't he…?

"I'm sorry," she told him tersely, not quite meeting his own suddenly mocking gaze.

Gabe relaxed slowly, a rueful smile finally curving his lips. "So what happens now?" He lightly changed the subject. "Do you go home and take a shower? Or do you have some other form of physical torture—exercise," he amended dryly, "in mind first?"

Jane smiled—as she knew she was supposed to do—at his deliberate slip. "Coffee, croissants, and the newspapers," she reassured him teasingly.

"Now you're talking!" He lightly grasped her elbow as they turned towards the road. "I could do with a coffee and a sit down."

"Oh, we aren't going to sit down yet," Jane turned to tell him smilingly. "I pick up the croissants and news-papers, and then I run home for the coffee. Usually," she added mockingly as she saw his instantly disap-pointed expression. "As you've obviously had enough running for one day, I'll make an exception today," she conceded, leading the way to the little patisserie down one of the side streets away from the park where she usu-ally stopped to buy her croissants on the way home.

As usual the door to the patisserie was already open and the smell of percolating coffee was wafting tempt-ingly out into the street. Several people were already seated at tables as they entered, sipping their coffee, and indulging themselves with the best croissants Jane had ever tasted—her own included.

It wasn't much of a place to look at from the outside, and Jane could see Gabe's eyes widen questioningly as she led the way through the serviceable tables and chairs to the counter beyond.

"Trust me," she told him softly.

"Without question," he conceded as softly.

The man behind the counter glanced up from his newspapers as he heard their approach, his handsome face lighting up with pleasure as he saw Jane was his customer. "Jane, *chérie*," he greeted in heavily accented

English, moving around the counter to kiss her on both cheeks. "Your usual?" he prompted huskily.

"Usual?" Gabe murmured beside her with dry derision.

She gave him a scathing glance. "I've brought a friend with me this morning, François." She spoke warmly to the other man as he looked speculatively at Gabe. "Two 'usuals', to eat in this morning, and two cups of your delicious coffee," she requested before leading Gabe firmly away to sit at a table by the window.

"First an Italian and now a Frenchman," Gabe muttered, with a resentful glance towards the handsome François.

Jane looked across the table at him with laughing, sherry-coloured eyes. "Multinational Jane, that's what they call me!" she returned laughingly. "Although I'm having more than a little trouble with a certain American I know!"

Gabe returned her gaze with too innocent aqua-blue eyes. "Me?"

She laughed softly at his disbelieving expression. "The part of the injured innocent doesn't suit you in the least, Gabe!"

"I—" He broke off as François arrived at their table, expertly carrying the two cups of coffee, two plates containing croissants, and the butter and honey to accompany them. "That looks wonderful, François." Gabe spoke lightly to the other man. "I'm Gabe Vaughan, by the way." He held out his hand.

François returned the gesture once he had divested himself of the plates and cups. "Any friend of Jane's is a friend of mine," he returned a little more coolly.

A coolness that Gabe had obviously picked up on as

he gazed speculatively across the table at Jane once the other man had returned to the counter to continue reading his newspaper. "Exactly how well do—"

"He's a married man, too, Gabe," she put in curtly. "Now eat your croissants!" she advised him exasperatedly, already spreading honey on one of her own.

"Yes, ma'am!" he returned tauntingly, turning his attention to the plate of food in front of him.

"At last," Jane breathed softly seconds later. "I've found a way to shut you up!" she explained as she watched the expression of first wonder, and then bliss, as it spread across his face after the first mouthful of croissant. As she knew from experience, the pastry would simply melt in his mouth, in an ecstasy of delicacy and taste.

"This guy could make a fortune in the States!" Gabe gasped wonderingly when he could speak again.

"This 'guy' is doing very nicely exactly where he is, thank you very much," Jane told him warningly. "Tempt him away from here at your peril!" She simply couldn't envisage a morning now without François's croissants to start her on her way!

Gabe took another bite of the croissant, as if he couldn't quite believe the first one could have been quite that delicious. "I'd marry him myself if he weren't already married," he murmured seconds later. "How are you on croissants, Jane?" he added, brows arched hopefully.

"Not as good as François," she answered abruptly. She didn't find any talk of marriage, even jokingly, in the least bit funny!

"Pity," Gabe shrugged, spreading more honey on what

was left of his first croissant. "I guess I'll just have to stick to François!"

He most certainly would!

Not that she didn't realise he had meant the remark to be a teasing one; it just wasn't a subject she could joke about. And certainly not with Gabriel Vaughan.

Of all people, never with him…!

CHAPTER TEN

"TELL me," Jane prompted derisively as they lingered over their second cup of coffee, "what would you have done if I hadn't turned up for a run in the park this morning?" She looked mockingly across at Gabe.

He shrugged. "I have faith in your determination, Jane, no matter what I may have said to the contrary the other evening!"

She put her cup down slowly, her expression wary. "My determination...?"

"You don't look in the least like a fair-weather runner to me." He looked admiringly at her slender figure.

And Jane didn't in the least care for that look.

"After that wonderful meal we had last night, I thought I ought to join you this morning," he added ruefully. "I just wasn't sure of your starting time, although I didn't think it would be too late, not with your work schedule," he added teasingly.

"You're certainly a persistent man," she said distractedly.

Gabe looked unperturbed. "Something I inherited from my father—"

"The politician," Jane recalled dryly.

"Retired," Gabe acknowledged ruefully, although he looked pleased that she had remembered.

"So he claims." Jane remembered that conversation

only too well. In fact, she remembered all of her conversations with Gabe. "I usually take a break from running at the weekends," she explained, still distracted by his persistence. "It tends to be my busiest time anyway. Although, as it happens, I do usually run later in the morning than this; today I'm up and about early because I'm catering for a lunch."

"To my good." He huskily acknowledged the breakfast they had just shared together. "It would have been even more pleasurable if we hadn't parted at all last night—but I realise I can't have everything!" He looked across at her with teasing eyes.

"You certainly can't where I'm concerned!" Jane dismissed laughingly as she stood up; she had virtually given up trying to stop Gabe coming out with such intimate remarks about the two of them—he took little or no notice of her protests, anyway! "Time I was going," she told him briskly. "I have work to do," she added pointedly.

"So do I, madam, so do I," he drawled in rebuke as he followed her back to the counter. "Let me—"

"My treat," she insisted firmly, handing over the correct money to François. "Gabe thinks you should go to the States and make your fortune, François," she told the other man lightly.

"And deprive myself of the pleasure of paying all these English taxes every year?" François returned with a Gallic shrug. "Besides, I have an English mother-in-law," he confided to Gabe with a pointed roll of warm brown eyes. "And an English mother-in-law has to be the most formidable in the world!" he added heavily.

"All the more reason to leave the country, I would

have thought," Gabe returned sympathetically, his eyes twinkling with his enjoyment of the conversation.

"There is no way she would let me take her two grandchildren with me, let alone her daughter!" François shook his head with certainty. "Not that my wife would be agreeable to such an idea, either," he added frowningly. "You know, ten years ago, when I first met her, she was very sweet and very beautiful, always agreeable. But with the passing of time she grows very like her mother...!" He gave another expressive Gallic shrug.

"Did no one ever warn you to look at the mother before marrying the daughter?" Gabe drawled mockingly.

"Er—excuse me?" Jane cut in pointedly on this man-to-man exchange. Did Gabe get on with everybody? It seemed that he was able to put most people at their ease, was able to adapt to any situation. Strange; three years ago she had had an impression of him being a much more rigid individual... "When the two of you have quite finished...?" she added ruefully.

Gabe looked down at her with mocking eyes. "Perhaps it would be a good idea for me to meet your mother...!" he murmured tauntingly.

But he had already done so! And, from the comments he had made to her after that meeting with the Smythe-Robertses, he had obviously liked both her parents.

"Sorry to disappoint you," Jane derided. "But I'm nothing like my mother! She's sweet and kind, and has been completely devoted to my father from the day she first met him!" She didn't think she was necessarily unsweet, or unkind, but she had one failed marriage behind her, and no intention of ever repeating the experience!

The two men laughed at her levity, although Gabe's smile faded once they were once again outside in the street, his hand light on her elbow. "You know, Jane, we can't all be as lucky with our first choice of partner as our parents have been," he told her gruffly. "In fact, I've often thought that my own parents' happy marriage gave me the mistaken idea they were all like that!" He shook his head in self-derision.

He could be right in that surmise, Jane allowed. She knew that she had viewed her own marriage, at age only twenty-one, to be a lifetime commitment to love and happiness. It had taken only a matter of months for her to realise that with Paul that was going to be hard work, if not impossible. But she had made the commitment, and so she had worked at the marriage. Unfortunately, Paul hadn't felt that same need...

"With hindsight, I'm sure our parents' marriages are the exception, not the rule," she said tightly.

"Probably." Gabe nodded thoughtfully, glancing at his wristwatch. "Now that's dinner and breakfast I owe you." He quirked dark brows. "Any chance we could start with the dinner?"

And end up having breakfast together the next morning...!

Gabe certainly had to be given marks for trying. After all, he had waited at the park for her this morning in the hope she would turn up. And she hadn't thought that a man like Gabe—rich, handsome, and available—would chase after any woman so persistently, let alone one who was obviously so reluctant to be chased! But perhaps that was the appeal...?

"I did tell you this is my busy time—"

"Even Santa Claus has some time off before the big day," Gabe reasoned persuasively.

"But as it happens," she continued firmly, "I'm free

this evening. It's very rare for me to organise a lunch and a dinner on the same day," she explained dismissively.

"And today you have a lunch," Gabe said with satisfaction. "My lucky evening!"

It could be. But then again, it might not be, not if all he was after was a conquest...

"And how do you know Father Christmas takes time off?" she asked inconsequentially.

Gabe burst out laughing. "I wondered if you would pick me up on that one!"

She would pick him up on anything she felt she should. But as she glanced at him she saw he was looking at his watch once again. "Am I keeping you from something? Or possibly someone?" she added dryly.

His mouth quirked. "As it happens—both those things! I have an appointment at ten o'clock, and after our run I need a shower before going to the office."

Jane's returning smile lacked humour. "Some other unlucky person whose business is in trouble?"

Gabe shook his head, looking at her with narrowed eyes. "I would like to know who gave you this detrimental version of my business dealings," he drawled irritably. "I could thank them personally!"

Not really! It was Paul who had told her all about Gabriel Vaughan and the way he did business, and he had been out of Gabe's—and anyone else's—reach for three years...

She shrugged. "It isn't important—"

"Maybe not to you," Gabe bit out tersely. "But it sure as hell is to me! I may have stepped in and taken a business over when it was in danger of failing— If I hadn't done it then someone else would have!" he defended harshly at her sceptical expression. "And at least with me the original workforce, and often the management too, would be kept on if they weren't the reason for the problem."

As he had with her father's company…except for her father, of course! "Somehow, Gabe, you don't strike me as a knight in shining armour—"

"I'm well aware of how I strike you, Jane," he rasped tautly. "And I'm doing my damnedest to show you how wrong you are!"

And in part, she realised with a worried frown, he was succeeding. Because several times in their new acquaintance she had been surprised by his actions, found them difficult to place with the ruthless shark she had originally thought him to be…

"Oh, to hell with this," he suddenly snapped impatiently. "Just tell me when and where this evening, and I'll meet you there. And try not to make it in yet another establishment where the male proprietor greets you like a long-lost lover, hmm?" he added grimly.

He was jealous! Of Antonio and François. He had been pleasant to both men; in fact, this morning she had noted how easy he found it to get along with people and put them, as well as himself, at their ease. And yet that continued show of relaxation hid another emotion completely.

"Caroline's," she told him, adding the address of her favourite French restaurant. "Hopefully we'll be able to get a table for eight o'clock," she added dryly. "Although that may be difficult this close to Christmas."

"Do I take it that Caroline is a female?" Gabe muttered warily.

"You do," Jane nodded. "But it's her husband Pierre who does the cooking," she added with a grin.

"I give up!" Gabe sighed disgustedly, glancing at his watch once again. "And I'm sure you'll have no trouble getting us a table—even if it is Christmas!" he dismissed exasperatedly. "I'll meet you there at eight o'clock. Now I really do have to go!" He bent and kissed her briefly on the lips before turning and running off towards the main road where, hopefully, he would be able to flag down a taxi to take him home.

Jane watched him go, ruefully shaking her head as she did so. The man had a way of first bursting in and then bursting out of her life!

And of kissing her whenever he felt like it!

He had dropped that kiss lightly on her lips just now, as if they were two lovers parting briefly to be reunited later in the day. Which was exactly what they were going to do. But they certainly weren't lovers!

Nor ever likely to be either...!

JANE sat at the table waiting, a frown marring her brow as she remembered the telephone message that had been left on her answer machine when she'd got in earlier.

"Janette, darling," her mother had greeted excitedly. "Such fun, darling! Daddy and I have decided to come up to London for the day, and we thought it would be marvellous if we could all have tea at the Waldorf like we used to. Daddy and I will be there at four-thirty. But don't worry if you aren't able to make it," she'd added doubtfully. "If that's the case I'll give you a ring in a few days' time."

A few days' time...! There was no way Jane could wait a few days before finding out what had prompted her parents to come up to London.

The London house had been sold three years earlier

along with the rest of their surplus needs, and with it most of their London friends had disappeared too. Besides, Jane knew there was little cash to spend on a day in London, let alone tea at the Waldorf...

Tea at the Waldorf had always been a first-day-home-from-boarding-school treat that she and her mother had indulged in, her father usually too busy to join them.

But that wasn't the case today, and luckily Jane had returned from catering the lunch to receive her mother's recorded message in time for her to get to the Waldorf.

A day in London...

Her parents rarely came to London nowadays, and when they did it wasn't done spontaneously, as this visit appeared to have been. And it was never just for the day; the two of them usually stayed with Jane for several days.

So here she sat, the troubled frown still marring her brow, the time one minute to four-thirty...

Her mother looked transformed as she entered the hotel, radiant in a fine woollen rose-pink suit, her hair newly coloured and styled, her smile graciously lovely as she greeted several other people she knew at the tables as she and Jane's father approached their own reserved table.

Jane's father looked the tall, handsome man she had known when she was a child and teenager, his smiles of greeting as warm as her mother's.

But Jane's feelings of pleasure at the change in her parents were tinged with trepidation as she wondered at the reason for that change...

"Darling!" Her mother kissed her warmly on the cheek as Jane stood up on their arrival at the table.

"Janette." Her father greeted her more sedately, but there was a teasing glitter in the warmth of his eyes.

"This was a lovely idea," Jane smiled as they all sat down. "Thank you both for inviting me."

But still her feelings of trepidation wouldn't be pushed aside. Although it wouldn't do to just blurt out her curiosity concerning their spontaneity. Besides, she didn't want to wipe out that happy light in the two faces she loved best in the world.

"Have you had an enjoyable day?" she asked casually once their sandwiches and tea had been placed on the table, the latter in front of her mother so that she could pour the Earl Grey into the three china cups. "It's a little late for Christmas shopping, and the weather hasn't exactly been brilliant for walking around the shops." There had been flurries of snow and rain most of the day, and the wind was bitterly cold.

"Everywhere looks so festive we didn't notice." Her mother smiled her pleasure. "I had forgotten how wonderful everywhere looks at this time of the year," she added wistfully.

Jane had barely noticed the decorations, she had to admit, not because she didn't like Christmas, but because until the evening of the twenty-fourth of December she would be worked off her feet providing other people's food for the festive season. Christmas Day she would spend with her parents, and on Boxing Day the round of parties and dinners would all begin again. But, yes, everywhere did look rather splendid, and, without her being aware of it until this moment, she was feeling lightened by some of the Christmas spirit herself.

And part of her now wondered just how much of

that was due to the presence of Gabriel Vaughan in her life…

She quickly pushed the question to the back of her mind, not wanting to know the answer. He couldn't be coming to mean anything to her; he just couldn't!

"Was there a special reason for your coming up to town today?" she queried as she took her cup of tea from her mother.

Her parents looked briefly at each other before her father answered her. "Actually, Janette, I had a business meeting. Don't look so surprised." He laughed at her shocked response to his statement. "I do still have some contacts in the business world, you know," he chided teasingly.

And most of those contacts hadn't wanted to know when he'd run into financial difficulty and had to relinquish his company. To Gabriel Vaughan…

But, whatever had transpired earlier today at this "business meeting", her father was transformed from that man already grown old at only sixty-one, his shoulders no longer stooped and defeated, that playful twinkle back in his eyes.

"I know you do, Daddy," she soothed apologetically. "I just thought—I believed—"

"That I had turned my back on all that," he finished lightly. "As most of them turned their back on me," he added tightly, the first time he—or her mother—had ever indicated the pain they had suffered over the last three years because of the defection of their so-called friends. "Retirement isn't all it's cracked up to be, you know," he added wryly, stirring sugar into his tea.

Especially when it had been forced on him!

But, nevertheless, her father was now sixty-one; he

couldn't seriously be considering fighting his way back into the business arena at this stage of his life...

Jane looked across at her mother, but her mother only had eyes for her husband: proud and infinitely loving. That love and pride in her mother for her father had never changed.

As it hadn't in Jane. It was just that she could see something else in her mother's gaze today, something she couldn't quite put a name to...

"Well, don't keep me in suspense, Daddy." She turned back to her father. "Tell me what you've been up to!"

"I haven't been 'up to' anything," he smiled at her frustration. "And I'm not sure I should actually tell you anything just yet," he added less assuredly. "Not until things are a little more settled. What do you think, Daphne?" A little of the hesitancy that had been with him so much over the last three years crept back into his face as he looked at Jane's mother for guidance.

"I think everything is going to work out splendidly," Daphne answered him firmly, one of her hands reaching out to rest briefly on his. "But I'm sure it can all wait until after Christmas," she added briskly. "You are still coming to us for Christmas Day, aren't you, Janette?" She looked across at her encouragingly.

Where else could she possibly be going for Christmas? Besides, she always spent Christmas with her parents. Even during the really bad times with Paul, Christmas had been a family time, when they had all been together, happily or not.

And she couldn't say she was particularly happy now with the way the conversation had been turned away from her father's business meeting earlier today. She never had been able to stand mysteries, and that dislike had been heightened during her marriage to Paul, when everything he did and said had become questionable. Until it had got to the stage where she'd stopped asking and he'd stopped telling!

"Of course I am," she assured them brightly. "But are you really not going to tell me anything else about what is obviously good news?"

Her father laughed. "Do you know, Janie, I haven't seen you pout like this since you were a little girl?" he explained affectionately at her hurt look.

Jane gave a rueful grin; maybe she had been trying a little too hard! "Did it work?" She quirked mischievous brows.

"Maybe back then," her father conceded warmly. "But you're twenty-eight now; it doesn't have the same impact."

She laughed. It was a long time since she had heard her father being quite this jovial. But she liked it. Whatever the reason for the change in him, and her mother, she could only thank whoever was responsible.

"Drink your tea, Janette," her mother encouraged briskly. "Your father and I have a train to catch in a couple of hours."

She sipped obediently at her tea; her mother was certainly starting to sound like her old self again too. In fact, it felt as if all of them were emerging from a long, dark tunnel...

"Why aren't you staying with me as you usually do?" she prompted lightly. "Do you have to rush back?"

"You're so busy, darling." Her mother smiled understandingly. "We don't want to intrude on what little time you do have for yourself. I know you never mention any young men in your life, but you're so beautiful, darling—more beautiful with your blonde hair, of course," she sighed, "but—"

"Now let's not start that, Daphne," her husband rebuked gently. "I agree with you, of course, but young women of today seem to change the colour of their hair depending on which outfit they're wearing! Janette may decide to be a flaming redhead by next week!"

"I don't think so, Daddy," she assured him dryly—although she was glad to have the subject changed from "young men" in her life! Until Gabe had forced himself into her life just under two weeks ago, there had been no man in her private life at all in the last three years. And she didn't think Gabe was at all the sort of "young man" her mother was talking about!

"Neither do I, really." Her father gave an answering smile. "And your mother is right, Janie—you are beautiful. And one bad experience shouldn't sour you for any future—"

"It did, Daddy," she cut in firmly. "There have been no young men, there is no young man, and there will be no young men, either!" She didn't consider Gabe a young man at all, and he wasn't in her life—instead he kept trying to pull her into his!

"And just how do you think I'm ever going to become a grandfather if you stick to that decision?" her father chided softly.

"Adoption?" she suggested helpfully.

"Now stop it, you two." Her mother tutted. "It's been a wonderful day, it's nearly Christmas, and I won't have the two of you indulging in one of your silly going-nowhere conversations. More tea, David?" she added pointedly.

It was wonderful to see her parents looking, and

being, so positive once again. And, Jane realised on her way back to her apartment an hour later, it was the first time for a very long time—three years, in fact!—that she had spent time with her parents without those feelings of guilt that had been like a brick wall between them.

Their lives were changing.

All of them.

Her own because of Gabriel Vaughan, she realised.

But if her parents were to realise, were to know that Gabe was the "man in her life" at the moment, albeit by his own invitation, how would that affect their own new-found happiness?

Not very well, she accepted frowningly. And nothing, absolutely nothing, must happen to affect her parents' mood of anticipation for the future.

Which meant, she decided firmly, that tonight had to be the last time, the very last time, that she ever saw Gabe...

CHAPTER ELEVEN

"I FIND it very difficult to believe, with the catering connections you seem to have, that you couldn't book a table at a restaurant for us anywhere!" Gabe didn't even pause to say hello as he strolled into her apartment. "So we're eating at home again, hmm?" He turned in the hallway and grinned at her.

Jane's mouth had dropped open indignantly at his initial bombardment as he came through the open doorway, but his second remark, and that grin—!

"What can I say?" she shrugged. "It's Christmas!"

Heavens, he looked gorgeous!

She had spent the last two hours telling herself that Gabe meant nothing to her, that they would have dinner together, and then she would tell him this was goodbye. And this time she intended making sure he knew she meant it!

But he did look so handsome in the casual blue shirt worn beneath a grey jacket, and black trousers.

It wasn't true that she couldn't get a table at the restaurant: Caroline and Pierre were old friends; they would have found a table for her even if they'd had to bring another one into the restaurant for her! But a restaurant wasn't the best place for her to say goodbye to him, especially if he should prove difficult—as he had done in the past... And so she had acquired his telephone number from Felicity and called to tell him they were eating at her apartment instead.

"I brought the wine." Gabe held up a marvellously exclusive—and expensive—bottle of red wine. "You didn't say what we were eating, but I guessed it wouldn't be beans on toast!" he said with satisfaction.

"You guessed it was eggs, hmm?" she came back derisively.

Gabe gave her a chiding look. "I've had a good day, Jane; don't spoil it by serving me eggs!"

She grimaced as she took the bottle of wine and went back into the kitchen where she had been when he'd rung the bell. "Everyone seems to be having a good day today," she murmured as she uncorked the wine, remembering her parents' happiness earlier. "Stay away from those pots, Gabe," she warned sharply as he would have lifted one of the saucepan lids. "Anticipation is half the fun!"

"I know, Jane."

She became very still, turning slowly to look at him. And then wished she hadn't. Gabe was looking at her as if he would like to make her his main course!

And she'd deliberately dressed down this evening, wearing a green cashmere sweater she had bought several years ago when she was still blonde, and a black fitted skirt, knee-length, not so short as to look inviting.

What she didn't realise was how much more the green colour of her sweater suited the new darkness of her hair, picking out those red highlights—she almost appeared the "flaming redhead" her father had referred to this afternoon!

"Glasses, Gabe," she told him through stiff lips.

"Certainly, Jane." He gave a mocking inclination of

his head before strolling across the kitchen, opening the correct cupboard and taking out two glasses.

Maybe having dinner at her apartment wasn't such a good idea, after all! Gabe was too comfortable, too relaxed, altogether too familiar with her home. And not just with her home, either...!

"What shall we drink to?"

While she had been lost in thought, Gabe had poured the wine into the two glasses, holding one out to her now.

"Good days?" he suggested huskily.

That had to be better than "us"!

This had not been a good idea. She could only hope the time would pass quickly.

"Why don't you go through to the sitting-room and pick out some music to play while I serve our first course?" she suggested abruptly, her usual calm having momentarily deserted her.

But then, when didn't it when she was around this man? It was past time to say goodbye to him!

"So why did you have a good day?" she prompted conversationally as they sat down to their garlic prawns with fresh mayonnaise, an old John Denver CD of hers playing softly in the background.

Gabe's gaze met hers laughingly. "Well, this morning I went for a run for the first time in two weeks—"

"Shame on you, Gabe!"

"Mmm, this tastes wonderful, Jane." He had just tasted his first prawn dipped in the mayonnaise. "I can hardly wait to see what we have for the main course!"

With any luck, his enjoyment of the food would stop him talking too much.

She could live in hope!

The wine, as she had already guessed when she'd seen the label, was beautiful—rich and silky smooth. Only the best for Gabriel Vaughan.

"Did you have a good day too?" Gabe looked up from his food to ask her, frowning at her derisive smile. "What…?" he prompted warily.

She gave a mocking shake of her head. "We don't have to play those sorts of games, Gabe," she told him dryly. "We're having dinner, not spending the rest of our lives together!" she explained scornfully at his puzzled expression.

"It starts with conversation, Jane, eating dinner together, finding out about each other, likes and dislikes, things like that. People don't leap straight into marriage—"

"I don't believe I mentioned the word marriage, Gabe." She stood up abruptly, their first course at an end as far as she was concerned.

"As I've already said," Gabe murmured, turning in his chair to watch her departure into the kitchen, "he must have been some bastard."

She didn't remember him saying any such thing! But, nevertheless, he was right; that was exactly what Paul had been.

Their used plates landed with a clatter on the kitchen worktop, her hands shaking so badly she'd had trouble carrying them at all.

What was wrong with her?

She had made a conscious decision this afternoon to tell Gabe this was definitely the last time they would see each other. One look at him and she knew her resolve had weakened. One smile from him, and she began to tremble. If he should actually touch her—

"Anything wrong—? Hell, Jane, I only touched your arm!" Gabe frowned down at her darkly as Jane had literally jumped away from the touch of his hand on her arm. "What the hell is wrong with you tonight?"

She had asked herself the same question only seconds ago!

And, looking at him, she was beginning to realise what the answer was...

No!

She couldn't have those sorts of feelings towards Gabe, couldn't actually want him to touch her, to make love to her?

But she did; she knew she did! And she hadn't felt this way since— But no—she hadn't ever felt quite this way towards Paul. She'd never trembled at the thought of him touching her, had never ached for his lips on hers.

But she'd loved Paul. She wasn't in love with Gabe. If she was anything, she was in lust with him!

Oh, God...!

"What is it, Jane?" he prompted again, his frown having deepened to a scowl at her continued silence.

She had to pull herself together, finish the meal—she doubted he would consider leaving before then!—and then she must make it absolutely plain to him that she did not want him appearing in her life whenever he felt like it; that there would be no more runs together in the park, no more turning up at her apartment, and no more impatient messages left on her answer machine.

And, most important of all, there would be no further occasion for him to kiss her!

"Sorry," she dismissed lightly. "My thoughts were miles away when you came into the kitchen, and I'm a little tired too, I'm afraid." She gave him a bright, meaningless smile as she voiced these excuses for her extraordinary behaviour, at the same time totally distancing herself from him as she crossed the kitchen to check on the food simmering on the hob. "If you would like to go back to the dining area, I'll serve our main course and bring it through in a few minutes."

She deliberately didn't look up at him again before she began to do exactly that, but all the time she busied herself with the food she was aware of him still standing across the other side of the kitchen, watching her with narrowed, puzzled eyes. And then, with a frustrated shake of his head, he turned and impatiently left the room.

Jane leant weakly against the table in the middle of the kitchen. She had never wanted any man the way she wanted Gabe!

And there was no way, simply no way, she could ever assuage this sudden hunger she felt for his kisses and his touch.

She had always thought of him—when she'd allowed herself to think of him at all—as a man who took his pleasure where he found it, and then moved on. But the one thing she had learnt about him since his reappearance into her life was that if Gabe wanted something, then he didn't relinquish his right to it easily. And she didn't doubt for a moment that, physically at least, Gabe wanted her as much as she wanted him.

And she also didn't doubt that to give him what he wanted wouldn't mean it would end there...

Goodbye was the word she had to say to him. Not angrily; it had to be said in such a way that he would never want to come back.

The ache inside her would go away, she assured

herself as she served the noisettes of lamb with tarragon sauce and the still crunchy vegetables from the steamer, and then everything could go back to the way she liked it—untroubled, and uncomplicated.

Why did that realisation suddenly hold no appeal for her?

Ridiculous. That was what this whole situation was— ridiculous! Thank you. And goodbye. Four words. Very easy to say.

But could she say them as if she meant them?

Her heart skipped a beat when Gabe turned to smile at her as she came in with the food.

Thank you. And goodbye, she repeated firmly to herself. She would say them. And mean them!

"Cooking dinner for us this evening has been too much for you," Gabe told her apologetically as she sat down opposite him. "I should have thought of that when you telephoned me earlier. You've already been at work today; the last thing you needed this evening was to cook another meal." He shook his head self-disgustedly. "The least I could have done was offer to cook for you." He sighed ruefully.

Jane knew from watching him the other evening that he was more than capable of doing it, too. But spend the evening at his apartment...? She didn't think so!

"Don't give it another thought, Gabe," she dismissed— knowing that he'd been thinking about it ever since he'd left the kitchen a few minutes ago. And the reason he had come up with for her skittishness was obviously that she had been working too hard. "Cooking for two people, and in the comfort of my own home, isn't work at all," she assured him.

"But the whole point of this evening was that I would take you out," he protested.

"You know, Gabe," she said softly, "I'm one of those chefs that's inclined to turn nasty if my food isn't eaten while it's still hot!"

He seemed on the point of protesting again for several seconds, and then he grinned, relaxing once again as he picked up his knife and fork in preparation for eating. "Never let it be said…!"

Jane ate sparingly, her appetite having deserted her with the realisation that after a couple of hours' time she would never see this man again.

How had he crept into her emotions like this—even lustful ones? *When* had he?

"—parents arrive in the country tomorrow, and I wondered if you could join us all for dinner tomorrow evening?"

Jane blinked across at him, having been lost in her own thoughts, and slowly took in what he had just said to her. His parents were arriving in London tomorrow? And why not? It was Christmas, and, from what he had said, he was an only child, too. But as for the suggestion of her having dinner with them…!

"I've told you, Gabe," she replied lightly. "This is my busy time of year. I'm catering for a party of thirty people tomorrow evening," she said thankfully.

"You work too damned hard," he bit out disapprovingly.

"I like to eat myself occasionally." She wryly pointed out the necessity for her to work. Maybe Gabe had forgotten what that was like; he was certainly in a financial position not to have to work any more, but she certainly wasn't!

He scowled heavily. "You shouldn't have to—"

"Now, now, Gabe," she cut in tauntingly. "Don't let your chauvinism show!"

"This isn't funny, Jane." He frowned across at her. "When I think—"

"I often think that the mere act of thinking only complicates things at times," she dismissed calmly, putting down her knife and fork, the food only half eaten on her plate, although Gabe seemed to have enjoyed his, his plate now empty. "Would you like your cheese or dessert next? People seem to vary in their preference nowadays, I've noticed."

"Actually—" he sat forward, leaning his elbows on the table as he looked straight at her "—I'd like an answer to my original question."

She raised dark brows. "Which question was that, Gabe?" But she knew which one it was. She also knew that she had no intention of meeting his parents, now or ever! After this evening she wouldn't be seeing him again, either...

His mouth quirked, and he gave a slight shake of his head. "It isn't going to work this time, Jane. I would very much like you to meet my parents," he told her bluntly. "And for them to meet you."

"Why?" she came back just as bluntly.

"Because they're nice people." He shrugged.

His parents wouldn't be the ones under inspection at such a meeting; she would. And she had been through all this once before in her life, eight years ago. She'd tried so hard at the time to win the approval of Paul's parents, little knowing that she needn't have bothered. The fact that she was the only child of very rich parents was the only asset she had needed in the eyes of Paul's parents!

It had never occurred to the elder Grangers that money could be lost more easily than it had been made...

Jane hadn't seen or heard from Paul's parents since just before Paul's death. On the one occasion she had attempted to telephone them they had claimed they would never forgive her for not even being at their son's funeral. The fact that she had been in a clinic at the time, having just lost her baby—their own grandchild—and that Paul had been in the company of another woman at the time of his accident, hadn't seemed to occur to them...

"Do you introduce all your friends to them, Gabe?" The derision could be heard in her voice.

He didn't even blink, his gaze remaining steady on hers. "The ones that matter, yes!"

She gave a humourless smile. "We barely know each other, Gabe. Did you introduce Jennifer to them before you married her?" she couldn't resist adding.

And then wished she hadn't! Jennifer had been his wife; their own relationship wasn't in the same category.

"As it happens, yes, I did." He relaxed back in his chair, smiling lazily. "My father was bowled over by the way she looked; my mother hated her on sight." He gave a wry chuckle. "I'm sure I don't have to tell you which one proved to be right!"

From what Jane knew of Jennifer Vaughan, men had always been "bowled over" by the way she looked. And the majority of women seemed to have disliked her intensely. Herself included.

"That can't have been easy for you," Jane sympathised.

"Nothing about that relationship was easy for me," he

acknowledged grimly. "And you're changing the subject again, Jane—"

"Because I don't want to meet your parents, Gabe," she sighed, becoming impatient with his persistence.

"Why not?" he came back as bluntly as she had minutes ago.

"Several reasons—"

"Name them," he put in forcefully, no longer relaxed, sitting upright in his chair, his gaze narrowed on her.

"I was about to," she rebuked softly; she did not want to get into an argument about this; she disliked arguments intensely. There had been too many of them with Paul. "Firstly, it puts a completely erroneous light on our friendship." She deliberately used the casual term, knowing he had registered that fact by the way his mouth tightened ominously. "And secondly," she added less confidently, knowing she was going to have that argument whether she wanted it or not, "I don't think the two of us should see each other again after tonight!" It all came out in a rush, so desperate was she to get it over with as quickly as possible.

Gabe raised those expressive dark brows. "And exactly what brought this on?" he questioned mildly.

"Nothing 'brought this on', Gabe," she returned exasperatedly. "I've been telling you to go away, one way or another, since the night we first met!" For all the good it had done her!

"Exactly," he nodded. "But this time you seem to mean it..." he said thoughtfully.

"I meant it all the other times too!" Jane claimed scathingly, wondering, in the light of the fact that she had now, inwardly at least, acknowledged her attraction towards him, whether she *had* really meant all those other refusals she had given him...

"Did you?" Gabe seemed to doubt it too!

Of course she had meant them, she told herself strongly. Gabriel Vaughan was a man for her to avoid, not encourage. Besides, she was sure she hadn't encouraged him. Not consciously, at least...

But subconsciously? Had she been forceful enough in telling him to go away? She had thought so at the time. But—

Enough of this! It was just confusing her.

She stood up abruptly, intending to clear their plates. And there would be no cheese or dessert. After this conversation, a little earlier in the meal than she had anticipated, she acknowledged, it was time for Gabe to leave!

"I meant it, Gabe," she told him forcefully. "I don't want to have dinner with you. I don't want to meet your parents. And, most important of all, I don't want to see you again! There, I can't be any plainer than that." She looked down at him with challenging brown eyes.

He coolly returned her furious gaze. "And what about the Christmas present I got for you today?" he said softly.

Present? He had bought her a Christmas present? "I think you were a little premature in buying me anything!" she told him impatiently. "But with any luck you'll have found someone else before Christmas that you can give it to instead—after all, there are still a few days to go!"

"Hmm, so we're back to the insults, are we?" Gabe murmured thoughtfully as he stood up. "The present was meant for you, Jane, not someone else," he bit out harshly, reaching out to clasp her arms.

Jane suddenly had trouble breathing, knowing it was due to Gabe's close proximity. "I don't—"

"Want it," he completed harshly. "You know, Jane, determination, and a certain independence of spirit, is to be admired in a woman. But not," he added dismissively as she would have made an angry reply, "when they are taken to the extreme of pigheaded rudeness! You went past that point several minutes ago," he added tightly.

"I—"

"Shut up, Jane," he rasped, pulling her effortlessly towards him.

"You can't—"

"Please!" he added with a groan, his head bending and his lips claiming hers.

Jane melted.

It was as if she had been waiting for this moment since he had kissed her so lightly this morning. And there was nothing light or distracted about this kiss; all Gabe's attention was focused on the passion that flared up between them so easily. Like tinder awaiting the flame. And it seemed they were that flame for each other...

Her arms moved up about his neck, one hand clinging to the broad width of his shoulder, the other becoming entangled in the dark thickness of his hair, her body held tightly against his, moulded to each muscle and sinew.

Without removing his lips from hers Gabe swung her up into his arms and carried her over to the soft gold-coloured sofa, laying her down on it before joining her there, their bodies even closer now, their breath mingling, Gabe's hands moving restlessly over the slenderness of her back and thighs.

Jane gasped softly as one of those hands moved to cup her breast, the gently sloping curve fitting perfectly against his own flesh, the nipple responding instantly to the gentle caress of his thumb, the tip hardening to his touch, a pleasurable warmth spreading through her thighs all the way to the tips of her toes.

She wanted this man!

Not like this, with their clothes between them, she wanted the naked warmth of his body next to hers, wanted to feel his hard possession, wanted to give him the same pleasure he was undoubtedly giving her.

His hand was beneath the woollen cashmere of her jumper now, and he was groaning low in his throat at his discovery that she wasn't wearing a bra, her breast naked to his touch.

Her breasts had always been firm and uplifting, definitely one of her better assets, and she rarely saw the necessity to wear a bra.

She groaned low in her own throat now as Gabe pushed aside the woollen garment, his head bending as his lips claimed possession of that fiery tip, his tongue rasping with slow, moist pleasure across her sensitive flesh.

She was on fire, offered no protest when, hindered by its presence, Gabe pulled the jumper up over her head and discarded it completely. Her gaze was shy as she looked up at him and he looked at her with such pleasurable intensity.

"You're beautiful, Jane," he murmured huskily. "But then, I always knew you would be!" he groaned before his head lowered, his mouth capturing hers with fierce intensity, passion flaring uncontrollably now, carrying them both on a tide that was going to be impossible to stop.

Not that Jane had any thought of bringing this to an end. She wanted Gabe as badly as he appeared to want her. She had never known such need, such desire, trembling with anticipation, knowing—

"Oh, Janie, Janie!" Gabe groaned as he buried his face in the warmth of her neck, breathing in deeply of her perfume. "If you only knew how I've wanted this, how long I've needed to hold and kiss you like this." His arms tightened about her as his lips travelled the length of her throat.

Jane felt cold. Icy.

Janie...

He had called her *Janie*. Only her father had ever called her by that pet name.

It could be coincidence, of course, Gabe's own arousal making him unaware of what he had just said.

Or just carelessness...?

Gabe tensed beside her, suddenly seeming to become aware of the way she had moved as far away from him as she was able on the confines of the sofa, slowly lifting his head so that he could look down at her, his expression—wary!

She wasn't mistaken.

It wasn't coincidence!

She moistened suddenly dry lips. "How long, Gabe?" she demanded coldly.

He frowned. "How long...?" he repeated, that wariness having increased.

She nodded, more certain with every second that passed that she wasn't mistaken in the conclusion she had just come to. "How long have you known exactly who I am?" she said plainly.

Because he did know.

She was sure now that he did.

So why hadn't he told her that days ago…?

CHAPTER TWELVE

"How long have you known, Gabe?" she repeated in a steady voice, fully clothed again now, standing across the room looking over to where Gabe still sat on the couch.

He drew in a ragged breath, running agitated fingers through the darkness of his hair. "I—"

"Don't even attempt to avoid answering me, Gabe," she warned harshly. "We both know—now—that you realise I was once Janette Smythe-Roberts!"

How long had he known? she asked herself again. And why hadn't he said so as soon as he made the discovery?

She literally went cold at the only explanation she could think of!

"You still are Janette Smythe-Roberts, damn it!" he rasped, standing up himself now, instantly dwarfing what had already seemed to her to be a space too small to hold them both.

She felt sick, had perhaps cherished some small hope inside her that he really didn't know. But his words confirmed that he did!

"Don't come near me." Jane cringed away from him as he would have reached out and touched her. "You still haven't told me exactly how long you've known," she prompted woodenly.

Or what he was going to do about it! He hadn't been

behaving like a man still out to wreak vengeance, but perhaps making her want him was his way of exacting retribution…?

Gabe gave a weary sigh, shrugging wide shoulders. "I realised who you were about thirty seconds after I came into the kitchen with Felicity last week," he admitted quietly.

Jane drew in a shaky breath, her arms wrapped about herself protectively. "That long? How on earth—?"

"Your hair may be a different colour, Jane," he rasped. "And your face has taken on a certain maturity it didn't once have. But it's still the same face I remember," he added huskily. "A face I'll never forget."

She shook her head disbelievingly. "But I never even saw you face to face until last week—"

"But I saw you," Gabe cut in firmly. "We were never actually introduced to each other, but I saw you at a party one evening with your husband."

Her husband. Gabe's wife's lover. The man Jennifer had left him for.

She sighed. "I don't remember that evening." She shook her head; a lot of the time before the accident was a blank to her, her misery as Paul's wife already well established.

"You looked beautiful that night," Gabe recalled softly. "You were wearing a brown dress, the same colour as your eyes, little make-up that I could see—but then, you don't need make-up to enhance your beauty. And your hair—! I had never seen hair quite that colour before, or that long; it reached down to your waist like a curtain of gold! I didn't need to be introduced to you to remember you, Jane—you stood out in that crowd like a golden light in darkness!"

Her mouth twisted scornfully. "Please stop waxing lyrical about me, Gabe; I was very unhappy at that time; I probably didn't even want to be there. I no longer loved my husband but felt trapped in the marriage—"

"Until he walked out of it!"

"Until Paul walked out of it," she acknowledged shakily. "To bc with your wife," she added hardly.

Gabe shrugged. "So the fairy story goes," he said dryly.

Jane gave him a sharp look. "There was no fairy-tale ending to that particular story—for any of us! And you've been playing with me for the last twelve days—"

"To what end?" he challenged harshly.

"I have no idea." She sighed wearily. "I presume for the same reason you tried to find me after the accident." She shrugged.

"The same reason. But not the one you think! And I backed off then when I heard the rumour that you had lost your baby," he rasped.

"Did you?" she said heavily, no longer looking at him but staring sightlessly at her music centre. The CD had long since finished playing. But neither of them had noticed that fact; they'd been too engrossed in each other at the time. Which brought her back to Gabe's kisses and caresses. Was he still trying to make someone pay for what happened three years ago? "Then you know that if anyone was a victim of my husband's relationship with your wife, Gabe," she bit out evenly, "it was my unborn baby!"

"Jane—"

"I told you not to come near me!" she flared as he made a move towards her, her eyes flashing in warning. "What did you think when you met me again last week,

Gabe?" She looked at him challengingly. "Did you see I had nothing left to lose and decide to hurt me in another way?"

He became suddenly still. "What way?"

"You tell me!" She smiled humourlessly. "Those conversations we had about Janette Smythe-Roberts." She shook her head disgustedly. "You were playing with me all the time!" she realised self-derisively. And all the time she had thought she was the one not being completely honest!

"I was trying to get you to defend yourself!" Gabe returned impatiently. "But you didn't do it," he added disappointedly.

"Didn't defend myself against being thought a cold-blooded, manipulative gold-digger? Someone who would take money from my parents and leave them almost penniless?" Jane looked at him scathingly. "As I told you once before, Gabe, you sweep through people's lives, uncaring of the chaos and pain you leave behind you—"

"That isn't true!" His hands were clenched angrily.

"Perhaps uncaring is the wrong word to use," she conceded disgustedly. "You're simply unaware of it! Which is perhaps even worse. What do you think happens to people when you've stepped in and bought their company, possibly their life's work, out from under them? Do you think they simply shrug their shoulders and start all over again?" she challenged.

"It's business, Jane—"

"So my father said when he tried to explain your behaviour to me!" she scorned. "But I call it something else completely!"

Gabe drew in a harsh breath. "Let's not lose sight of

the real villain here, Jane," he rasped. "And it wasn't me!"

Paul... It always came back to Paul. And with thoughts of Paul came ones of Gabe's wife Jennifer...

"If you're going to blame Paul for this then let's include your wife in it too," Jane said with distaste. "Who do you think he was trying to impress with his gambling and high living?"

Gabe became suddenly still. "I accept Jennifer's blame—"

"Do you?" Jane gave another mirthless smile. "She was beautiful, immoral, utterly uncaring of anyone but herself. She knew of my pregnancy, too, because Paul had told her, but it made no difference when she decided she wanted my husband—"

"Jennifer couldn't have children herself," Gabe put in softly. "She'd had tests. She was infertile. Pregnant women represented a threat to her."

Jane felt the momentary sadness that she would for any woman unable to have children of her own. But it was only momentary where Jennifer Vaughan was concerned. "That didn't give her the right to entice away the husbands of those women!"

"I agree." Gabe sighed heavily. "But it's an inescapable fact that that's exactly what she did. With dire results in your particular case."

Jane stared at him as she fully registered all that he had just said. "Are you telling me that that wasn't the first time Jennifer had done something like that?" It seemed incredible, but that was exactly what it sounded like he was saying!

He ran a weary hand across his brow. "Jennifer was

a very troubled woman. The fact that she couldn't have children—"

"I asked you a question, Gabe," Jane cut in tautly.

He looked at her steadily. "I believe I've already told you that Jennifer was much more interested in other women's husbands than she was in her own—"

"But pregnant women in particular?" Jane persisted.

"Yes!" he acknowledged harshly, turning away. "To Jennifer there was nothing more beautiful than a pregnant woman. To her they seemed to glow. More importantly, they carried life inside them. A pregnant woman became the ultimate in beauty to her."

"That's ridiculous!" Jane snapped. "Most pregnant women don't feel that way at all. Oh, there's a certain magic in creating life, in feeling that life growing inside you," she remembered emotionally. "But for the most part you feel nauseous, and in the beginning it's a nausea that never seems to stop. And, added to that, you feel fat and unattractive—"

"Pregnant women aren't fat," Gabe cut in softly. "They're blossoming."

"That's a word only used by people who aren't pregnant," Jane put in dismissively. "Believe me, most of us just feel fat!" And that feeling hadn't been helped, in her case, by the fact that Paul had obviously found her condition most unattractive!

"Maybe," Gabe conceded with a sigh. "But to a woman who has never been pregnant, and who never can be, that isn't how pregnancy appears at all. Oh, I'm not excusing Jennifer's behaviour—"

"I hope not," Jane told him tightly. "Because it isn't a good enough excuse as far as I'm concerned!" She had lost her baby—the only good thing to come out of her marriage—because her husband had left her for Jennifer Vaughan, and the two of them had subsequently died together in a car crash. There was no excuse for that!

"It isn't a good enough excuse for any woman," Gabe accepted heavily. "But it's what Jennifer did."

"Then why didn't you leave her?" Jane frowned. "Why did you stay with her, and in doing so condone her behaviour?"

A nerve pulsed in his tightly clenched jaw. "I didn't condone it, Jane. I would never condone such behaviour. But I thought that by staying with her I could—" He shook his head. "I don't believe in divorce, Jane," he told her abruptly. "And neither did Jennifer," he added softly.

She became suddenly still, her frown deepening. Jennifer didn't believe in divorce...? "But she left you..."

Gabe sighed. "No. She didn't."

"But—"

"I know that's what Paul told you three years ago, and it's what everyone else thought at the time too, but I can assure you, Jennifer was not leaving me." He shook his head. "There were so many times I wished she would," he admitted harshly. "But I was her safety net, the let-out when any of her little affairs became too serious. As Paul did..."

Jane was having trouble absorbing all of this now. Was Gabe really saying what she thought he was?

Paul had said he was leaving her, that he and Jennifer were going to be together.

"Are you telling me—?" She ran her tongue over suddenly dry lips. "Are you saying that Paul and Jennifer weren't going away together?"

"That's exactly what I'm saying." Gabe nodded grimly. "Jennifer was furious the day of the accident. Paul had telephoned her to say he'd left you, and now he expected her to do the same to me. She met him that day only so that she could tell him what a fool he was, that she had no intention of leaving me, that he had better hurry home and make it up with his wife before she decided his leaving had been the best thing that ever happened to her! Her words, Jane, not mine," Gabe told her bleakly.

But it had already been too late for Paul to do that. She might not already have realised that Paul's leaving "had been the best thing that ever happened to her", but Paul had been in too deeply in other ways to backtrack on his decision. As her father's assistant, he had stolen money from the company, and in doing so had brought that company almost to the point of ruin.

"I've often wondered if it was an accident," Gabe murmured softly, as if partly reading her thoughts.

Jane looked at him dazedly. Not an accident? What was he saying, suggesting? But hadn't she just told herself there had been no way back for Paul, that he had already burnt his bridges, both professionally and privately? But could he have thought that there was no reason to carry on? No, she wouldn't believe that! Paul had been too selfish, too self-motivated, to take his own and Jennifer's lives.

"It's something we'll never know the answer to," Gabe continued gently. "Probably something best not known."

Jane agreed with him. That sort of soul-searching could do neither of them any good. No matter what the reason for doing so...

"Love is a very strange emotion," she said dully. "It appears to grow and exist for people who really don't deserve it." And Jennifer Vaughan certainly hadn't deserved Gabe's, or any other man's, love. And yet who but a man in love could ever have thought her the "perfection" he had once called her?

"Death is rather final," Gabe muttered. "But you're still well rid of Paul Granger!"

"I've never—" She shook her head. "We're getting away from the point here—"

"Maybe I caught that from you." Gabe attempted to tease, although he couldn't even bring himself to smile, let alone encourage her to do so. "What is the point here, Jane? You tell me." He shook his head. "Because I've certainly lost it!"

For the main part, so had she! Except that Gabe had known exactly who she was for the last twelve days. And for reasons of his own he had chosen to keep that fact to himself!

She looked at him coldly. "The point is that for me the past is as dead and buried as Paul himself is. Why do you think I've been asking you to go away for the last twelve days? Because you remind me of a time I would rather forget," she told him bluntly.

Gabe looked pale now. "I didn't imagine what happened between us a short time ago—"

"It's been a long time for me, Gabe," she said scornfully. "My marriage may have been a mistake, but despite all that I'm still a normal woman, with normal desires, and you—"

"Just happened to be here!" he finished disgustedly. "Is that it, Jane?"

No, that wasn't it! She had met plenty of other men

over the last three years, much more suitable men, men just as handsome as he was, just as interested in a relationship with her. And she hadn't responded to any of them, hadn't allowed any of them as close to her as this man had got in a matter of days.

But to find the reason for that she would have to delve into her own emotions. And she had already done enough of that where Gabriel Vaughan was concerned.

"That just about sums it up, yes!" she confirmed hardly. "It probably has something to do with the time of year, too," she added insultingly. "Let's face it, no one likes to be on their own at Christmas!"

And strangely, despite the fact that this Christmas was actually going to be no different from the last three she had spent with her parents, she had a feeling she was going to feel very much alone...

What had Gabe done to her? What was it that she felt towards him? Because it was no longer that mixture of fear and apprehension she had felt before .

Gabe gave a pained wince at her deliberate bluntness. "I had better make myself scarce, then, hadn't I?" He picked up his jacket, but didn't put it on. "That way you still have time to meet someone else before the big day!"

Although his words hurt—as they were meant to do!—Jane offered no defence. Nor did she try to stop him as he walked out of the door, closing it softly behind him.

There would have been no point in stopping him. They had said all that needed to be said. Probably more than needed to be said!

And she still had no idea why Gabe had pursued her so relentlessly for the last twelve days. She felt he had offered no real explanation for such extraordinary behaviour when he had known all the time she was Janette Smythe-Roberts.

Two things she did know only too clearly, though.

One; Gabe must have loved his wife very much; he must have done to have tolerated her behaviour. Secondly—and this was against all that she had tried to do for herself for the last three years—she didn't need to delve into her own emotions to find out why she had responded to Gabe in the way that she had. She had known the answer to that question as soon as he had closed the door behind him...

Somehow—and she wasn't sure how such a thing could have happened—she had fallen in love with Gabe!

Stupidly.

Irrevocably!

CHAPTER THIRTEEN

JANE made the drive to her parents' home on Christmas morning with more than her usual reluctance. The last few days, since Gabe had walked out of her life for good, had been such a strain to get through, and as a consequence she looked paler than usual, despite the application of blusher.

And even in those few days she had lost enough weight for it to be noticeable. She had put on a baggy thigh-length jumper, burnt orange in colour, and styled black trousers, in an effort to hide this fact from her parents. But there was nothing she could do to hide the gauntness of her face, or the dull pain in her eyes that wouldn't go away.

She had let Gabriel Vaughan get to her. Not only that, she had allowed herself to fall in love with him.

Maybe that was what he had hoped for, she had told herself over and over again in the last few days, when not even her work could blot him from her mind and senses. If it was, then he had succeeded, even if he wasn't aware of it.

At least, she hoped he wasn't aware of it. That would be the ultimate pain in this whole sorry business!

Jane drew in a deep breath after parking her van, forcing a bright smile to her lips as she got out and walked towards the house. It was only a few hours of forced gaiety; surely she could handle that? After all, it was Christmas Day!

"You're looking very pale, darling," her mother said, sounding concerned, kissing her in greeting as she did so.

"And you've lost weight, too," her father added reprovingly after giving her a hug.

So much for her efforts at camouflage!

"You're both looking well too," she returned teasingly. "And one of your Christmas lunches, Mummy, should take care of both those things!" she assured them lightly.

"I hope so," her father said sternly. "But first things first—a glass of my Christmas punch?"

"Guaranteed to put us all to sleep this afternoon!" Jane laughed, finding she was, after all, glad to be home with her parents on this special day.

"I sincerely hope not." Her mother smiled. "We have guests arriving after lunch!"

It was the first Jane had heard of anyone joining them on Christmas Day, but even if company was the last thing she felt in need of she was glad for her parents' sake. Whatever it was her father had become involved with on a business level, it had obviously given their social life a jolt too; it was years since they had spent Christmas with the house full of people.

Besides, company would take the pressure off her.

"In that case, I suggest we drink our punch and open our presents." She had brought her parents' presents with her. "And then I can help you cook lunch, Mummy," she offered—Mrs Weaver always spent Christmas with her sister in Brighton. "Windy, cold place this time of year", the housekeeper invariably complained, but

Jane's parents insisted she must be with her family at Christmas-time.

"Busman's holiday, Janie?" her father teased.

Her smile wavered for only a fraction of a second. The last person to call her Janie had been Gabe. No, she wouldn't think of him any more today! Her parents were in very good spirits, and she would allow none of her own unhappiness to spill over and ruin their day for them.

Which proved more than a little difficult later that afternoon when the "guests" turned out to be Gabe and his parents!

It hadn't even occurred to Jane to ask who the guests were going to be, having assumed it was friends of her parents whom she had known herself since childhood, friends she could feel perfectly relaxed with.

A tall, handsome man, dark hair showing grey at his temples, entered the room first with her mother, her parents having gone together to answer the ring of the doorbell. Her father entered the room seconds later with a tall, blonde-haired woman, elegantly beautiful, her soft American drawl as she spoke softly sending warning bells through Jane even before Gabe entered the room behind the foursome.

Jane was dumbstruck. Never in her worst nightmare could she have imagined her parents inviting Gabe and his parents here on Christmas Day! They barely knew Gabe, let alone his parents, so why on earth—?

But even as she stared disbelievingly across at Gabe, his own gaze coolly challenging as he met hers, Jane knew exactly what Gabe and his parents were doing here. That day, when her mother and father had come to London so unexpectedly, had also been the day Gabe had told her he had an important business meeting he had to get to for ten o'clock...!

Gabe was the person who had offered her father some sort of business opening, was the reason why her father looked so much younger, and her mother looked so much more buoyant!

He couldn't! He couldn't be going to hurt her parents all over again? He—

No, she answered herself confidently even as the idea came into her head. The man she had come to know over the last two weeks, the man she loved, wouldn't do that.

Then why? What was it all about? What did it all mean?

"Think about it a while, Jane." Gabe had strolled casually across the room to stand at her side, his tone pleasant, but those aqua-blue eyes were as cold as ice.

Like the blue of an iceberg Jane had once seen in a photograph...

"Really think about it, Jane," he muttered harshly. "But in the meantime come and say hello to my parents."

The trouble was, she couldn't think at all; she wasn't even aware that she was being introduced to his father, although she did note that he was an older version of his son, the only difference being that on the older man the aqua-blue eyes were warm and friendly as he shook her hand.

Marisa Vaughn, although aged in her early sixties, was undoubtedly a beautiful woman, possessed of an air of complete satisfaction with her life.

Jane found she couldn't help but like and feel drawn to both the older Vaughns.

"Janette is such a pretty name," Marisa Vaughn murmured huskily. "It suits you, my dear." She squeezed

Jane's arm warmly before turning away to accept the glass of punch being poured to warm them all.

"Janette has just suggested the two of us go for a walk," Gabe put in loudly enough that the four older people could hear him over their own murmur of conversation. "Would any of you care to join us?"

"Excellent idea." His father nodded approvingly. "But after the drive this fire—" he held out his hands to the blazing warmth of the coal fire "—has much more appeal!" He grinned at his son.

"Take my coat from the hallway, Janette," her mother told her. "We don't want you to catch cold."

She didn't want to go for a walk, had made no such suggestion in the first place, but with the four older people looking at her so expectantly she didn't seem to have a lot of choice in the matter. Not without appearing incredibly rude.

"I thought it best that you say what you have to say to me away from our parents," Gabe bit out once they were outside in the crisp December air, walking over to the paddock where Jane had once kept her horse stabled.

She wasn't sure she could say anything to him, wasn't sure she could speak at all. She was still stunned by the fact that he was here at all. She had thought she would never see him again…

And how she had ached these last few days with that realisation!

How she ached now. But with quite a different emotion.

"Why, Gabe?" she finally managed to say.

He had been staring across at the bleak December landscape, a little snow having fallen in the night, leaving a crisp whiteness on everything. "Why did I come here today with my parents?" he ground out. "Because we were invited, Jane," he responded harshly. "It would have been rude not to have accepted." He turned back to look over the paddock.

Jane looked up at his grim profile, his cheeks hollow, his jaw clenched. As if waiting for a blow...

She swallowed hard. "I didn't mean that." She shook her head. "Why did you try to find me three years ago?" She felt that if she had the answer to that she might, just might, have the answer to the whole puzzle...

He looked down at her again, frowning slightly now. "I thought you already knew the answer to that one," he rasped scathingly. "I was out to wreak vengeance, wasn't I? On a woman who had not only been deserted by her husband because of my wife, but had also been bombarded with reporters because of the scandal when the two of them died together in a car crash. Not only that, that woman had also lost her baby! That's the way it happened, isn't it, Jane?" he challenged disgustedly. "You see, I've been doing some thinking of my own!" He shook his head. "My conclusions aren't exactly pretty!"

She still stared up at him, couldn't seem to look away. She loved this man.

"I—" She moistened dry lips, swallowing hard. "I could have been wrong—"

"Could have been?" Gabe turned fully towards her now, grasping her arms painfully. "There's no 'could have been' about it, Jane; if that's what you thought, you were wrong!" His eyes glittered dangerously, a nerve pulsing in his cheek. "In fact, you're so damned far from the truth it's laughable. If I felt like laughing, that is," he muttered grimly. "Which I don't!"

She had done a lot of thinking herself over the last few days, and knew that somehow, some way, there was something wrong with what she had believed until two weeks ago, when she'd actually met Gabe for the first time. Maybe Gabe had been devastated by Jennifer's death, but the man she had come to know wouldn't blame anyone else for that death; he'd known the destructive streak that had motivated his wife better than anyone.

So if he hadn't wanted retribution all those years ago, what had he wanted...? It was that Jane wanted—needed—to know.

"Gabe, I was wrong," she told him chokingly, putting her hand on his arm, refusing to remove it even when she felt him flinch. "I know that now. I know *you* now."

He shook his head. "No, you don't, Jane. Not really."

And now she never would? Was that what he was saying?

She didn't want that, couldn't bear it if she were never to see him again after today. The past few days had been bad enough, but to go through that pain all over again...!

"Gabe, I'm trying to apologise. For what I thought," she explained abruptly.

"Accepted." He nodded tersely, his expression still hard. "Can we go back inside now?" he added gratingly.

"Why are you helping my father, Gabe?" She refused to move, knowing that once they were back inside the house Gabe would become a remote stranger to her. And after telling him for days that that was what she wanted him to be it was now the last thing she wanted.

He gave a rueful grimace. "So you know about that

too now, hmm?" He nodded dismissively. "Well, obviously I'm up to something underhand and malicious, entangling your father in some sort of plot—"

"Gabe!" Jane groaned her distress at his bitterness. "I was wrong! I know I was wrong! I'm sorry. What else can I say?" She looked at him pleadingly.

He became very still now, looking down at her warily. "What else do you want to say?"

So many things, but most of all, that she loved him. But how cautious she had, by necessity, been over the last three years of her life held her back from being quite that daring. What if he should throw that love back in her face?

She chewed on her bottom lip. "I think your mother likes me," she told him lightly, remembering what his mother's opinion of Jennifer had been.

His expression softened. "You're right, she does," he acknowledged dryly. "But then, I knew she would," he added enigmatically.

"Gabe, tell me why you tried to find me three years ago!" She tried again, because she was still sure this was the key to everything. "Please, Gabe," she pleaded as he looked grim once again.

"Do you have any idea what it's like to love someone so badly you can't even see straight?" he attacked viciously. "So that you think of nothing else but that person, until they fill your whole world? Do you have any idea what it's like to love someone like that?" he groaned harshly. "And then to have them disappear from your life as if they had never been, almost as if you had imagined them ever being there at all?" His hands were clenched at his sides, his face pale.

She was beginning to. Oh, yes, she was beginning to!

And if he could still talk about his dead wife like this, still felt that way about her, then her own love for him was as worthless as ashes.

She drew in a deep breath. "I'm sorry Jennifer died—"

"Jennifer? I'm not talking about Jennifer!" he dismissed incredulously. "She was my wife, and as such I cared what happened to her, and could never actually bring myself to hate her—I felt pity for her more than anything. I hadn't loved her for years before she died. If I ever did," he added bleakly. "Compared with what I now know of love I believe I was initially fascinated by Jennifer, and then, after we were married, that fascination quickly turned to a rather sad affection. Beneath that surface selfishness was a very vulnerable woman, a woman who saw herself as being less than other women—I've already explained to you why that was. So you see, Jane, I felt sorry for Jennifer, I cared for her, but I was not in love with her. Before or after she died," he said grimly.

"But—" Jane looked at him with puzzled eyes. If it wasn't Jennifer, then who was this mysterious woman he loved...? "That perfect woman—the woman who evaporated, disappeared before your eyes." She painfully recalled what he had told her of the woman he loved. The woman she had for so long assumed was Jennifer...

"What about her?" he echoed harshly.

Jane shook her head. "Where is she? *Who* is she?"

Gabe looked down at her with narrowed eyes, his expression softening as he saw the look of complete bewilderment in her face. "You really don't know, do you?" He shook his head self-derisively, moving away from her to lean back against the fence, the collar of his jacket turned up to keep out the worst of the cold. "I was at a party one night—one of those endless parties that are impossible to enjoy, but you simply can't get away from. And then I looked across the crowded room—that well-worn cliché!—and there she was."

Jane couldn't move, could barely breathe now.

Gabe was no longer looking at her, his thoughts all inwards as he recalled the past. "I told myself not to be so stupid," he continued harshly. "Love didn't happen like that, in a moment—"

"At first sight." Jane spoke hoarsely, remembering he had once asked her if she believed in the emotion. She had said a definite no!

"At first sight," he echoed scornfully. "But I couldn't stop watching this woman, couldn't seem to look anywhere else. And as I watched her I realised she wasn't just beautiful, she was gracious and warm too. She spoke to everybody there in the same warm way, and there was an elderly man there, who had been slightly drunk when he arrived, but instead of shying away from him as everyone else was she sat next to him, talking to him quietly, for over an hour. And by the time he left he was slightly less drunk and even managed to smile a little."

"His wife had died the previous month," Jane put in softly. "That evening was the first time he had been out in company since her death. And people weren't shying away from him because he'd had slightly too much to drink; it was because they didn't know what to say to him, how to deal with his loss, and so they simply ignored him." She remembered that night so well—it had been the last time she had gone anywhere with Paul, because, ironically enough, a few days later *he* had been dead.

Gabe nodded abruptly. "I know that. I asked around who he was. Who you were. You were another man's wife!"

She was that perfect woman, the woman who had seemed to disappear, evaporate. And after the accident, after losing the baby, that was exactly what she had done!

Gabe had been in love with her three years ago! Not a man on a quest for vengeance, but a man on a quest for the woman he had fallen in love with at first sight at a party one night!

"You were another woman's husband," she reminded him gruffly.

"Not by the time I came looking for you." He shook his head firmly. "The first time I saw you, I accept we were both married to other people, and in those circumstances I would never have come near you. I didn't come near you. And maybe I did act with indecent haste by trying to find you after our respective partners were killed," he acknowledged grimly. "But, as it happened, my worst nightmare came true." He looked bleak. "You had disappeared. And, no matter how I tried to find you, someone would put a wall up to block my way. After three months of coming up against those brick walls, of finally discovering that you had lost your baby because of what happened—"

"That was the reason you did a deal with Richard Warner rather than buy him out, wasn't it?" Jane said with certainty.

"A horror of history repeating itself?" Gabe nodded. "It was too close to what happened to you three years ago."

Jane gasped. "You weren't responsible for my miscarriage—"

"Maybe I could have done something to stop Jenni-fer." He shook his head. "Who knows? I certainly didn't. So I tried to convince myself I had imagined you." He sighed. "I went back to the States, buried myself in my work, and told myself that Janette Granger was a myth, that even if I had finally got to meet you, speak to you, you would have hated me; that it was best to leave you as a dream, a mirage. The only trouble with dreams and mirages is that they transpose themselves over reality." He grimaced.

"No normal woman can possibly live up to a dream one. And for me no woman ever has."

He turned away abruptly, staring out across the empty paddock. "When I met you again so suddenly two weeks ago. You were everything I had ever thought you were. And I was sure that you knew me too, but I thought—stupidly, I realise now—that if you could just get to know me, realise I wasn't a cold-hearted ogre, you might come to— Oh, never mind what I thought, Jane," he rasped. "I was wrong, so very wrong."

"My name is Janette," she put in softly, pointedly. "Janie, if you prefer; it's always been my father's pet name for me."

Gabe loved her. At least, he had loved her three years ago... Had the reality lived up to that dream?

He turned back to look at her. "That night, at your apartment, I called you Janie..." he realised softly.

"You did," she nodded. "And I don't know what you're trying to do to help my father—"

"I'm putting him into Richard's company as his senior manager," Gabe told her gently. "Richard is good at PR work, and your father is good at the management level; together they should turn that company around in six months." He swallowed hard. "You were right about me; I had no idea of the financial difficulties your father had three years ago, of the debts he had to pay—"

"Paul's debts," Jane put in hardly. "My father did that for me. And what you're doing for him now has transformed his life—his and Mummy's. I could love you for just that alone," she added shyly.

"Don't, Jane—"

"But I don't love you for that alone," she continued determinedly, eyes very big in the paleness of her face as she looked up at him. "I love you because you're warm and funny, caring and loving. And when you kiss me…!" She gave a self-conscious laugh.

"When I kiss you," Gabe agreed throatily, "I'm back to that first night I saw you; I can't think straight, can't see straight, all I know is you. With every part of me. Oh, Janie!"

She needed no further encouragement, flinging herself into his arms, both of them losing themselves in the sheer beauty of loving and being loved.

How long they remained like that Jane didn't know, finally laughing gently against the warmth of his chest, where he had cradled her as if he would never let her go again.

"All we have to do now is find a way to explain to our respective parents that we're going to be married." She chuckled softly. "Considering my parents don't even realise we know each other—"

"Marriage, Janie?" Gabe looked down at her searchingly. "You love me that much?"

And more. Marriage to Paul had been possession and pain; with Gabe it would be sharing and love. With Gabe, she had no doubts about making such a commitment. No doubts whatsoever.

"If you'll have me." She nodded shyly, suddenly wondering if he was prepared to make such a commitment again after his disastrous marriage to Jennifer.

He let out a whoop of delight, picking her up to swing her round in the snow. "Oh, I'll have you, Janette Smythe-Roberts, Janette Granger, Jane Smith. All of you! I love you, Janie, so very much." He slowly lowered her to the snow-covered ground. "And my parents already know how I feel about you, have known for some time that I left my heart behind in England three years ago," he acknowledged ruefully. "As for your own parents, they only want for you what will make you happy. And I certainly intend doing that! So will you marry me, Jane? Soon!" His arms tightened about her. "It has to be soon!"

He had already waited long enough, his pleading expression told her. And so had she, she realised weakly. "As soon as it can be arranged," she assured him huskily. "I can't wait for us to belong to each other. And my father was asking me only the other day when I was going to give him grandchildren...!" She looked up at Gabe hopefully.

"Children... *Our* children, Janie," he groaned, his hands trembling as he held her. "*Soon*, Janie. Oh, yes, very soon!"

CHAPTER FOURTEEN

GOLD.

Bright, shiny, *warm* gold.

Her hair, returned to its natural colour for almost a year now, flowed like liquid gold over Gabe's fingers as he played with the silky tresses, his attention so intense he hadn't realised Jane had woken beside him in the bed and lay looking up at him.

It had been a good year—a year in which they had married and moved into a house of their own in London. Initially Jane's time had been filled with choosing the décor and furnishings, and soon—very soon!—her time was going to be filled with their son or daughter.

Being with Gabe, as his wife, was the deepest happiness Jane had ever known—falling asleep in his arms every night, waking still held in those strong arms, and spending their days busy in each other's company. Both sets of parents were constant visitors, eager for the birth of their first grandchild. As Jane and Gabe were.

"Good morning, my love." She greeted her husband huskily, warmed by the pleasure that lit his face as he realised she was awake.

He kissed her lingeringly on the lips. "I've just been wondering what I ever found to do with my time before I had you to look at and love," he admitted ruefully. "You're so beautiful, Jane," he told her shakily.

She laughed softly, reaching up to gently touch his cheek. "At the moment I look like a baby whale!"

His hand moved to rest possessively on the swell of her body that was their unborn child. "To me you're beautiful."

And she knew he meant it, that he had enjoyed every aspect of her pregnancy, been a part of all of it, as far as he was able. And since Felicity and Richard's son Thom had been born six months ago, the other couple now close friends who visited often, Gabe had been practising changing nappies, much to baby Thom's disgust.

"You were very restless last night, darling." Gabe frowned down at her concernedly now. "Do you feel okay?"

Jane grinned up at him. "As okay as I can be in the early stages of labour," she informed him lightly, knowing that the slight cramps she had had in her stomach the evening before had deepened during the night, although not seriously enough yet for her to need to go to hospital, which was why she had been napping on and off during the night, preparing herself for the much heavier labour she was positive was imminent.

Gabe shot out of bed so quickly Jane could only lie and stare at him, moving up to lean on one elbow to watch him as he raced around the bedroom, throwing on his own clothes, before puling her own out of the adjoining wardrobe and laying them down on the bed.

"Gabe...?" She finally stopped his rushing about. "It's going to be hours yet—"

He came to an abrupt halt, sitting down on the side of the bed, gently clasping her shoulders. "I'm not taking any chances with you, Jane," he told her emotionally. "If anything should happen to you—"

Jane placed her fingertips lightly against his lips. "Nothing is going to happen to me," she assured him confidently. "We fell in love with each other against all the odds; nothing could possibly happen to part us now," she said with conviction, sure in her own heart that they were meant to be together. Always.

"I love you so much, Jane," he choked. "My life would be empty without you!"

"And mine without you. But that isn't going to happen, Gabe." She was absolutely positive about this, felt sure they were going to grow old together. "Nothing is going to happen in the next few hours except we're going to have our own darling little baby." She gave him a glowing smile. "But perhaps you're right about going to the hospital now." She began her breathing exercises as a much stronger contraction took her breath away. "I think the baby has decided that today would be a good time to be born!"

And six hours later, when their daughter Ami was born, with Jane's golden hair and Gabe's aqua-blue eyes, they knew that their world was complete.

"She's gorgeous, Jane." Gabe gazed down wonderingly at their tiny daughter, each tiny feature perfect. "I can't believe you're both mine." He shook his head.

"Believe it, Gabe," Jane told him emotionally.

As she believed.

In Gabe.

In their marriage.

In their for ever...

* * * * *

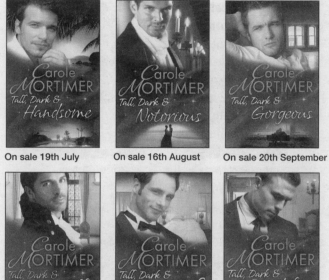

The Correttis

Introducing the Correttis, Sicily's most scandalous family!

On sale 3rd May

On sale 7th June

On sale 5th July

On sale 2nd August

Mills & Boon® Modern™ invites you to step over the threshold and enter the Correttis' dark and dazzling world…